D0145630

RULES OF
HONOR

ALSO BY MATT HILTON

Joe Hunter Thriller Novels
Dead Men's Dust
Judgement and Wrath
Slash and Burn
Cut and Run
Blood and Ashes
Dead Men's Harvest
No Going Back
Rules of Honour
The Lawless Kind

Joe Hunter Thriller Short Stories
Six of the Best (E-book)
Dead Fall (E-book)
Red Stripes (E-book)
Instant Justice (E-book)

Stand Alone Novels
Dominion
Darkest Hour
Mark Darrow and the Stealer of Souls
Preternatural
The Shadows Call

MATT HILTON

RULES OF HONOR

A Joe Hunter Thriller

Down & Out Books
3959 Van Dyke Rd, Ste. 265
Lutz, FL 33558
www.DownAndOutBooks.com

Cover design by JT Lindroos

ISBN: 1937495930
ISBN-13: 978-1-937495-93-0

This one is for Jordon

1

'Stay in bed, I'm going to take a look.'

'I'll phone the police.'

'No. Just wait until I check things out. It was maybe just the wind.'

'That wasn't the wind, Andrew.'

'Maybe not, but it's too early to call the police. Just wait and I'll go see. If I'm not back in two minutes, call then.'

The woman watched her husband pull a robe over his bulky shoulders, then move for the closet in their bedroom. He opened the door and reached for the top shelf, from which he retrieved a locked box. Inside the box was a relic of her husband's past. He glanced at her briefly, an apologetic look, but then withdrew the gun that winked dully in the lamplight. Inside the box was a rapid loader, and Andrew fed the six bullets into the gun with precision. Done, he looked at his wife again.

'It's only a precaution,' he whispered, closing the cylinder and latching it tight.

'Be careful...'

His wife had switched on the bedside lamp, but the rest of the house was in darkness. As he eased open the door and peered into the upstairs hall he pressed his body close to the opening to stop light spill. He paused there a moment, allowing his eyes to adjust to the dark. Then he slipped out into the hall, surprisingly agile for a man of his advanced years. Andrew was a septuagenarian but looking at him most would guess he was at least ten years younger. His height had barely been touched by the years, and he still had the broad shoulders and heavy arms of his youth. His knees bothered him these days, but not now while a bubble of adrenalin coursed through his frame. He went along the hall with the gun held close to his side. He didn't concern himself with the guest bedrooms or the bathroom

1

because the sound that had woken them had definitely come from below in the living room.

Recently there had been a spate of burglaries in the neighbourhood, the cops putting down the breaking and entries to drug addicts looking for cash, credit cards and items easily pawned. Andrew and his wife, though they weren't rich, were wealthy enough to attract the attention of a sneak thief. That angered Andrew: he'd worked hard all of his life, even put his safety on the line, to make an easy retirement for him and his wife. No sneak thief was going to take anything from them.

A lifetime ago he'd fought in Korea, had survived the worst that war could throw at him, and for decades afterwards had striven to be the same soldier. He had failed to protect his girl child, who'd succumbed through illness, and one boy following suit with a military career had been killed in the line of duty. So now he was more determined than ever that he would not fail his wife and allow some punk to invade their home and take their lives' worth. He was old but he'd lost none of his military acumen and thought himself more than equal to a drug-addled thief.

From the head of the landing he peered down the stairs.

Moonlight flooded the vestibule at the bottom, a skewed oblong cast from the window in the front door stretching across the floor. Within the light grey shadows danced, but Andrew recognised them as the trees in his garden dancing to the breeze. He took the stairs one at a time, avoiding the third step down that was prone to squeak under his weight. As he descended the stairs he looked for the blinking red light on the alarm box on the hall wall, but it was steady. Whoever had found a way inside was clever enough to dismantle the alarm. Or they knew the code and had turned it off. There was only one other person who knew the code, but he wasn't prone to dropping in uninvited like this in the dead of night. Alone the sound they'd heard wasn't proof that an invader was in their house, but the dead alarm now solidified it. Andrew considered going back upstairs and telling his wife to telephone the police immediately, but something halted him. Pride. Foolish pride perhaps, but he wasn't the type to run from danger.

Some would have been tempted to call out a challenge, but Andrew knew that it would be a mistake. A desperate drug addict might run for it, but then if Andrew had managed to corner him then his desperation might turn violent. Better that he initiated any beating than the other way around. He went down the stairs, paused to check the alarm box and saw that the guts of it had been teased open and a wire clipped onto the exposed workings to form a loop in the system. The alarm had been negated, but the automatic signal to his service provider would not have kicked in, as it would if the wires had been merely torn out. If he'd stopped to think for a moment he'd have realised that it was too sophisticated a method for an addict only intent on his next fix. But he wasn't thinking he was reacting. Threat demanded action.

He glanced once towards the kitchen but discarded it: a thief would go for the living room where the possibility of rich pickings was greater. He moved along the short hallway and saw that the door to the sitting room was ajar. Always conscious about home safety, fire and smoke being the worst threat to sleeping inhabitants, he was always careful to turn off electrical appliances and to close doors tight. He had got it down to a bedtime routine and knew he'd closed that door tightly, as he did every night. He paused there listening. He thought he heard a soft footfall, but it came from above, probably his wife. Placing a fingertip to the door, he teased it inward, the revolver held steady against his hip. Then, without warning he shoved the door hard and stepped quickly into the room, sweeping the familiar space for anything alien.

There was nobody to be seen.

If not for the jerry-rigged alarm he'd have thought he'd been mistaken, that the noise that woke him was nothing but wind throwing the garden furniture around the yard. He wondered if the burglar had heard him as he'd risen and had made himself scarce. But in the next instant he knew that he was wrong.

A cold metallic tickle behind his right ear made him halt.

'You know what that is, don't you, old man?'

Andrew nodded slightly, a minute movement because he didn't know how hair-triggered the gun pressed to his skull was.

'Mine's bigger than yours,' whispered the voice over his

shoulder. 'I suggest you drop that old revolver and kick it back to me.'

'Okay, son, take it easy now.' Andrew lifted the revolver and flicked the latch to open the swing-out cylinder. He rattled the gun and allowed the shells to tumble out and clatter on the hardwood floor.

'Not good enough.' A fist was jabbed into Andrew's back, directly above his left kidney. Pain flared through the old man, sending a white flash across his vision. 'Now, as I said first time, put down the gun and kick it back to me.'

'It's useless,' Andrew said, desperate not to relinquish the weapon having placed some spare rounds in his robe pocket.

'Is it?' The man clubbed Andrew across the back of his head and sent him sprawling into the living room.

As he fell the revolver was knocked from Andrew's hand. In the seconds afterwards it didn't matter because he used both hands to cover the split in his scalp. 'Son of a bitch.'

'You see,' the man said. 'Even an empty gun can be a good weapon.' He levelled his semi-automatic handgun on Andrew's chest. 'Not that mine's empty.'

Andrew struggled up to a seated position, grabbing at a settee for support. He could feel blood trickling through his hair. He looked up at the man, squinting to try to make sense of the face.

'Who the hell are you? What do you want?'

One thing Andrew was sure about: this was no addict looking for a quick payday. The man was large and solidly built, dressed in black jeans, black jacket and a black baseball cap. Backlit by the meagre moonlight in the hall he looked like a living silhouette.

'If I answered your first question, you'd probably guess the second.'

'If you're after money, you've come to the wrong place. You'd be better off...'

'I'm not here for money.'

'That's good, son, because I'm old and haven't worked in years, I don't have much to get by on.'

'Save it,' said the man. 'You're wasting your time trying to make conversation. I know what you're trying to do: humanize

4

yourself in my eyes, making me think twice about doing you harm. You're wasting the few breaths you have left.'

Andrew was thinking clearer now and studied his surroundings for a way out of this. He didn't like what the man had just said, it sounded like he had only one agenda. No way was Andrew going to sit on his ass and offer his would-be killer an easy ride. He thought of his wife upstairs and knew that she'd be next, but not if he did enough to alert her to the danger, and slowed the bastard down. He looked for something to use as a weapon.

'Don't even think about it.'

Andrew returned his gaze to the man. He'd stepped inside the room and was looming over Andrew. The gun was held steadily, the barrel aimed directly at Andrew's face. 'I want you to know why I'm here, why I'm about to kill you. It'd be a shame if I had to put a bullet through your skull before I showed you this.'

From his jacket pocket the man took out a cell phone. He'd readied it beforehand, and he held out the glowing screen so that Andrew could see the photograph on the screen. Andrew screwed his eyes to help focus the picture and saw that in fact it was a photograph taken from one much older. The image was of a man in uniform, sepia in colour. It was many decades since Andrew had seen that face but he recognised it and knew who this man might be.

'Who is it?' Andrew tried, but he knew the man recognised the lie.

'You don't remember? Well that's a shame, because he's waiting to greet you in hell.'

The man's voice had risen in pitch and volume, and Andrew knew that the rest of his life could be counted in seconds. He coiled himself, ready to call out, to fight back, to do *something*.

Andrew squirmed round so that he was partly side-on to the man. To anyone uninitiated to violence it might seem that the old man was frightened and trying to make himself a smaller target. 'You do know what he did?'

'Oh, so you're admitting that you know him now?' The man put the phone away and from his pocket took out a long tubular object. Andrew recognised it as a sound suppressor. It was both a bad and good sign. It meant that the man was not a first time killer and had come prepared, but also that he did not want to raise an alarm by firing indiscriminately.

'He deserved everything he got,' Andrew said.

'No one deserved *that!*' The man screwed the suppressor onto the barrel of his gun with a few practiced twists. He did it blindly, but couldn't deny the natural reaction to glance at it once, to make sure he'd secured it correctly. It was only a brief second of inattention, but Andrew took advantage of it.

From his side-on position he could chamber his left leg, and he shot it out, aiming with his bare heel at the man's shin. Better that he aim for the knee, but he didn't have the range. His heel struck bone, at the same time as he swung his other foot to hook behind the man's ankle. Andrew scissored his legs. An untrained man would have been upended, giving Andrew time to swarm on top of him and to snatch away the gun. Unfortunately this man had come with violence in mind, and though he was staggered, he was agile enough that he was able to disengage his trapped leg and to hop aside...bringing round the gun.

'No!'

Andrew's yell wasn't out of fear of the bullet destined for him.

A slight figure had appeared as a shadow behind the man, one arm raised in the air. With all of her strength his wife brought down a plant pot she'd lifted off a hallway dresser. The man had somehow felt her presence behind him and was already turning. The plant pot struck him on the shoulder, but it was nothing to the man. He continued his turn and swung with the barrel of the gun, striking the woman across the side of her skull. She hit the floor quicker than the falling plant pot, which shattered in a way that Andrew feared her skull had. The man gave one disdainful look at the woman before turning his attention back to Andrew.

He took a step back. Andrew had come up from the floor much faster than a man of his age should have been able.

'Bastard!' Andrew came at him with animal ferocity, throwing two solid punches at the man's chest, but both fell short. 'If you've killed her I'll—'

6

The man shot him: three rapid bullets to the chest.
Andrew staggered at each impact.
'*This time* you'll do nothing,' the man sneered.
Andrew collapsed to the floor, jammed in the doorway. He didn't look at the man now, but at his wife. She lay on her side; her head cradled under one arm. He could barely see the rise and fall of her shoulder as it rode each breath.
'Please,' he moaned. 'Take me, but don't harm my wife.'
The man snorted.
'Why not? It's your lying wife's fault it came to this.'
He shot Andrew again, this time in the head.

2

It was misty in San Francisco.

The mist was nothing unusual, because it was a regular occurrence in the bay area. Something to do with the humidity coming in from the Pacific and meeting the cool air sweeping out from the U.S. landmass, or vice versa. Whatever the phenomenon, it had coalesced into low-lying clouds. Today it had formed out on the water, a huge embankment that had followed the shorelines, obscuring from view the world famous Golden Gate Bridge before pushing in to shroud Alcatraz and on to similarly veil the Bay Bridge. Above the mist I could still make out the tallest points of the Bay Bridge, against the backdrop of a starry sky. The thrum of traffic over the bridge was muted, a background accompaniment only. On the Embarcadero traffic was light, and none of the famous cable cars were in sight. Pedestrians were few as well, but there were street people camped out next to a large fountain that looked as if it had been erected using the leftover concrete from an overpass. Most of the street people were tucked under sleeping bags, shopping trolleys piled with their belongings forming wind breaks behind them. One of the homeless guys was an early riser like me, and he was rooting through some boxes outside a pizza shop. He had shuffled past a minute earlier without noticing me, which went a long way to prove my disguise was working.

I was wearing a thick parka jacket picked up from a military surplus store, plus jeans and a pair of boots that looked like they'd seen a thousand miles, and a wool cap pulled down around my ears. I'd gone unshaven for three days. To complete my disguise I'd rooted around in an open Dumpster and allowed the stink to percolate. I was sure that no one but another hobo would come within ten feet of me from choice.

It was very early, an hour or two before dawn, but I wasn't

feeling it. I'd only flown in from Florida two days before, and my body clock swore it was actually midmorning. I was wide-awake and intent on the job at hand. I saw the man I'd been waiting for immediately.

He was a large man. Maybe a shade over six feet, but big in other ways: big shoulders, big arms, big chest and waist. He was also big in the local criminal underworld, but still a few rungs from the top. He was dressed for purpose in a windcheater jacket: not a defence against the chill but to conceal the gun holstered beneath his left armpit. He was called Sean Chaney, a strong arm of the resident criminal fraternity. He looked half-asleep, which suited me fine.

As he moved by, I fell into step a dozen yards behind him. He didn't glance at me, and wouldn't be concerned if he did. All the homeless people here knew who he was, what he did for a living and didn't hassle him for change. He walked alongside the Hyatt, a huge structure of tiered rooms and balconies to make the best of the view across the bay. The Embarcadero Centre was on our right; a three storied shopping mall that spanned several blocks of the city. Apart from security lighting all of the shops remained in darkness and there was no one else around. My boots scuffed the ground, and to me sounded like canon fire, but Chaney seemed oblivious and carried on to the corner of the hotel and took a left. Coming round the corner after him, I saw him check his watch and his pace picked up.

Valets on the hotel door watched Chaney stride past, but didn't give me as much as a glance: it said something about human nature to me. There was a junction in the road here, and it was a boarding point for the cable cars that carried tourists up and down Nob Hill, but Chaney didn't approach the stop but headed for the stairs down to the underground BART system. I counted to ten then followed down. He was already past the ticket machines heading for the southbound platform. There was no one else in sight, but I wasn't worried. The big man was rubbing his eyes and yawning expansively. I fed coins into the machine, took my ticket and then shuffled towards the platform. This time Chaney did look at me, but it was a glancing blow that didn't stick. He went back to yawning, turning away from me with uninterest. I slouched against a wall, at the opposite end of the platform.

The Bay Area Rapid Transport system is on the ball at all hours of the day and night, and it was little more than a minute before the train squealed into the station. Chaney was at the doors in a second, rocking on his heels while he waited for them to open. He squeezed inside even as the doors hissed open. I waited a few seconds more, then clambered aboard the second carriage along. There was a middle-aged Chinese woman sitting in my carriage and she gave me a brief fearful look, before quickly averting her eyes. She was sitting with a couple of bags on her lap and as I moved past her she pulled them tight to her chest like a shield. I cringed inwardly, thinking about how I'd frightened the woman, but it was neither the time nor the place to reassure her she was in no danger. The only person in danger on this train was Chaney.

The next carriage along was deserted.

I moved through it as the train pulled out of the station and began swaying along the tracks.

Coming to the next connecting doors, I paused.

Peeking through the glass I could see Chaney midway along the carriage. He was facing my way, but had taken out his cell phone and was involved in checking the screen for messages. He didn't see me, and was totally oblivious of the other person who had entered the carriage from the far end. He'd obviously had it too easy of late and had lost the intrinsic paranoia necessary for a criminal.

My friend Jared Rington moved along the carriage with an easy pace, but even from this end I could see the muscles working in his jaw, an old knife scar standing out as a white slash against his tawny skin. Rink hadn't gone to the trouble I had. He wasn't disguised, and didn't see the need. He wanted Chaney to know who was coming for him, and who his executioner was going to be. The only compromise to his usual colourful attire was a pair of black leather gloves. Chaney had his back to Rink, but my friend isn't the type to do a hit from behind. Rink's voice was muffled, but I still heard his sharp command: 'Stand up you piece of shit.'

Chaney dropped his phone and went for his gun, already turning as he rose.

Rink struck him with the edge of his hand, a chop to the side of the big man's neck. Uncontrolled the blow could kill, but Rink had tempered the force. It was still enough to stagger Chaney and while he was weakened, Rink took the gun from him with a practiced twist of the wrist. Chaney grunted something, continued his turn and tried to grapple for the gun. Rink hit him again, a sweeping elbow strike that contacted with Chaney's face and knocked him back a few steps. Rink followed him, bringing up the Glock he'd liberated to point it directly at Chaney's forehead.

Time I did something.

I hit the button and the door swept open.

As I entered the carriage my view of Rink was slightly obscured by Chaney's thick body. I had a horrible feeling that Rink would shoot, and the bullet would go directly through Chaney's skull and hit me. I sidestepped, placing myself in the open next to the exit doors. Rink was taller than Chaney, and I knew he'd seen me from the slight narrowing of his eyes. That was all the notice he gave me, though, because his attention was on the man he was about to kill.

I brought up my SIG Sauer P226 and pointed it at Chaney's back. My other hand I held open to Rink.

'Don't do this, brother,' I said to him. 'Chaney's a piece of shit, but he doesn't deserve this.'

Rink didn't even look at me. Nausea squirmed a passage through my gut.

'Don't,' I said again.

'What're you going to do, Hunter?' Rink's eyes never left Chaney. 'Shoot me?'

'I don't want to,' I said.

'That's something, at least.' Rink ignored me then and took a step nearer Chaney.

The enforcer reared back on his heels, bringing up his hands in a placating motion. 'Whoa! What's this all about?'

'I'm about to kill you,' my friend snarled.

'Rink. Don't do it.' I hurried towards him. 'Don't cross the line, brother.'

'It's too late for that, Joe.'

I knew then that there was less than a heartbeat to spare.
I fired.

3

Rink is more than a friend to me. He is more like a brother, and I love him as such. When he's thinking straight he'd die for me, as I would for him. There's no way on earth that I'd shoot him and he knew it. So I did the first thing that came to mind. I shot Sean Chaney instead.

I shot him to save his life.

My bullet struck him in his left thigh and he dropped like an ox in a slaughterhouse. He bellowed like one too, his hands going to the wound in his leg. The speed at which he'd collapsed saved him the bullet that Rink was about to put in his skull. My friend blinked over the top of the writhing man at me.

'What the hell'd you do that for?'

'To save you from making a big mistake.'

'There's no mistake.' Rink turned the gun on the fallen enforcer, but I could see a flicker of doubt worming its way across his features.

By now I was alongside my friend and I put my hand on his wrist.

'Trust me,' I said.

He continued to train the gun on Chaney, but I could feel the doubt in his body now, and finally he allowed me to press the gun down.

'It wasn't Chaney,' I said. 'It wasn't him or any of his guys.'

'And you know that how?'

I flicked a cautionary nod. 'Later, okay?'

At our feet the enforcer was sitting with his back against one of the bench seats. His jaw was set in a grimace of agony as he grasped at his wounded leg, and his eyes were brimming with fear as he watched us. He made a mistake of opening his mouth.

'Who the fuck are you? Do you realise who you're messing with?'

Rink rounded on him.

'You've just got a goddamn reprieve, punk. Now shut your hole!'

Chaney looked at me. 'You shot me, you bastard. You should've let your buddy kill me, 'cause I'm gonna...'

'Going to what?' I glared down at him. 'I barely scratched you. You're an ungrateful piece of crap; I've just saved your life.'

'Says who?' Chaney struggled to get up, leaning on the bench with a blood-slicked hand. 'The way I see it your buddy is too much of a pussy to shoot. If he was gonna do it, he'd have goddamn done it. Just wait 'til I get up and—'

I kicked his support arm from under him. Chaney went down on his backside with a solid bump. Anger flared, shame at what he perceived as the ultimate humiliation. He began to struggle up. Rink and I shared a glance and it was just like old times, before all this started. I shrugged at him. Gave him the go ahead.

Rink turned up the corner of his mouth in a smile. Then he slapped the butt of the Glock against Chaney's skull. The enforcer was out cold before he'd slumped all the way to the floor.

'What now?' Rink looked at me.

'We get off at the next station and make ourselves scarce.'

'Thought you'd maybe explain yourself first.'

'There's no time.' I left Rink while I searched the floor and came back a moment later, pocketing the flattened round I'd put through Chaney's leg.

Rink grunted. 'That's why I wore gloves and used his gun. No forensics to worry about.'

'As if that would make a difference? Doesn't look like you made an effort to avoid the CCTV cameras.'

'They'd have seen a big guy with black hair, but only the top of my head. Could be one of a thousand dudes, even in this shirt.' He tugged at the collar of his bright Hawaiian number that was only partly hidden by a black leather jacket. It would look like a warning beacon anywhere else but here: there was still a large contingent of hippies and arty types in San Francisco who sported much gaudier attire. Rink nodded at me. 'I see you're still dressing as classy as ever.'

I was pleased to hear the tongue in cheek insult; it meant my big friend was back, thinking a little clearer than before.

'It's academic now,' I said, referring to the concern about forensics. 'Chaney isn't going to call the police. He didn't die, and when he wakes up he's going to realise how lucky he's been. All that talk was just bluster. Fear. He'll keep quiet. But that won't mean a thing if we're still standing round here when we reach the next stop.'

Rink crouched down and pushed the Glock into Chaney's holster, then arranged his coat so that it was hidden from view. Then he followed me through the carriages, away from where the Chinese woman sat oblivious to what had just occurred. We were pulling into the next station at Montgomery Street and I could see that some bleary-eyed passengers were waiting on the platform.

'What's the time?' I asked.

Rink calculated. 'Has to be coming up six o'clock by now.'

'Good. Some of the shops should be opening. Don't know about you, Rink, but I need a strong cup of coffee.'

'What you need is to get rid of that coat. It smells like someone took a crap in it.'

The doors opened and we had to stand aside to avoid a suited man who rushed aboard, already conducting business on his Blackberry. He didn't give us so much as a glance and went for the nearest seat. We got off the train and moved for the exit stairs. The train was already moving away and, as it moved parallel to us, I glimpsed into the carriage where we'd left Chaney. He was still sound asleep. Probably he wouldn't waken until the train reached the terminus at San Francisco International Airport. Wherever he'd been heading this morning, he was going to be late for his appointment.

I dumped the coat first chance I got. The jeans and boots should have gone in the Dumpster with it, but they were all I had with me. I threw the wool cap in with the rubbish, made do with smoothing down my hair. It was short so didn't look too bad. The shirt and canvas jacket I'd worn beneath the coat weren't filthy, so I looked reasonably dressed and wouldn't be kicked out of the coffee shop we headed for. Rink was silent as we strode across a thoroughfare beginning to swell with foot traffic as people headed for their work places. Rink is the epitome of the strong, silent type—until he gets going—but this morning his silence was deeper than normal. I could feel it like a living thing, caged for now but ready to be let loose to ravage and tear.

I gave up smoking and hard liquor years ago, but the old habits had been replaced by my over-reliance on strong coffee. I ordered the largest cup on sale, got a fruit smoothie for Rink. The shop had only just opened its doors and the barista was overworked. As soon as he'd delivered our drinks he continued stocking the shelves we'd disturbed him from doing. That suited us: there were no other customers and we could speak in private. We took a table where we could see the entrance and out of the front window, so there'd be no surprises. It was an old habit I'd been unable to lose.

'I saw you.'

'Thought you might've,' I said, cupping my drink with both palms. 'But you were still going to go ahead with the hit?'

'Thought you might try to stop me.'

'I did.'

'Yeah.'

'If you were determined enough to kill Chaney there was nothing I could've done about it.'

Rink closed his eyes briefly. 'No. But I'm glad you did. You said I made a mistake: I trust you. But you'd better tell me how or I'm going back for the punk.'

I took a long swallow of coffee. 'Chaney is a thug; there's no denying it. And I don't doubt that he deserves the bullet you planned to put in him, but it wasn't him.'

'How can you be so sure?'

'I went back and talked with your mom again, Rink.'

'She told me it was Chaney.'

'She was...uh, lying.'

Rink's forehead creased, but it wasn't at my suggestion that his mother was less than the symbol of virtue and goodness he believed, but that my words had struck a chord in him.

'Not lying per se,' I went on, 'but guessing: putting two and

16

two together and getting five. As you know, there had been some trouble with Chaney's lot throwing their weight around, so it was only natural that your mom should mention him to the police, and to us when we got here. But she's had more time to think and she doesn't believe that Chaney's the one responsible any more. For a start, she doesn't believe that a clown like him could've done what he did.'

'No,' Rink said. 'Now that I've met him and tested his mettle, I don't think so either. But it doesn't make a difference to me, Hunter. Someone is responsible and I'm gonna find him. And when I do, even you won't be able to stop me next time.'

'As if I'm going to try? I'll be right there beside you, brother.'

Rink hadn't even looked at his smoothie until now, and he chugged it down. 'You went back to see my mom. How is she?'

'Hurting. Physically and mentally. She was more concerned about you running off the way you did than anything else. She was frightened that she sent you after the wrong man and asked that I stop you from making the biggest mistake of your life.'

'Chaney wouldn't have been a loss...to anyone.'

'Maybe not, but the way you went about it, there'd have been only one suspect. Your mom didn't want to see you going to prison for the wrong man.'

'That'd put a wrench in the works...no way I'd find the right one then.' Rink squinted at me. 'I take it the disguise wasn't for my sake?'

'I had to get close to Chaney in order to find you. Like many, he's blind to anyone he deems beneath himself. It worked. I was able to find him, and he led me to you. Had a feeling that you'd do him on the early train where there was little chance of collateral damage. But I wasn't positive and decided I'd shadow him for as long as it took you to make a move. Would've made life much easier if you hadn't done a runner from the hospital, or if you'd answered your bloody phone when I called you.'

He curled a lip at my ear bashing. Usually the tables were turned the opposite direction. Then he grew melancholy, and his hooded eyes sparkled with unshed tears. 'Didn't want to bring you down with me, brother.'

'Jesus, Rink! It's your dad we're talking about here. I want to avenge his murder as much as you do.'

17

4

'I'll wait outside, Rink. I think it's important that you speak with your mom alone.'

'She'll be glad to see you, too.'

'I know, but there'll be time for that later. You need to speak with her in private. There's something she wants to say, but my guess is it's for your ears only.'

I watched as Rink headed into the intensive care unit, then went to stand in the parking lot, kicking my heels against the kerb while I killed time. The hospital was nestled at the foot of Potrero Hill in the city's Mission District, considered one of the finest public hospitals in the U.S. I didn't doubt it. Now that the early mist had burned off, I was happy to feel the Californian sun on my face, but that wasn't why I chose to wait outside. I preferred things that way.

Though I respect doctors, nurses, in fact everyone in the medical profession, I hate hospitals. For me a trip to a hospital usually means that I'm injured, or someone I care for is hurt, suffering illness, have already perished or soon will. The smell is often enough to cause a negative reflex surge inside me, but then it's been said that the olfactory sense has the greatest memory. It isn't so much the anti-septic smell that raises my gorge but the underlying odour of pain. It's a distinct aroma that has dogged my memories most of my life.

Visiting the hospital this time there was one thing that made me grateful, and that was the fact that Rink's mom was on the mend, her injuries not as life threatening as we'd first feared. She had suffered blunt force trauma, most probably from the barrel of a gun, but thankfully she'd been struck a glancing blow. It had been enough to rip her scalp, to scar the bone beneath, but not split her skull completely. The blow had knocked her unconscious, left her with concussion and a throbbing headache, but nothing lasting. The surgeons' greatest fear was that there could be an internal bleed, but MRI scans had shown her brain to be uninjured. Their second fear was that the elderly lady's underlying health problems might kill her. For some years now Yukiko had been suffering cardiac problems, and the concern was that her failing heart might not be strong enough to sustain her recovery: particularly when she was told her husband had died. Yet, Yukiko had surprised us all and was much stronger now. Probably the relief of seeing her sole surviving child by her bedside helped. Yesterday, when Rink had made off from the hospital, Yukiko had looked at me and I had recognised terror in her face. She had outlived her husband, and two children; she did not want to outlive her youngest boy. She had made me swear that I'd bring him back safely to her. I'm glad that I was able to do that and to give her some comfort.

I hoped now that Yukiko would repay that debt by telling Rink the truth about who had murdered his dad.

I waited an hour.

When Rink was a no-show I feared that he'd sneaked off again on another uncharacteristic rampage. But I was doing him an injustice and so I waited some more.

Another hour later Rink finally approached. Since flying in we'd hired a rental car, and without looking at me he headed directly for the silver Chrysler. I fell in step with him, arrived at the car at the same time.

I leaned on the roof of the car, caught my friend's eye. 'Well?'

'She's doing fine. The doctors say she'll be able to go home in a day or two.'

'That's good,' I said, and meant it. 'But that's not what I asked.'

Rink nodded me inside the car. I'd have offered to drive, but things were usually this way with us. Rink didn't trust me to stay on the right side of the road. Ordinarily he'd make some jibe, but not now. He started the car and pulled away, and he didn't have a destination in mind judging by the way he paused at the exit. Finally he took a left, for no other reason that it was as good as any direction.

'She swears she doesn't know who killed my dad.'

We'd been there when a detective had attended her bedside and recorded a statement. Yukiko had related how she and Andrew had been wakened by a noise and her husband had gone downstairs to investigate. She had followed him down and seen a man in black standing over Andrew, a gun in his hand. The man had his back to her and she'd taken the opportunity to arm herself with a plant pot. The trouble was he'd heard her approaching and had struck her unconscious. That was all she could recall, despite all the detective's attempts at teasing further detail from her. That was when she'd mentioned some trouble with Chaney and his friends and suggested that he might have had something to do with her husband's murder. The detective had noted her words down, then left, and Yukiko had drifted into a fitful sleep. A few minutes after that and Rink had slipped away. At first I'd thought he'd snuck off somewhere to be alone, to grieve in private, and I gave him some space. But that only lasted until Yukiko had roused from her sleep and asked for him.

'Do you believe her?'

Rink nodded. 'She told me that she mentioned Chaney to the cops because she thought he deserved extra notice from them, but that was all. She was also about to say something else but her nurse came in and she clammed up. I tried to press her on it afterwards, but she wouldn't say anything. She changed the subject, started making preparations for my dad's funeral.' There was a hitch in his voice at the end, so I allowed him a moment or two of reflection.

'She doesn't know who killed your dad, but she knows why.'

Rink turned to me for a second and I barely recognised him.

'Yeah,' he said, 'that's what I figure.'

'So why won't she tell the cops? Why not tell you?'

'Giri.' Rink looked at me again and this time his face was set in stone. 'My mom is a firm believer in the old ways.'

Giri. I turned the Japanese phrase over in my mind. It was a concept rather than a single word, and one I was familiar with. Not that it was a phrase easily translated in the west. Some have said that it means "duty" but it goes much deeper than that. It is better defined as "moral obligation", or a debt of gratitude where self-sacrifice outweighs the pursuit of happiness.

Basically, Yukiko believed she owed someone her silence, and fulfilling her obligation countered bringing her husband's murderer to justice. Sometimes *giri* has been called the "burden of obligation", and I could see that it was true in Yukiko's case.

'What about the *giri* she should show towards your father?' Immediately I wanted to retract the question. 'Shit. Ignore that, Rink. That was pretty insensitive of me.'

'Yeah,' he said, without expounding. I wasn't sure which of my statements he was agreeing with.

Hitomi Yukiko's parents had been Japanese, staunch traditionalists raised in a land that was still governed by an Emperor, whose rule was defined by a static feudal order that had existed and defined Japanese society for centuries. Even when they had moved to the U.S. the Hitomi family had continued to practice these ancient values, and had passed them down to their girl child. Even Rink, raised in the U.S., with a Scottish-Canadian father, held strongly to some of his grandparents' teachings. I knew what was going through his head: if anyone held a burden of obligation to his father, it was he. By default that burden extended to me and I'd do everything I could to help my friend repay it.

'So what's the plan?'

Rink concentrated on the road ahead. It was probably so that I didn't see the tears in his eyes. 'As soon as the police release his body I'll see to my father's funeral. Then I'll avenge him.'

It was a simple plan, but those were the type I preferred.

5

Jed Newmark was drinking alone. Other drinkers in the bar on Stanyan Street surrounded him, but he'd chosen to ignore them and hunched over his drink at the bar. For a start he shared little in common with the young professionals who spent less time on drinking than they did their cell phones. He was twice the age of the next oldest person in the bar, and that was the bartender. During the 1990s Cole Valley had grown popular with dot-commers, so much so that many of the original residents had moved out to make way for the young and affluent. Now some of those yuppie types were approaching their middle years, but they were still young punks to Jed. He felt old. Recently some young pup had heard his name and asked if he was any relation to Craig Newmark, the internet entrepreneur responsible for founding the San Francisco-based website Craigslist. Jed had played along and had said yes. 'Are you his dad?' asked the young sycophant. Shit, Jed had thought, Craig Newmark has to be in his sixties by now.

He cupped both hands around his glass, just a drop or two of whisky left in the bottom, peering over at his reflection in the warped mirror beyond the shelved liquor bottles. He looked toad-like, short, squat, and round faced. His mouth drooped down at the corners, but didn't help smooth out any of the wrinkles round his puffy eyelids. To be honest, it was a wonder he hadn't been mistaken for Craig's granddad.

He finished his drink, pushed the empty glass from him and slipped some dollars in the general direction of the bartender. Without even a nod of appreciation for the tip he'd added, the bartender continued serving martinis to a middle-aged couple further along the bar. Feeling invisible, Jed walked out of the bar and into late afternoon sunlight. He blinked against the unfamiliar glare, before setting off for his apartment a couple of blocks south on Carmel. He was returning to an empty home.

His wife, Rose, had died three years ago. Stomach cancer had spread to her liver where it did more damage than the hard liquor he'd consumed over the years ever did to his. Jed was alone in the world now. No children. No friends. That was different until very recently, but then Andrew Rington had been taken during a senseless bout of violence in the man's home.

Jed muttered to himself as he walked. The liquor he'd downed had thrown a cloak of cotton wool over him, fogging the pain of grief he'd felt at the news of Andrew's murder, but it was still there like an itch at the back of his head that he couldn't shake. Fucking senseless. How could such a good man as Andrew Rington be gunned down in his own home? What had this world become?

He had known Andrew and Yukiko for more than forty years. He knew the couple when they had lived in Little Rock, Arkansas, way back before the birth of their youngest son, Jared. They had been good friends, and more so because Rose and Yukiko got on so well, having grown up in the same neighbourhood of San Francisco as children. Jed had lost contact with the Ringtons for a few years, after him and Rose moved back west, and had been surprised to hear from Andrew a few years ago when they too planned to move back to Yukiko's childhood home. Rose didn't live too long afterwards, but it had been a happy reunion with Yukiko while it lasted. It had helped his wife through the final painful days of her illness. Jed and Andrew occasionally took themselves down to Fisherman's Warf to cast a line in the sea, or to simply sit on the benches and spend a couple hours of companionable silence watching the antics of the sea lions out on the jetties near Pier 39.

He felt the sting of tears and wiped at his cheeks with the back of a wrist.

He'd shared good memories with Andrew.

Then again, they also shared bad memories.

The basement.

He shook his head. Don't go there, he commanded himself.

The Cole Valley district originally grew up around a streetcar stop at the entrance to the Sunset Tunnel. Now that area at the intersection of Carl and Cole Streets was the neighbourhood's small business district, and Jed still managed a tiny flower boutique Rose had opened there. He had closed it the morning he'd heard of Andrew's murder and hadn't been to the shop since. He couldn't go on neglecting it like this, but he still could not face work today. He wouldn't be able to be polite to his customers and that wouldn't do. Neither could he go to the shop drunk as he was. Tomorrow, he promised, he'd go in and design a wreath fit to place on his friend's grave.

The home he'd shared with Rose was on the upper floor of a three-storied Victorian, the lower levels now rented to staff from the University of California. This time of day his neighbours would not be home, and he was glad that he wouldn't be required to make small talk on the stairs. He pushed into his apartment having no memory of the walk back. Inside, the air-conditioning was turned too high, the air chilly. Nevertheless he shrugged out of his jacket and hung it on a hook in the closet next to the front door, and kicked off his shoes and placed them on a shelf. It was an old habit adopted from his wife who had always had exacting housekeeping standards. He worked his feet into a pair of slippers, and then headed along the short hall passing the sitting room. Old age had brought intolerance to him, and he hated the cold. It played havoc with his joints. He decided he'd turn up the central heating before the mist returned and with it the ache to his bones. Perhaps a nice hot cup of coffee wouldn't go amiss either. He entered the kitchen and placed the makings in his Mr Coffee machine and set it dripping. Like many of the items in the apartment the machine was a relic of earlier times, a gift bought for him by Rose back in the mid-1970s and carted round with them ever since. Thinking back on when she'd presented the machine to him, he smiled sadly. He was a fan of Joe DiMaggio, and his wife thought it apt that he received a gift endorsed by the former baseball star. It was those little naïve touches of hers that had made him love her so much. Feeling maudlin, Jed fetched his favourite mug, placed it next to the hissing machine and then headed for the sitting room to deal with the heating.

A panel in the sitting room controlled the central heating; it was on the wall to the left as he entered. Concentrating on the task at hand he pushed open the door, twisted towards the panel. It took a second for his booze-addled brain to notice that something was out of place. He turned from the panel to look at the figure standing across the room from him with his hands clasped at his lower back.

'Who are you?' Even as the question rolled from his tongue it became redundant, because the man had lifted his chin and Jed got a good look at his features.

'I see you know that already,' the man replied.

Jed looked around the room, as though checking that nothing else was out of the norm. It was a wasted act, because it wouldn't matter in the long run.

'What do you want?'

The man snorted out a lough. 'I think you also know that.'

These days Jed was a florist, another thing he'd adopted and embraced from a life shared with his gentle wife, but he hadn't always been. As a young man he'd had a very different skill set and the instincts he'd carried then surged to the surface now. He bunched his fists. 'It was you. You killed Andrew Rington.'

'It's kind of obvious, isn't it?'

'You murderous son of a bitch!' Jed took a step forward.

The man brought his hands from behind his back, and with them the silenced handgun he pointed at Jed's face. He smiled. 'Isn't that what they call "a pot calling the kettle black"?'

The gun spat, but Jed didn't hear it. The bullet took out the back of his skull before the sound reached his ears.

6

The sun was beating down from a sky devoid of clouds, the heat trickling like warm honey beneath my formal clothing. For the occasion I'd doffed my usual casual attire in favour of shirt, tie and black suit. Most funerals I've ever attended have been dour events conducted under leaden skies, and it felt unusual to feel the sunlight dance on my face. To banish the unfamiliar sensation I kept my head tilted down, but that was more befitting the ceremony at any rate.

I was like a brother to Rink, as I've said, and by virtue of that relationship a second son to Yukiko and Andrew Rington, and I'd been allotted a place at the graveside. Rink was supporting his mom under the protective arch of his arm, and I stood to her other side. I felt a little awkward standing there in my stiff new suit and could have done with someone else to hold on to. Ordinarily my girlfriend, Imogen, would have been beside me, but not now. In the past few months we'd kind of drifted apart, the spells where we didn't see each other, or even speak on the phone, growing longer. I'd told her about Andrew's murder, and she'd been saddened, but hadn't offered to join me at the funeral. I took that as her way of cutting me adrift. It had been coming, and my skipping off to the other side of the continent was as good an excuse as any. Partly I was happy she was moving on, partly I was disappointed that our relationship had come to an end. It was a depressing fact that we'd got together due to a violent death and now we had parted because of another.

There were few other mourners. Not that Andrew wasn't well liked or that he had no friends, but that had been a thing of the past. Most of his contemporaries were now in graves of their own and it's a sad reflection that the longer one lives the less people there are to mourn your passing. The vicar presided, saying a prayer. Having helped us to lower the coffin, the four pallbearers supplied by the undertaker service stood back from the grave. Opposite us were two elderly ladies, friends of Yukiko, and three old guys who were passing acquaintances of Andrew. Behind us stood two more mourners. A thin old man with watery grey eyes and an aquiline nose who had introduced himself as Lawrence Parnell, and another heavyset old man with a bald head mottled by fine scars called Rodney Faulks were Andrew's only genuine friends in attendance. I'd noticed Yukiko share nods with both men, before she'd frowned then searched the graveyard for someone else. When the missing person didn't appear her features had gone from grief to mild concern. But now, as the vicar made the sign of the cross over the coffin to a soft chorus of "amen" from the mourners, I saw that her attention had returned fully to her beloved husband's interment.

The cemetery was on a sloping hill, encircled by a stone retaining wall and towering eucalyptus trees. Between the trees was a view of the Golden Gate Bridge, the blue waters of the bay and the rolling hills of the U.S. mainland beyond. It was a picture perfect view but held no interest for me. Though I had my head tilted in respect, I was peering from under my brows, watching. I didn't doubt that there could be plain-clothed police officers out there somewhere, because it was standard practice at funerals of murder victims. Occasionally a killer liked to turn up at a funeral, mingle with the mourners and take perverted satisfaction from the grief they'd caused. Over the top of rows of headstones I didn't see anyone suspicious, but then I didn't have a full field of vision.

A small bowl holding earth was passed around. Yukiko was first to sprinkle dust on the coffin, as well as a single lily she'd brought for just that purpose. Rink followed, then I took a pinch of dust and sprinkled it over the coffin. Once we had done that we moved away, with Rink still cradling his mom and it was my first opportunity to scan the space beyond the Spanish Revival-styled rostrum and up towards the entrance drive where we'd left the funeral cars. There were a couple of people up there, but they could have been visitors to other graves showing us a few minutes respect by keeping their distance. We headed that way and as we approached the couple moved deeper into the cemetery. They were a middle-aged couple carrying a wreath and of no concern. Something else caught my eye though. There was a large saloon car idling on the road outside the front gate. Even from this distance I could make out the silhouette of a head turned our way, but nothing of the features. The last thing anyone wanted was violence at a funeral, but I wondered if this was Andrew's killer. More than anything I wanted to slip away from Rink and Yukiko, and go over there and check. But I didn't; for all I knew it was a cop scoping us out. I just lifted my head and stared at him. A hand came out of the front passenger window. I didn't flinch: it was empty, I could tell. The hand furled into a fist and knocked a short rhythm against the door. Then the engine roared and the saloon car peeled away from the entrance and took off at speed.

'Who was that?'

Rink had come silently to my shoulder. His mom was in the capable hands of her two lady friends, blissfully ignorant of what had just happened as she accepted their hugs and condolences.

'I was just wondering the very same thing,' I said.

'You think it was Chaney?'

'No.' I'd credited Sean Chaney with more intelligence than this. From the way we handled him on the BART carriage he must have realised he was wholly outclassed. I was confident that he hadn't run to the police to complain about us, because he would have had to come clean about why he'd made an enemy of us. He was a mug, but not an idiot.

'If the cops questioned him about my dad's murder he'll know where to find us. No way that bastard's going to bring trouble to my mom's house.' Rink was building a case for pre-emptive action. I wasn't usually averse to the idea, but this time we'd have being targeting the wrong person.

'It wasn't Chaney,' I repeated. 'His head wasn't fat enough.'

'You should've let me shoot Chaney, saved everyone a heap of trouble.' He checked on his mom. Yukiko looked frail and bewildered, not an image I'd ever had of her before. Before this she had always epitomized strength and tranquillilty, but now she was jittery as she glanced back and forth between her concerned friends, then she would look elsewhere, and again I got the impression she was searching for another face.

'Forget about him,' I said. 'Let's concentrate on finding the man who did murder your dad.'

He scowled, but knew I was speaking sense. 'You think that was him? That asshole in the car?'

'I doubt it.'

'But it could have been, and we just missed our opportunity to catch him.'

'We'll have other opportunities,' I said. 'In places less public than this.'

He understood what I was saying. When we did find the murderer, we didn't want a bunch of innocents caught in the crossfire. We definitely didn't want witnesses.

'Got to see to my mom first,' he said. 'Then we'll get started.'

Ordinarily a wake would have been held to honor Andrew's memory. However, having just come out of hospital, and still weakened by her injuries, Yukiko was in no state to play host to a gathering offering their sympathies. Rink had taken the decision that his dad's memory was honor enough and that a wake wouldn't help his mom's recovery. But he saw some value in having someone close by her.

'I'm going to ask her friends to stay with her for a while. It will do her good. She won't talk to me about losing my dad, but she might with them.' Rink walked away, approached the trio of elderly ladies and I saw him kiss each of them on the cheek. I allowed him the privacy, taking the opportunity to scan the cemetery once more. The three acquaintances of Andrew had already climbed into their respective vehicles and were pulling away. Lawrence Parnell and Rodney Faulks were still near to Andrew's grave. They had their heads bowed in silent reflection, but they weren't looking down at the grave, but towards Yukiko. They were possibly waiting for the right moment to say their condolences, but I wasn't sure. Parnell glanced my way. When he saw me watching, he offered a nod and a grimace of a smile before dipping his head. I thought that during the brief interaction there was fear in his face. Perhaps he was feeling his mortality and that the ceremony had made him consider his own short future. But I felt that there was something else.

I walked towards the two old men.

Rink had briefly introduced us earlier, so there was no need of names now. I offered my hand to Parnell, and then to Faulks. Both men shook hands with the hearty manner that spoke of mutual respect. Faulks gestured at the grave. 'It's a terrible way for such a good man to go,' he said.

'Was a time when nobody would have got the drop on him. Andrew was a tough guy, the toughest guy I ever knew. Such a shame.' Parnell swiped at his face with a palm, dashing away tears. 'I can't believe that some sneaking little thief did that to him.'

Parnell had heard the findings of the police investigation. It was early days yet, but already the homicide detectives had decided that Andrew fell victim to a burglary gone wrong. The fact that there were no signs of entry, and that nothing had been taken seemed beside the point. Theories of how the burglar had found an unsecured door, had entered but was then disturbed before having chance to steal anything were still being bandied around.

'You don't think that's the case?' I asked.

Parnell and Faulks shared a glance. There was something hidden and furtive in their features.

'It was Sean Chaney, if you ask me. If not him, then someone he put up to it.' Parnell glanced once more at Faulks, gave him a sharp look and Faulks nodded in agreement. Parnell went on. 'You probably heard from Yukiko that one of our buddies was having trouble with Chaney's crew. They were leaning on him for money, so Andrew was waiting for them next time they visited Jed's store. He saw them off the premises if you, uh, get my meaning?'

I smiled gently. I knew exactly what he meant. Even in his late seventies Andrew Rington was no slouch.

Faulks took up the story. 'See, Chaney's all bluster. He backed down from Andrew, but to save face he made threats on the way out. Told him things weren't finished with, that Andrew would have to watch his ass.'

'The cops already cleared Chaney. I'm guessing he had a solid alibi,' I pointed out.

'Like I said,' Parnell said. 'He must have put one of his buddies up to it.'

I didn't comment. It sounded feasible, but not quite the truth either. These old men had their suspicions about the real killer, but they weren't yet ready to voice them. I knew then that their suspicion had been the source of the fear I'd read in Parnell's glance.

Faulks leaned in conspiratorially. 'I heard that Chaney is limping around all of a sudden. I think that maybe Andrew's boy has already had a word with him?'

Again I didn't comment. But both men understood the reason for my silence and now they smiled as gently as I had.

I wasn't smiling now though. Something was bothering me, and it had nothing to do with how these men were diverting me from the truth. 'The friend Andrew helped out...?'

'Jed Newmark,' Faulks offered.

'I'd have thought he'd have been here to show his respect. Particularly if Andrew lost his life after sticking up for him.'

'Yeah. We're surprised he isn't here, too,' Parnell said.

I watched Rink help his mom into one of her friends' car. As she prepared to slide into the back, she took one last look around. Even from this distance I could tell there was more concern than disappointment on her face. Yukiko was expecting to see Jed Newmark here as well, and was worried when he had not turned up. Considering that Jed was the source of trouble involving Chaney, perhaps he'd stayed away out of a feeling of responsibility over Andrew's death. Maybe he couldn't yet bring himself to face Yukiko out of misguided guilt. Or—and this was what troubled me most—fear of further retribution from Chaney had made him go into hiding.

'Are you friends with Jed as well?'

Both men shared that look again. Then Parnell said, 'Yeah. We all go way back.'

'You keep in touch with him?'

They nodded.

'When did you last speak to him?'

'Couple of nights ago,' Faulks offered. 'We had a few drink's together, to remember Andrew.'

'How was he?'

'Broken-hearted like the rest of us,' Parnell said.

'Not feeling guilty?'

'What's he got to feel guilty about?' Parnell looked at me sharply. But then he lowered his gaze, started scuffing the turf with a toe. I waited for him to add more but he didn't. I turned to Faulks but he wouldn't meet my eye either. All I got was a view of his suntanned pate, criss-crossed with fine white lines.

'Where does he live?' I asked.

Faulks told me an address in Cole Valley, giving me general directions of how to get there. Suddenly my reason for asking hit his friends simultaneously, and now they were looking at me earnestly.

'You don't think something has happened to him?'

'I hope not, Mr Parnell,' I said. 'But we won't know without checking.'

'You want us to come with you?' Faulks offered. Once upon a time the guy was possibly handy in a scrap, but now his heavy body was sunken, his knees bowed. A hindrance rather than a help. Parnell still appeared reasonably fit for his age, but he was lucky if he weighed eight stones wet through. Force of will didn't mean a thing when someone could pick him up with one hand and throw him across a room.

'No,' I said, thinking of a good enough reason to turn them down. 'I don't doubt that you can handle yourselves, but if Chaney and his lot are hanging around, I'll have my hands full. I won't be able to look after you guys as well. I was talking about me and Rink going there.'

Both men turned to see Rink walking towards us. They appraised him, maybe comparing him with the memory of his father. Both Parnell and Faulks seemed happy with the comparison. Parnell said, 'If they have hurt Jed, what will you do?'

'Stuff like that's best left unsaid,' I told him with a wink. 'I wouldn't like to drop a conspiracy to murder charge in your lap.'

They didn't reply, but shared that furtive glance of before.

7

Homicide Detective P. Wayne Tyler of the SFPD was more formal than his partner who introduced himself simply as Gar Jones.

The four of us were grouped on the landing outside Jed Newmark's third floor apartment in a converted Victorian in Cole Valley. It was a tight squeeze: Rink's huge, and Gar Jones wasn't a little man either. He wasn't as muscular as Rink, but he was as tall, with square shoulders topping a solid, raw-boned frame. Standing side by side they practically blocked the hall. Tyler was a slighter man, dark and handsome and dressed in a sharp suit and tie. He was alongside me, waiting while the CSI team finished up and we could go back into the apartment. He kept flicking an inquisitive glance my way, but when I looked he'd turn away quickly.

There was a scuff of movement on the stairs below us and from the stairwell appeared men from the Medical Examiner's office. They were lugging a gurney and body bag. We spread out, allowing them to squeeze by us and approach the apartment door. A CSI tech waved them inside and we all followed suit. If the body was being released from the crime scene it meant that it was safe for us to enter. Rink and I had already agreed to allow the CSI team to run tests on us: fingerprints, shoe prints, fibre samples, but only for the purpose of eliminating us from their enquiries. It was a necessary evil, having entered the apartment when we'd found the door ajar on our arrival. When we had called out and received no answer from Jed Newmark we'd gone in. The smell had hit us before we reached the living room, and it was no surprise to find the bloating corpse lying in the centre of the room.

Jed had been shot in the face at point blank range. The bullet had exited and taken with it a considerable chunk of his skull. The blood spatter pattern showed he'd been standing a little to

the left inside the entrance to the room. The spent bullet had
buried itself in the doorjamb. Other bullets were in Jed's back,
fired into him when he was already belly down on the floor and
dead. They had been fired in an act of overkill: that or cold
anger. To me it meant that the shooter had come here not only
to murder Jed, but also to punish him. The similarities with
Andrew's murder didn't escape either Rink or me, or the
detectives who we called in shortly after.

Tyler and Jones had treated us with suspicion—and rightly
so. But when we related how we'd come directly from a funeral
to check on the deceased's missing best friend it relaxed them a
tad, but not much. It didn't take much deduction to figure that
Jed had died sometime the day before, so it didn't put either of
us out of the frame for his murder. For a second or two I
thought Rink was going to go nuclear on them, but to my
surprise he'd merely grunted and acquiesced to the detectives'
theory. Now he was simply going with the flow, but I knew
why. If we started jumping around and shouting the odds, we'd
most likely have the cops hounding our tails and no way would
we be able to avenge Andrew, and now Jed. It was apparent
that the murderer of both men was one and the same, but I
didn't think it had anything to do with Chaney. We had to play
our cards close to our chests, otherwise we'd be hobbled by the
SFPD and never find the one responsible.

A CSI tech had dug the bullet out of the jamb, had bagged it
as evidence. He showed it briefly to Tyler.

'Nine mil?' Tyler asked.

The tech nodded.

I was thankful that we'd come directly from the cemetery,
and therefore without our sidearms. My SIG was loaded with 9
mm Parabellum ammunition and could have caused an
awkward moment if the cops chose to search us for a possible
murder weapon. Coming in earlier, Tyler and Jones had done a
preliminary inspection of the body and they had concluded
from the entry holes that the bullets had been 9 mm: Tyler
looked pleased that they'd guessed correctly. It didn't mean an
awful lot because many guns use the same ammunition, and
didn't help identify a possible suspect without a gun to compare
it to.

The CSI team had concluded their examination and collected all the evidence they were going to. The men from the MEs office moved in to bag and tag Jed. It was a cold description of their duties, but at the end of the day was what it was. As they went about their business I turned to look at Rink. It must have been hell for him to witness and I knew what must have been going through his mind, his father having died so recently in similar circumstances. I considered asking him to follow me out of the room but Rink wasn't one to be mollycoddled. In the brief moment my attention was off the proceedings I missed something. When I looked back the two detectives were crouching down over Jed's corpse, peering at something that had until now gone undetected. I shared a quizzical glance with Rink and we both stepped in for a look at what had caught their attention.

It was a photograph in a gilt-edged frame.

Tyler pulled on latex gloves, handed to him by one of the CSI men.

He teased the photo out from under Jed, and then paused to look at the carpet where it had lain. Because the shots fired into Jed's body had been done so post mortem there was little blood beneath him, but there were some dots on the carpet underneath where the photo had been found. I don't consider myself a detective, but even I could tell that the photo frame had been slipped beneath the body after Jed was already dead.

Tyler looked once at Jones, confirming that his partner had caught the significance too, before noticing us looming over them. 'Do you mind keeping your distance? In fact, I'm not even sure I want you in the room.'

Continuing our show of compliance we stepped back, watching as Tyler sealed the photo in an evidence bag, then signing it over to the CSI team. Unless the killer was supremely stupid he would have been wearing gloves when placing the photo, but there was always an off chance that there were fingerprints on the frame. I doubted it: but the frame was a clue of sorts to me, and more for the photograph's subject than the physical item. On the way over here, Rink had told me a little about Jed Newmark, that he was a widower whose wife, Rose had died a few years earlier. Rose had been a friend of Yukiko's but I hadn't realised until seeing the picture that she too was Japanese. A theory was beginning to rattle around in my head, gaining momentum, but it wasn't something I wanted to mention to the detectives. Rink's words came back to me. '*Giri. My mom is a firm believer in the old ways.*' I had begun to wonder how far that "burden of obligation" stretched.

Detective Jones left his partner to approach us. He was smiling faintly as he tucked his thumbs into his belt, shoved back his shoulders. 'There's stuff you guys know but aren't telling us. Want to get down to business and save us the run around?'

We shared a look, and I allowed Rink to reply for us. 'All I know is that someone murdered my dad, and now his best friend, and the SFPD doesn't seem to have a goddamn clue who's responsible.'

Jones shook his head. With his strawberry blond curls and a splash of freckles across his nose, he looked much younger, and less experienced than his position as a homicide detective dictated. But his face took on harder edges, and he didn't look as amiable as before. He looked into Rink's eyes and didn't flinch. 'When your father was killed you were in Florida. We checked. We know that you—' he gave me a cursory nod '—and your friend weren't involved directly, but we also found out a thing or two that raised a red flag. As much as you've covered your asses, and it seems someone with influence has kept you both from being thrown in jail, our colleagues out east aren't idiots. They know that you're responsible for a number of violent crimes—*fatally* violent in some cases—and that you have made some dangerous and brutal enemies in the last couple years. There has been a certain lassitude shown towards your actions, primarily because those that you've gone up against probably deserved what they got, but when those actions bring trouble to *our city* the SFPD aren't the type to turn a blind eye. We don't endorse vigilantism here.'

'You haven't just had someone close to you murdered,' Rink said. 'Maybe you'd think differently then.'

Jones ignored the retort. 'The way I was beginning to look at things, this was your entire fault: someone with a beef with you chose to attack you through your family.' He gestured at the bagged corpse being loaded onto the gurney. 'Now I'm not so sure. I can't see any reason why they would then target Mr Newmark. Not unless there's something I'm missing?'

Did Jones believe that Jed Newmark was Andrew's murderer, and that we'd done the old guy in out of revenge? If so, he wasn't saying, but it would add validity to why it had become necessary for us to consent to forensic examination. I didn't think that was the case, though: if we were deemed suspects we'd have been arrested at the get go.

'Whatever you're missing, we are too,' Rink said.

Jones puffed his cheeks out, before exhaling noisily. 'Forgive me, Mr Rington, but I think you're feeding me a line of bullshit.'

'That's your prerogative. I don't care. All I care about is finding the man who killed my dad.' His gaze flicked to the gurney being trundled past us. 'And Jed Newmark.'

'That's what we all want. But there's something else that we demand...'

'If we learn anything, we tell you immediately?'

'Yes. I'd hate to think that you chose to exact your own brand of justice: if that were to happen—'

'The SFPD wouldn't turn a blind eye. Yeah, we got that already.'

Detective Jones unhooked his thumbs, allowing his jacket to swing closed over the gun holstered on his belt next to his detective's shield. 'I'm glad we're all clear on that.'

'Crystal,' Rink said. I could smell the testosterone in the air.

'Just the way we like it.' Jones glanced over at Detective Tyler and the men shared a less than subtle nod. Jones allowed his features to relax, and the easy going smile crept back into place. 'We appreciate your cooperation on this. Makes it much easier for everyone involved.'

Including the murderer, I thought, but elected to keep my opinion to myself.

Jones indicated one of the CSI techs. 'Don't forget to speak with my colleague before you leave. In fact, why don't you go with him now? You can use the kitchen over there.'

We'd been dismissed like chastened schoolboys from the 'principal's office. Not that either of us minded. We'd wasted enough time there as it was. As soon as we were done with the forensics guy, we could get on with what needed doing. After we'd changed our clothing and shoes and put on gloves.

8

In South Dakota, at 8:30 p.m. on the day of Andrew Rington's funeral, Dan Lansdale was sitting in the bleachers of his grandson's Little League stadium. The description of "stadium" was too grand because it wasn't much more than a diamond set in well-trampled sun-dried earth, a lean-to dug out and a chain-link fence, surrounded by triple-tiered rows of wooden benches on metal scaffolding. But it was known as "The Stadium" by the local townsfolk and had been since Dan was a boy. When he was a kid he'd taken his first practice swings out on the same diamond, observed by his grandfather in turn. He wasn't watching his own grandson now: the boy was home with his parents, as he should be this late in the evening. Dan had come here because it held such fond memories for him, thinking they might push aside the terrible things he'd been forced into recalling since hearing of Andrew's murder.

The sun was low in the heavens, setting fire to the low-lying clouds shrouding the nearest peaks of the Black Hills. Occasionally Dan turned his gaze away, blinking until the colours etched onto his retina faded, before looking west again. He was sitting in the tiny town of Whitehead, far enough off Interstate 90 that sightseers heading for the nearby national park and Mount Rushmore missed it, but his mind was on his deceased friend in San Francisco. Occasionally it drifted to a different place but he was quick to shove the thoughts away. He chose to dwell on better times, or at least attempted to because thoughts of *the basement* kept coming back to him.

Dan had been born here in Whitehead, into a large Evangelican Lutheran family, and but for a spell spent abroad had lived here most of his adult life. Whitehead was his sanctum, the place he felt that his other life had no business invading and until the telephone call he'd received a couple days ago it had left him alone. Being a religious man, he had no truck in the concepts of fate or karma, but believed that a man's sins would come back to repay him tenfold. He was therefore unsurprised when he heard the soft thud of footsteps and turned to see a man approaching across the deserted baseball ground. Though he wouldn't admit it, Dan had come here for more than the purpose of reminiscing. He had suspected that he was next on the list and didn't want to be found at home where his wife could be hurt the way Yukiko was when the man had gone for Andrew.

Dan didn't get up.

There was no point in trying to run, not with bad legs that required the support of a walking stick these days. But that wasn't the reason: he fully accepted that he was about to die and wouldn't give the man the satisfaction of chasing him down like a coward.

As the man approached he kicked up dust, small zephyrs lifting dust devils in his wake. The man was wearing a black jacket over a plaid shirt, jeans and boots. He had a baseball cap pulled down low, and sunglasses that reflected the burning clouds. He stopped ten feet from Dan and regarded him through the links in the fence. The effect of the sunglasses added to the man's soulless scrutiny. The image took Dan way back to that basement again, and how he'd struck a similar set of glasses from a man's face. He wished now he could do likewise, but even with the added reach of his stick the man was out of range.

Without saying a word his would-be executioner pulled a folding knife from out of his jacket pocket. He was wearing gloves, the latex type favoured by surgeons. The blade also reflected the fiery sky as the man opened it.

'You shot Andrew Rington.' It wasn't a question, or recrimination; Dan was simply stating a fact.

'That's right. I shot Newmark and Tennant as well.' The man watched the colour drain from Dan's features. 'I see the news about your other two buddies hasn't reached you yet.'

'There aren't many of us left...'

'No. Soon there won't be any.'

'And what will you do then, when this misguided crusade ends? You'll go back to your normal life? Have you stopped to think about that? Can it ever be normal again?'

'I doubt it. I'm beginning to enjoy being judge, jury and executioner. There's still a penance to pay. My life has been hell; maybe I'll make *others* suffer the way I have.'

Dan hung his head. 'I accept now that what we did was wrong. I've made my confession, begged forgiveness from God, but from the fact you've shown up here, it seems my prayers went unheard.'

'Don't expect leniency from me either.'

'I don't. I accept my punishment. But please...' Dan lifted his head to stare directly at the man. 'Stop then. There's no need for anyone else to get hurt. There's been enough killing already.'

The man shook his head, an almost sad motion that wasn't conveyed by his sneer. 'It can't stop here.'

'It can.'

'It can't and I won't stop.' The man held the knife close to his hip. 'Not while there are three still alive. And I won't stop while the other ones who concocted those lies breathe either.'

'They weren't lies,' Dan said as the man approached him, pushing through a gate in the fence. He pointed an arthritic finger at the murderer. 'And you know it.'

The man kept on coming, hopping up onto the first tier. The first sign that Dan's accusation struck a chord was in the way his jaw tightened. Then there were his words. 'I chose to bring a knife here because there was a danger a gunshot would be heard, that a knife was a more silent way of killing you. I wasted my time. For what you just said, you're going to scream, old man.'

Dan lowered his head. He put aside his walking sticks and clasped his hands in his lap. Perhaps he was praying for strength, the fortitude to deny his killer. But once more God didn't appear to be listening.

9

Following the murder of Dan Lansdale his killer left South Dakota and returned to San Francisco, arriving late in the evening. The clothing he'd worn—as well as the murder weapon—had been discarded in a Dumpster behind a roadside diner thirty or so miles from the scene of the crime, as he'd made his way to catch his flight. He now wore jeans, over a grey button-down shirt and casual jacket. His only baggage was a carry-on holdall, containing an innocent change of clothing, a toiletry kit and a well-thumbed thriller novel he'd skimmed through on the flight home. Since reclaiming his holdall from where he'd hidden it, he had placed his cigarettes, wallet and cell phone in his jacket pockets. But that was all he carried. He was a big man, but there was nothing distinctive about him that would attract attention, or even more than a cursory glance from any airport staff. He walked out through the arrivals exit confident that no one had paid him any attention.

He had three choices: he could take the BART into the city, hail a cab or plump for the next bus to come along. He had taken precautions while in South Dakota, ensuring there was no record of his visit to Whitehead, having hired a car under false credentials and paying his bill in cash. Back at this end there was of course a record of his flight, but he'd already told a couple of his work colleagues that he was heading off on a hiking trip for a couple of days, and that he was going to visit Mount Rushmore. His trip to South Dakota was no secret, only his real agenda. The chances of his presence in the state being flagged against the brutal murder in a backwoods town would be nil. Nevertheless, the fewer points on his trail that could be identified the better, so he had elected to leave his car at home and travelled to San Francisco International Airport via public transport, so there was no record of his vehicle in the airport car park. Now he thought he might have been over-cautious, and all it meant was a slow return home. He was wiped out from the adrenalin buzz, needed rest, but was due in work at six the following morning. He decided to taxicab it to his house in Clarendon Heights, despite the cost of the fare.

One bonus was that the roads were quiet this late in the evening and the cab was winding its way up Market Street and ready for the turn onto Twin Peaks Boulevard before he realised how close to home he was. Minutes later he was outside his house. He climbed out of the cab yawning, paid and thanked the driver and gave him a hearty tip. Then he trudged up the slight incline towards his house. He checked the mailbox on the way up, but found it empty. He was pleased: even if there had been mail it would have had to wait. Killing was tiring work, he'd found.

His house was a narrow wooden structure with a peaked attic and a veranda at each of the three floors. Built just after the great earthquake it showed its age in the slight lean of its walls, the faded paint on the rails and in the way in which the front porch steps had drooped at their centres. His grandfather built the house and—though he'd never lived here—his father had inherited it. When his father died, it had been passed on to the son. The killer had never wed, had no family, but he didn't feel out of place in a house large enough for an extended family. As a child he'd grown used to the seclusion, because after his father disappeared there had been only him and his mom, and for all the notice she gave him he could have been alone in the world. Until she brought home her male drinking buddies, that was, and suddenly he was the centrepiece of their evening entertainment. The cigarette burns on his body had scarred him less than those wounds on his mind.

When all this was over with, when he'd sufficiently punished the others, then maybe he still would have purpose. Dan Lansdale begged him to stop killing, even when he'd slipped the knife between his ribs and twisted it, the old man had pleaded that he end his killing spree. But he would not. Once vengeance was his, he would take his fight to those sick-minded bastards his mother had introduced him to. He had trained all of his adult life for this, acquiring the skills that would ensure he'd never be a victim again: it would be a shame to waste them.

It was cool inside when he entered the house, and dark. He flicked on lights as he progressed through the house to the kitchen. He wasn't hungry. In fact, the only thing he would do before retiring to bed was this one simple task. He found the upright refrigerator, and he placed one finger against the sheet of paper stuck to it, holding it in place while he reached with his other hand for the pen swinging below it on a piece of string. He gave the pen a shake to get the ink flowing to the nib, leaned close and scored out the fourth name on his list. He wasn't even half way through the list yet, but even he had to admit that having only started this thing a fortnight ago, he was well ahead of schedule.

He looked at the next names on the list, blinking away the weariness in order to bring the writing into focus. Who next? All three targets lived here in San Francisco, two of them in the same apartment block. Perhaps he should leave them until last, otherwise the connection might be made between his victims and bring the cops down on him before he was finished with the third. That wouldn't do. He had to send every last one of them to the grave.

The thought settled him and he made his way up to the room he'd commandeered as his bedroom at the uppermost level. He could have used any of the larger rooms on the intervening floors, but this was as far away as he could get from the basement cellar. Ever since dealing with Tennant, and hearing the truth from the punk, entering basements had made him slightly uneasy.

He took off his jacket and boots, but that was all he had the energy for and slumped back on the narrow cot he'd dragged up there. His fatigue was the effect of an adrenalin dump, and was not physical as such. In the morning he'd be fresh and ready to go again. When he woke up he would put himself through the rigorous exercise regime he'd set himself, pump himself full of energy and the desire to take the next step in his plan. For motivation he peered up at a profusion of photographs pinned to the wall over his head. They swam in and out of focus. His eyes were slipping shut, but he forced himself to lean over and hit the switch on his alarm clock. He hoped for a deep and dreamless slumber. There was no chance of that, though: as soon as his eyes fluttered closed the flames built behind their lids and the blood and screams soon followed.

10

'So where do we go from here?' I asked.

'Only one place I can think of,' Rink said.

On the way back, Rink telephoned his mom and had her driven home by her friends. As we sat in the living room, Yukiko had gone to the kitchen and busied herself with preparing a meal. We could hear the clatter of pots and pans, and it was apparent that Yukiko was taking out her frustrations on a large metal utensil.

'Maybe I should talk to her,' I offered. 'I still think she's finding it difficult looking you in the face.'

The corners of Rink's mouth jumped, but it wasn't a smile. He dipped his head, and the way his hooded lids obscured his eyes made it difficult to see how my comment affected him. But that was obvious.

For all that Rink had inherited his mother's Japanese looks and colouring, he was still very much his dad's image. It had to be difficult for Yukiko to look at her son without experiencing another pang of loss for her husband. Before he could refuse, I stood up and headed for the kitchen. As an out for his mother's emotions, I closed the door behind me, shutting Rink away so he could have his own privacy.

I found Yukiko leaning over the sink, both palms pressed tightly to the work counter, her elbows locked. If she didn't support herself so I guessed her knees would have given way and pitched her to the floor. Her shoulders were shuddering, though I couldn't hear her weeping. For a second I almost turned away, but didn't. I brought a chair from the table and guided Yukiko into it. At first she resisted, her back forced ramrod straight, but as I placed a comforting arm around her she relented, and sat down. I found some tissues and handed her a bunch. She used them to hide behind.

I waited.

All I offered was my silent companionship, but it must have helped.

Yukiko finally came out from behind the emotional crutch of the tissues to blink up at me. Tears trembled on her lashes, but her gaze was now steady. She was nearing eighty years old, was small and petite, but for a second or two she looked as tough as steel. 'Forgive me, Joe. You must think me a silly old woman.'

'That's not what I think. Not at all.'

Her hair was white, cut close to her head in an elfin cap. The soft amber hue of her skin was spared the mottle of age, and was relatively wrinkle free. She was immaculately dressed in an off-white silk sweater and slacks. She looked like a woman thirty years younger and the beauty that must have struck Andrew all those years ago was barely diluted. Even suffering the grief of losing her husband, she struck an image of steadfast calmness. Sadly, I knew that the image was born of the etiquette instilled in her all her life. It would have been easier for me if she had wailed and beat at her breast in anguish.

'Then you must think me selfish.'

I shook my head, before pulling over another seat and positioning it in front of her. I sat, leaning on my elbows, clasping my hands.

'I know you have personal reasons for staying silent, Yukiko. And I respect your wishes.'

'But?' Yukiko smiled sadly. 'I hear the "but" behind your words. You are not unlike Jared in that respect.'

'You know who murdered Andrew.'

'I do not.' There was no reproof in her words, it was a simple admission—I believed—of her futility in trying to find answers to her own questions.

'But you have your suspicions on *why* he died.'

Yukiko didn't answer.

I shifted, leaning that bit closer. I reached for her hands and held them in mine. She bunched her fists around the tissue and briefly I wondered if I'd overstepped the mark. But then I felt her hands relax and noted the slump in her shoulders.

'If I tell the police then I will bring harm to others.'

'I'm not asking that you tell the police. Tell me.'

'I know what you would do, and what Jared would do. I do

not want this to continue, Joe. I'm sorry, I can't tell either of you.'

Giri, I understood, was a matter of honor, and it was okay for one of a western mentality to scoff, but it was *everything* to Yukiko. It had been difficult enough for her to admit that she held some knowledge about her husband's death, but now there had to be a war raging inside her.

'This man, the one who murdered Andrew, is without honor,' I said. 'You have no obligation towards him. Whichever way you look at it.'

Suddenly Yukiko pulled out of my hands. Her back was tight to the seat. I thought she was about to slap my face.

'I do not protect *that pig*!'

I understood what we had missed then. Whatever obligation Yukiko felt she owed it was to her husband. Not only that, but to Jed Newmark and perhaps others. I sat, watching her, waiting for her to gather herself. Either she would strike me for the dishonor of my words, or she would fold.

Thankfully it was the latter.

She stood up, and leaning against the counter for support, she made her way to a drawer. She opened it and drew out a rolled newspaper. She returned to her seat, sat down before offering me the paper. I unfurled it.

'Page fifteen,' she said, her voice barely a whisper.

Before turning to the page she'd indicated I took a glance at the cover, saw that the newspaper was almost a fortnight old. I looked up from it to find Yukiko staring at me. I nodded and she mirrored the gesture. She had suspected something was coming for the best part of two weeks, but had kept the secret to herself. Maybe I was wrong: she would have shared this with Andrew at least. I thumbed through the sheets to the correct page. Yukiko pointed at a column on the bottom of the page. The story was accompanied by two photographs: that of a fire crew sifting through the wreckage of a house consumed by fire, and, inset into it, the face of an elderly man.

I read the accompanying story, sensing that Bruce Tennant would prove to be an old friend of Andrew and Jed Newmark. Fire crews had been summoned to a decrepit flophouse in the Tenderloin district, reacting to reports of smoke billowing from its cellar. Before they could arrive on the scene the ensuing fire had claimed most of the building, and it was only afterwards, while they were searching through the wreckage, that the body of Tennant had been discovered in the cellar. He was burned so badly that it had taken a post mortem examination to confirm his manner of death. It wasn't the flames but three bullets fired into him at point blank range: two in the heart and one in the head. A police spokesperson gave an official comment, but reading between the lines it was suggested that Tennant—who had recently been released from prison—was known to have made several criminal enemies and that it was possible that his past had caught up to him. Maybe they had a point, but I was beginning to think that the repercussions came from a past much further back than the police intimated.

I took one last look at the face of Tennant, before lifting my gaze to Yukiko. She had sat without comment, waiting for me to finish. Her mouth opened slightly, but that was all. She looked down at her hands, her chin tilted away from me.

'I'm taking a guess here,' I said. 'Bruce Tennant was a friend of Andrew and Jed?'

Yukiko shook her head. 'No, he wasn't a friend. He was just someone they knew once. Someone whose life connected to theirs—to ours—but he was never a friend.'

I frowned. 'How were they connected?'

'It is this that I have most trouble admitting to. If I say, then it will become apparent what they did. Then the others will be harmed.'

'Not if we figure out what's going on and stop the man responsible.'

'You're not listening to me, Joe. Just like Jared, you assume that all problems can be solved by force.'

Her comment stung, but she had a point.

'The ones I wish to protect face more than the threat of murder. They face imprisonment, ruination, and shame. Not only them, but also their loved ones will suffer. It is to all these families that I owe my silence. Do you understand?'

'You said that I assume, but now you do, Yukiko. The people you protect are only at risk if the story is made public. Rink and me aren't in the habit of talking to the police. What you have to remember is that the same people are in danger from this killer.' I held up a hand to stop the admonishment I saw building in her. 'You said that even their families would suffer: they'll suffer even more if their loved ones are murdered the way the other three were.'

Yukiko nodded, and her eyelids drooped. A single tear ran down her cheek and hung off the side of her jaw. 'Four,' she said.

When I didn't respond, she looked up at me. 'While at my friends' house I made a decision and I telephoned those I knew were in danger. Sadly, I was too late to alert one of them. Daniel Lansdale was stabbed to death yesterday evening.'

I tasted bile in my throat. I had to swallow it down, when all I wanted was to snap at Yukiko. If she'd told us what was going on, then maybe we would have been able to save Lansdale. Maybe we would have been able to save Andrew and Jed too.

She must have read the reproof in my face because Yukiko slapped her thigh. The noise caught me unawares, causing me to flinch.

'When I read about Bruce Tennant, I did not realise what his death meant. It was many years since we last spoke to him; he was not the type of man we wished to keep as a friend.' She didn't expound, but I had read that his criminal disposition had ensured he was in and out of prisons most of his adult life. 'Even when Andrew was murdered I wasn't sure,' Yukiko went on. 'But with Jed's murder, there could only be one thing that tied all of them together in a way that they each would be targeted by this killer. With Dan Lansdale also a victim, I am now positive...but only *now*, Joe.'

I didn't bother placating her: I'd been caught and was guilty as charged. Instead, I said, 'I take it that neither Bruce Tennant nor Jed Newmark have any surviving families? You felt that your silence was justified in that there was no one in their lives that you could hurt by talking. You were hoping that the killer would end things there, that he'd be finished with the murders, that by keeping quiet it would all just go away? What about Lansdale? He has a wife, children?'

'They still need protecting from the past, Joe. Daniel was murdered, but they need not learn what he did. It would destroy them: can't you see that?' She glanced at the door to the living room, and I knew what she was thinking. Whatever secret she held, it might destroy Rink too.

'Nothing you tell me would change Rink's opinion of his dad. He loved him dearly. He idolised him—' I allowed a smile to slip into place '—almost as much as he idolises you. Nothing you can tell me will make him think otherwise.' I leaned forward and took her hands in mine as before. This time she turned them over so that we could entwine our fingers.

'Tell me,' I urged, 'then we can figure out who is responsible and stop him from hurting anyone else. By saving them, you're not betraying anyone, least of all Andrew.'

Yukiko looked once more to the closed door. Then she nodded, a gentle gesture, and I could see that some kind of peace had flooded over her. They say a problem shared is a problem halved, but even I had not steeled myself for what she soon told me, and to be honest I wasn't sure how I was going to break to Rink what I learned.

11

Hitomi Yukiko was afraid of the big men with knives on their guns. She tried to keep away from them, to avoid their cold stares. She was only a child, but even children weren't safe, she'd been warned. It seemed like she had run and hid from these men for as long as she could remember. Even the vague recollections of when she was a little girl held images of men with knives on their guns. She had been in her mom's arms when the soldiers came, forcing them from their home. Her parents had begged to stay, proclaiming their loyalty to their new country, but their words had fallen on deaf ears. She had snatched memories of their belongings piled on the street outside their home in Japan Town, in San Francisco, and men in suits and buttoned down collars greedily hauling them away, their father staring in dismay at the pittance of dollars shoved into his hands. Then there was the train journey. They had been crammed alongside hundreds into the carriages, small bags all they were allowed to carry. The soldiers were on the train, and others waited for them when they finally arrived at the sprawling camp that she later learned was in a place called Desha County, in Arkansas. The camp terrified her with its rigid conformity, the rows of barracks-like buildings ringed by tall fences topped with barbed wire. Her young mind had not made sense of why they must stay at this place and she had wept and asked her father to take her home. Her father had approached a soldier, seeking answers, but had been knocked to the ground instead. She still had nightmares about the man bending over her dad, aiming the long knife on his gun at her father's chest.

Her dad was taken away. Yukiko had cried for his return and her mom had hushed her and told her he'd been taken to a place called Tule Lake. Yukiko thought that a place with a lake must be much nicer than somewhere called Rohwer Relocation

Center. Four years later she was old enough to learn the truth, that Tule Lake was a segregation facility in the Rocky Mountains, where those deemed troublesome or dangerous were held. Her dad was a gentle man, not troublesome at all, and Yukiko had blamed herself for having got him in trouble. She had asked one of the soldiers when her father could come back. The man had laughed at her—brutal and harsh—then spat on her. Wiping his hot spittle from her cheek she told him he was a nasty man. The soldier had jabbed at her with his long knife and she had fled screaming. He had laughed even louder.

Yukiko hid from the soldiers from then on, avoiding them as best she could. It was difficult, because she was forced to work alongside the women with guards watching their every move, even when they were in the communal eating, laundry and washing areas there was always a soldier on the door.

Yukiko couldn't remember when first she met Rose Kurihara. It must have been back in San Francisco, because she could never think of a time when her friend wasn't in her life. They were much the same age, with a shared background, and they had bonded within days of arriving at Rohwer, becoming inseparable. They were best friends, almost sisters, and they ran together. They had both learned to hide from the men with long knives. But there was one time when Rose did not hide in time.

'He raped her? A child?'

Yukiko hung her head in shame. 'I watched. I was hiding under a pile of laundry in the washroom. He had come in while Rose was bathing, but I had already done so and was drying myself. When I heard the springs on the door, I quickly dropped down and crawled to where the used towels were bundled. I tried to call out to Rose but she could not hear me for the running water. I saw the soldier walk into the room and watch Rose. She did not know he was there. He had the eyes of a snake, the way they slithered over her nakedness.'

I did not want to picture the terrible deed that followed, but it was unavoidable. I felt sick, even contemplating that a grown man would do such to a child. I found that I was now hanging my head in shame, mirroring Yukiko, as if somehow I had failed to protect Rose too.

The soldier was a big man, a giant. His uniform was dusty from being on guard duty, with dark rings of sweat under his arms and down the centre of his back. Sweat glistened on his brow as well, and he had licked his lips. Perhaps he tasted the salt—or was he imagining how sweet Rose would taste when he ran his tongue over her body?

Rose was oblivious to his presence. She was washing the soap from her hair, and humming a tune that was lost amid the splash of water.

Yukiko thought that if she only stood up, then the soldier would know he had been seen and would go away. But she was too afraid. What if he grew angry that she had hidden herself and punished her? She looked at his gun and the wicked length of steel that rose a foot in length from its tip. That knife could go all the way through Yukiko with many inches to spare.

The soldier had walked slowly towards Rose, and Yukiko saw how violently his fingers were trembling as he'd reached to touch her raven hair. Yukiko fought down the urge to shout out a warning her gaze bouncing from the tips of the giant's fingers, to the gleaming tip of his knife. When he grabbed Rose's shoulder, Yukiko had to cover her mouth with her hands. Rose had jumped. Not immediately frightened because perhaps she thought it was only her friend playing a prank on her. Then her head had come up and she'd looked into the face of the soldier. She was small, waif-like, the nubs of her breasts barely an indication on her chest, yet she had thrown an arm over them, the other hand covering her modesty down below. The soldier didn't waste time with speech: there was no attempt at calming her—in his eyes she was his to do with as he pleased. He placed his rifle down and reached for her, grabbing her at her shoulders and lifting her from the shower stall. Rose was stricken with terror, her mouth wide but emitting no sound. The giant still clamped one hand over her face, encircling her with his other arm and lifting her over to a bench against one wall. There he continued to press a hand tight over her mouth, while his other fingers pulled at the buttons on his trousers.

Yukiko paused in her tale, unable to voice what happened, and I was glad. I did not need the details to know what Rose must have endured. The old lady was shaking, the memories so vivid in her mind that she must have felt transported back through those years and was once again that tiny girl, hiding beneath a pile of dirty laundry, watching her best friend being violated by a monster.

I touched her on her knee.

'You were a child, Yukiko. There was nothing you could do to stop him. Don't blame yourself, okay.'

'I should have done *something*. Even if I'd shouted and run away, it would have made him stop. He would have feared repercussions, because I know now that he was an aberration— only one of a few men who were beastly towards us. He would have been punished for his crime then....instead of later.'

I now knew where Yukiko's story was leading, but I did not want to rush her to the conclusion.

'I helped Rose as best I could. I got cloths and cleaned her. She was bleeding, Joe, from down there: a small girl bleeding as if she was a woman. Afterwards Rose swore me to silence. She felt dirty, afraid, that somehow she was to blame for what that monster did to her. She thought that if the truth were told then she would be seen as spoiled and she would be disowned by her family, like a used vessel that was no good anymore.'

'But by keeping her secret you were also inadvertently allowing this man to get away with what he did. It must've been a terrible thing for you to carry, being so young yourself.'

'Yes, a terrible burden, but it was worse than that, Joe. Later I learned that the soldier had raped other girls. One lady died. Not at his hand but indirectly. She was so ashamed that she took her own life. She was found hanging in a store closet. Her death wasn't so much covered up as it was simply ignored. Life was hard in the internment camps, and she wasn't the first to choose death over such a brutal and disheartening existence. But *we* knew. Rose and I, for we had been watching the monster watching her and knew what he'd driven her to.'

'Her death was never investigated fully?'

'No. People died from inadequate medical care, others from the high level of emotional stress they suffered. The lady was just another statistic, Joe, that's all any of us were back then. We thought that the commanders suspected that something was going on, but they chose to turn a blind eye. Finally—following the lady's suicide—someone must have decided to take action because he was moved away. I heard later that he had been sent to Tule Lake. It is stupid now, but I feared that he would hurt my father. I know now that he was a coward, and it was only helpless girls and ladies he had any interest in.'

I was cold. I had a ball of ice at my core and the more Yukiko explained the harder it grew. I knew about this dark episode in American history, but like many had not given it much thought. When Japan attacked Pearl Harbor on December 7th, 1941, U.S. citizens had feared another attack and war hysteria had seized the country. Pressure was placed on President Roosevelt to sign Executive order 9066, and under the order 120,000 citizens of Japanese descent were forcefully removed from their homes and placed in internment camps, on the unfounded fear that they would spy for the Japanese. More than two thirds of those interned were American citizens and half of them were children. None had ever shown disloyalty to the U.S. During the course of the war ten people were convicted of spying for Japan: ironically all of them were Caucasian. These days, people are horrified that Nazi Germany ran similar concentration camps—and rightly so—but no one wants to accept that we were also guilty of similar crimes. It made little difference that the U.S. government later apologized, paid reparation to those families affected, because it would never make up for what they suffered at the hands of their own people.

Rink once told me how he'd come to be born and raised in Little Rock, Arkansas. Having been forced into swearing fealty to the U.S., the Japanese internees were finally allowed to return home in January 1945. Some of them, angered by their treatment, had returned to Japan, but some had stayed. However, their previous home was no longer available and, instead of returning to San Francisco from where they hailed, Yukiko's family had settled in Arkansas, after her dad was returned to them. It was much later when Yukiko had met a young Scottish-Canadian soldier called Andrew Rington and gave birth to the first of three children. Rink had mentioned how Yukiko always felt that Little Rock held no attachment for her and that she would one day return to the West Coast, to her home in San Francisco.

I found it sad that the horror that she'd endured then had continued to dog her the rest of her life. And it had finally killed her husband.

'Tell me about this beast,' I said. I couldn't bring myself to call him a soldier.

12

By 1970 Charles Peterson was onto his third marriage and it was no more successful than his previous two. In fact, if anything it was the worst position he'd been in. Each successive failure had brought him down, first from a homeowner, to a man renting a squat, and now to this trailer on a patch of dusty ground surrounded by discarded electrical equipment he'd intended to fix up and sell but hadn't got round to yet. There was that old place of his father's out in San Francisco, but his wife had refused to pick up sticks and move halfway across the country, so here he was stuck in this shit hole in the middle of nowhere. His latest wife was called Michaela, twenty-three years his junior, and already too old for his taste. He thought that before long he'd have to get shot of the bitch and go trawling for someone much younger. But he was stuck for now—at least until the brat was old enough to kick out onto the street with her. The useless bitch had purposefully done it, he thought: forgot to take her pills. She knew he had no love of babies, the last thing he wanted making his life more miserable being a squawking toddler. Shit, how could a man think with all that howling going on, let alone find a fucking job to support them? His ass-wipe life was all her fault, and she'd asked for the smack in the jaw he'd given her earlier. Let her run off for a few hours, it'd do her good—see what she was missing. It certainly pleased him to have the trailer to himself for a while.

He was lying on the bunk, feet up, his hands crossed across his large belly. There was a Lucky Strike smouldering in the corner of his mouth, and a can of Bud balanced between his wrists. He was savouring the smoke and the brew, making them last because there was none left. Michaela best get her scrawny ass back soon and bring him more of each as he'd warned her to do. A TV played at the end of the trailer, the black and white

58

picture flickering and rolling—a Sergeant Bilko *rerun was airing, but he could hardly make it out. He fancied himself as a fixer-upper, but had put off the jobs waiting outside; he thought that maybe he should see to the TV first. Too much like hard work, he decided, and drew on the Lucky all the way down to the stub. The TV continued to flicker, the blue light flashing on his spectacle lenses. Phil Silver's was giving the little fat guy hell and Peterson laughed to himself, a bitter sound: the programme was nothing like his days in the army, far too naïve for that.*

He heard the soft thrum of an engine.

It wasn't his beloved family returning to him, which was for damn sure. This engine sounded healthy, unlike their old Dodge that drank oil by the bucketful. Peterson was concerned. Sometimes some of the kids from the nearby town came out and took pot shots at the old machines standing on his lawn like sentries. Usually they used catapults or air rifles, but once one of them had used his daddy's pump action and blew a hole through the back end of the trailer. Pity that seven-months-pregnant Michaela was sleeping at the other end at the time, it would have saved him the trouble he was having now. Still, he couldn't allow the little punks to blast holes in his trailer, not when enough wind whistled through the cracks in the windows as it was. He flicked the stub of the cigarette into the neck of the empty Budweiser can, reached languidly for the length of pipe he kept down the edge of the bunk for just such an eventuality. He swung his legs out, sitting up, grunting. Then, cursing, he went to the door to see who was calling round this late of an evening.

As he opened the door and stepped down onto hard dirt, the vehicle swept up the short drive towards his plot. It came to a stop, its lights almost blinding him. Peterson placed a hand across his forehead, shielding the light off his glasses. 'You kids think you're coming in here shooting up the place again...I'll whup your goddamn asses!' For effect he wagged the length of pipe.

Beyond the first one, another vehicle pulled into his drive. From its size and blocky shape he could tell it was a van. The van pulled up alongside the car, that Peterson now recognised as an Oldsmobile: one of those station wagons with the wooden trim running the length of it. It was difficult to see beyond the glare of headlights but he thought that both vehicles carried a number of passengers. Suddenly Peterson didn't feel so sure of himself anymore. Had Michaela gone and told her family what he'd done and rounded up her brothers and cousins to teach him a lesson? Nah, that wasn't it; the car and van were too nice to belong to trailer park scum.

'Hey! This is private property and yous guys are trespassing. You best get away off my land, okay.' Peterson didn't like the high-pitch of his voice, but there was nothing for it. He was frightened. This wasn't right.

Doors came open in the station wagon and he saw four figures move behind the headlights. He was still trying to make them out when the doors of the van swung out and another two figures joined them. Another man was still in the driving position of the van, and as Peterson lifted his club a second time the van began to roll back. As he watched, the driver completed a three-point turn, so that the back of the van faced him. The two that had climbed out went and opened the doors.

Peterson was confused. But he was no fool. He knew the shit had hit the fan and he was up to the neck in it. These weren't kids out for a little drunken fun, these were grown men. He had caught glimpses of their faces, but they meant nothing to him. What the hell did they want from him?

'Charles Henry Peterson.'

He heard his name called out and flinched from it. The words had sounded like condemnation.

'What do you want with him?' Again his voice was higher than he'd have liked. 'You cops or something? If that's the case, you've come to the wrong man. I haven't done a goddamn thing.'

'Are you Charles Henry Peterson?'

'That depends what you want him for?' He tried to make light of the situation. 'If he owes you money, then, hell no.'

'It's him, all right.'

The four men from the car came forward. Peterson watched them. One of them was a big man like himself, the other three smaller. He glanced at the pipe in his hand, figuring his chances if he whacked the big one first. Then he saw the guns in their hands.

'Drop the pipe,' the big man said.

'What the hell's going on here? Tell me who you are and what you want.'

'I want you to drop the pipe.' The big man had an odd accent, a soft burr to it that Peterson didn't recognise. 'Otherwise I'll shoot you in the gut and then take it away myself.'

'Hey, take it easy, will you?' Peterson was loath to give up his only weapon, but he didn't think the man was bluffing. He let it fall and it thudded heavily on the hard-packed dirt.

'Kick it away.'

Peterson toed the pipe away, taking things easy because his feet were bare.

'Good,' the big man went on. 'Now walk to the back of the van.'

'What're you going to do?'

'Do what I said: walk to the van.' The big man lifted the gun so it was aiming directly at Peterson's face.

'Okay. Okay. I'm going, you don't have to wave that hawgleg in my face.'

The others had been silent until now, but Peterson heard whispers pass between the group. He daren't look at the one force-marching him to the van, but he glanced back and forth, searching the others for any sign of pity. He didn't find any.

He was still approaching the rear of the van when two of them moved close. They grabbed him by an arm apiece, forcing his wrists behind his back. A third one joined in, wrapping a heavy hemp rope around his wrists, pulling it so tightly that the rough fibres scored the flesh from him. Peterson yelled, finally building the courage to fight back, even though it was hopeless.

'What the hell are you doing to me? Get off!'

'We're just going to take a little drive,' a voice said by his ear—one of the men holding him. 'Taking you somewhere that you haven't been in a long, long time.'

'What are you talking about?'

The big man grabbed him by his chin and twisted his head round. From this angle Peterson could now see into the rear of

the station wagon. He could make out two more figures in the back, sitting on their knees in the luggage space. The two women stared back at him, and their gazes condemned him to hell. One of them he didn't know, but the other...
A sack was forced down over his head.

'You went along with the men, you and Rose?'

'We had to. We were the only ones prepared to do so. The other wives did not wish to see what happened, happy only in that the rapist finally paid for what he had done.'

I scrubbed my hands through my hair, glanced once at the closed door and wondered what the hell Rink was doing. Partly I was glad he wasn't hearing this, but another part wished he were there so I wouldn't have to go over it again.

Rose Kurihara met Jed Newmark at the same dance hall where Yukiko met Andrew. Jed—another soldier on furlough from Korea—had fallen deeply for the pretty Japanese girl and had pursued her until she had accepted his hand in marriage. They had spent many happy years together, but of late the subject of babies had come up. They had tried to conceive but to no avail. They had watched Andrew and Yukiko have their first child—a girl—who sadly died shortly after birth, then a boy that had thrived, and now Yukiko was pregnant with their third. At first they believed that they were placing too much pressure on themselves to conceive, but then the subject of medical health had arisen. Tests showed that Rose was unable to bear children, the reason being scar tissue build-up from internal damage suffered years earlier. It had been a terrific blow to Jed, not only that he'd never be a father, but also that his beautiful wife had been violated as a child. Rose had been forced to tell the awful truth of what had been done to her by Charles Peterson all those years earlier. That would have been the end of it, had not Jed spoken to Andrew. Fearful that Yukiko had suffered similarly Andrew had confronted her and learned the entire shocking story. Being a man who believed that family was everything, he could not let the brutality go unpunished. Yukiko and Rose had contacted the other girls who had been harmed by Peterson—the plan to bring the man to justice—but some of them feared the repercussions and the scandal the story would bring should they speak in an open court. Respecting their wishes, Andrew and Jed had concocted another plan. They had contacted the husbands and brothers of the women instead. They formed their own lynch party.

Charles Peterson had no idea how long he was in the back of the van. Hooded, his arms bound, his body aching from where he'd been bodily lifted and slung onto the hard bed of the van, he could do nothing but feel sorry for himself. Never once did he feel regret for despoiling the girls, his only regret being that his past had finally caught up to him. He had tried to plead, but his begging had fallen on deaf ears, had earned him a kick in the gut from one of those guarding him. Another time he'd been pulled over onto his back, held prone, and one of the enraged men had punched him in the balls. He kept quiet after that, his only sounds the soft sobs he couldn't hold in.

At one point during the night, he wondered if Michaela had returned to the trailer with the boy yet. Would she realise something had happened to him and call the police? Little chance of that! She would be glad he was out of the way, probably hoping that he never came back. Bitterly he wondered if she had anything to do with this. Wouldn't surprise him, though he'd no idea how she'd have any knowledge of his former life. Whatever, he couldn't hope for her to send anyone to his rescue. He was alone and couldn't think of a way out.

Finally the van stopped.

Peterson wasn't relieved: he'd rather the van kept on going forever.

The sack muffled his captors' voices, but he could hear the urgency in them, and his sobbing rose to a high-pitched wail.

Someone leaned close. 'Don't expect pity, you bastard. Did the little girls cry like that when you were tearing their insides apart?'

The doors were opened and cold air bit into his sweat-sodden clothing. Hands grabbed him and he was hauled out. They didn't take away the sack, only marched him bare-footed across soil littered with jagged stones. Recalling the words from moments before he bit his tongue to hold back the yelps, but he couldn't and was crying again by the time he felt smooth stone beneath his soles. Someone pushed him forward and he stumbled, finding nothing but air beneath his feet now. He fell face first down a flight of stone stairs, his body whacking painfully on every step.

Feet clattered down behind him and hands seized him and dragged him up. Peterson was moaning, not so much from pain, but from realisation that the end was getting near. He wasn't religious in any sense, but if there was a hell he knew where he was heading. Hell on earth in the next few minutes, at least.

His captors were still speaking among themselves, partly in argument, but he could not hope that any of them were having second thoughts. They forced him across a floor that rang hollowly to their footsteps. Then he was twisted around.

'Do you know where you are?'

Peterson recognised the voice of the big man. He was too fearful to answer.

'Let me show you.'

The sack was yanked from his head and Peterson blinked at the invasion of light. His spectacles had been knocked askew, and there was nothing he could do to right them. Someone had brought a flashlight and was flicking its beam around a small room with bare concrete walls daubed with faded graffiti. The ceiling was low overhead with wooden beams upholding a floor of warped planks. Peterson had no idea where he was.

'Don't you recognise it? You can't have forgotten about your time at Rohwer?'

The big man was standing in front of him, pointing up at the ceiling. 'The buildings are gone now. They've been gone for years, demolished and carted away and hidden: struck from history for the shameful things they were. But this cellar survived. We found it easily enough. A girl who was raped in an adjacent building showed us where she used to hide from you, Charles.'

'No, no, it wasn't me. You've got the wrong man. Whoever put you up to this is mistaken.'

A different man came forward. 'Are you calling my wife a liar?' Flat-handed the man struck him across the cheek. The

blow was more a shock than it was painful: there was
something decidedly insulting about a slap—men traded
punches, girls slapped.
    'I'm not saying that...just that she's made a mistake.'
    Yet another stepped forward. 'I guess mine is mistaken too.'
    This man struck him, and the slap tore the glasses off
Peterson's face and sent them spinning on the floor.
    Hurting, Peterson stared back at the line of men standing
before him. There were seven in total. Only seven. He was glad
that all that he had hurt had not come back to haunt him.
    One of the men was holding a chain.
    Another carried a stool.
    Yet another a gasoline can.
    They walked behind him and Peterson did not have the
courage to look. He heard the stool thud into place and then
one of them step up onto it. When he heard the links of the
chain rattling over the ceiling beams he closed his eyes. He was
still standing thus when the chain was looped round his neck.
    'Take a step back, Charles.' It wasn't the big one now, but a
stocky man whose face held more than a touch of the orient in
it.
    Peterson mewled, but did as he was told.
    'Now step up.'
    'No, please. Oh God, no!'
    'Do it!'
    One of those behind him, the one who had carried the
gasoline, grasped Peterson by his shoulders and pulled him back
and up onto the stool. As he did so, the man snapped. 'My
name is Tennant. I want you to take that name with you when
you die, so you know who it was that killed you. Motherfucker,
you deserve worse than this for what you forced my sister-in-
law to.'
    'I don't know what you mean!'
    'You don't, huh?' Tennant struck him in his lower back.
'You don't remember raping a young woman who was so
ashamed she took her own life afterwards.'
    'What? Who...your sister-in-law? But...but you're an
American!'
    'So was she, you sick bastard!'

'They were the enemy!'

The big man suddenly held up a hand. 'Finally we're getting to the truth.'

'No,' Peterson cried. 'That's not what I meant. I'm not admitting to—'

Tennant struck him in the back again, pain flooding him, digging into his liver like a lance.

The Asian holding the chain reeled in the slack. The screech of links over wood was harsh, like the breath that caught in Peterson's throat. 'Don't...do...this...'

But they did. He was first dragged onto the stool, where he stood, unbalanced and stumbling, but only for as long as it took Tennant to kick away the legs. The stool broke with a snap, tilted sideways and Peterson was suddenly dancing in space, the chain digging mercilessly into his throat. Blood pounded in his head, his eyes bulging, his tongue pushing from between his teeth.

He did not see, but some of the men turned away, sickened by what they bore witness to. Others only watched him coolly. Tennant was laughing. Even through the torment, Peterson heard one of them say: 'Jesus, he's not dying quickly enough.'

'Don't shoot him,' Tennant snapped. 'Let the bastard die in agony.'

'No,' said another, the soft burr evident, 'we're not the animals he is, let's just get this over with quickly.'

A gun blasted.

13

We couldn't look each other in the face.

Yukiko was sickened by what she'd related, while I was bilious for another reason. I've never been known for my liberal views: when it comes to rapists and murderers there's only one thing good for them in my opinion. But, I was gutted by the fact that good people had been pushed into doing something totally out of their natures. It made me wonder now if Andrew had suffered the guilt of what he'd done. The burden he must have carried for the last four decades must have weighed heavily on him. There have been times when he and Rink have been at odds, and I could imagine the reason why he didn't approve of his son following my vigilante lead.

'They summarily executed him,' I finally said. My voice was flat. I wasn't being judgmental. How could I be?

'That was always going to happen,' Yukiko admitted. 'But things got out of hand.'

'When Andrew shot him?'

'No. That was an act of pity. Despite what Peterson did to all those children, Andrew wasn't the type to torture the beast. To do that would be to stoop to *his* level. No, I'm talking about Tennant.'

'What did he do?'

'You might remember that one of them carried a can of gasoline into the cellar. Andrew brought it so they could burn their clothing afterwards, to get rid of any trace evidence. Tennant had other ideas.'

'He set Peterson on fire?'

Yukiko dipped her head, placed her hands over her face. 'The flames were roaring behind them as the men fled the cellar. They were shouting and arguing and I could tell the decision to light the fire was *unpopular*. I saw Andrew strike Tennant before the others could stop him. I did not hear what was said, but I guessed that Tennant had doused Peterson and set him on fire...before he died.'

'Jesus,' I said, more a sound of disgust than prayer.

This revelation clarified two things for me. It explained why Andrew and Yukiko hadn't remained friends with Tennant in the following years. Plus, it made sense of the *modus operandi* of Tennant's subsequent murder. Whoever was responsible was re-enacting the killing of Charles Peterson.

'Four of the original seven have already been killed,' I said, conscious that Yukiko's husband was one of them. 'Andrew, Jed, Tennant, and Daniel Lansdale: who are the other three?'

Yukiko bit her lip, deciding. She must have come to the conclusion that to keep these names from me was pointless. After all, her secret was out now, and the only way things could ever end was if she told me everything. 'You met two of them already: Lawrence Parnell and Rodney Faulks. The final one is called Yoshida Takumi.'

Having met Parnell and Faulks, I immediately discarded them as having any part in the murders—other than that either man might be next. But it was the first I'd learned of Yoshida and wished to know more.

Yukiko made a sound of scorn, but it wasn't for Yoshida but for my unspoken hypothesis. 'There you go assuming things again, Joe. Takumi is a fine and noble man. He was there to avenge his sister's honor. He is not responsible for what has happened since.'

'It has to be someone who was there, Yukiko. How else would they have knowledge of how Peterson died in order to re-enact it?'

'I assure you that Takumi is not responsible.'

'How can you be so certain?'

'He was injured during the Korean War, fighting for *this* country. He took shrapnel in the gut, but that is not what exonerates him from blame. Though, indirectly it does. As he aged, his injuries came back to plague him: problems with his liver and pancreas. A side-effect being he became an insulin dependent diabetic. Complications have arisen in the last few years, blindness for one. Two years ago, he lost both legs to amputation. He has been in a wheelchair since, and is cared for round the clock by his granddaughter. Do you still think he is the one?'

'Where is he now?'

'You will not let it rest even after what I've just told you?'

'It's not that I think he's responsible—how could he be? But I'm pretty damn sure that he's in danger. No way am I going to allow him to face a murderer alone.'

'He lives with his granddaughter as I said, I will give you his address.'

'You said you telephoned to warn the others: you included Mr Yoshida in this? What about the granddaughter?'

'I did not tell her. My words were for Takumi alone.'

'I understand why you wouldn't tell her, but if she's with her grandfather then she could also be in danger. It makes things difficult for us. Me and Rink can't watch everyone.'

'There are the others, too. Lawrence and Rodney. They are equally in danger.'

'And there's you, Mom.'

We spun to find Rink standing in the doorway. His gaze looked haunted as he stared back at us. He rapped a knuckle on the doorframe. 'This old house has thin walls. And I've got good ears. I've heard everything that's been said, even from the length of the hall.'

Yukiko got up. She looked like she wanted to go and hug him, but instead crossed her hands across her stomach and stood with her head bowed. 'Despite what you heard, your father was a good man.'

'I know, Mom.' He glanced at me, and I could read the pain in his features, but it wasn't at finding that his father had once murdered a man. 'The truth is, there's nothing he did I wouldn't have done myself.'

'That is what frightens me, son.' Yukiko moved towards him and Rink opened his arms for her.

'You needn't be frightened. I won't let this man hurt anyone else. Definitely not you: I love you, Mom.' Rink hugged her, and it was touching enough that I was forced to turn away. I even blinked a couple of times so that when I looked back it was with clear vision. Rink bent so he could kiss Yukiko on the top of her head, then he looked at me. 'There wasn't seven people involved when Peterson died; there was nine of them. Rose Newmark and my mom were there as well. Rose died a few years ago and is free from this killer, but my mom's still at risk.'

Yukiko shook her head, pressing away from him gently. 'I was there when your dad was killed; the opportunity was there to kill me too. I do not think I'm in any danger.'

'Mom, the bastard struck you in the head with his gun. I don't mean to insult you, but you're an old lady now, in poor health. What are the chances he expected you to survive? Maybe he thought that you were already dead, but once he learns otherwise...'

14

Sometimes he could still feel his toes. Occasionally they tickled, and the sensation was a pleasant reminder. But at other times pain would flare, and if he could get up and run from it, he would. It was phantom pain only, residual memory imbued in his brain, recollections from before the nerve endings were severed when the surgeons took away his legs. There was no escaping the bad memories.

He laughed at that.

No indeed.

For more than forty years he'd tried to put aside the shocking developments that had escalated in the cellar of the deconstructed concentration camp. As often as had all the others there—barring that borderline psychopath, Bruce Tennant—he regretted allowing his hatred and self-righteous fury to get the better of him. It was right that a monstrous child rapist had received his dues, and that the brother of one of the violated girls should bear witness when that happened, but still, it had been a difficult scene to stomach. When he was first contacted by Andrew Rington he did not know the man, but one thing he was sure of was that he was speaking with someone who was both honorable and admirable, despite the course of action he had suggested. Takumi was only a toddler when his family had been 'relocated'. He was too young at the time to remember the events at Rohwer, but in the years following the war, when his family returned to their home on the west coast, he had watched his once beautiful sister dissolve into a pitiful figure, a wreck of humanity compelled by neurosis and paranoia to an early grave. When Rington told him what his sister, Kazumi, had suffered at the hands of Charles Henry Peterson, he knew that the abuse was at the core of her suffering, and the disintegration of her self-worth. Her slow death sentence was levied the moment that monster first laid his filthy hands on her. To avenge her he'd willingly gone along with the other aggrieved family members. They all burned with fury at the injustice that Peterson had gone unpunished, but none could have guessed to what it would lead them to do.

After that night, once all had been sworn to silence, they had parted company. Takumi knew that some of the men were friends and that they would continue to associate with each other, but Takumi was a stranger to them, and was glad that it was so. He had left the stench of burning flesh behind, and tried ever since to expunge it from his soul. But—like the phantom pain—it would never leave him. There was always something to remind him, and he knew that was the way of sin.

He wasn't surprised when Yukiko Rington telephoned yesterday. He knew his time on earth was nearing its end, and understood that he would be judged and made to pay for his wrongdoing before taking his final rest. His Buddhist teaching said: "For every event that occurs, there will follow another event whose existence was caused by the first, and this second event will be pleasant or unpleasant according to its cause." Well, however he tried to vindicate his actions in the cellar, there was no getting away from the fact that they were unpleasant. According to Yukiko, four of the co-conspirators had already been served their dues, and it would be only a matter of time until karma came knocking at his door. It was ironic that evil begat evil, and that it chose further evil to punish those involved. He wondered how that circle could ever close, but suspected that it was an impossibility.

His granddaughter, Melissa, had resisted him when he suggested she go out with her friends. She had told him that the movie would last two hours, but that she would be gone for at least four. No way would she leave him alone for that length of time. Takumi had then played the "grumpy old guy" card, and sent her off with a flea in her ear, snapping at her that he was quite capable of sitting in a goddamn chair for a few hours, and by suggesting otherwise she was being both dishonorable and spiteful. Melissa had acquiesced, but only on the understanding that he have his cell phone in his lap, her number on speed dial and only the press of a button away. It was a game that they both played, but one that appeased each that they had retained the upper hand. Takumi smiled at the memory of the kiss she'd laid on his forehead, before she had rushed happily to join the friends waiting outside in the taxicab.

He was happy that Melissa was out of the way. He was only sorry that she would be the first to find him dead.

'I may be blind, but I'm not deaf.'

He heard a second click from behind him. The first had been subtler, but it was the inescapable sound of bodyweight adjusting on a loose floorboard. He was familiar with the sound. When Melissa would sneak in to check on him without wanting to alert him to her presence, she had learned to step over the loose board, but often forgot that her perfume was a dead giveaway. The interloper did not wear expensive cologne, he smelled of sweat and leather.

'I know you are there,' Takumi said again. He picked up the cell phone and hit a button. It was not to alert Melissa, quite the opposite. He hit the red button to turn it off. Then he reached for the table his wheelchair stood alongside and placed the phone down in clear view of the man behind him. 'There,' he said, 'you have nothing to fear. Come forward.'

Still he got no reply. Takumi placed his hands on the wheel rims, held one in place, twisted the other. He turned abruptly so that he was facing the intruder.

'You can hold your breath, but not forever. I know you are there...I can smell you.'

'Can you smell this?'

Takumi reared away, avoiding the acrid stink so close to his nostrils. He recognised the unmistakable tang of cordite. The intruder had placed the barrel of a gun under his nose, and it was evident that it had been fired recently. Once he'd regained his composure, Takumi smiled. If he were facing death it would be with a brave heart. He reached out, placed a finger against the barrel of the gun and pushed it aside. He squinted up at his would be tormentor. Despite what even Melissa believed Takumi was not totally blind. He still had a sense of colours, and could make out the blurred outlines of larger figures, albeit as though peering through moving fog. Darkness hovered over him, the man leaning close, his face an indistinct paler blob at the top.

'I'm surprised,' the man said.

'That I'm not afraid of you?'

'No. I'm surprised that you're the only Jap in the bunch. I kinda expected more of you to be involved.'

'Why would you?'

'It was Jap bitches who told the lies that had an innocent man murdered.'

'You speak like you do not like Japanese people.'

'I don't. And I don't like Americans who consort with them either. What I especially don't like is Jap murderers. That's why I don't like you.'

'You are misguided.'

'How's that?'

'Peterson wasn't innocent. Far from it. You are avenging a sex offender...a *child* rapist.'

'So you say, *Jap*. But I've heard no proof of that. On the other hand I got all the gory details from Bruce Tennant of what you and those other bastards did. Way I heard it, you were the one who held on to the chain while he was strangled to death.' The man moved, walking round Takumi, forcing the old man to follow his progress by pushing at the wheels. 'I was going to pay you back in kind until I got a look at you. Kind of pointless hoping to watch you dancing in the air, isn't it?'

Takumi snorted.

'Any way, I didn't bring a chain with me...just this.' The gun barrel tapped against the side of Takumi's jaw. He swiped at the barrel then wished that he hadn't. He missed and the man laughed at his blind grope. He made himself a promise he wouldn't react the next time, he wouldn't give the man the privilege of laughter.

'You know something?' The man continued his slow walk around Takumi. This time the old man didn't turn with him. 'When first I saw you, saw the suffering you're going through, I decided to let you live. I think what you have to put up with now is preferable to the quick death I was going to give you. But...' He laughed. 'I've changed my mind. I'm still going to kill you. Not with my gun, though.'

Takumi heard a clatter alongside him. He tried to make sense of the movements swarming through his fogged gaze. It was futile, but still natural to try to look when he should have relied on his stronger senses. By the time he understood what the man was up to and tried to swat his hands away it was too late. The man had already moved.

'Hmmm, a diabetic, eh?'

Takumi sighed. He should have moved the damn insulin pen. Before leaving for her movie date, Melissa had prepared his next dose of Humulin-S, setting the insulin level on the dispenser so that all he had to do was jab the needle in and press the plunger.

'I've seen these before. Always wondered what they were. They look just like a pen these days—huh? Not like a syringe at all. Is that to make it more socially acceptable for when you're injecting in public?'

Takumi didn't answer. His Bushido resolve to meet his death face on wavered for the first time. He hated that his condition had affected him so badly, taking his eyesight, taking his legs, and prior to this had dreaded succumbing to further complications. His doctor had warned him that his likely prognosis was renal failure, followed most probably by a heart attack. When first the killer of his co-conspirators had mentioned the gun, a flare of hope had risen up in him: better a clean death while confronting an enemy than wasting away in agony. Now that he understood what his tormentor planned, he was horrified.

Damn him, though, Takumi would not show his fear.

'Just shoot me and get the hell out of here.'

'No. Why waste good bullets?'

Takumi heard the click, click, click that was so familiar—and so despised—as the man charged the dispenser. By the number of clicks he'd ratcheted the pen all the way to the top. Knowing Melissa she'd have left him a full pen: that meant that there was 300 ml of insulin—more than plenty to send him into hypoglycaemic coma, from which there'd be no waking up.

Takumi tensed, trying to pinpoint the man's whereabouts. His heart began to beat ferociously, his adrenalin kicking in, and Takumi thought that his body was his worst enemy of all, for his raised pulse would only aid the effects of the insulin. Despite his earlier resolve to show no fear, he cried out, began swiping randomly to push away his killer.

He felt the sting of the needle as it punctured the side of his neck. It was as if a wasp had stung him. He slapped at it, but found the man's hand as he pushed down on the plunger. In desperation Takumi dug his nails into flesh and tried to tear the hand loose. The man only laughed and continued to depress the plunger. Takumi realised too late that he had not found skin, but leather gloves—the source of the man's scent when first noticing his presence in the room.

'This is almost too easy,' the killer said, stepping away. 'I came here hoping that you were some sort of karate master and that I might have my hands full in a one on one battle. I was looking forward to the challenge. Instead, you're about the most pathetic of them all.'

'You bastard! You *evil* bastard!'

'Hah, what happened to the inscrutable Jap reserve I've heard about? When you're about to die, Japs're no braver than anybody else.'

Takumi grabbed at the wheels of his chair, twisting round. Not to face the man but searching for his side table. He scrabbled his fingers along the top, searching for the cell phone he'd placed there.

'Looking for this? Oh, sorry, I forgot you can't see. If you're looking for your phone, I've got it right here.'

'Please...'

'What? Please *what*? Please help you?' Something clattered against a wall and Takumi thought that the phone had been thrown across the room. He continued to scrabble at the table, his fingers meeting things that were normally so familiar but in his panic unidentifiable. He could not find what he was seeking for. Takumi began yelling in frustration.

The wheelchair was yanked round. The man leaned over him, grabbing hold of his head and holding him tightly. 'Shut up! Shut up, goddamnit, or I'll cut your fucking tongue out.' Takumi felt the man shake him savagely. 'Good. That's better. Now if you scream again, I won't finish things with you. I'll wait here for your pretty little granddaughter to come home. Do you understand what I'm saying? Do you understand what I'll do to her.'

'Leave her be, she has nothing to do with this.'

'Shut up. You have no say in what I do. All you're going to do is sit there and die, you old Jap bastard.'

The man shoved Takumi's head to one side, then stepped away. 'How long does it take for that insulin to work? I'd have thought it would be kicking in by now. Let me see your face.'

Takumi wanted to resist, but suddenly he felt a sinking feeling in his entire being, like someone had opened a valve and his blood was spilling out of him. He was familiar with the symptoms associated with hypoglycaemia as his blood sugar levels began to drop. Ordinarily, he would call to Melissa and she would bring him a sugary drink, or some hard candy to suck on and he would stave it off. Never had it come on as rapidly as this before. Heat burned a swathe up the centre of his back. Conversely the sweat popping out on his brow was icy cold.

'Shit. I've never watched a yellow man turn white before. I think you're fucked up, old man.'

Takumi began to shiver. It didn't manifest outwardly, the sensation was internal, his cells craving energy. The phantom pain was back. But now it travelled up from his ghost legs, through his thighs and into his lower abdomen. A cramp knifed its way into his stomach.

'Are you hurting? What a pity. Well, if it's any consolation it's nothing to what you're going to feel next.'

Takumi wasn't thinking straight. He tried to wheel his chair past the man and into the hall. If he could get to the front door and shout for help, there was the hope that a passer-by would hear him and come to his assistance. A boot jammed against the chair, held it in place.

'Where are you going?' The man kicked the chair back again. 'I'm just getting the fire started. Just imagine what it's going to be like: you slipping into a coma, knowing that the flames are going to eat you alive. I don't think you'll feel it, but I bet that's even worse. Jesus, just the knowledge that you're burning alive and can do nothing about it...that must be terrible? Just think about that. Think how *he* must have felt.'

A spasm racked Takumi, drawing his hands into claws. Never had his hypoglycaemia reached this low level before. He had been told that if ever his blood sugar levels should drop off the scale then convulsions would follow. Well, it was apparent he'd reached that point. Not that he was conscious of that, because with the convulsions his brain activity went haywire. He jack-knifed out of the chair and sprawled on the floor. The man was so close that his boot bumped against Takumi's body as he stepped over him. The old man tried to grasp at it, but he was already too late, his fingers unresponsive. Groaning he rolled onto his back, trying in vain to see where the man was. In his fogged vision a new colour blossomed. It was yellow, then flared to orange, contracted to red as he screwed his eyes tight. Heat wafted over him, but it was a sensation he could no longer make sense of. He groaned again, as fresh pain lanced through him. Its source wasn't his amputated legs this time. He could not pinpoint the agony; it was everywhere at once, his every nerve ending screaming out. Darkness began to descend in his mind, a ragged blanket of feathers cascading out of the sky. He was almost thankful that unconsciousness was coming, but his killer had been right. Knowing that the fire was going to sear the living flesh from his bones struck terror into his heart and he began to scream. Yet—like the agony—the screams were internal, centred in his mind and soul.

15

It was my first trip to San Francisco's Japan Town. I had been to the more famous China Town with its dragon gate and profusion of glittering shops and restaurants, but this was more to my taste: less tacky. Driving up Geary Boulevard I was surprised to see the impressive edifice that was the Cathedral of St Mary's of the Assumption, while just a tad further along there was the Japan Town Peace Plaza, with a beautiful five-tiered pagoda dominating the square. I would have liked to have abandoned the car and taken a walk through the commercial area, but didn't have the luxury of time. It was the day following Yukiko's revelation concerning a four decades old murder, and even after all that time there wasn't a second to spare.

It was apparent to us all that any remaining members of the lynch party led by Andrew Rington was now in dire danger, and from the speed at which the killer's agenda had escalated, I didn't think that Yoshida Takumi had much time left. Rink was loath to leave his mother's side—understandably—but had also taken on the task of locating both Parnell and Faulks, so it fell to me to go and check on their elderly Japanese friend. Yukiko remained adamant that we could not share what we'd learned with the police, and we'd concurred. If the truth came out, prison time was on the cards for all four surviving members— Yukiko included. I wasn't sure that an invalid in a wheelchair would escape the law either. Though their crime was horrific, the same psyche that drove me to wage war against the bad guys of the world said that Charles Peterson deserved everything he got. Two wrongs never make a right: true, but where did that leave the issue when a third wrong had been added to the mix? Maybe what I was prepared to do to protect the conspirators was required to balance the equilibrium again.

I took a right on Webster, then started watching for the turn

I'd need to take me to the neighbourhood where Takumi lived with his granddaughter. Yukiko had given me the address, but also his telephone number. I thought it was a good idea to phone the man, so he'd be expecting my arrival. I didn't want him getting the wrong impression when a stranger turned up at his door. Using my hands-free kit, I dialled, listened to a recorded message stating that the phone was switched off. That didn't immediately concern me, but I still thought it odd that Takumi's lifeline to the outside world was not in good working order.

On his street, I slowed, counting down the house numbers. I found his place about mid-way along, a pretty two story home, painted duck-egg blue with off-white doors and window frames. The garden was tiny, but well maintained, with neat shrubs and flowers around a central water feature. There was a flight of wooden steps up to the front door, but alongside them a ramp had been installed to allow easier access for the disabled man. I wondered if his granddaughter wheeled him out here on occasion to pass time with the pleasant tinkle of water as a backdrop.

I looked up at the windows. All I could see was the reflection of the overhead sky, the windows opaque beneath the blue. But, I got a sense of movement behind the living room window, as if someone was watching me. I waved, showed a smile, before getting out of my car. I only hoped that Takumi wasn't waiting for me with a loaded gun when the door was opened. Still offering the smile, I made my way towards the steps. Before I reached the first, I detected a soft rumble from inside the house. I didn't discern the sound for anything unusual, but the following bang made me flinch. It sounded as if someone had exited the house in a hurry, kicking open a door at the side of the building in their haste.

Instilled habits caused me to swerve to the right, and I took half a dozen hurried paces to the corner of the house. I was just in time to see a large man vault over the back fence and into a neighbour's yard. Under any circumstances the man's actions would have been suspicions; with the recent events in mind, I'd no doubt who the fleeing person was. I called out harshly, saw the man glance back at me, his face twisted into an angry scowl, but then he fled alongside the neighbouring house and was gone. Before I knew what I was doing I was racing after him. This was my chance to catch the bastard, stop him once and for all.

I barely made it past the side door when I skidded to a halt. Undoubtedly I'd disturbed him while here to do harm to Takumi. Was I already too late to save the old man, or was there something I could still do? Following the killer's previous MO I thought that Takumi would be past helping. I spurred after the killer.

Something made me stop. I looked back at the house. As I'd charged past the side door there'd been an aroma that my brain had recognised but not realised the significance of while otherwise engaged in the chase. Now I understood that the smell was smoke, and—as he had at Bruce Tennant's house—the killer had employed fire to kill his latest victim. As much as I wanted to pursue and bring down the killer, I charged back towards the house and yanked open the door.

A plume of oily smoke billowed out. I crouched low, seeking its source but a draft was pushing the smoke from elsewhere and out of the open portal. There was no time for anything else: throwing my arm across my mouth and nostrils I went in, staying low to make the most of the oxygen close to the floor. I was in a narrow vestibule with open doorways giving access to various rooms. One of them was a kitchen and yet untouched by flame. I ignored it, heading deeper towards the front of the house. I called out, shouting the names of Takumi and his granddaughter, Melissa. Neither of them replied. The smoke was acrid, and growing denser as I approached the end of the hall. I dropped to my hands and knees, making quicker progress now that most of the smoke was above me.

The heat from the living room was already intense. As I paused in the doorway I could see dirty orange flames writhing up the walls, the fabric of the curtains, and over the furniture.

'Takumi! Melissa? Can you hear me?' I ended my shout with a hacking cough, covered my face with my jacket.

I could see neither and again got no reply. I was sure though that at least one of them had to be here, otherwise why would the killer have lit the fire?

The smoke stung my eyes, and I could feel the prickle of heat. Minutes ago I'd looked up at the windows, thinking their opacity was due to reflection but knew now that it was the smoke in the room that had made the interior nigh-on invisible. The swirling smoke was the source of movement I thought I'd detected, not someone peering back at me. No one could have been standing at that window, not with the blazing flames and poisonous smoke invading their lungs. They'd have been dead in seconds. What were the chances of anyone surviving this long? Then I saw the wheelchair and immediately noted that it was empty. On all fours, I scrambled towards it.

The heat was tremendous, but I ignored it. Grabbing at the wheelchair my hand fell on bare metal, and I hissed, drawing away from the heat that seared my palm. I searched around, pushing aside a small table, and then bumped up against a settee. The settee was on fire and I quickly moved away from it. The choking smoke was now barely inches above my head, and I could feel the poison seeping into my lungs. I began to cough and splutter but wasn't ready to give up yet. I found the wheelchair again, and this time pushed it out of my way, so I could get to the other side.

I didn't realise I'd squeezed my eyelids tight until my groping fingers fell on a malleable form and I had to open them to identify who I'd found. Takumi was lying on his back with his hands clenched at his chest. I feared he was already dead, but I could hear his rasping breath, and as I climbed up his body could feel that he was slick with sweat, so much so that his clothing was steaming. Lying almost face-to-face, I shouted at him. His eyelids flickered but that was his only response. His features were very pale, waxy, shining with perspiration. I placed my unburned palm to his forehead and felt he was icy cold—despite the fire raging only feet away.

I'm no doctor, but being a soldier and fighting enough battles over the years, I had some knowledge of battlefield injuries and could lend a helping hand to aid a wounded comrade. Right then I was at a loss. I couldn't find a wound on Takumi's body, nothing to indicate what he was suffering from, and at first thought his unresponsiveness had to be down to smoke inhalation. Then I noted a smear of blood on his neck, and wiping it away could see a tiny pinprick in the skin. It immediately welled up with a fresh bead of blood and I understood that he'd been jabbed with a needle of sorts. A drug? What?

I recalled Yukiko's words from when I'd suspected that Takumi could be the killer. How she had explained that he'd been injured, and complications from his wounds had brought on type-one diabetes. It was apparent to me that Takumi was in some sort of shock, and that it was most probably down to having been given an overdose of insulin. Shit! Where the hell did that leave me? I possessed a rudimentary knowledge of the condition. My mother, Anita, has type two-diabetes, and though nowhere near as severe could still suffer the same debilitations of an insulin dependent person. I recalled that my mother always had a contingency treatment nearby should she slip into hypoglycaemic shock. Risking being burned alive, or dying from the poison building in my lungs, I began scrabbling through the detritus on the floor. I vaguely recalled seeing something over near the settee, when I pushed aside the small table. Grabbing at Takumi's clothing, I hauled him over there with me.

I was nearly blind, my eyes streaming, but thankfully the few inches at ground level was still untouched by the smoke. I lay flat, sweeping my hands through the clutter and my fingers grasped at a cylindrical object about the size of a fountain pen. I dragged it close, but immediately identified the object as an insulin dispenser and of no use to me. I threw it away in disgust, thinking it was probably the intended murder weapon. I continued scratching my way through the other items spilled from the table.

'Yes,' I hissed. I'd found a bright orange tubular object this time, and without pause I pulled off the cap, even as I shook it furiously. The orange tube disgorged a syringe. An inch long needle sprouted from one end, and without pause I jammed it through Takumi's clothing into his abdomen and depressed the plunger. If I'd guessed correctly then I'd administered the hormone glucagon without which Takumi would most certainly perish. If it were anything else it might kill him outright, but that was the prognosis any way, if I did nothing.

I didn't expect a miraculous cure, and I was right not to. Takumi showed no signs of recovery, did not respond as I shook him and shouted in his ear, but at least he now had a chance. It would only last seconds if I didn't do something to get us clear of the fire and smoke. I grabbed him under his armpits and heaved him tightly to my chest. Then it was decision time. Try to drag him back the way I'd come in, or do something equally as risky but less time consuming? I've always been one for economy of motion. Takumi was a stocky fellow, even sans his legs he weighed as much as I did, but I was driven with a strength born of necessity. I heaved him over my shoulder, came to my feet all in one motion then ran. If we struck any furniture it would be our undoing—but we didn't. I headed directly for where the conflagration was at its highest, then bent forward shielding my head with one forearm and Takumi's back with the other. The flames licked over us, but it was only for the briefest of seconds. Then we struck a hard surface that only resisted us momentarily before our combined weight and momentum shattered the front window and we sailed out into space.

The smashing of the window ensured a reaction. Oxygen sucked back in through the side door, tunnelled down the hallway and into the living room, and sought to escape via the same exit we left by. It did so inferno hot and we were carried on a blistering wave of flames as the living room exploded.

There was no easy or safe way to land while carrying another figure over my shoulder and I trusted to luck to see us through. We crashed through the water feature, upsetting a figurine at its centre, smashing our way through the bowl of the pond beneath and then landed with jarring force on the lawn. The grass was pitched towards the road and we rolled together, still caught in an ungainly embrace until a fence abutting the sidewalk checked us. I was underneath, and though I hurt like hell, I was thankful that I took some of the force away from the old man as we collided with it. Gently I pressed him over, feeling for his neck, checking for telltale signs that his spine had snapped during our crash to earth. I couldn't find any. Being unconscious, and therefore pliable, he was probably in a fitter state than I was for taking the fall. I felt for a pulse, found one but it was faint and rapid. I hauled him up to my chest once more and then carried him like a sack of wet cement to the gate and out onto the sidewalk.

The house was belching flame and smoke, the fire now snaking up the front of the house towards the upper floor. I checked Takumi was as comfortable as he could be, then began to walk back towards the house. Was Melissa inside? I had no way of knowing. Two probabilities struck me: if she was there when the killer arrived he would have silenced her in order to carry out his assault on Takumi; if she'd been elsewhere in the house and avoided the killer she would have been screaming for help by now. I heard no screams. I took a step back and went to assist the old man. I could only hope that his granddaughter had been away on some errand or other and was safely out the way, because there was no way I could return inside for a second try.

Voices began to filter through my dulled hearing and glancing up I saw people approaching. They were neighbours, Japanese predominantly. The man I'd seen leaping the fence at the back, for all he'd only turned briefly towards me, had been a Caucasian, and he'd been larger than any of the people moving towards us.

'Call nine-one-one,' I yelled. 'Get an ambulance here now and tell them an elderly male is in hypoglycaemic shock.'

People were gawping, looking from me to the fire that now engulfed the front of Takumi's home. An elderly couple came forward to assist me, but that wasn't what I wanted.

'Call nine-one-one, damn it!' I yelled at the top of my voice. The couple backed away, stunned by my ferocity, but didn't reach for their phones. It stood to reason they probably didn't have a cell on them, but it didn't matter anyway, because I could see others beyond them speaking animatedly into theirs. From some distance I caught the first warbling strains of responding sirens, and I sank down next to Takumi.

'Come on, come on,' I urged the unresponsive man. 'Don't let that bastard beat us. Live, Takumi. For God's sake, live!'

16

I hadn't realised it at the time, but I must have struck a forbidding figure when yelling at Takumi's neighbours earlier. When fire trucks turned up at the scene, I'd handed over the medical care to their first responders, not that there was much the fire crew could do without the correct medication, but at least they got some oxygen into the old man by way of a mask. It sustained him until the ambulance arrived shortly after and he was quickly loaded aboard, intravenous drips inserted into him, and another mask placed over his mouth and nostrils. I told the paramedics my suspicions that the old man had over-dosed on insulin and that I'd loaded him with glucagon to counteract it, but I mentioned nothing of the suspect I'd seen running from the house. The crime wasn't their concern, only looking after the victim. The ambulance took off at speed, leaving the fire crews to contend with the blaze, and me, the other patient. Luckily I'd only a few shallow nicks in my face and forearms from crashing through the window, but I gladly accepted a suck on the oxygen tank as well. I hacked my lungs up for two or three minutes afterwards. It was only when I moved out of the way and stood alongside my car and caught a reflection in the windscreen that I realised just how awful I looked. My hair was full of splinters of glass, dust and blades of grass from the lawn. It had also been singed in a couple of places. My face was smeared with much of the same and also streaked with soot. Blood from my wounds had congealed amid the mess, dark runnels from forehead to chin, making me look like a watercolour painting of a nightscape gone wrong. That was just my head: the rest of me was in no better shape. Added to the filth, the bitter stench of smoke clung to me, not to mention the equally bitter stink of sweat that had flooded out of me during the time in the house.

Despite all of that, people approached me, shaking my hand,

patting me on the back. To them I was a hero. I didn't expect or even want the acclaim, but it did no harm to smile politely and wave down the adulation. I was frustrated, wanted to get to my car and conceal my weapon before the cops arrived. Coughing and spluttering, I excused myself and made my way over to the Chrysler and popped the trunk. The fire was still burning brightly, and the structure growing unstable, despite the fire crew's attempts to save it. I busied myself by pretending to look for something until the opportune moment arose. The roof tilted at one corner, then came crashing down: the resulting cloud of sparks and smoke that belched into the sky was fascinating enough to catch everyone's attention and I quickly squirrelled my SIG out of the way beneath the spare wheel. I closed the trunk and walked to the far side of the street, made sure my car was a good distance away from me for when the police arrived.

I had considered leaving prior to their arrival, but knew it would be no use. There was no sense in having me chased across town, as a possible suspect in an arson case. It was best I waited and told a plausible enough story to appease them.

I expected a patrol car to respond and gather witness statements. I hadn't banked on Detectives Jones and Tyler arriving on the scene. Even as they clambered from their car, I could tell Gar wasn't happy to see me. He gave me dead eyes all the time they spoke with the fire chief, then he left his partner to march towards me.

'Why doesn't it surprise me to find you here, Hunter? Seems like we've a mini-crime wave going on in our city and everywhere I look I see your face.'

His comment wasn't particularly accurate, but it would have been pointless telling him so.

'Who says there's been a crime?' I asked.

He jerked a thumb at the burning house. 'What does that look like?'

'An old man, having taken the wrong dosage of medicine, making a careless mistake with a cigarette?'

'Bull shit.' He prodded me in the chest. 'I knew it last time, and I know it now. You're involved in what's going on here and you're sure as hell going to tell me the truth.'

'I don't know anything. I just came by to call on a family friend, realised the house was on fire and dragged Mr Yoshida into the clear. We'll have to wait until he recovers before we'll learn how the fire started.'

'Bull shit,' he said again, a man of little imagination when it came to cursing. 'You know what happened here.'

'All I know is that I just saved a man's life. I could do without being treated like the bad guy.'

'You want me to treat you like a goddamn hero? Bull shit! For all we know *you* started that goddamn fire. You ask me, you're our prime suspect.'

I was tempted to echo his catch phrase, but didn't. 'Why would I do that, only to carry Mr Yoshida outside like that? If I was trying to murder him, would I have given him an antidote and then risked my own life by jumping through a window with him on my shoulder?'

'That's my point! How'd you know to be here and come to his rescue? You were checking on a family friend? My ass. Seems way too convenient if you ask me. You're up to your neck in this, and I'm going to find out the truth.'

'Are you going to arrest me?'

He considered it, but then shook his head. 'No, not yet. I'm in a good mind to, but not yet.'

'Good. Then I've got nothing more to say to you.'

'The hell you haven't. You're a material witness to a crime and you are going to speak.'

'Sorry, *Gar*, but that's all you're getting from me. I'm going back to shower and put on some clean clothes. When you feel like being a bit more civil, in other words you ask me nicely, then maybe I'll be prepared to pay you back in kind.'

'Bull shit!'

'The only bullshit here is your attitude,' I told him— remaining calm. 'Come and find me when you're done throwing your weight around.'

He reared back, puffing out his chest, the way I recalled from our first meeting. His mouth opened and closed a couple of times, but nothing issued from him. Not until I turned to walk away. He called after me, trying to reassert his position in front of the few members of the public who'd born witness to his accusations. 'Yes. Thanks for your time Mr Hunter. I'll be in touch.' He spoiled his chances of vindicating himself in their eyes by adding, '*Real* soon.'

Despite brushing Detective Jones off, he wasn't someone to underestimate, and I wasn't deliberately trying to piss him off either. The sensible thing to do was to cooperate with him, tell him about the figure I'd seen running from the house and to work to bring the killer down together. But to do that would be to betray Yukiko and the others, so I chose the option of silence. It risked the detective dogging my every step, and putting paid to any hope I had of running my own enquiries into the killer's identity, but it was preferable to throwing Yukiko and her friends to the wolves.

I started my car, drove away, having to wind my way through the fire trucks and hoses blocking the street. As I passed Gar Jones he was staring at me again, and the dead eyes were back. His partner only gave me a cursory glance, but when he recognised me, I thought he nodded and his look was one of grudging respect. The fire chief standing beside them waved at me, and he was without doubt appreciative of what I'd achieved. I waved back, but kept going. I'd just cleared the last fire truck when I saw a taxicab speeding towards the scene. The cab pulled up and the rear door flew open and a young woman bolted out. She passed within feet of me and I got a look at her face a moment before she cupped her hands over her mouth to stifle a cry of horror. There was little in her features to indicate her racial heritage other than a slight tilt to her eyes that gave her an exotic look, but I made an educated guess that she was Takumi's granddaughter, Melissa. I thought about stopping the car and going to her, to reassure her that her grandfather wasn't stuck inside the burning house, but decided against it. I would allow the detectives to give her the news. I wasn't after her thanks, I was only thankful that the girl had not been near when the house went up. I drove on, a smile curling at the corners of my mouth.

If Takumi was lucky, and if I'd managed to administer the glucagon in time, I was hopeful that he would pull through. I'd managed to deny his killer another notch on his gun belt, and that pleased me. But I was angered that I'd had the bastard in my sights and had not taken him down. I wondered what the possibilities were that I could pick up his trail, catch up with him and drop the bastard in his tracks, and decided that they were nil. He'd be long gone by now, and with only the briefest of glances at his face I'd never be able to identify him even if he was standing among the crowds watching all the drama. Coming to that conclusion, the smile slipped away.

I'd told Detective Jones more than one white lie. I'd no intention of showering or changing my clothes. I'd a more urgent task. I wanted to be at Takumi's side when he woke up. Going to the hospital in my present state might raise eyebrows, but it was also good cover: I'd look more like a patient than anything else and would be able to get closer to him than if I turned up groomed and fresh-faced. The cops would be heading there next and I wanted to be gone from the hospital before they arrived. I drove, mulling over what I'd speak to Takumi about. I just couldn't prioritise what I would broach first: if he knew the identity of his enemy or the necessity to keep quiet about him when questioned by the detectives. I wondered if his sense of *giri* was as strong as Yukiko's.

17

He should have shot Takumi and had been done with it. He knew now that his split-second decision to go for the grandiose and painstaking death he chose was stupid. He wasn't even positive that the 300 ml of insulin would be enough to kill the old man; understanding that it was all determined by how high his blood sugar levels were to start with. He vaguely knew that insulin dependent diabetics balanced everything by food intake versus insulin. For all he knew the old man had been stuffing himself with candy before he arrived and needed the equivalent of the injection he'd given him just to take him back to normal. He should have punched the crap out of Takumi, using his knuckles on the Jap's head the way he'd pounded the heavy punch bag in his gym this morning. That would have pleased him, given him a sense of satisfaction, and then a bullet in his skull would have ensured death, and the fire would have put a cap on it. He was mad at himself, for allowing his anger to overshadow his good judgement. Now he couldn't be sure if Takumi was dead. The stranger that turned up at the most inopportune of moments could have dragged him to safety. And who the hell was he any way?

He had run when he should have stayed.

He was more than a match for most men in a fight, and he could have smashed the stranger and left him in the fire too. Yet the noise of him beating the stranger to death could have brought out other witnesses, and he couldn't allow that.

He should have turned round and shot the man as they'd peered at each other over the top of that fence. The retort of his pistol would not have raised an eyebrow in the neighbourhood, not when it was filled with senile old farts. That would have stopped any hope of rescue for Takumi. But at the time he had been more concerned about the man getting a good look at him and describing him to the police, and instinct caused him to flee.

Until now he'd taken great care and had left behind no clues as to his identity. He had prepared for this, had worked hard to gain the skills necessary to fulfil his mission—martial arts practice, hours spent on the shooting range, placing himself in the most conflict-laden situations he could find—now he'd threatened it by being careless. Next time, he would make sure that death was immediate, and he'd be gone before anyone knew that another of Charles Peterson's murderers had been executed.

He wasn't a coward. When he'd run, he'd only done so for as long as it took to be sure he wasn't being followed. The stranger had obviously rushed back to the burning house. Deeming it more suspicious for a grown man to be running through the streets, he had slowed, meandered his way back to his vehicle at a casual pace. He was still near enough to the location so that he could hear the responding sirens, but far enough away that no one would associate him with the fire a couple of blocks across town. Back at his car he had a spare jacket—the one he wore at work—and a baseball cap and sunglasses. He drove a block over before stopping and changing into them. Now he looked nothing like the man who had been seen running from the house fire and believed he'd attract no attention if he went back there.

He was confident that the members of the murder ring would not speak with the police: to do that was sentencing themselves to prison. All of them were old enough that they would never see a day of freedom again. But he had to wonder if the presence of the stranger was more than what it seemed. Had one or more of them sought assistance, perhaps hired a private operator to protect them? It was feasible and made his task all the more difficult, but not yet out of reach. The presence of a tough guy did not frighten him—he'd been around tough guys all his adult life, and hadn't met anyone he couldn't beat—and he was sure that he was the man's equal. No, he was more than equal, because he wasn't constrained by the same rules that a private security guard was. Another advantage was that the man had no idea who he was, or where or when he would strike next. It would be a simple enough matter to discover this man's identity and to kill him.

There was no time like the present to get started.

He pulled into Takumi's street two blocks south of the fire, then drove along to the next intersection, and parked in a vacant spot. SFFD fire trucks blocked the road and most of his view of the activity on the street outside the burning house. But he was in time to see the ambulance pull away, its lights flashing and siren wailing as it bore its patient off to hospital. He chewed his lip. The fact that the ambulance was in a hurry probably meant that Takumi was still hanging on to life and they intended getting him to hospital as quickly as possible. He sorted through the figures moving about in a clot on the opposite sidewalk, discarding the fire crews, and those who looked like neighbourhood residents. He saw a man who looked a little worse for wear, his face and clothing darkened with soot and dirt. He'd only had a second or so to look over the fence at the stranger before fleeing, but there was no denying it was the same man. He had to consider that the stranger had managed to get Takumi out of the fire, and was now waiting around to make his report to the police.

The man peeled away from the crowd, and approached a silver Chrysler parked near to the front of Takumi's house. He popped the trunk, delved in it, and then in one swift movement dipped his hand into the small of his back and shoved whatever he'd taken out into the trunk. There was no doubting what the man was concealing: a gun. He didn't want to be found with it when the cops arrived. Speaking of whom, he saw a nondescript sedan car approach from the far end of the block. When it parked, two guys he made as detectives step out. One cop was tall and raw-boned, with strawberry-blond curls, the other slighter, darker, more austere. They approached the fire chief, but after a moment the big one peeled away and approached the stranger. He had seen enough posturing in his lifetime that he could read their body language. The two men had history, and none of it good. Judging by their short discourse there was a pissing competition occurring between them, and the stranger won hands down. He watched the big cop muttering behind his back as the stranger walked away and got in his Chrysler. The guy pulled away from the kerb and began wending a route between the fire trucks.

His decision to follow was a no-brainer. But he wasn't about to drive through a bunch of cops and fire fighters who might spot him and note him for later. He backed up, and spun the wheel, taking him on to the intersection where he raced to the next block over. He paralleled Takumi's street, racing the car along it to make the next intersection. Something must have slowed the stranger down because his Chrysler was only now crossing the next intersection up. At the next block they'd both be back on Geary Boulevard and he was confident he could tuck in behind the stranger there and follow him to where ever he was going. He pushed across the intersection as soon as the silver car was out of sight, giving the sedan throttle and beating the other to the main road. He was fortunate in that there were no other cars ahead of him, because the traffic lights were on stop, but he nosed far enough into the junction so that he could see the Chrysler turn and come down the hill towards him.

As it happened the stranger was halted by a red light. That made things awkward. They were now stopped at right angles to each other, and a simple glance from the man could be his undoing. He wasn't that concerned: the man had no hope of recognizing him now, disguised as he was. But there was a more pressing problem. His light had turned green. If he stayed put he'd probably attract attention, some impatient driver behind him would begin honking a horn to get him moving. He had no option but to turn left. Due to his positioning on the road though, it appeared that the stranger was heading down Geary past Peace Plaza, so once he was a block down he pulled in and parked at the side of the road. Within thirty seconds the Chrysler drew up at the next lights down, and he found himself peering at the stranger from no more than fifteen feet away. Luckily the man did not glance over at him—he was talking animatedly, probably on a hands free telephone that he couldn't see from this angle. Pedestrians crossing the road were oblivious of the man, wrapped up in their own worlds, and did not notice that he looked like an old time chimney sweep, his face soot-blackened.

The lights changed and the Chrysler swept forward. Another car came in behind it, then a truck emblazoned with Kanji symbols, but after that a gap presented itself and he pulled out sharply to continue the pursuit. While the lights had stopped the Chrysler, he'd memorized the number plate. He had his ways and means and would find out who the car was registered to later. But only out of interest, so he could learn his name, because he fully intended killing the man beforehand.

He followed, trying to decide his best strategy. Should he wait until the man returned to his employer so he got a full idea of whom it was that was trying to protect himself from him? He could kill the stranger—beat the living crap out of him—in front of his employer just to prove a point. Or just do the man at first opportunity and have done with it? He decided on the second: why complicate matters? He was going to kill every last one of the murderers, and having this man in his way was only slowing him down. He pulled out his pistol and placed it in his lap, and as he drove, reached for the glove compartment and pulled out the sound suppressor he'd employed on previous occasions. The silencer was a little corrupted, but out here on the noisy streets it wouldn't make that large a difference. At the next stop, he fixed the suppressor in place and laid the gun across his lap. Then he followed once more.

He was surprised when the Chrysler took a right and headed for the north end of town. He had expected that the stranger was heading back to either Faulks or Parnell's place, but now it looked like he had another destination in mind. He glanced at the clock on his dash. Time was counting down: he had somewhere he had to be in a little over an hour and a half. No time like the present then.

He moved across lanes, paralleling the Chrysler, but two vehicles back. Then he began to speed up. He lifted the gun, readying himself. He was coming adjacent to the stranger's car, could see him in profile. He lifted the gun a little higher, waited for them to approach the next intersection where the lights were turning red. Excellent, he thought. But it was a fleeting emotion, because sitting on the corner was a SFPD squad car. He quickly dropped the gun in his lap, and faced forward. Forced into no other option, he'd to pull up alongside the Chrysler. He continued to stare forward, sure that he was being scrutinized by both the stranger and the cop on the corner. He gripped the steering wheel with both hands, digging his fingertips into the leather, cursing under his breath.

As the lights changed, he was a little heavy-footed in his frustration to get away and the car lurched ahead, gaining distance on the Chrysler. Not to worry, he thought, because being in front of his quarry there was less chance the stranger would make him. The fact was he'd just earned a positive advantage. He gave the car gas and sped ahead, aiming to make it through the next lights before they turned and get a couple of blocks lead. The traffic was heavy this far down into town, but still flowing along sharply. At his first opportunity, he swerved into an empty space, jammed his gun inside his jacket and stepped out onto the sidewalk.

Standing out of sight he waited, watching as the Chrysler came down the hill towards him. The car wasn't coming at great speed, but that pleased him: it made for an easier shot.

18

The big man caught my eye. He was wearing some kind of uniform jacket, over black trousers and black boots. His hair was hidden beneath a ball cap, emblazoned with a motif I couldn't make out from here, and his aviator-type sunglasses obscured much of his upper face.

It wasn't his clothing, or even the fact that I couldn't see his features under the peak of the cap and glasses that drew my attention. It was the feeling I'd seen him somewhere before, and very recently. I was just mulling his appearance over when he appeared to stiffen as I drove towards him.

He stepped out from the doorway where he'd hid, and I saw his right hand grab towards his jacket, then make a snapping motion downwards, before the hand began to come back up. Subconsciously my mind was working on hyper-drive.

His action wasn't something that many would even notice, never mind recognise for what it was, but I'd been on both ends of an attempted hit enough times to instantly yank down on the steering wheel. It was an injudicious move in that it sent the car sideways into the oncoming lane but at least I was moving away from his line of fire. The bullet he fired starred the windscreen. It also ripped a chunk out of the passenger seat headrest and buried itself in the upholstery of the seat behind. At least it missed my head and I was still alive. That of course could change any second.

It was approaching mid-day, and the traffic was in full flow. There were cars in the oncoming lane, plus a bus loaded with tourists, and a wagon hauling livestock. Hit any of them and the bullet would have done its trick anyway. I sawed the wheel, whipping around the first car, seeing the astonished face of its elderly male driver peering back at me. A younger man drove the next car, and maybe he saw my driving as a challenge because he also started yanking down on his steering. Luckily he went one way and I went the other, but our back ends clipped and for a moment it felt like my Chrysler went airborne. Professional that he was, the bus driver was already braking, his tyres sending up black smoke, but it wouldn't make much difference if he broadsided me. I hit the throttle, streaking by the front of the bus towards the sidewalk, which thankfully was clear of pedestrians. The high kerb almost ripped my tyres from the rims, but I made it up onto the sidewalk just as the bus rammed the back end of my car. The Chrysler spun with the impact, rocking me wildly in my seat, the belt snapping tight against my collarbone. The noise was horrendous, but while I still had hearing it meant I wasn't badly hurt—even though some say it's the last sense to leave a dying person. The collision kept my car moving, throwing it around and now the other side took the brunt of the hit as it slammed into a metal signpost. The post wasn't enough to check the car, and it continued on its awkward trajectory and only halted when the back end caromed into a boutique selling women's lingerie.

Stunned, I watched as the bus continued forward another thirty yards or so, juddering to a halt with fresh jets of black smoke off the asphalt. There was more noise and I snapped round, seeing the livestock truck bearing down on me. The driver had locked up the brakes, causing the rig to jack knife. I could imagine the panic-stricken bellowing of the cattle inside it as it teetered on one side, sliding unchecked towards me. Any second now and tons of metal and beef would be joining me among the bras and briefs. There were too many variables working against me; the seat belt; the door jammed tight against the shop front; the two or three seconds until the truck hit. But I had to try to save myself. I didn't go for the belt or the door because there was no point. I did what most people would do out of instinct: I threw my hands over my head and scrunched low in the seat.

There was an irony attached to what I saw as my impending death, insofar as that it was going to be much worse than if I'd just taken the shot to the head that was originally on the cards. Distractedly I watched it coming from under my laced forearms. The trailer hit the row of shops, collapsing walls and doors and shattering plate glass. The day was full of glittering shards of light as glass rained everywhere. The slatted box containing the cattle was wrenched into an absurd angle but at least it didn't flatten and squash the poor beasts inside. The cab kept coming, and still it was enough to destroy my car. The cab hit, crunching the back end of the Chrysler into a concertina, but also served to wrench the front away from the shop front. Then all movement ceased and I slowly unfolded my arms from over my head. I was looking into the dark space formed by the triangle of jack knifed truck and trailer, my car wedged firmly, but almost untouched at the front.

Beyond all chance I'd survived, but how long would that last if I stayed put in my seat? The man who'd taken the shot might try again: except I couldn't see how, considering I was completely surrounded by the wreck of the truck and the collapsed storefronts. I took a moment to check for injuries. There was fresh blood on my forehead, but a quick dab of the finger showed me it wasn't serious, just a few shallow nicks from the flying glass. My shoulder hurt like hell, a result of the seatbelt bruising the flesh—or maybe from the tumble I'd taken earlier. The air bags had performed, but now they'd deflated and lay like withered balloons throughout the interior of the car. Pale dust and particles of glass still hung in the air. I blinked some clarity into my vision; saw that I was well and truly jammed inside the car. With some effort I extricated myself from the seat belt and hauled my legs out from under the steering column. Leaning over the seats I saw where the round had cut through the headrest then buried itself in the upholstery. It was the only evidence of what had just occurred, but I wasn't going to mention it to the police who'd already be en route to the scene of the collision. Remarkably—but for the bullet scar—the windscreen had survived the series of smashes. I chambered my right knee, kicked back; finishing off what the bullet started and smashed the windscreen. I went backwards through the hole, trailing nuggets of glass with me, and rested a second or two on the steaming bonnet. Then I sat up, looking for a way out.

The truck's cab was wedged firmly to the back of my car, as well as buried a foot or two in the boutique shop, while its trailer made a wall that helmed me in and was likewise jammed into another store front beyond me. Big brown eyes rolled my way from between the slats, and here and there I saw a pink tongue flecked with froth. The cattle appeared largely unhurt, which I was happy about: it was enough to suspect the poor things were on their way to the slaughterhouse without them becoming ground beef beforehand. Maybe the accident had won them a reprieve...I wanted to think that was the case.

Clambering off the bonnet, I felt the effects of the smash in my muscles. It was going to hurt tomorrow, worse the day after that. While I was able, I crouched low and looked for a way out under the trailer. On the far side I could make out the feet of other road users rushing to aid the truck driver, but they were almost obscured by the curtain of urine and dung splattering on the asphalt. I didn't relish crawling out that way, so decided to head the opposite direction, through the lingerie shop. First though, I grabbed my cell phone from the cradle in the front. It concerned me that I'd to leave my gun behind, but it was under the spare wheel in the trunk, and the trunk was a squashed mess of metal.

Under normal circumstances I had an aversion to dealing with cops. It had nothing to do with a dislike for them, in fact the truth's the exact opposite because I respect them for doing a thankless and dangerous job, but we don't always sing from the same hymn sheet when it comes to dealing with the criminals of the world. It didn't escape me that Gar Jones was already champing at the bit to find something he could use against me, so I'd no desire to hang around and wait to be taken down town while he tried to find some way to blame me for everything. I looked for a back way out of the shop, and had found my way into a rear stock area filled with boxes and hanging garments when I stopped.

The Chrysler was registered to me at the rental company, and if the cops found it empty then Jones would assume my guilt, decide I'd fled the scene of the smash because I had something worse to hide and would hunt me down like a sick dog. Shit, I could do without the hassle. But then again, if I went out there on the street and waited for the cops to arrive, what was to say that the gunman wouldn't try for another shot? Ordinarily I'd welcome the chance at getting even with him, but not while there were so many innocent civilians around. It ill behoved me to admit it, but it made sense to hold tight and let the cops do their thing, but it wouldn't be out there where I might draw gunfire.

Guessing it would be some time until anyone found their way inside the boutique, I sat down on a stack of boxes and pulled out my cell phone. Prior to the crash I'd already brought my friend up to speed on what had happened at Takumi's house.

'Rink?'

'You rang me, Hunter. Who else did you expect?'

'Right,' I said. 'Someone just took a shot at me.'

'You okay?'

'I am, but I doubt the rental company are going to be happy when we return the car.'

'The hell has happened now, Hunter?'

'Let's say that things might take a bit straightening out down at the precinct.'

'Shit! The cops have taken you in?'

'Not yet, but I'm thinking it's kind of inevitable if Jones and Tyler turn up.' I told him what had happened and about the resulting destruction. Earlier I was worried about the welfare of the cattle in the trailer; I hadn't stopped to consider if there were any human casualties. It appeared that the lingerie boutique must have closed for the lunch hour, because there was no staff around, but I couldn't be sure of the other shops that had been destroyed. I hoped that everyone had made it through the crash unharmed.

'Someone shot at you, you said?' Rink went on. 'Same guy that was at Takumi's?'

'Has to be, from what I glimpsed of him,' I said. 'At least we've learned something about the killer. I'm guessing he isn't a pro. He wouldn't have aimed through the windscreen at me if he was, he'd have waited for a better shot.'

'You're sure it was him and not one of Chaney's mob?'

'How would any of Chaney's guys know where to wait for me? I think the bastard followed me from Takumi's, got ahead of me, then laid in ambush. I should've noticed him. Maybe I did...'

'How's that?'

'He was wearing some kind of uniform. I'm pretty sure the bastard was in a vehicle alongside mine at one point. It's when I was talking to you about what happened at Takumi's. Hate to admit it, Rink, but I was kind of distracted. I made a mistake dropping my guard like that.'

'Hey, we're not all perfect. Even I made a mistake going after Chaney.'

'Maybe I shouldn't complain, then? Not if even you are fallible.'

Rink grunted, almost a laugh.

'At least he tried for me this time and not one of the others. I'm happy about that.'

'You enjoy being shot at?'

'Helps keep the blood moving, Rink.'

'So long as it's not moving across the goddamn floor.'

There was a ruckus from outside, the sounds of vehicles, men and women shouting, some officiously, some not. San Francisco's finest were on the scene.

'Look, Rink. I don't see a way out of this other than cooperating with the cops.'

'You're gonna tell them someone tried to put a bullet in your head? You know where that'll lead them: right back to the murders again. They'll demand answers this time, Hunter.'

'They can demand all they like. I'm going to tell them about the wasp that flew in my open window, and how I'm frightened of the nasty little critters.'

'Yellow Jacket,' Rink corrected me. 'We call them Yellow Jackets here.'

'Whatever they're called it buzzed right by my ear and out of panic I lost control of the vehicle.'

'And that lame story would work for you with the cops over in England?'

'Probably not, but it's all Gar Jones will get from me. Something *did* buzz by my ear, so I'll be able to make it sound plausible.'

'Except he'll know you're talking bull shit.'

'Yeah,' I said, considering how fond Detective Jones was of the term. 'What could I be looking at here, if he tries to push things?'

'Just hope that nobody was killed or you could go down for ten years.'

'I'm pretty sure there was no one injured.' I thought about the truck driver and how I hadn't heard anything from him after the collision. Hopefully he was okay, but if not then I'd have trouble keeping quiet about the shooter. That was something I would rather avoid, because it would ultimately lead back to Yukiko and the events of forty years ago. 'Otherwise I'm going to have to go with the Fifth Amendment. What's he going to do, rubber hose the truth from me?'

'Last I want is you locked up, Hunter. You came here to support me and my mom, I never expected you'd end up in this crap.'

'If it happens, it happens. I'm not going to say a word that will get your mom in trouble—the problem is, I'm kind of stuck now for getting to Takumi in time. I can't guarantee he won't speak once he comes round.'

I heard talking in the background, Yukiko saying something, but Rink placed his hand over the receiver and I couldn't make out what she said. When Rink came back on seconds later, there was something in his voice I didn't like. 'I don't think we need worry about Takumi, Hunter. He's kept the secret all these years, and he's not going to say anything now.'

'How can you be sure?'

'My mom's just taken a call from Melissa. Sorry to tell you this, brother. But everything you did was for nothing. Takumi was pronounced dead on arrival at hospital. The bastard got another one of them.'

19

The rental car was a complete wreck. All I took from it were a couple of discs I'd slotted into the CD player when Rink wasn't around: Howling Wolf and Doris Day—talk about two opposite ends of a spectrum. Then I rooted around with the tip of my fingers and dug the bullet out of the upholstery in back. I dropped it surreptitiously in my pocket so that the guy from the auto-shop didn't see, then went to scrawl my signature on the obligatory paperwork. While he was busy processing the documents, I excused myself and returned to the car. A little pushing and shoving later, and I managed to yank free my SIG and I concealed it under the tail of my jacket. Thankfully, Homicide Detectives Jones and Tyler were still tied up at Takumi's place, and it was down to regular patrol cops to deal with the multiple pile-ups: if I was lucky the detectives would never hear of my involvement in the smash. When I walked away I wasn't doing as well as when the cops had put me through their sobriety tests earlier. Back then I could walk in a straight line, but I was still riding on adrenalin. Now, a couple of hours later, my muscles were cramping up and it felt as if my spine had been replaced with rubber. My head was thumping as well, and not all of it was down to caffeine withdrawal. I wondered if I'd suffered whiplash during the crash. I'd been thrown all over by the numerous collisions and vaguely remembered my head rattling around. Somehow, I thought, the pain would get worse before it eased.

On foot, I crossed to a drug store and stocked up on Tylenol before seeking the solace of a nearby Starbucks. After the cops arrived on scene and we'd gone through the obligatory tests, I'd been interviewed into a notebook, where I'd made no mention of the mystery shooter. The cop had slapped me a ticket of some kind that I shoved in my pocket. It looked as if my 'wasp defence' wouldn't get me out of this one, but, because there were no casualties involved, I wasn't looking at prison time. I didn't expect that any charges would actually be laid and this would end up a matter for the respective insurance companies involved. Because there had been no hint of an actual crime, I wasn't arrested or the vehicle searched, so my weapon didn't become an issue. No one came forward to report hearing a gunshot, or seeing the shooter, but that didn't surprise me: any bang that would have followed the gunshot would have been lost among the racket of the subsequent collision. Left to my own devices, I'd hailed a tow truck to remove the rental from the shop front, before calling Rink with an update. I told him I'd get a cab back to his mom's place, but he was adamant he was coming to fetch me. When he gets that way, it's pointless arguing. I told him which auto-shop was towing me and to look for the nearest coffee shop to it.

On entering the coffee shop, I'd caught a couple of uneasy looks from the barista, and I'd made my apologies for my state of dress, telling him I'd just been in a car wreck. After that he was more sympathetic and offered me my first coffee on the house. I made use of the bathroom, washing the soot and blood from my face, and was a little more presentable when collecting my coffee. I splashed it with some half-and-half to add a hint of colour then downed a trio of painkillers. The first cup barely hit the sides of my parched throat. I ordered another cup but went without whitener this time. I sat nursing my brew while I waited for Rink to come and collect me. All of the tables were taken so I was sitting on a stool in the window, but that suited me. I'd see when Rink arrived. There was a narrow ledge to settle my cup on and I dumped the CDs beside it, hiding Doris under Howling Wolf: my street cred protected. The bullet I'd prized out of the back seat was a weight in my pocket that niggled at me, and, though it probably wasn't the ideal location for an examination, I dug it out. Bouncing it in my palm, I concluded that it was a standard 9 mm commercially produced round. So what did that mean? It reinforced my theory that the shooter wasn't a pro and more likely to be some punk who'd got his hands on the first available handgun. But then I had to consider the sound suppressor fixed to that gun: they weren't readily available, which meant he had some kind of connections.

I thought of the clothing the man was wearing. Recalling the jacket and cap, they both were emblazoned with motifs or badges, though too far away for me to identify. It struck me as a uniform, but not one I was familiar with. It was similar to a cop's uniform but that wasn't it. Could it have been the uniform of a security company? Some private security guards carried sidearms, and were often ex-cops or military personnel, with possible access to contacts capable of supplying a suppressor. Then again, men of either profession would have most likely done a better job of shooting me. They'd have waited until I was adjacent to them, then shot through the side window where there was less chance of missing, before firing off a few more rounds to make sure I was dead. The man who targeted me had done so in a rush and afterwards he'd made himself scarce before the cops arrived. Considering it was a good half hour following the crash before I was back out on the street, there was a firm possibility the gunman was unaware he'd missed killing me. If that was so it gave me a distinct advantage.

I peered through the coffee shop window, wishing that Rink would hurry up, because the advantage would only last for so long. Pretty soon my would-be killer could check on the number of reported casualties and realise his poor excuse for a hit had failed.

My second coffee was finished and a third on the shelf by the time Rink pulled up outside the shop. His usual mode of travel tends to lean towards sporty model cars, but he arrived in a modest saloon car. I watched him climb from the car, as languid as a big cat. He caught admiring glances from a duo of office girls walking by. Rink winked and flashed them a grin that was pearly against his tawny skin. Beats me why the girls found him attractive: dressed in a bright orange bowling shirt with alternating cobalt blue panels down the front, he made my eyes sore looking at him. Rink never fails to amaze me. Visit his home, his office, or anywhere else associated with him, and you'll see a space so minimalistic that you'd think he'd never moved in. But when it comes to his choice of clothing and flashy cars...well. No one would guess he was in mourning.

But then, first impressions can be deceiving and Rink was living proof. He came forward, hitching his jeans on his lean waist. His hooded eyes cut through the glare off the window and settled on me, and I saw his grin slide back to the face of a man in grief. I held up my cup and got a shake of his head in reproof.

'You want a refill?' he asked, grabbing a bottle of something from a cooler as he came inside.

'Don't mind if I do,' I said, downing the dregs of my current cup.

'Gonna have to peel you off the ceiling before long,' he said.

Rink believes I drink too much coffee. He's probably right, but it's one of the few comforts I'll allow myself in an otherwise Spartan lifestyle. That and the occasional Corona are my only vices these days. He came back from the counter with his bottled smoothie and another brew for me. He settled them on the shelf and dragged a stool closer. I saw him regard the CDs then he used a thick finger to shove Howling Wolf off Doris Day. He raised an eyebrow at my choice in music. Okay, so I have more guilty pleasures than coffee and Corona. Call me a sucker for *Secret Love* as well.

Settling on the stool, he angled himself so he could get a view of who was coming and going through the door. I had also subconsciously sat so that no one could surprise me with a sudden appearance. Perched dead centre of a plate glass window wasn't ideal when there was a gunman out there, but how else would I be able to watch the road and buildings opposite? Not that I expected trouble here; it was like I'd assumed already, that the killer had bailed long before the cops showed up.

'I think it's time we step things up a notch.' Rink twisted the cap off his smoothie, and then leaned back to drain the bottle. He placed the empty bottle on the shelf, and then gave me a quick glance, wondering at my silence.

'It'd be a little easier if we knew who we were up against,' I said.

'I vote we go and find out.'

'Yeah. I agree. But who's going to tell us? Your mom's already made it clear she has no idea who's behind this.'

'Now that Takumi is dead, there are only two other guys who know what happened back at Rohwer. I think we should start with them.'

He was correct. Recalling our conversation at Andrew's funeral, I'd suspected that Faulks and Parnell knew more than they were letting on. Since then, I'd believed they'd held their tongues for the same reason Yukiko had, so none of them ended up in prison, but now I wasn't so sure. I pulled the strip of Tylenol from my pocket. 'Couple more of these and I'll be good to go.'

'You're sure? I can call on them if you're hurting.'

'I'm okay, Rink. I just need to stave off the headache I'm getting from looking at your shirt.'

'What's wrong with my shirt? I can't mope around forever; I need to get motivated. I've dressed for purpose, is all.'

'Purpose?' I stepped off my stool, stretched, feeling the recent collision in all of my bones. I reached for my coffee and downed it, as if it would help lubricate my aching frame. 'What purpose could a shirt like that have...apart from inducing nausea?'

Rink smiled, his hooded gaze giving my soot-smeared jacket the once over. 'That's why I stick so close to you, Joe,' he said. 'The invaluable fashion advice you give me.'

'Fair point,' I conceded.

Standing, Rink picked imaginary lint off my shoulder. Then he shook his head in mock derision and led the way out of the coffee shop. It was good that he was able to joke again, in the last few days I'd missed my friend's mockery. I followed, walking stiff-legged and working a kink out of my neck. Physically I wasn't up to scratch, but mentally I was definitely ready. Before, I'd thought of the killer from a third party perspective, where I was there to help protect others. Now that the killer had targeted me, things had just grown personal.

20

On the way across town I checked my SIG for damage. My rental had been a scene of total carnage, a mangled heap, but the spare wheel had offered protection to my gun. I found it to be untouched and in full working order. I didn't expect to utilize it while speaking with Parnell and Faulks, but I shoved it away in its usual place down the back of my trousers. You never could tell.

The car Rink had commandeered was his dad's. It had been parked in the carport alongside the house. There were some of his personal belongings on the dash, mundane items, but it made me wonder how difficult Rink had found it driving the car, if it felt like his dad's ghost was peering over his shoulder the whole time. Maybe he'd had to steel himself before climbing inside, but then perhaps not. He'd dressed—as he'd pointed out—for the purpose of moving beyond the grieving stage, and maybe driving his dad's car was an exercise in catharsis too. They were tiny steps in the right direction, but I doubted Rink would feel better until his father's murderer was in the ground.

Rink had learned their addresses from his mom, and told me that both old guys lived in the same apartment block. Apparently they had been friends before and had stayed in touch after the events in the cellar at Rohwer. Both men had previously lived at family homes in different districts of the city, but after their respective wives had passed away, Parnell had moved to the smaller apartment block. Out of a need for companionship, he had talked Faulks into joining him and his friend had taken an apartment at first opportunity. They'd both been there for three years now. It didn't surprise me to find that their wives had been Japanese, and also interns of the relocation camp in Arkansas. It seemed a majority of the Japanese-American families forced out of their homes and transported across country had been from San Francisco. Unlike Andrew,

Jed, Dan and Takumi, neither of these men had a background in the military. They had spent their lives in mundane, blue-collar jobs, where there was little need to practice their fighting skills. I wondered if there was a reason they'd been left to last: was it because they were the least dangerous foes, seen as the easiest targets and the killer had gone for the most able first? Then again, why target Bruce Tennant at the outset? As far as I'd learned Tennant was a low level criminal with no appreciable skills other than an ability to become an aggressive drunk at the drop of a hat. Then again, I had to consider Yukiko's version of the story: Tennant had been the most vicious of all when dealing punishment to Charles Peterson. Perhaps that was why his murder had been particularly brutal in turn. It was Tennant's death—and how closely it resembled Peterson's—that made me think the killer must have known what occurred down in that cellar. Yukiko had kept the secret all these years, her burden of obligation weighing heavy on her while she protected everyone else, but I wondered if any of the others had been less secretive. Loose lips sink ships, they say. Maybe one of the conspirators had given up the secret in a moment of weakness. They were all growing old, perhaps feeling their mortality, and required to unburden themselves of their sins before meeting their maker. How else could the killer have learned about Peterson's fate, and therefore chosen to avenge him?

The apartment block where the two old men lived wasn't as high-rise as the name suggested. Hayes Tower was only six stories tall. In the unpretentious residential area of Potrero Hill, it was an unremarkable building, surrounded by others equally commonplace. It did look clean and utilitarian, and I guessed that's all the elderly men required these days. Rink parked his dad's car in a side street that dead-ended at the warehouse-style doors of a Christian book depository. If the car was going to be safe, I couldn't think of a more apt place to leave it than under the watchful eye of The Almighty.

Rink had rung ahead. He'd asked that both men meet us at one apartment, and found that his request was academic. Since hearing of Jed Newmark's murder both men had spent little time apart, the less able-bodied Faulks seeking solace—and a spare bed—in Parnell's apartment. It made sense for both guys to watch each other's back, and made them a more difficult target for the killer. Then again, if he was ballsy enough, the killer could take them both out at the same time.

Parnell lived on the uppermost floor of the tower. I've never been a fan of elevators: not from any sense of claustrophobia but because I saw them as death traps for the unwary for anyone in my business. Back when I was hunting terrorists, quite a number of men had died as the doors of an elevator slid open to find me waiting for them with gun or knife in hand. For that reason I took to the stairs, and Rink joined me without comment. He came from the same school of thought.

We went up the stairs, pushing through fire doors at each level, all the way to the top. The building was designed to make the most of the balmy weather, with the access corridors, open to the elements, running along the back of the building. At the front the rooms came with small patio-type balconies, and on arrival I'd noted that some residents had capitalised on the sunshine and planted gardens.

On the way up we didn't relax our guard. The chances of the killer making an attempt on Parnell and Faulks so soon after the events at Takumi's house were slim, but you never could tell. But we made it to the top floor without incident and followed the corridor along the sunless side of the tower. Parnell's apartment was the second from last at the northern end of the building. Rink leaned on the doorbell, but then didn't wait before rapping loudly on the door. A soft scuff of shoes on tiles answered.

'Who is it?'

The voice was Parnell's, and it held a gruff edge. Perhaps he thought by acting tough he would frighten off the killer. There was little chance of that, but at least the old guy had enough sense to take precautions.

'It's Rink and Hunter. Open up.'

There was a rattle of chains, then the click of a deadbolt. The door swung inward and Parnell peered out at us, his gaze as watery as the first time I met him. He nodded us in, but then leaned past us, searching back along the corridor. 'Your mom didn't come with you, Jared?'

'My mom's safe where she is,' Rink assured him. Before coming to collect me from the coffee shop he'd dropped Yukiko at one of her friends' place, and she was currently surrounded by enough family members to deter the killer from trying for her there. Rink caught Parnell by the elbow and tugged him inside. 'Lock the door again, Lawrence.'

'You don't think the bastard's out there do you?'

'He's somewhere,' Rink said. 'Could be closer than any of us think.'

The entry vestibule was short and opened directly into the living room. The space was tastefully decorated, but there was also an edge of neglect about it, with grit and fluff on the carpets, and dust motes dancing in a slash of light coming through the front window. On the right I could see a pair of stockinged feet sticking out at the base of a settee, a coffee table with a cup on top directly in front. As I moved into the room, Rodney Faulks began to struggle out of the settee, his face fearful. He was holding an empty plate, dotted with crumbs, and he almost dropped it in his haste. I waved him back down again. Recognizing me, and Rink following, he relaxed a little. He slumped back down, settling the plate on the coffee table. Evidently he needed to be doing something to occupy his mind. He reached for his cup and brought it to his lips. He watched us over its rim, waiting while we positioned ourselves in the room. There was one other easy chair, in which Parnell sat, but we didn't feel like squeezing up alongside Faulks on the settee so stood in the middle of the room, looking down at the old men. Faulks placed his cup down, and I thought he'd barely wet his lips. I recognised the movement as a nervous reaction: Faulks was probably unaware he'd even picked the cup up. Checking on Parnell, I saw he was much steadier than his friend. In fact, he looked positively defensive. Not surprisingly: he was aware that we knew what had happened to Charles Peterson, and their part in his slaying. He was possibly ordering an argument in his mind to convince us that what they did was correct. If Charles Peterson were guilty as charged, then he'd find no disapproval from me. There was only one guy out the bunch I'd have taken umbrage with and he was already dead...paid back in kind so to speak.

'Before we go any further,' I said, 'let's not get hung up on the past. We don't care who did what to whom; all we're interested in is stopping the latest murders. We've been on the back foot for too long and that's going to change.'

A look of consternation crossed Faulk's features and he grabbed at his cup again. Colour flooded his features, and swept up and over his bald pate, causing the faint scars to stand out like ridges on his scalp. I wasn't sure if it was through shame that we'd learned his secret, or that the disclosure would bring him further danger. Once I'd credited the old man with more strength, but now I could tell he was almost folding under the stress. Parnell, in contrast, simply looked resigned, and bowed his head over his folded hands.

'We were worried that you'd think the worst of us,' he sighed.

'How could we do that without thinking bad of my parents?' Rink asked. He didn't have to add that such a notion was unspeakable to him.

'Who is it? Who is the killer?'

'We don't know. That's the god's honest truth. We haven't got a clue.' Parnell waved a hand, taking in the room, but his gesture was more encompassing than that. 'Could be anyone.'

'No,' I said. 'He has to have a vested interest in this. These killings aren't down to random chance; they're pinpointed, directed at the men who executed Charles Peterson. The killer is personally avenging his death, or working on behalf of someone intent on doing so. You guys investigated Peterson before you hunted him down to his trailer, you must have looked into his background, his family, those kinds of things. Is there anyone there that could be responsible?'

'You're asking us to remember details from over forty years ago.'

'It's a small ask in return for your lives,' I said.

'Give us some names,' Rink put in. 'I have a friend I can put on to them, who'll check them out and—if they're there—find the leads we need to identify the killer.'

Faulks placed his cup down, and this time it rattled emptily. His anxiety had forced him to drain his cup in one long gulp this time. 'Only one person I can think of.' He looked over at

Parnell, as though seeking permission to go on. They must have been talking about the very subject before we arrived, and had yet to come to a decision what to tell us. Perhaps they'd decided to feel us out first, see how we planned to use the information before they specified anyone. Parnell only frowned. Faulks said, 'It has to be Peterson's son. Nicolas.'

Both Rink and I had wondered about the boy. When Peterson had been snatched from his trailer, he'd been shacked up with his third wife, Michaela. Yukiko had mentioned that there was a boy-child living with them, and that they'd timed the grab for when the mother and toddler were out of the way. The theory Yukiko held was that they probably did his wife and child a huge favour getting rid of the abusive man, but who knew? A child as young as Nicolas was at the time could have a different viewpoint concerning his absent father.

'The boy would be full-grown now, probably in his early forties. That would fit with the description of the man I saw at Takumi's house, and also later on the road.' I shook my head. 'How would he know what happened to his father? More pertinently, how could he have learned who was responsible for killing him?'

'Who else could it be?' Parnell said.

I hadn't a clue. But Rink was the better detective than I was. 'I'll get Harvey on to it. I'll have him check out the son, see where he is, what he's up to these days. It'll be simple enough to dismiss him as a suspect once we have all the facts.'

'What about us?' Faulks asked. 'What are we supposed to do in the meantime: just sit here and wait for the bastard to show up?'

Rink looked around the apartment, taking in the windows, the thin walls. The only good thing it had going for it was its elevated position, but it was about as defensive as a shoebox. 'Maybe you should both think about moving.' Before either man could mount a defence, he added, 'I'm only talking about going to a hotel for a few days, somewhere outside the city. I've a couple guys I can bring in. They'll keep an eye on you while we get on with stopping the killer.'

On the drive over we'd talked about our plan, and Rink had put things in motion by way of a couple of telephone calls.

Velasquez and McTeer were employees of Rink, ex-cops, and good guys to have around. They'd helped us during previous dangerous episodes and had proven trustworthy and capable. Also we'd pulled on our mutual friend, Harvey Lucas. Harvey had been conspicuous by his absence at Andrew's funeral, but he was currently neck deep in a job of his own and could not get away. He had promised that he would hook up with us at first opportunity, in order to correctly pay his respects. When he heard what was happening here he said he'd drop everything, but we'd put him off. He was best placed—being an inhabitant of Little Rock—to look into the situation at his end, despite his offer to hop on the first flight out here. If anyone could track down the current whereabouts of Nicolas Peterson it would be him.

'When will your friends arrive?'

I looked at Faulks, could see the poor man was terrified. 'Don't worry; we're not going to leave you alone. Rink's going to fetch Yukiko and place you in the same hotel. We'll be there with you the whole time until McTeer and Velasquez arrive. They're on the way here now and should be with us some time this evening. Hopefully by then our other friend will have found something for us to work on.'

'We'll get our things together.' Parnell stood up slowly, leaning on the arm of his chair for support. It struck me then how fragile and vulnerable these old guys were. Whatever they did forty years ago wasn't an issue now. They had been acting in good faith, punishing a man who'd escaped justice for his terrible crimes, and didn't deserve to go through any of this now. I realised that my purpose had just changed. First I'd come as an emotional support for my best friend, then to a would-be vigilante avenger. Now it seemed I was back to doing something I preferred: I was a protector. The term was more desirable than 'vigilante', considering the actions of the killer. In his mind he was serving vigilante justice and more than anything I wanted nothing to do with his type.

21

Rink's cell phone began ringing.

We were on our way out of Parnell's apartment, ready to flank the old guys as we ushered them to the car. Ordinarily Rink would ignore the call, but he was conscious of having left behind his mom, and from the way he snatched it out his pocket and juggled it to his ear he was fearful something had happened to her. Before he hit the answer button he glanced at the screen. He paused. 'Unrecognised number,' he said.

I held back Parnell and Faulks. 'Give us a minute, okay,' I said, sending them back into the apartment.

Rink was about to discard the call, but I saw him frown. For all he knew it was one of his mom's friend's calling from their place. He didn't have either woman's name stored in his contacts. He hit the green button.

'Hello.' That was all he'd offer. I watched his eyes pinch, and he looked at me, shaking his head. 'No, sorry, I've no idea where he is right now. Maybe he's back at my parent's house. Last I heard he was going to shower and change after pulling an old man from a house fire.'

Rink listened. He rolled his eyes my way, said, 'I'm not at home; I'm at a friend's place. Why do you need to know that? Right. Well, if you've already been by my parents' house you'll know he isn't there when he didn't answer the door. I'm sorry I can't help you.' He listened again. A mock joviality came over him. 'Yeah, sure I will. As soon as I hear from him I'll tell him to come and find you, Detective Jones.'

Rink held the phone away from his ear and I could hear a raised voice at the other end. I couldn't make out everything but I think I heard the term "bullshit" repeated more than once—but then again I could have just been filling in the gaps.

Putting away his cell, Rink said, 'That was your favourite homicide detective looking for you.'

'What the hell does he want now?'

'With Takumi dying the investigation has been stepped up. He says you're a material witness to the crime and requires you to go in and give a statement.'

'Did he mention the crash I was involved in?'

'No. The chances are he hasn't pieced that together yet. Detective radios are usually on a different wave band to the regular patrol cops. Unless the dispatcher or any of the cops on the scene decided to inform him personally he won't have heard about the crash. What are the chances they would bother? A traffic collision isn't in a homicide detective's remit.'

'I didn't tell him or Tyler about the man I saw running from the scene, only that I'd found Takumi and he'd apparently overdosed on insulin and accidentally started the fire.'

'They've probably had a preliminary report from the hospital. You told me that the killer jabbed him in the neck with a syringe: one look at that and the doctors would have suspected foul play. I don't like the sound of this, Joe. I'd hate to think the cops are trying to set you up for Takumi's murder. If that happens we're going to have to come clean.'

'No way,' I said. 'We do that and your mom and those two old guys in there will be arrested. I'm not going to let that happen.' I made a decision. 'Fuck Gar Jones! I'm not going in. He can wait until this is over with.'

'That could cause us more trouble than it's worth. We're gonna be hard put staying under the radar while we deal with the killer. It'll be nigh-on impossible if you're named as a murder suspect and every cop in San Francisco is looking for you.'

He was right. There was nothing for it. I'd just have to go in, answer Jones's questions and make sure I didn't incriminate myself. If he wanted to try anything funny, then I'd just have to deal with it. The detective was only doing his job: misguided in his thinking as he was, I couldn't hold it against him. When all came to all, we both wished for the same end result: that the murderer preying on the elderly residents of the city was stopped. It would only be our method that would differ.

'Okay. I'll go in and speak with him. But not before we've got everyone safely out of the way. Come on, let's get this done.'

Faulks was lurking in the hall, but Parnell had gone back inside the living room. I called out, waved to Faulks and he passed on the instruction to his friend. They both came out lugging overnight bags. After the doors were locked, Rink led the way and I covered the rear. The book depository dominated the land to the left, with a good yard extending part way behind Hayes Tower. There were a couple of vans parked in the lot, but I couldn't see any workers. The rest of the grounds had gone to fallow, dusty and bare, with only a few clumps of weeds capable of eking out a living in the poor soil, and a mound of discarded junk up against a wire fence. Beyond the fence were similar apartment complexes. None were as tall as Hayes Tower—possibly why it had been given the lofty name— but high enough that a sniper could take a position on a roof to pick off anyone leaving Parnell's flat. I didn't think the killer had the skills necessary to make a shot though: plus it didn't fit his pattern. His MO definitely leaned more to the up-close-and-personal-type kill. When looking back at each of the other murders, each had been brutal and nasty. He was driven by a need for vengeance and I guessed that he was the type who took pleasure in doling out pain: shooting someone from a distance wouldn't cut it for him.

I doubted he was anywhere nearby. After I disturbed his attack on Takumi, he had responded quickly, but that was down more to chance and opportunity than it was planning. After witnessing the carnage his attempt on my life had caused, it was probable that he'd headed off to reorganize himself for his next attack. But you never can tell with people driven crazy by a cause. We had to remain vigilante and protect our charges at all times.

As it was, we made it down the stairs without incident. Rink's father's car was where we'd left it and it was untouched. We loaded the old men in the back and had them scrunch low so they weren't obvious targets. Then we were off. It took us all of two blocks to spot the tail we'd picked up.

'Don't look back,' I told our passengers.

'Who is it? Is it him?' Faulks' words came fast and fearful.

'If it is he's got himself a buddy,' I said.

The sand-coloured sedan had been parked opposite Hayes Tower. As soon as Rink pulled out onto the street, its engine had sparked to life and its driver had sawed on the steering to fall in behind us. On its own it wouldn't have meant much, the presence of the car being a possible coincidence, but it wasn't. It just happened to come too soon after Detective Jones's call to Rink for my liking. Our shadow was undoubtedly cops, sent to Hayes Tower for one of two reasons: either they had learned of the connection between our charges and the murdered men and had come here to bring them in, or they suspected they were next to be hit and were here watching for the killer. I wondered who their main suspects were and didn't like what I came up with.

'How'd Jones get your number, Rink?'

'From my mom. He told me he traced her to her friend's house. When he told her he needed to speak to you, she gave him my number. You think he had a trace placed on the phone?'

'Yeah, I do. That phone call was to confirm we were where he expected. I'm guessing that him and his partner are going to hotfoot it over here, and he called in the nearest cops available to back them up. But it looks like we've surprised them by leaving so soon. It explains the over-reaction of the surveillance team, the way they pulled out so sharply to follow us.'

'You want me to pull over? It doesn't make sense to have the cops on our tails as well.'

I knew that I wouldn't say anything to incriminate us, and trusted Rink, but the old men in the back couldn't be counted on to keep quiet about the murders. It was unfortunate that we'd pressed them for a possible suspect, because once the detectives started pushing for answers, one of them would blab. Faulks probably. Although such a revelation would let us off the hook, our investigation would be effectively stymied and no way would Rink get pay back then.

'There's no sense in all of us being grabbed,' I said. 'Once you've got Faulks and Parnell out of harm's way, I'll contact Jones. Best we lose these jokers for now though.'

'Was thinking the very same,' Rink said. He smiled into the rear view mirror. 'Best buckle up guys, things could get a little bumpy.'

Until that point he'd been driving sedately, obeying the strict speed limit. He dropped gears, pressed the throttle and the small car lunged forward. Glancing in the wing mirror I watched the cops respond. Their sedan was larger and more powerful than ours. I saw its front rise inches as it accelerated in pursuit. The streets here had been laid to concrete, and our tyres rumbled as they struck each connecting section. Rink was soon travelling fast enough that the corresponding thrum sounded like a rapid heartbeat. Despite that there was no way we could outrun the cop car. But what we lacked in power, we gained in manouevrability. Rink hit a perfect handbrake skid, taking us ninety degrees so that we sat side on to the approaching cop car. Then he hit the gas again and shot across the opposite lane, entering a narrow service alley. Dumpsters and trashcans were parked adjacent to the buildings on our left, allowing for foot passage down the alley. There was just enough room for us to squeeze through, but no way could the larger vehicle follow. Looking in the mirrors I saw the cop car screeching to a halt, passing the mouth of the alley before it could fully stop. Then it reversed back quickly and the cops stared at us barrelling away from them. In the next instant they took off at speed, seeking to cut us off when we exited onto the parallel road.

'Now,' I told Rink.

He screeched the car to a stop, threw it into reverse and then we were travelling backwards almost as quickly as before. We lost a wing mirror, left a Dumpster rocking in our wake, but then we blasted out into the original street once more, causing another car to make diversionary tactics to avoid striking us. The man driving the car hit his horn, shook his head at our recklessness. With plenty of time to do all that, I didn't know what he was complaining about. Rink popped another handbrake turn and took off back the way we'd just come towards Hayes Tower. At the first intersection he took a left, slowing down now so that we didn't attract attention. He travelled three blocks east, before turning left once more. We were now four blocks over from where the cops would expect us to be, and heading in a different direction. As we approached a set of traffic lights they were turning red, and Rink slowed, tucking in behind a UPS van. Just as we did so a police patrol car whipped across the intersection, its sirens shrieking as it headed off to join the hunt for us further down town. When the lights changed, Rink followed the van across the junction, peeled round it as it began to slow, and took off again at a regular pace.

'That was almost too easy,' I said, not believing our luck.

'They might have tried a little harder,' Rink grunted. 'I didn't even get a chance to do a *Bullitt* down Nob Hill.'

Laughing, I checked on our wards. 'You okay, guys?'

They both peeked up at me from where they'd scrunched down in the seat. Faulks' mouth was opening and closing like a fish. Parnell chewed at his bottom lip. 'You two boys are insane,' he wheezed. 'You can't run from the cops like that!'

'All in a day's work for us,' I told him. I smiled to show I was only joking. 'It was important for your protection that we got away, don't forget. It's much better for everyone if we can bury the killer without the cops ever learning who he was. It's the only way to save you ending your days behind bars.'

I left the rest unsaid, but Parnell got it. He knew that if the cops pulled him in he'd end up telling them about the cellar. He shut his eyes, and I wondered if he was weeping. I glanced over at Faulks. He was staring into vacant space. Or maybe he was looking back into the past. I left them to their reminiscences and turned back to Rink. 'You'll struggle getting your mom out now. The cops will probably be watching her after this.'

'Good. While the cops are around it means she's safe from the killer. We can concentrate on getting our buddies here outta the way.'

I hadn't considered that.

We took the Bay Bridge out of the city, Rink hurling his cell phone out of the window and into the water below in case Jones was tracing its signal. We bypassed Oakland and Alameda on the Nimitz Freeway and headed into San Leandro where we would be well placed for when McTeer and Velasquez arrived at Oakland International. We cut across town to meet the MacArthur Freeway, followed it for a mile or so south and then took a road into Chabot Regional Park. The area was a golfer's paradise, with no less than three courses in the immediate vicinity and the hotel we headed for was more expensive than anywhere the police would expect us to flee. The hotel was set out to individual lodges that had great views across Lake Chabot to where redwood trees dominated the craggy skyline. While Rink confirmed the booking, paying for a full week's stay on a credit card, I took over driving duties and took the old men to their lodgings. There was no fear that we'd be traced by Rink's credit trail—the card was registered to a shell company he'd fed money into, set up for just this kind of emergency—but there was always the chance that someone might recognise Parnell or Faulks if the police chose to flash their pictures to the desk staff. It was a shame that we were in such a beautiful location, because they could not make the most of it. For the next few days they would have to stay inside while their babysitters did all the coming and going.

While I escorted them inside, and got them settled, Rink made his way to the lodge on foot. It didn't escape me that Rink was rather distinctive, much more memorable than either of the anonymous old men, but he had taken precautions, shedding his gaudy shirt for a plain T-shirt he'd fetched from the trunk, and hiding his hooded eyes behind reflective sunglasses. I watched him approach the lodge through a window, walking slightly bent over, his hands in his trouser pockets. He didn't look anything like his normal self, which was good.

'Everyone comfortable?' He straightened up as he came in, pulling off the shades and hooking them in his collar. He made a quick scan of the lodge, and found it to his liking. Parnell and Faulks were positively out of them comfort zone, though. They stood at the centre of the main room, looking abashed, as though they'd just been caught red handed in a place they'd no right being.

'How the other half live,' Parnell said, casting his eye over the luscious furniture and décor. 'This must cost an arm and a leg.'

'Make the most of it,' Rink said. 'I can guarantee you'll be sick of the sight of it in a couple of days' time. Joe's told you that you can't leave, yeah?'

'Could think of worse places to be locked up.'

'A gilded cage is still a cage,' Faulks put in. 'Not that I'm ungrateful, Jared, but how long do you think we're going to have to stay here?'

'Hopefully it won't be too long. But who can say? It depends on how fast we locate this bastard and take him out.'

I clapped Rink on his shoulder. 'You'll be okay on your own for a while? I'd best go and get things over with. Jones isn't going to wait forever before he puts out an APB on us. Best that I go and speak with him before he makes it impossible for us to move around.'

'Take the car,' Rink said. 'I'll order a rental and have it delivered here. No, wait. On second thoughts, the cops we gave the slip to would have put out a description, maybe you'd best get a cab.'

I tossed him the keys. There was a phone on the wall, and I chose to use it rather than my cell. If Jones were resourceful enough he would already have requested a call log made from Rink's phone. It was at the bottom of the bay now, but mine could still be traced if he found the number. I opened my cell, took out the battery and snapped the SIM card in two. It was one thing throwing myself to the wolves, but I didn't want them finding the others.

I pulled my SIG out and handed it to Rink. Not a good idea to take it into a police station with me.

Then I walked out towards the exit gate, discarding the parts of my cell phone in a trashcan on the way. My cab arrived shortly after, and I gave the driver instructions to take me back into San Francisco. We took a different route back via the San Mateo toll bridge and Bay Shore Freeway, until I asked him to stop on the corner of 8th Street and Mission. I paid the driver, plus extra for the toll charge, and gave him a decent tip. I wasn't too lavish with the cash, because I didn't want him to remember me, but the guy had come a long distance out of his way and had to go back again. As soon as he'd pulled off, I began looking for another cab, and flagged the first to come along.

'Police station on Vallejo Street, please.'

The driver was a bit of a wise guy. 'Normally when I pick

someone up looking like you they want to avoid the cops.'

I'd washed, but my clothing was still dirty and smelled faintly of smoke. The guy probably thought I was a street person. 'I'm good for the fare, if that's what you're worried about.'

'I ain't worried, just saying.'

Climbing into the cab, I pushed twenty dollars at him. 'That's for the fare up front.' Then I slipped him another ten bucks. 'That's for the good advice. But drive there anyway.'

'Your funeral, buddy.'

'Let's hope it doesn't come to that.'

22

When he'd shot at the stranger he had made a big mistake. It wasn't the act of shooting itself, because that had achieved the desired result. The suppressor on his pistol had muffled the retort and hadn't attracted any untoward attention. All witnesses had turned at the sound of screeching tyres as the stranger took evasive action, and their attention held as traffic began to pile up on the street. He had to wonder what the outcome would have been if he'd shot the stranger on one of the fast moving freeways as opposed to a surface street. As it was the carnage went way beyond anything he had anticipated. He would have liked to check that the stranger was dead, but the magnitude of the crash meant that patrol cars would be responding very quickly. He could not see how the man could have avoided certain death. A cattle truck flattened his car, and even if he had survived the bullet he'd have suffered tremendous injuries. Dead or not he'd be in no shape to offer protection to the next people on his list.

No, the mistake he'd made was in wearing his uniform while out on the street. It was stupid and reckless, and could identify him if anyone had indeed witnessed the shooting, or his quick run back to his car and subsequent speedy getaway. His work clothes weren't distinctive in themself—it wasn't as if it was a police officer's uniform or anything else immediately identifiable—but it wouldn't take much tracking down by a determined investigator. He had been acting on impulse, he recalled. The uniform had offered good disguise as he'd fled from Yoshida Takumi's house, but he should have shed it before shooting at the stranger. He wouldn't make another amateurish mistake like that again.

It was hours later now, and still he wore the same jacket and cap. As soon as he was out of here he would ensure they were well out of the way at home when he went for the next target.

He couldn't keep his mind on his job for the distraction of thinking about tonight. He had to plan every move, make sure that there were no slip-ups. This time he would not mess around but get in, kill his next victim and get out again. The cops weren't fools and would be closing in. It was only a matter of time until they recognised the pattern and zoned in on the remaining conspirators and took them into protective custody: he couldn't imagine how he would get at them then. Unless he dropped an anonymous tip—told the police what the bastards had done forty years earlier. If they were arrested and subsequently sent down, well, things would be different then. They would be out of the way, incarcerated behind bars, but there were always ways and means where a prison was concerned. Money placed in the right hands, a door *accidentally* left unlocked, a guard willing to turn a blind eye, and many a prisoner's life had been ended in a welter of violence.

Earlier he'd thought about ringing in sick, taking the day off to plan and recoup after the disaster at Yoshida's place, but it was imperative that he not attract any unwanted attention. Best that he kept up his usual life and not give anyone a reason to question what he was up to outside of work. There were a number of nosey people around here and he didn't want any of them putting two and two together. If he stuck to the programme, separated his paying career from his vocational work then he should be fine. When all of this was done, and he avoided discovery, he would still need his job. Despite bragging to Daniel Lansdale about continuing his mission he had no intention of pushing the issue too soon. Revenge is a dish best served cold, he'd heard. Once the conspirators were all punished, he'd be happy to go back to his normal work for a while, before seeking out those others deserving of a visit from him. Before setting off on his crusade, he had been a relatively law-abiding man, and if he hadn't learned the horrible truth from Bruce Tennant he would most likely be now. However things had changed and there was no going back to the person he used to be. The thrill of the chase was all encompassing at present, and if he slipped back into his normal life he would miss the excitement. He got some action during his ordinary day-to-day duties, and though he occasionally fed his desire for violence, there was a line he was not allowed to cross. He did not wish to endanger his employment here, he needed a wage because killing required an income. Plus, he owed a lot to this place: who'd have thought it would have led to the discovery of those responsible for murdering his father?

Bruce Tennant wanted more alcohol. He was barely tipsy and wished nothing more than to be speechless, so that when he returned home he'd be oblivious to the stench and grime, so that when he lay down to sleep he wouldn't be conscious of the bugs crawling over his face, let alone the noises from his neighbouring apartments. He had spent all the cash he'd scratched from his pocket, and had managed to scam a couple of drinks from one of his drunker barfly buddies, but then he'd allowed his temper to get the better of him and began mouthing off. The barkeep at the Dynamo had grabbed him, told him there were no more warnings and had thrown him out on the street. He had to learn to keep his goddamn mouth shut: one of these days it was going to get him in real trouble.

He stumbled along, aware of the hobos sitting in doorways, their hands out, handwritten notes begging for change. More than once he thought about rolling one of them for their takings, but he knew where that would lead. Before long he'd be spending more time in their company, and soon he'd be sitting alongside them with his hand out. There was a 7-Eleven on the corner of his street. He went in, lingered around the counters. An Iranian teller watched him the entire time, and he stumbled outside again, his opportunity to boost a bottle or two missed. As he came out the door, swearing under his breath, a big guy had blocked his path. The man had grunted something—almost like an exclamation—before shoving past and into the shop. 'A little fucking manners wouldn't go amiss,' Tennant shouted at him. Then he recalled his earlier resolve to mind his mouth, and he loped away before the guy could chase him down.

This part of the city was rundown. That was an understatement if ever he'd heard one. It was downright shitty. He had no right to complain, of course. It was his own fault that he'd ended up here, and having been kicked loose from prison only weeks before he should feel damn fortunate to have found a landlord willing to give a room to an ex-jailbird. He didn't feel lucky. His house wasn't fit for rats, let alone human habitation. The fact that it was all he could afford was beside the point, and it didn't mean he had to be happy about the arrangement. He shared the house with two other men. Both were drunks, and he trusted they were out in the bars, mooching free drinks in exchange for raunchy stories. He was going to get his head down—it would be impossible if either were home. One of them was so deaf he had to yell even when speaking to himself. The other fancied himself the Great Caruso and sang freakin' opera at the top of his voice.

He had a key to the front door, but it was pointless. The frame was so warped that the components of the lock didn't meet. As he usually did, he grabbed the handle, twisted it, and shoved with a shoulder against the door and it popped open. He closed the door in reverse. His heels scuffed through a drift of accumulated trash: mainly crushed beer cans and flyers, unopened bills and soiled clothing. There was no light bulb in the hall, but enough ambient city light came through the grimy window at the top of the stairs to guide a path through the junk. He passed the Great Caruso's room on the left, and the door to the basement on the right. He lived on the second floor. The stair carpet was threadbare, holed in places, and a trap for the unwary. But he'd learned to navigate the danger spots— even drunk—so went up the stairs, grasping the rail for support. He had only made it part way up when he heard the door shoved open. Shit, his plans of dropping off to sleep now were scuppered. He swung round, a warning that his house mate keep the fuck quiet building on his lips.

The figure blocking the doorway wasn't either man he expected. Both his housemates were shrunken gnomes; this man was large and stockily built. It wasn't the first time some street punk had found their way inside, looking for somewhere out of sight to administer their drug of choice. Twice in the past fortnight, Tennant had had to kick bums back out onto the street. He started down the stairs, glad that he was only on the cusp of drunkenness because it meant he was at that stage where he could be as galled as he wished, but retained enough of his faculties that he could deal with a dangerous situation. 'Hey, buddy, the street's back that way. Now turn the fuck around and get outta here.'

The man didn't reply, only bent down and heaved a large rucksack inside. Maddened, Tennant stomped down the stairs and into the hall. The house had three rooms, a shared kitchen and communal bathroom. There was the basement but it was a damp hole good for growing mold and nothing else. There was no room for a fourth lodger. 'You can forget about moving in, buddy. Get your bag outta here and try somewhere else.'

The man closed the door. He was now lost in the shadows of the hall. Tennant halted. In the brief moment as the guy had turned to shut the door he'd caught a glimpse of his features in the streetlight from outside. It was the big guy who he'd almost collided with at the door of the 7-Eleven. Suddenly Tennant didn't feel as sure about himself as before.

'You followed me back here, for what? Okay, I owe you an apology. I shouldn't have mouthed off like that. I'm sorry. Now let's leave things at that, buddy.'

The man stepped forward.

'Okay. That's as far as you come, buddy. Now, I've apologised,' Tennant puffed up his chest and bunched his fists, 'but now it's time to leave.'

'I'm not finished here,' the man replied.

'Yes,' Tennant said, stomping forward, 'you are.'

The fear that pricked him at the appearance of the stranger had been pushed aside by the false courage of the liquor in his veins. When the whisky took hold like that, Tennant wasn't afraid of any one. Not even a big punk who invaded his house. Tennant went to grab the man, to force him back out onto the street.

He barely saw the man move. He hit Tennant with some Bruce Lee move; his knee flicking up, his lower shin whipping up and around to slam against his skull. Stars exploded in his vision and he tasted copper on his tongue. Tennant bounced off the wall, but fought to stay upright.

'Son of a bitch!' he hissed, his fingers against the welt growing on his forehead.

The man's leg flicked again, this time under Tennant's arms, and the ball of his foot found the soft spot beneath Tennant's sternum. The wind was powered from his lungs, and his diaphragm recoiled at the trauma. Gasping for breath, Tennant retreated.

He heard a clink of metal as the man set down his bag. The movement was unhurried, as if Tennant was below contempt.

Tennant backed up to the base of the stairs, searching for something to use as a weapon, his heels digging through trash. His boot clanked against an empty beer bottle. Tennant ducked and came back up, holding the bottle by its neck. He lifted the bottle like a club.

'Come any closer and I'll break your head,' he snapped.

There was a sound like someone coughing and the bottle shattered in his grip. Flying shards cut at his flesh, glittered in his vision. Tennant's hand came open in reflex and the stub of the bottle fell back to the trash. The man came forward, and the slash of amber light filtering down from the window landed in a bar across his face. Below it something glinted bluish in the man's right hand. Cordite drifted in the air, a stink stronger than the rankness already imbuing the atmosphere.

Tennant had seen enough guns in his lifetime to recognise the semi-automatic in the man's hand. The tubular object screwed on the barrel was something he was only familiar with from action movies and TV cop shows. The guy hadn't simply followed him from the convenience store, he understood. The man had been following him before that. He had been spying inside, checking what he was up to, and Tennant had surprised him when he'd brusquely shoved out the door. The guy had been after him, and had an agenda that didn't include finding lodging in this crap hole. Tennant knew enough that he was in real danger. As tough as he thought himself, he had no chance against a gun. He turned and fled up the stairs.

He didn't get far.

A hand grasping Tennant's jacket collar followed rapid footsteps. Tennant was no lightweight, but he was yanked off his feet, fell backwards and was dragged back down the stairs. Stunned, he blinked tears from his eyes as the man leaned over him.

'Where do you think you're running off to?' the man asked.

'Who are you, man? What do you want?'

'I've come to say hello. Your old pal, Mitch told me where to look you up.'

Mitch? He had to be talking about Mitchell Forbeck, his cellmate during his last six months inside. They had both been paroled the same week, but Tennant hadn't seen him since. He'd had enough of Mitch to last him a lifetime and had said goodbye and meant it. Why would Mitch send this guy after him? He didn't owe Mitch a damn thing, and their parting had been amicable enough. So, who was this guy: a friend of Mitch's? He doubted it: Mitch didn't have friends. Tennant attempted to study the man's face. There was something vaguely familiar in it, but he was positive he didn't know the man personally. Was he another inmate, someone he'd pissed off during their time behind bars?

'Why'd Mitch send you here?'

'Because I asked him to. Of course, I had to motivate him a little, the way I guess I'll have to with you.' The gun was pressed to Tennant's forehead. 'Now stand up. Don't try anything funny, or your brains will decorate the floor.'

Recalling the state of Tennant's home his threat was moot, because he had no intention of killing him outright. He had learned that Tennant was a braggart, and that while in prison he'd regaled his cellmate with tales of his criminal activity. All prisoners were guilty of embellishment, and Mitchell Forbeck had surmised that Tennant was building himself a tough rep, to assure he was not someone to be messed with when he'd told him about hanging and then burning a man alive in a cellar in Arkansas. Mitch didn't believe Tennant, but he thought he could win points with the warden if he slipped him the nod. He didn't get to see the warden himself, but two prison guards who reassured him that Tennant was blowing hot air out of his ass. The guards had sent Mitch back to his cell, cowed like a whipped dog for wasting their time, but they must have mentioned the story to another guard. From there the tale had grown fleetingly, before it was lost once more among all the other rumours bubbling around the general population. That was when the wild story had reached his ears and he knew that it was true: the man allegedly murdered shared his name. By then the originator of the admission was forgotten, but Mitch Forbeck's inclusion was still bandied around. Mitch had been released from prison by then but he took no tracking down. All it took for him to learn the name of the braggart from Forbeck was to shove his gun under the punk's chin. He probably didn't need to shoot him dead afterwards, but it was possible that Mitch recognised him, and he had already proven himself to be the type to go stool pigeon.

Prior to that moment he had never killed another man, but it had proved surprisingly easy when he was driven by such pure rage. His life had been shit. Mother was a drunkard and those she brought into their home had been scum. He had known more *stepfathers* and *uncles* than he could count, and the beatings he took from them were the least of their sins he'd allow himself to recall. He went through his childhood hoping that his real dad would return, take him away from the horror, save him. When he discovered that his father had been thwarted from doing so by thugs led by vile lies he had resolved that Forbeck would not be the last to die at his hand.

It was a colossal coincidence that he should end up at the same prison as a man with information about his father's demise, especially after so many years. He had truly believed that he'd never avenge the murder, thinking that the conspirators had to be so aged by now that they would already be in their graves.

After he'd found out Tennant's identity, and tracked him back to the ramshackle house, it had pleased him to learn the names of all the lynch party, and more so that they—all the men at least—were still in the land of the living. What he hadn't expected was for Tennant to be so forthcoming in the description of his father's suffering. Perhaps it was because the asshole expected to die in agony and wished to take away some of the satisfaction from his punisher by basking in the gory details. Or maybe it was simply the man's nature to brag, even if it meant further torment before he died.

* * *

'I burned that sick motherfucker! It's what the bastard deserved. I wasn't like the other pussies that were having second thoughts. If I hadn't thrown the gasoline over him I'm sure they'd have let him down, and rushed him to the nearest hospital to have his bullet wound seen to. Not me, though, no fucking way!'

The man listened to Tennant's rant, dispassionately.

'Do you hear me, you sick fuck? I burned your precious daddy. You should have seen him dance. Jesus! The screams. How half of Arkansas didn't hear him I'll never know. He was a fucking coward in life and he was a fucking coward in death.'

The man was sickened by Tennant's lies. He had everything he needed from him—the names of each of the murderer's, and a full description of each of their respective crimes. He did not need to listen any longer. He pulled tight the chain-link noose. Tennant gagged. His eyes bugged. The chain would strangle him completely, but not immediately. First Tennant must endure the agony of the links tearing into his flesh. He would like to allow the bastard to suffer the torture, but Tennant's sickening false condemnation of his father had piqued his anger. He kicked the stool from under Tennant's feet.

Tennant dropped like a stone, the links of the chain snapping around his throat, bunching up folds of grey skin beneath his clamped jaw. His tongue was forced between the gaps in his teeth, forming small blood-red balloons. His legs kicked and spasmed.

The man shot Tennant in the chest.

Then he began to pile the trash from the cellar floor around Tennant, watching him all the while. The bastard's eyes were dulling, even as they bulged from their sockets. He leaned down, flicked his cigarette lighter and gave flame to the pile of trash.

The chain ensured that Tennant couldn't scream, but he tried anyway, a keening noise that escaped him like steam as the flames danced up his legs and caught in the fabric of his trousers.

'Who's the fucking coward now?' the man asked him, before firing once more into his chest.

Still, Tennant lingered. He was shuddering as the flames writhed over him.

The man shot him in the head.

23

Studying it from outside, the police station on Vallejo Street was about the prettiest I'd ever had the pleasure of visiting, but once through the doors I forgot all about the tasteful architecture and concentrated on the reason why I was there. If I ended up in a cell, staring at the bare walls and featureless steel door I'd have ample opportunity to think about the lovely views I was missing while killing time.

I approached a desk sergeant. In movies and books, desk sergeants are always trying to do ten tasks at once and barely give the time of day to someone making an enquiry. Often they are bad tempered and shout a lot. Seems that the sarge here bucked the cliché somewhat. He was a rosy-faced guy, chubby in the shoulders and neck. All he needed was a white beard and he'd make an ideal department store Santa Claus. He was leaning on his fists, watching my approach, offering me a 'come hither' smile. 'How can I help you, sir?'

'I'm here to speak to Detective Jones, if he's available?'

'Detective Jones? My, my.' He looked down at some list pinned beneath the level of the desk, running a finger down it. 'We have three Joneses here, can you be more specific?'

'Gar Jones,' I said. 'Homicide.'

The sergeant tapped the sheet. Smiled at me. 'Of course, our friend Garforth,' he said. He reached for a telephone, raised both eyebrows my way. 'Your name please, sir.'

'Joe Hunter,' I said. No reason to lie.

His lack of recognition was a good sign; it meant that Jones and Tyler had not yet put out that APB I was worried about.

The sergeant spoke into the phone. He only frowned mildly at me once before hanging up. 'You're in luck, Mr Hunter. Come on through.' He opened a flap in the desk, and unlatched a swing gate to allow me passage. As I stepped past him he made the counter secure once more, before indicating a door to his left. 'Follow me, please.'

Just because the sarge was polite didn't mean he wasn't setting me up for an arrest once I was out of public view. If he was going to put the cuffs on me once we were through the back then so be it. I wouldn't resist. There was no sense in making the situation more awkward than it already was.

As it was, when we passed through the door there was a female patrol officer coming down the hall, her arms filled with investigation files.

'Ah, Officer Brockovich! You've timed it just right.' Without waiting, the sergeant reached and took the folders from her. 'Will you escort this gentleman to the Homicide office for me? He's here to see Gar Jones.'

The cop gave me the once over, checking out the state of my jacket. She glanced at the sarge and they both raised their eyebrows. The sarge possibly winked at her, but from the angle I couldn't tell. Whatever signal he gave her, she smiled sweetly and asked me to follow her. Can't say that I minded: she was a looker with a curvaceous figure that her uniform couldn't conceal. If anything her utility belt helped accentuate her hips and the way in which they swayed.

'The sarge seems like a decent feller,' I said.

Without turning she said, 'He's one of the better bosses.'

'So...what do you make of Garforth Jones?' To be honest, I'd believed Gar was the shortened form of Gary, and the name was an odd one to my ear.

'I couldn't possibly comment. It would be unprofessional of me.' She turned and flashed me a conspiratorial smile. It would have been better if her eyetooth hadn't glinted; it would have made it look less like a shark attack.

'Sounds like I'm in for a pleasant time,' I said.

'Yeah,' she said. 'You have my sympathies.'

She led me down a utilitarian corridor, passing closed doors and then into an open space dominated by cluttered desks. There were a handful of detectives making calls, or trawling through information on their work terminals. One man was sitting on the end of a desk, swinging his feet as we walked in. It was as if we'd caught him skiving duties and he stood up quickly. For a second it looked like he would cut us off, but Officer Brockovich anticipated him. 'Gar's expecting us.'

The detective scrutinized me up and down, before jerking a thumb over his shoulder. 'He's back there in the confession box.'

The confession box? I thought it was station slang for an interview room, but I guessed wrong. When Brockovich knocked and then opened the door, I saw the detective was referring to the dimensions of the room. I'd been in larger store cupboards. There was barely room for the desk and computer, let alone the husky form of Gar Jones whose chair was jammed sideways on to the desk. He was hunched over the monitor, tapping at the keyboard with one index finger: it couldn't have been easy on his posture. He stood up sharply, and I was prepared for him to start on me immediately. He surprised me by sticking out his hand to shake. Taken off guard I accepted his hand without thinking. 'Thanks for coming in at such short notice,' he said. Then he held up a finger. 'Give me a second, huh?'

He leaned back into the confession box and snared his jacket off the back of his chair. As an afterthought he locked down the computer screen. Then he stepped out into the squad room. He gestured towards the exit door and the corridor we'd just come along. 'We'll go somewhere a little more comfortable. Can I get you anything? Water? Coffee?'

'A coffee would be great,' I said, thinking that if he was leading me to somewhere where an arrest was more easily contained then I might as well have a decent brew before being thrown in a cell.

He nodded. Then to Brockovich, he said, 'Do the honors will you, Kathy? Bring one for Tyler and me as well, okay? We'll be in room five.'

'Of course,' she said brightly, but she couldn't help the twist of her mouth. I wondered if it was at Jones' ill-concealed sexism, or the inherent 'them and us' competition that existed between detectives and uniformed officers in most police stations. I decided on the latter.

'Much appreciated,' I said to her, and meant it.

She only jerked her head haughtily. I watched her go, smiling sadly to myself. I was once close to a uniformed policewoman and Kathy Brockovich brought her to mind. Kate Piers had worn a different uniform, and her beat was the breadth of a continent away: she was also dead. But there was enough about this woman to bring her to mind. I shook the memories loose. Gar Jones was looking at me. He must have misread my interest in his colleague, because he grinned conspiratorially, nudged me with his elbow. 'Easy on the eyes, right?'

'I've met plenty worse looking cops.' I met his gaze, watched his grin slip a little. But then he got that I was joking—albeit at his expense—and his grin broadened. 'Come on. There's an even uglier one waiting for us down the hall.'

Gar Jones hadn't yet decided on his best play to get through to me. He'd tried amiable cop, bad cop, now it looked as if he was going for the good cop routine. I preferred people who were true to themselves, even if they were obnoxious, and this buddy-buddy style of his struck me as a lie. He led the way from the squad room and into the hallway I'd earlier traversed. The doors were numbered consecutively, mirroring the one opposite, but each office was designated "A" or "B" depending on which side of the corridor it was on. We headed for 5A.

Gar swung the door open without knocking, and went in. I was a pace behind him. We caught Detective Tyler posed as I'd found Jones minutes earlier, typing furiously at a laptop. Unlike Jones he'd learned to type correctly, and all fingers were flying at the keys. He looked up from his work, saw me, and sat back, pushing out from under the desk. He didn't get up. He did however lean across to offer his hand.

'I have coffee coming,' Jones announced. Having shook with me, Tyler sat back and folded his hands across his stomach. He acknowledged Jones' proclamation wryly. He waited for us to sit, then, as an afterthought, flipped the screen down on his laptop so he could see us over it. I made a cursory inspection of my surroundings. The office was about fifteen by ten feet, not huge by anyone's standards, and about the size of most interrogation rooms I'd been in. But the computer, the desk and drawers, the in-tray and the memo notes on the walls reassured me this was nothing of the sort. I looked for CCTV cameras, but if they were there they were well concealed. There was an archaic monitor on another table in the corner behind Tyler, plus a DVD machine, but that was all. It was a workplace, and it allowed me to relax a little. There was still time for the detectives to arrest me, but it wouldn't be here.

'Thanks for coming in, Mr Hunter.'

'Just plain Joe,' I said, 'or Hunter. Whatever you prefer.'

'Okay, Joe. Then you can call us Gar and Ty. Let's keep things informal, shall we?'

'Depends on why I'm here. Will I need legal representation?'

'For performing a heroic deed? Why would you?' Tyler eyed me squarely. His words would have held more reassurance if they hadn't been delivered so dryly. 'Sadly your efforts were wasted. Yoshida Takumi passed away en route to hospital. He succumbed from the overdose of insulin despite your actions with the Glucagon. Maybe it was best: his lungs may never have recovered from the smoke he inhaled. He'd have suffered.'

'I suppose it was better going that way than burning alive,' I said.

'Yeah. Good job you were there, otherwise we'd never have known what happened to him.' Tyler unfolded his hands, placed one on the desk, and began distractedly scratching at the wood with a fingernail. 'What exactly were you doing at Mr Yoshida's house?'

'Visiting.'

'You said that already,' Gar said. 'You didn't say why you would do that. You said he was a family friend, but that's not entirely true is it?'

'Only if you wish to be awkward about it,' I said. 'Yukiko Rington asked me to check in with him. She wanted me to tell him about her husband's death, and to reassure him that she was okay.'

'Why not ask her son to do that? Instead of a relative stranger?'

'Rink has more on his mind than running errands.'

'Just seems too much of a coincidence that you just happened along at the most opportune of times. I mean, what are the chances?'

'Beats me,' I said. 'What are your thoughts on the subject? You're obviously not considering me a suspect otherwise I doubt we'd be going through this rigmarole without you having read me my rights.'

'We don't think you're a suspect in Yoshida's murder, but we think you know much more than you're letting on.'

'Yeah.' I looked across at Gar. 'He made that clear already.'

I expected my words to get a rise out of Jones, but he merely pursed his lips. I returned my attention to Tyler.

'We're after the same thing here, Joe. We want to find the person responsible for the brutal murder of a significant number of our elderly residents. We know that's also what you want. We could help each other out.'

'I'd love to help, but I don't know a damn thing.'

I felt a shift in mood. The mock friendliness was about to go out of the window. Jones said, '*You* made that clear already. But we're not having any of it.'

'Fair enough.'

Before the recriminations could start flying there was a knock at the door. Kathy Brockovich poked her head inside. She was lugging a tray with three mugs of coffee. She felt the charged atmosphere. She looked at the floor. 'You want me to leave these here?'

Tyler indicated his desk, shifting his laptop over to make room. He didn't thank the woman; maybe she had grown not to expect it. She placed the tray down without any ceremony and scuttled out of the room.

'Do I still get to drink my coffee?' I asked.

'It's here now. Knock yourself out.'

I took mine black. Neither detective reached for theirs.

'Here's the deal,' Tyler said.

I watched him over my cup, the steam wafting up my face.

'You tell us what you know and we let the assault on Sean Chaney slide.'

I was surprised to hear he'd learned about that, but didn't let it show.

'Sean who?'

He didn't bother expounding. He opened his laptop and hit some buttons. He twisted it around on the desk so that I could see it. There was a small movie file centred on the screen. Tyler hit another key and the picture expanded, filling the corners. I immediately recognised Rink and me stepping off the train at Montgomery Street Station. The image was taken from a wall-mounted camera. I was relieved, for a moment I thought the image was going to be a recording from inside the BART carriage. I watched the events unfold. At no time did either of us look up and offer a full on view of our faces, but it'd take a blind man not to recognise us—even dressed in the shabby clothes I was wearing.

'Well?'

'*Well* what?'

'You're denying that was you and Jared Rington?'

'It was us all right: I just don't see any assault.'

Tyler did his magic with the computer, bringing up a different file. On this one, it showed Sean Chaney boarding the BART at the Embarcadero stop. A few seconds later, I darted into the next carriage along. Tyler raised a quizzical eyebrow at me, but I was unmoved. He brought up a third file, which I guessed was from a camera at the airport terminus. Chaney stumbled from the carriage, dragging his left leg, one hand clamped down hard on it but failing to stem the flow of blood that dotted the platform.

'I still don't understand what you're talking about.'

'You followed Chaney on that train; a fight broke out; Chaney ended up with a bullet in his leg.'

'Where's the CCTV footage that proves that?'

'Unfortunately the system inside was down. Someone stuck a post-it note over the lens to block the view. I'm guessing it was you.'

Actually, I'd had nothing to do with that, but I wondered to what ends Rink had gone to cover his tracks that he hadn't told me about.

'Were my fingerprints on this note? You can see from the guy on the video that *he* isn't wearing gloves.'

'Don't take *us* for idiots, Hunter.'

'I'm not. But where's your proof? Did this Sean Chaney make a complaint?' I knew that he hadn't, otherwise they would have already read me my rights and shaken his statement under my nose. I drank my coffee.

Tyler shut down the computer. If that was all the leverage

they had on me, then they were on a losing streak. 'We know exactly what happened inside that carriage. Okay, no one has gone on record to say so, but we know what went down and why you were both there. You were looking for whoever was responsible for murdering Andrew Rington. That's also what we are doing.' He opened a drawer in the desk, having to shuffle back to make room. He pulled out a folder and handed it across to Jones. Jones opened it and held it out. I'd to place down my mug to take it from him.

There were two columns of names.

The victims were listed down one side of the page, their wives, and sisters, in one case a sister-in-law, down the other. I noticed immediately that Dan Lansdale and his wife had been added to the list. Parnell and Faulks were conspicuous by their absence though. I wondered if they had been deliberately left off the list so that I wouldn't realise the cops were on to them. Funnily enough, neither detective had referred to us snatching the old guys from under their noses yet. There was one name I didn't recognise. He didn't have a corresponding female name alongside his. I had no idea who Mitchell Forbeck was, or what he was doing on there. Having perused the list, I looked across at Tyler.

'We've been trying to discover the connection between all the victims. What is it that strikes you as obvious here?'

'Each of them are related to Japanese women.' There was nothing else I could say, without being totally obstructive.

'We noticed that very early in our investigation, however we didn't think it was that large a coincidence. Many men here have Japanese wives, and vice versa: we're an open community in that regard. At first we were looking to identify something about the men, trying to connect them. Some are friends, but then there are others who aren't. So we started looking at the women instead.'

Feeling very uneasy about the way his story was heading, I didn't ask. Tyler had already made his mind up to lay all his cards on the table. 'Each of the women on the list have one thing in common. As youngsters, they were relocated under Executive Order nine-zero-six-six to an internment camp in Arkansas during the Second World War.'

'Wasn't everyone of Japanese descent shipped from here to POW camps? It's a pretty tenuous link.'

Tyler ignored me. 'It's a link all the same. When you vector in the fact that each of these women were friends, who remained in contact after the war, then you have to consider that it must have some bearing on the current situation. As you said earlier, you went to check on Mr Yoshida at Yukiko Rington's behest. We did a little checking of our own. It appears that Yukiko contacted a number of the men on our list. Frankly it was what brought us to discover that Daniel Lansdale was murdered over in South Dakota. He was stabbed to death a couple of evenings ago. It was a different MO to the previous murders, but that isn't so unusual now that the perp has changed his method. He injected Yoshida with an overdose of insulin, then set fire to his house, so it appears to us he's not particular about how he kills his victims, rather he's only interested in killing them. Period. It's the reason *why* we can't figure out. We know it's because of the women, we just can't decide how.'

'We think you know more about that,' Jones put in. 'There's something we're missing here. All it takes is one hint, and we'll be able to put it all together. Come on, Joe. Work on this with us.'

Guilt assailed me. I wished I could say, and help these cops to do their jobs. It mattered most that the killer was stopped from hurting anyone else—but there was no denying it: I owed *giri* to Yukiko and to her murdered husband. More than anything I owed Rink an opportunity at revenge.

'Sorry, guys,' I said. 'But I'm at a loss for any idea.'

143

24

Melissa Yoshida was sitting opposite the sergeant's desk as Detective Jones ushered me out of our meeting. I wouldn't have noticed her, had not Jones given her a slight wave, and told her he'd be ready to speak with her in a few minutes.

'Thank you, Detective,' Melissa responded. 'I'm fine here.'

She wasn't fine: she looked distraught and little wonder. I hadn't anticipated that she would be called in for questioning, but it was obvious when I thought about it. Jones and Tyler were trying to piece together the killer's motive and Melissa could possibly tell them something important. I doubted it. If Takumi had been anything like Yukiko then he had kept his secret to himself.

I felt guilty for some reason, as if I should apologize to her for not doing more to save her grandfather, and the shame hit me like a punch to the gut. I averted my face, doing my best to avoid notice. Maybe I'd have got away clean if Detective Jones hadn't said: 'Stay in touch, Mr Hunter. Anything you learn, I'd like to hear about it.' He handed me a card with his telephone number on it.

The gregarious desk sergeant unlatched the flap to let me out, smiling and nodding, and as I moved into the public area I felt Melissa's gaze on me. I couldn't help glancing over at her, and our eyes met and stuck.

She was already getting up off the public bench, approaching me. She was dressed in a black trouser suit over a purple blouse, with her dark hair pulled back and barely a trace of make-up. Though I knew her to be in her early twenties, she appeared more mature, and—dare I say it—very pretty, despite her sadness. She was clutching a small purse against her abdomen, her head to one side as she studied me. It was as if she recognised my face, but how was a mystery to me. I'd only seen her that one time when she'd leapt from the taxi and ran

144

towards the burning house and she hadn't looked at me then. I pulled up, casting a glance behind me to check Gar Jones had gone: he wouldn't appreciate his key witnesses talking. Then again, that could have been his intention. Maybe he'd conspired that we'd meet. Perhaps he thought I'd share what I knew with the woman and he'd be able to tease the information from her. The best thing I could have done was smile, turn away and walk directly out of the police station.

Her gaze caught mine again though, and I waited for her to speak.

'Excuse me,' she said timidly. 'Are you Joe Hunter? Only I just heard the detective say your name and thought...'

There was no getting away now, not without appearing rude. 'I'm Joe Hunter, yeah.'

She nodded, holding her bag even tighter to her body. Her face tipped down, and briefly I expected it to rise with a look of recrimination. It didn't, when she looked at my face her dark eyes shone. She traced the lines of my forehead and nose, settled briefly on my mouth, then her scrutiny returned to my eyes and stayed there. I was aware I was a tad unkempt, but it didn't seem to faze the young woman. In fact, my appearance seemed to satisfy her. As if I fit an image she'd conjured in her mind.

'You're the one who saved my grandfather from the fire.'

Her words were more statement than anything else. They surprised me, and I partly expected her to finish by saying I had not done enough. She didn't.

'I'm glad that I bumped into you,' she said. 'I wanted to say thank you. If it weren't for you...'

I didn't have the words to answer. I still wasn't sure where this was leading. Maybe she misread my reticence to reply as humility instead of shame. It was an awkward moment, and I tried to say something. 'I...I only wish I could have done more.'

Melissa shook her head; a smile flickered at the corner of her mouth.

'You risked your own life to save him.'

'Yeah, but...'

Melissa surprised me again by reaching out and touching me on my chest. It was an intimate gesture, the delicate touch of her fingertips over my heart conveying more than any number of words could.

'It was an incredibly brave and selfless act. If my grandfather was still around he would've said thank you, but, well, that's my responsibility now.'

'It's okay,' I said. 'I don't deserve your thanks. I only did what anyone else would've done. I'm sorry it wasn't enough.'

'You know that isn't true. The detectives told me what you did—all of it—trying to save my grandfather. Most people would've given up long before you did.'

I shook my head softly.

Melissa smiled again, but it was laden with sadness.

'Please, Mr Hunter. Accept my thanks, even if it's only on behalf of my grandfather. He would have it no other way.'

'Okay.' I nodded, only barely. I put out my hand to accept hers and she held on.

Then I received surprise number three as she leaned in and kissed me on my cheek.

Melissa smiled again, this time more openly. 'Thank you,' she said.

'I, uh, thank you,' I said, the memory of her lips tingling on my skin, as I held her hand. She blinked, as if realizing how forward she'd been. Detective Jones forestalled her any further embarrassment, poking his head out of the back office door.

'Miss Yoshida, are you ready to come through?'

We both looked at him, releasing our handshake.

'I'd best go,' Melissa said.

I caught a frown from Jones and understood he'd had no part in our meeting. It was a simple act of fortune.

'Nice meeting you,' I said.

'It was.' She smiled shyly again.

Melissa walked away and I caught myself watching her. I waited for her to glance back, and when she did I was glad everything about my trip to San Francisco wasn't all doom and gloom. I left the station feeling lighter than I had in days.

Once back out on Vallejo Street I flagged a taxi. I asked to go to Fisherman's Wharf, which, as the crow flies, wasn't far distant. The area is a famous tourist attraction with a plethora of themed restaurants, whacky museums and a huge aquarium.

Even in the off-season it still teems with visitors—therefore it was a good place to lose any tail my newly found detective buddies might send after me. I wandered among the crowds of jostling tourists, checking for a surveillance team and saw nothing suspicious. I joined a queue for another taxi, fending off guys offering to carry me in their carts that they pulled along behind bicycles. Finally I made it into a cab and gave the driver directions back to the lodge at Lake Chabot.

I was surprised that Jones and Tyler had allowed me to leave so soon. Part of me had been expecting to be hauled down to the cells: it was always a good way of getting someone to talk, locking them in a cell for a few hours with no other company than the bare walls to stare at. But they seemed deflated at my failure to cave in, and after only a few more questions had allowed me to leave. Jones didn't even offer a veiled threat when he saw me out of the office. What was apparent to me was that they were under pressure from the higher-ups and—apart from that half-arsed attempt at coercing me into their way of thinking by threatening me with an assault charge—they'd decided I was of better use to them as an ally rather than an enemy. As I'd been led from the office I believed their friendly approach was all a sham, and I was under no illusion that they might haul me in again, maybe going for the thumbscrews or rubber hose method next time. But then I'd met Melissa Yoshida, and from her reaction the detectives must have told her only good things about my part in her grandfather's brief rescue. The cops' attitude seemed to have changed. Nevertheless, I expected a tail to be put on me, so they could keep tabs on my whereabouts for when they decided to up the pressure. But I was confident now that the tail wasn't there.

It made me think once again about the sand-coloured car and its two occupants who'd followed us from Hayes Tower. We had assumed they were cops. Now I wasn't as certain. To be honest, I always thought that we had given them the slip far too easily, and had to consider now that it wasn't a police surveillance team watching us but someone else. Who could it be? My first assumption was that if it was the killer, then he had help. That was something none of us had anticipated. Yet I didn't think that was the case. Someone else was interested in

Parnell or Faulks, then? No, that wasn't it either. They'd been after Rink and me. We were the obvious targets of scrutiny, and I could only think of one other person in San Francisco who had any interest in us. Some guys, it seemed, would never take good advice. You'd think that having been shot in the thigh, it would have taught him he was punching above his weight, but Sean Chaney hadn't yet got the message. Chaney was a distraction we could do without, but also a complication that could get in the way of finishing this with the killer. We couldn't take the war to him without bringing the cops down on us, but neither could we ignore Chaney. For a second or two I thought about employing McTeer and Velasquez as more than chaperones for Parnell and Faulks: perhaps they could visit Chaney on our behalf. But I discarded the idea immediately. The situation was bad enough without getting our friends involved.

I pushed the issue to the back of my mind. First and foremost we had to identify and deal with the murderer. Concentrating on the local thug didn't help me do that. So I focused instead on what I'd learned during my time with my detective buddies. I have an ability to snapshoot scenes, for full recall later. I'd memorized the list of names they had shown me, and the one that stood out most of all was Mitchell Forbeck. Who was he? What connection did he have to everything that had gone on to date? One thing I was sure of was that Yukiko had never mentioned his name to me. Was he a suspect? No, because he was on the list of victims. I was confident that he was connected somehow, otherwise the cops wouldn't have included him, I just couldn't fathom how. That was a mystery for later.

I figured out how Parnell and Faulks were excluded from the list. Tyler had said they'd checked on Yukiko, and saw from her telephone log that she had been in communication with the other victims shortly before their deaths—except in Lansdale's case where she was too late. She had told me that she had tried to warn them of her suspicions and had telephoned the other members of Peterson's lynch party. Well, there'd been no need to phone Parnell or Faulks when both men were already aware that they were in danger. Ergo, the cops didn't know about them yet.

The killer did know about them, though, so it was imperative we keep them safely tucked out the way. My mind went back to that sand-coloured car. How the hell had Chaney learned about the old men, and sent his guys to Parnell's place after us? The answer was obvious enough: I'd been standing with the old boys at the cemetery during Andrew's funeral when that odd incident with the man in the car occurred. If he was one of Chaney's men then he must have noted them, and the cars they drove, and found them through their licence plate numbers. But that was crediting Chaney with connections in law enforcement and that I didn't believe. More simply Chaney's man could have been lying in wait and had followed Parnell or Faulks home after the ceremony was over.

Without the need for diversionary tactics, my taxi took the more direct route to Lake Chabot by the Bay Bridge, then down the MacArthur Freeway. I was still mulling everything over when it drew up outside the reception building. I gave the driver a decent tip on top of the fare, and he pulled away, possibly heading out towards Oakland International Airport to pick up a return fare to the city.

Rink was waiting for me at the front porch. He'd set himself up on a bench where he had a great view of the lake and forested hills beyond. The afternoon sun was slanting through the nearby treetops, and Rink had found himself a warm spot. I sat down next to him, crossing my heels and folding my hands at my waist. It was the first time I'd relaxed in days.

'Are the old guys settled in okay?'

'Yup. I ordered them room service and they're making the most of it as we speak. How did you get on at the station?'

'Well, as you can see I wasn't arrested.' I brought him up to speed about my chitchat with the detectives. How they tried the lame attempt at threatening me into compliance, followed by their plea for help. I told him about the list. 'They're not far from putting everything together, Rink.'

'Crap. Don't mention anything about that to our old buddies in there, or to my mom. They're frightened enough without the threat of going to prison hanging over them.'

'They won't hear anything from me,' I reassured him.

Next I shared my suspicions about who was trailing us in the sand-coloured car. I saw an argument forming in Rink's mind and anticipated him. 'They were amateurs who had no idea how to follow us without being seen. Plus they fell for the oldest trick in the book when you pulled that stunt in the alley. Any cop worth their salt would've radioed in another car to cut us off and stayed put to stop us coming back that way.'

'They did call in another patrol car. Do you remember: it tore past us at that intersection on its way downtown?'

'Could have been a pure coincidence. A patrol car on a totally different call just happened to go past at the opportune time, and we assumed that it was after us.' I laughed to myself. Receiving a puzzled frown, I explained. 'Your mom warned me that I assume too much: maybe she's right.'

'Yeah, my mom's a wise one, all right. Pity she wasn't as wise when she sent me after Chaney. Would have saved us all a heap of trouble now.'

'That's supposing I'm right, of course, and it was Chaney's lot that was following us.'

'Has to be him, doesn't it? Jesus, Hunter. We've fought assassins and serial killers who've proven less a pain in the butt than Chaney's turning out.'

'He's not worth wasting any more time on.'

'Unless the punks he sent after us try something, I'm with you. But before we leave San Francisco, I'm putting that asshole in his place.'

I let it go. I mentioned the name that had struck me as out of place on Tyler's list of victims.

'Mitchell Forbeck,' Rink repeated the name. 'Never heard of him. But I'll have Harve check on him, see if he can figure out how he's connected.'

'Have we heard from Harvey yet?' It didn't escape me that both Rink and I had destroyed our cell phones—pointlessly it turned out, because it was apparent now that the police hadn't fixed a trace on Rink's signal as we'd feared—but there was always the landline inside.

'I'm still waiting on him getting back to me. Before you ask: yeah, I did call him and give him the number here.'

'What about the guys?'

I was referring to our friends flying in from Florida. Rink

glanced at his watch. 'Still a few hours until they get here.'

'So what do we do?' More than anything I hated inactivity. The next few hours were going to be a drawn out hell for me.

Rink plucked at the sleeve of my jacket. 'You should take that shower you've been putting off for hours, otherwise the bad guy's going to be able to sniff us out.'

25

It was approaching evening in Arkansas. A strong breeze had kicked up; bringing with it a grey haze of drizzle that smeared the windscreen like grease. The wipers batted at it ineffectually, causing blotches that only hindered visibility. Harvey Lucas pressed buttons to drop his window and peered out across fallow pastureland, trying to locate the house he was certain lay out there somewhere. Spatters of rain flicked across his face and he grunted in annoyance. Coming all the way out here to the sticks had seemed like a good idea at the time, but now he wasn't so sure. But a lead was a lead and he couldn't turn his back on it. His friends were relying on him.

Through the gloom he could see a telephone pole. It leaned to one side, the wires taut on one side, lazy the other. At its base was a rickety wooden fence, almost overgrown by couch grass. There was no other reason for their presence out here if it wasn't to serve a homestead. The road was unpaved, a muddy trail full of potholes and ruts, and he could make out the occasional impression of tyre tracks at its edge. He'd no way of telling how old the tracks were, but it was at least evidence that another vehicle had driven this way in the recent past. He dropped the window lower, leaning out for a better view than his blurred windscreen offered. Cursing, he ducked back inside, swiping rain from his face. The moisture made a dark satin on the cuff of his suit jacket, and he cursed all the more. He should have dressed in something less expensive for a trip out to the wilds, but he hadn't expected to go all Daniel Boone to find the goddamn place.

His Lexus wasn't designed for these kinds of roads. He took things real easy, negotiating the deeper ruts by way of mounting the grass verge with two wheels. He felt nervous in a way conflict didn't affect him, concern for the under carriage of his car outdoing that of his own well-being. There was always the possibility that he would not be welcomed out here: the kind of trailer trash he sought weren't known for their love of black men. Especially not educated, well-dressed black men who were apparently financially much better off than they were. He should have kitted himself out in some old hiking gear, and perhaps left his luxury car well out of sight. He sprayed the windscreen with wash, flicked the wipers to full but it didn't really help. Gripping the steering, he leaned forward, muttering under his breath.

A couple of hundred yards away treetops began to dot the horizon. He glanced out towards where the telephone lines drooped and followed their angle, noting that they converged with the tree line in front. He expected that the trees surrounded the house, planted there to offer some protection from the elements. His discovery added no urgency to his progress, because the road was growing less maintained the nearer he got to the house.

Finally the road began to rise, following the contour of a hill. Here some gravel had been spread to aid traction and he pushed upward and over the crest. His headlights picked out an indistinct but relatively geometric shape beyond a stand of pine on the downslope. He thought his decision might prove injudicious, but he pushed the car on and pulled directly into a small yard at the front of the house. A pickup truck shared the space, but from the way it listed on a punctured tyre he didn't think it had moved any time lately. He cast a jaundiced eye over the place, noting the ramshackle and unloved house before him. It was more a shack than anything else. Planks that had once known paint had been left to darken and warp under the elements. The shingles on the roof looked like scabs the way they peeled in places, flapping in the breeze. The only stone structure on the site was a chimney where moss had nestled in all the seams. He couldn't detect any light from behind the shutters. If he'd come all the way out here on a fool's errand...

Harvey reached for the glove compartment and flipped it open. Inside was his Glock 19 in a snap holster. He took out the gun, released the magazine, checked the load and then reinserted it. He racked the slide. Pulling back the tail of his suit jacket, he clipped the holster and gun to his belt. Better safe than sorry.

He looked again at the house, then twisted to scan the nearby copses of trees, looking for anywhere else people could be. This wasn't a working farm though, so all he found was an equally ramshackle carport across the yard. There was no room for a car beneath it, the space was dominated by junk and garbage. As much as he loathed doing so, Harvey got out the car, turning up his collar against the cold rain. Shit, his hand-tooled, Italian leather shoes were going to require attention after this. He jogged across the muddy yard, and clumped up onto the porch. The planks settled beneath his feet with a groan.

Harvey rapped on the door, gently at first. 'Hello,' he called. 'Anyone home? Miss Douchard?'

Receiving no reply he knocked harder, feeling the door rattle in its frame with each contact with his knuckles.

'Miss Douchard? Hello, my name's Harvey Lucas. I'm a private investigator out of Little Rock, and I only have a couple questions for you.'

He wondered if Michaela Douchard had heard the approach of his car engine and had shut off the lights to deter visitors. It was a gamble offering his identity like that, but he knew how some of these people hated cops and didn't want to be confused for one. They probably didn't get guys looking like him turning up at their door, unless it was to serve a warrant. 'Miss Douchard, I'm not here for any kind of trouble. I just need to locate your son.'

With no reply, he moved along the sagging porch, hearing the ominous moan of resistance and expecting to crash through it at any second. He paused at one window. The rain pattered from the shingles overhead making it impossible to hear anything from inside. He couldn't distinguish one shadow from another as he peered through a chink in the shutters. He went to the corner and leaned out. The chimneystack blocked his view to the rear, but he could see overgrown weeds and brambles grew wild all the way up to the side of the building, offering no route through. He backtracked to the opposite end and found a path formed of hard packed dirt. Shivering as a gust of wind sent rain against his face, he stepped down and followed the side of the shack, looking for a back way in. There was another window at the side of the house and he found that the shutters hadn't been closed as securely here. He teased them open, and leaned close to peer through the glass. Curtains, old, floral, a tad dingy, on the other side foiled his view. He went on to the back. Behind the house he found the secondary garbage dump, discovering a large trench that was almost full of trash. He could smell rotting food, not to mention faeces on the breeze. The stench was unbelievably bad. How could anyone live in a place like this? He turned quickly back to the front of the house, not really sure he wanted to gain access now.

Still, he returned to the front door and knocked harder than before. This time the door shook enough that the unsecured latch sprung and the door creaked inward. Harvey averted his face as a sour odour crept out.

'Hello? Anyone home?'

He pressed the door open and leaned inside. The interior was in darkness and he could make little out beyond the shapes of furniture. Stepping in his toes caught on a carpet that rucked up beneath him. He shook his foot loose and took another step inside. 'Miss Douchard? Nicolas Peterson? Anyone home?'

He stood still listening, allowing his vision to acclimatize to the deep gloom. That sour odour was all around him, sending a shudder of disgust down his spine. Goddamn stench would cling to his clothing no matter what he did afterwards. But there was nothing for it. Placing one cupped palm over his mouth, he reached for his Glock with the other, resting his hand on the butt. He moved though the living area towards a secondary room, the one that he'd failed to see into from the side of the building. He guessed the place beyond the door would prove to be Michaela Douchard's bedroom. There was a scuffmark near the base of the door, brighter than the rest, at odds with the grimy surface. He didn't bother calling out this time, and simply rested his hand on the knob, twisted it open.

The stink in the living room was bad, now it was ten times as bad, a hundred. There was nothing worse than the stench of a rotting corpse to put you off your dinner. Harvey turned his head aside, controlling the gag reflex, then forced himself to look back. From his pocket he took out his cell phone, using the light to illuminate the scene.

There wasn't one corpse here but two.

One was on the unkempt bed, semi-clothed in a nightdress over the top of a dull grey bra. The nightdress was ripped, as though someone had grabbed its wearer by the shoulder and then thrown her down without releasing it. There were two wounds in her upper chest, the edges blackened and puckered as though the bullets had been fired at point blank range. There was also another wound and Harvey turned away from it, despite bearing witness to many gunshot wounds in the past. This final bullet had torn most of Michaela Douchard's bottom jaw off, leaving the lower half of her face an open, suppurating sore. Harvey turned from her to look at the man who was lying over her feet, his chest and head in the dark at the far side of the bed, his hands trailing to the floor.

As much as he hated to, Harvey approached. He could see where a bullet had passed through the man's torso, blowing a hole in his lower back. There was another wound in his left shoulder, and it was close enough to the heart that it would have proved fatal. The man's face was still hidden. Harvey reached for his lank brown hair, taking a bunch of it in his fist, and he used it to lift and turn the man's face towards him. Following death his blood had pooled and settled by the laws of gravity, causing his face to become a large, purple hematoma. Nonetheless, there was enough in the features that Harvey recognised the dead man. He'd looked at a photograph of him enough times so that he would know when he located him. One thing he was sure of now: Nicolas Peterson wasn't the murderer his friends Joe and Rink were hunting.

26

'It looks to me as if they've been lying out there for the best part of a fortnight. We've had a cooler than normal spell of weather out here in Arkansas that's helped slow down decomposition, but they were still well gone. There aren't too many insects around at the present, Hunter, but if it was the height of summer, I don't think there'd be much more than bones left.'

Rink had left to check on his mom, with the intention of picking up McTeer and Velasquez on his return trip to Lake Chabot. So it was down to me to take the call when Harvey rang with news of his shocking discovery. I had placed a silent bet that the man behind the murders had to be Charles Peterson's son, Nicolas, but apparently I'd lost my stake.

'Two weeks, but you could still identify them?'

'Okay, we can't be positive until the cops get through with all their tests, but, yeah, I'm pretty sure it's Nicolas and his mother. The fact that Nicolas was carrying his driving license in his wallet helped me identify *his* remains.'

'You called the cops?'

'No. I didn't think that would be a good idea. I'd have had a problem explaining to them why I was looking for Nicolas, and it would have come back on you guys down the line somewhere. I've left them as I found them. They've been out there for a couple weeks already, another few days won't make that much of a difference.'

'You think it was our guy that killed them?'

'I discovered that Nick Peterson wasn't the most law-abiding guy going. He had a rap sheet for various offences the length of my arm: small time stuff really, theft, assault, but he was also a known drug dealer. There's always the chance that he upset one of his clients or suppliers, but I don't think so. Reading the scene, the main target was his mom, and Nicolas tried to protect her.'

'Maybe he wasn't such a bad guy after all,' I said cynically.

'The way it looked to me was someone turned up at their house but was allowed inside without any fuss. The front door was undamaged, so was the living room. I noticed that the door to Michaela's room had been kicked open, and I'm guessing that Nicolas had taken refuge in the room and tried to keep the killer out. He was shot in the gut and the killer had grabbed his mom and thrown her down on the bed. He shot her point blank, Hunter, three times and must have been straddling her at the time. I think Nicolas must have tried to drag the killer off his mom and was shot again, this time through the chest. The way it looked was as if the killer was holding him up close at the time, put the gun to him and blasted him to death. It was kind of personal, up close stuff, if you ask me.'

'And the likelihood is that he knew his victims, huh? You said he was allowed inside the house and the fight didn't start until the killer approached the bedroom. If Nicolas had a criminal record he was likely as suspicious and paranoid as every other small time crook we've ever met.'

'That's what I was thinking. There are no guarantees, of course. The killer could have come in disguise, maybe posing as an official and gained access that way.'

'Yeah, but what are the chances, Harve?'

'Slim. I'm only playing devil's advocate.'

'So what else have you been considering?'

'Heading out your way. Trouble is I'm still tied up with this damn job for the next couple days.'

'You've done your bit for us, we both appreciate it.'

'Good. You shouldn't complain when you get my bill for a new pair of shoes.' Harvey laughed to himself. 'Seriously though, I wish I was there with you guys. There's little excitement here in Little Rock now that Petoskey's no longer around.'

I grunted out a laugh of my own. I killed Sigmund Petoskey a few months ago, kicked him out of a helicopter piloted by Harvey after the bastard kidnapped and tortured Rink. Petoskey was only a small cog in a plot to find and murder my brother John, but he'd got everything he deserved.

'You don't think discovering a couple of murdered people rates as exciting?'

'The smell kind of dampens my enthusiasm.'

I knew what he meant. I've been around corpses for most of my adult life, but you never get used to the stench of human decomposition. Maybe it's an inherent trait, an instinct programmed at birth, that we all find it abhorrent. It's a reminder of our mortality and that we all end up as fertilizer at the end of our lives.

'I'm at a loss here, Harve. I was full sure that Nicolas was our man, but now I'm back to square one.'

'Not exactly. We still know that everything goes back to what Rink's dad and his friends did to Charles Peterson. Either someone who was there is involved or someone has learned what happened and wasn't happy about what they discovered. My guess is that's the reason why Michaela was targeted. She knew that Charles was snatched out of the trailer, but she didn't report it to the cops.'

'She didn't?' The news took me by surprise. I'd automatically accepted that she had reported Peterson's disappearance and that the police had discovered his remains. Yukiko had never made it clear either way: I'd gone and bloody *assumed* it again.

'There was never a police report made. As far as I can tell, Peterson's still buried out there in that cellar because Michaela chose to keep quiet about him going missing. Reading between the lines, she was best shot of him, and maybe she decided the same thing. The way my mind's working is that the killer found out about that and went to show her how mad that made him. Nicolas, I'm guessing, was just unlucky to be home when the guy showed up at their door.'

'So what else are you thinking, Harve? It's obvious you've come up with another theory...'

'I got to thinking that the killer must have an individual stake in all this. He's either being paid by someone who has, or he has, a very personal reason for killing everyone involved in Charles' death. He'd have to be a *very good* friend of Charles to do this, or he has to be family. I don't see why any other person who would go to these extremes otherwise.'

'Any friends of Charles Peterson would be old by now, the guy I saw running from Takumi's house was only in his forties. I'm guessing it has to be the latter. It might also explain why he managed to get inside Michaela's house without any problem. C'mon, Harve, what aren't you telling me?'

Harvey chuckled. 'Michaela Douchard was Charles Peterson's third wife. Both previous relationships were reputedly childless, but that wasn't so. Charles' second wife was carrying his baby when he ran off to shack up with Michaela. It was a boy, Hunter. Born after the divorce came through, and named after his mother. His name is Markus Colby.'

The revelation came like a punch to my gut. It had to be him.

'Where is he now, Harve?'

'We've a slight problem there, Hunter. I've been unable to trace him beyond his high school years. Markus Colby has dropped off the face of the earth, the way his dad did all those years ago.'

'Maybe you've been looking for records under the wrong name. By the sound of things, the killer hasn't accepted that his father deserved what happened to him. It's not unusual for a kid to sanctify an absent father, and form some sort of fantasy image of him. Maybe that's what set off this rampage: he discovered his dad was a piece of shit and has rebelled against it. Maybe that's why he has to kill everyone involved; not out of vengeance, but to protect the image he has built of Charles in his own mind. Go back and look again, Harve. But, this time, look for him under his dad's surname. Look for Markus Peterson.'

27

The sun had gone down, yet there were no lights on in either Parnell or Faulks' apartments. Both of them must have heard of the others' slayings by now and realised that they were next, so it was unsurprising that the remaining two men had gone into hiding. It was a problem that he hadn't thought through well enough, and couldn't see how he would be able to trace them now. San Francisco was a huge city with many places where they could hide, God forbid that they had fled the city itself. It was a blip in his plan for ending the lives of all those involved in his father's murder, but only that. They would not stay away forever, and would have to return to their homes soon enough. He'd already been in both apartments earlier and found that all their belongings seemed intact: maybe they'd hurriedly packed an overnight bag but that would have been all. Their clothing was still hung in wardrobes, their shoes and underwear, toiletries and even medication all still there. He hoped that one or the other of them would attempt to sneak back under the cover of darkness to fetch more of their belongings and at that time he could follow them back to wherever it was that they were hiding. He had parked his car in a dead-end street, near to a book depository that had closed for the day. He had spun the car first, parking nose out so that he could keep an eye out on the street. Initially he decided he would give it an hour or two, and if neither man showed, then he'd reassess the situation— maybe go after the old Jap bitch instead.

He thought of how he'd missed his opportunity to finish the lying whore the first time, but he was certain that when he struck her with his gun barrel he'd heard her skull crack like an egg shell. He should have put a bullet or two into her to make sure, but at the time he was more intent on punishing her husband. His mistakes were not those a professional assassin would make, but he didn't consider himself anything other than a son paying back the murderers of his father. He was allowed to make a mistake or two. Like he had with Takumi: he should have shot the cripple and had done, but thankfully everything had worked out there. He had heard the news that the old man had perished en route to the hospital, so in the end he was happy with the result. Pity his actions a short time later hadn't finished as well. After firing at the stranger he was certain that the man had been killed, but he had heard nothing about any fatalities from the multi-vehicle pile-up he'd caused. The stranger was still out there somewhere and he had no idea who he was—or how dangerous. That was a little worrying, he had to admit, but it was nothing that would deter him from his task. Markus Colby owed entire commitment to avenging his father.

He had only caught a series of brief glances of the stranger, first as he'd run from the burning house, then later as he'd played cat and mouse with him through the city streets. But he had fixed the man's description in his mind. He was certain that neither of the two who had pulled their car into a parking slot opposite Hayes Tower was the guy who'd dragged Takumi from the fire. His first concern was that they were cops, and he thought about leaving the scene, but when neither of them climbed out of their vehicle, but sat watching the tower block he concluded that they were there for a different reason than law enforcement. Maybe the stranger had survived the crash, but he had been injured, and these men were his replacements. Had these newcomers arrived with the purpose of watching for his arrival, with the intention of taking him out? Or had they come at Parnell or Faulks' behest and were checking things out prior to going inside to fetch their belongings? Markus decided he'd wait and see.

The men in the vehicle were tough guys. They had the kind of faces that had been on the end of more than one whupping, lumpy with scar tissue and their noses flattened, and one of them had cauliflower ears. They had thick necks and broad shoulders. One of them gripped the steering wheel with hands that looked capable of strangling a steer. Markus knew their type, but wasn't afraid. He knew that tough guys were nothing when held under the threat of a silenced pistol. He guessed that they were muscle brought in as protection, but they wouldn't stop him. They were the ones in need of protecting from him.

He watched for another quarter hour. Civilians wandered the street, heading uptown, or making for the shortcut along the far side of Hayes Tower to get to the social housing scheme round back. Markus ignored them all, watching the two tough guys as they in turn watched the tower block. Occasionally one or the other would glance his way, but he was invisible to them behind the tint of his windscreen. Markus thought that if these men were here on Parnell or Faulks' behalf, then he could sit it out, wait until they drove away and then follow them back to their base. He fully expected that he'd find one or other of his quarries there. It was a full twenty minutes later before one of them got out and went to the back of their car. The one inside popped the trunk and the other leaned inside. Markus couldn't make out what happened next, but when the guy straightened up he was holding something inside his coat, gripping the item tightly with his elbow. He nodded to the other who joined him on the road. The first passed something over and it was hidden beneath the second man's jacket. Both men then glanced at the uppermost floor. Markus followed their gaze, but from his angle couldn't determine what had caught their attention. The tough guys jogged towards Hayes Tower.

Markus slipped out of his car.

The two men disappeared inside the tower block, heading in by the communal entrance, the glass doors swinging lazily in their wake.

Markus didn't immediately follow: he angled across the street for a better position and looked up at Parnell's room. Immediately he recognised a difference from his visit earlier. Then the curtains had been closed tightly, but now they had been opened a hand's span. Someone must have gained access to the apartment, most likely approaching over the waste ground and sneaking into the building via a secondary entrance at the rear. Markus smiled to himself. This was the opportunity he'd been waiting for. Then he paused.

If the big guys were protection brought in by one of the old men, then why had they been out here at the front and not accompanying him, as Markus would expect? Why—when noticing movement inside the apartment—had they collected their weapons from the trunk and gone inside? He couldn't imagine why, but he'd swear that the thugs had an opposite agenda to what he'd first credited them with. They weren't here to protect the old guys, but to hurt them. Scowling, he headed for the entrance door. He wanted to see Parnell and Faulks dead, but not at someone else's hand: where was the vengeance in that?

He slipped in through the glass doors, easing them shut behind him and stepped into a dim foyer. In his jacket pocket was his silenced gun. He placed his hand on the butt but did not draw it. There was always the chance that another of the tenants might meet him and the last he wanted was for them to start hollering about an armed man on the loose in the building. He scanned the foyer, then walked to the base of the access stairs. He listened but there was no indication that the tough guys were making their way up the stairs. He returned to the elevator. The bulb in the direction arrow had blown, so there was no external sign to show that the elevator was on its way upward, but he placed the flat of his hand against the metal doors and felt a faint vibration. He could hear the soft thrum of machinery from beyond the doors. Immediately Markus bounded towards the stairs and rushed upward.

As he pounded up the stairs he didn't stop to think that the men were here for anyone other than his would be victims. They had definitely been watching Parnell's apartment, and the movement of the curtain was what had brought them from their car. The stairs doglegged back and forth, and at each level allowed access to a corridor open to the elements along the rear of the building. He ignored the first few landings, but the higher he went he had to be more careful. He'd momentarily lost count of the flights he'd ascended and it was important that he scope out each landing in case one of the tough guys had exited the elevator on Faulks's floor. When he detected no movement he continued up. At the penultimate level he paused, catching his breath. There he withdrew his gun, careful that he didn't snag it on his clothing. He checked the action and was confident that all was in order. He went up the final flight of stairs at an easier pace, picking the spots where he placed his feet to avoid making any unnecessary noise.

Coming to the final level, he pressed himself into the doorframe, out of sight of anyone in the corridor, and peered through glass made practically opaque by the number of greasy fingerprints smearing the window. The elevator doors were approximately twenty feet away and were closed. Beyond them he could make out two bulky figures moving along the hall, attempting to be cat-footed, but still cumbersome from the way they were bunched together. Markus thought about rushing along the hall behind them and shooting them before they knew he was there, but the noise would most assuredly alert his targets, who would already be on high alert. Should he approach them in another manner—his gun hidden—and take them out silently. He was confident that he could handle the two of them, even though they carried clubs. Their weapons would hinder them in the confined space, whereas he'd have plenty of room to deliver a couple of larynx crushing blows. The idea was tempting but he chose to wait, his finger hooked around the trigger of his gun, observing the men as they took up position to each side of the second to last door. There was no doubt now that they had come for Parnell. But with their weapons of choice they had not come to kill him: he would enter the apartment after them, kill them, and then take Parnell at his leisure.

Markus crouched slightly, attempting to find a cleaner spot on the window. When he could find none, he took the decision to push the doors open a little and he watched the action through the gap down the centre of the swing doors. He was in time to see the nearest man rap softly on the door. Immediately the tough guy slipped out of the way of the door: possibly so he couldn't be seen if anyone checked through a spy hole. Markus couldn't recall if there was a peephole or not. When there was no reply the two guys huddled together, but their words were merely a sibilant hiss from this distance. One of them backed up, placing his hips to the small wall that formed the balustrade. Then he lunged forward, lifting his knee and crashing his heel close to the door handle. His first attempt to kick open the door failed, so he lifted his knee and booted it again. The clatter of a chain snapping and the links scattering on the floor was loud even to Markus's ear. The door swung inwards this time, and crashed off a wall. Immediately the two guys charged inside.

Markus didn't stop to think. If they were here to harm Parnell and Faulks, then he had seconds to respond or they would get to his targets first. He thrust through the swing doors and charged along the hall.

He could hear the stamps of the men as they surged into the apartment, the thud of doors being thrown open, and the sounds were almost Markus's undoing. He was concentrating on them so much that he almost missed the final door on the landing being pulled open and a man stepping into sight. He thought that the man was possibly a concerned neighbour, checking on the sounds of commotion. But then it struck him. He knew the face that briefly turned to regard him. He saw the man's eyes widen in recognition, and in the next instant the man's hand was coming up and it was clutching a handgun. Unlike the two tough guys who'd mounted their attack with the finesse of charging bulls, this man moved with professional calm. The man centred his gaze on Markus the way he had in that moment when they'd glanced at each other over the fence in Yoshida Takumi's back yard. The stranger aimed his gun at Markus's chest.

Markus also lifted his gun, but he wasn't quick enough. He fired, but it was a moment after the stranger had already done so. Markus had no way of knowing if his aim was on target, because his reaction was to throw himself to one side. It didn't save him: the bullet struck his side like a hammer blow. Caught mid-dive the impact spun him and Markus caromed against the low wall.

Pain flared through him, a white flash of agony lancing through his senses. He wanted to scream but the pain ensured his teeth were clamped tight. Before this he'd had no idea of what being shot felt like, but he knew now. He wondered if he was dying, his mind racing, rage boiling up because he'd been thwarted before completing his mission. The wind was caught in his lungs, his throat pinching tight, and then the world tilted.

He could see the evening sky, the clouds a bilious orange tinted by the city lights. Then his vision was filled with the lights of the buildings opposite, and they were slipping and arching, following his sideways pitch as he tumbled out over the balustrade. Everything moved with a lazy calm, and Markus looked down at the hard packed dirt of the fallow ground behind Hayes Tower.

Then the earth rushed up to meet him.

28

So that's Markus finished then.

That was my acerbic thought as I watched the killer tumble from the sixth-floor balcony and plummet from sight.

My next thought: Rink's going to be pissed at me.

After Rink had collected McTeer and Velasquez from the airport and they had taken over the minder duties, I'd briefed him about Harvey's discovery, and the likelihood that our enemy was Charles Peterson's firstborn son, Markus Colby. Discovering that Markus was so hell bent on destruction that he'd murdered Michaela Douchard, and even his half-brother, Nicolas, it stood to reason that he would not stop until he'd had his day with Parnell and Faulks. His agenda had escalated exponentially, and neither of us believed he'd allow more than a couple of days to go by without trying to get at one or the other of them. He had no way of knowing that we'd already snatched the old guys out from under him, so the probability of him launching an attack at Hayes Tower was a firm possibility. We'd arrived just as dusk was falling, leaving our car in a lot on the far side of service yard bordering the Christian book depository, and entering via the rear of the building. We had foregone Faulks' place, electing instead to set up a trap at the highest and most defensible point on the upper floor. Parnell informed us that his neighbour who held tenancy of the final apartment on his level was currently out of town, visiting relatives down in Los Angeles. I jimmied the flimsy lock and set up in the neighbouring apartment while Rink ensconced himself in Parnell's. Two pay-as-you-go cell phones we'd picked up on our way in allowed us to keep in touch, and to coordinate a pincer movement for when the killer showed.

We hadn't expected for our unknown friends in the sand-coloured car to take up observations again. We had waited for them to make their move, but apparently they were stalling until there were no witnesses out on the street. Finally as evening had settled in, Rink had made a decision.

'Let's find out what these jokers want and who the fuck they're working for.'

He had jerked aside the curtains, ensuring that they noticed the sudden movement.

I had angled myself so that I could watch from the neighbouring window and saw the guys exit their car and tool up. The guy who leaned inside the trunk to fetch their weapons concealed his actions, but I still caught a glint of steel before he shoved the items under his coat. Whatever they were bringing to the party it wasn't handguns: they looked more like steel bars. I thought that they weren't here for either of the old men, but to extract information from them about where to find us. Rink's warning had been explicit to Sean Chaney, but it seemed that his buddies weren't the type to listen. As the second guy collected his weapon from his friend, he looked up at Parnell's window.

The two men had then headed quickly for the tower and I'd moved for the front door, waiting for their arrival. Cracking the door open I'd heard their approach along the corridor, listened as they'd knocked at Parnell's door, hopeful of drawing the old man into their clutches no doubt. When I heard the first boot smash into the door I drew my SIG, held my breath, waited for the second crash as they went inside. Immediately I pulled open the door and went to follow them in. Damn the stupid fools, but they'd diverted us from our main objective.

My reaction to the killer's presence was pure instinct, but I couldn't tell if I'd hit him or only his clothing before he spun over the railing and plummeted out of sight. Training told me to check that he was dead, but friendship was a more powerful deciding factor and I leapt after the two thugs who by now were cornering Rink.

I passed through the short vestibule in less than two seconds, noting distractedly that the doors to the anterooms had been thrust open, as the men had made their search of the apartment. The door to the living room stood wide, but the room was in darkness but for the narrow strip of city light leaking through the chink in the curtains. The two men were big and blocked much of my view, but I could tell from their stance that they hadn't found whom they were expecting. But whom they had found was a boon of luck.

There were words: recriminations and threats, but my mind was working on another level and didn't order them into any sense. It didn't matter. If they were here for a fair fight, then maybe I'd have been happy to oblige, but they had come to force information from helpless old men, so the rules didn't apply. I slipped into the room behind them.

Rink had placed his gun down, out of reach of the two bruisers, and was beckoning them forward with his curled fingers. His face was set in a manic grin, and I understood that he had not yet gone beyond the madness his father's murder had placed in his mind. He could have easily disarmed them by threat of his gun, but no: Rink wanted to fight these punks. I slipped my SIG into my trousers.

Fair enough, I thought, as I lunged at the nearest one.

At the same time Rink went for the other.

There was no time for checking Rink's tactics; I was too busy with my own. The big guy reacted to my presence by jerking away, but immediately swiping at my skull with his metal bar. I ducked and closed with him, getting within the arch of his weapon and jamming his arm with my elbow. I jabbed a knee into the soft flesh of his inner thigh, a hand's width above the knee. His leg buckled, but he didn't go down. That was okay, because I was more intent on disrupting his balance for a follow up strike than to put him down on the floor. The guy should have dropped the bar, because it only hindered him. He tried to twist it around and took a couple of cracks at my skull, but the bar couldn't reach. With my defending arm, I jammed the heel of my palm solidly below his right ear. My free fist pounded into his solar plexus in a right hook. He massively outweighed me, but that meant he was easily manoeuvred when off balance. I struck upwards now, employing my palm heel against his chin, smashing his teeth together and rocking him back on his heels. As he backpedalled my left hand struck a knife-edge blow to the mound of his forearm and his numb arm could no longer hold the unwieldy bar. It fell with a hollow thud on the carpet.

The big guy was more dangerous now, but he didn't know it,

and I didn't give him an opportunity to use his strength or size. I shot a kick into his knee, choosing to attack the one previously softened up. His leg twisted awkwardly, yanking and ripping the tendons in his hip, and the guy let out a shout of pain as he began to collapse. As he dropped down to my size, I whipped the point of my right elbow into his cheekbone, and the force of the blow, plus the tremendous impact in his skull spun him to the floor. If his leg had been twisted badly before, now it was in a grotesque position. I'd never dislocated anyone's hip by striking their head before, but I wasn't particularly impressed. Feeling mildly nauseated by what I'd done to the man, I spared him the boot to the balls I was lining up and turned to check on my friend instead.

I was just in time to see Rink drive his heel into the second man's gut and send him five feet backwards to crash against the living room wall. The big guy rebounded, but it only meant he met Rink's fist as my friend spun and back-fisted him across the jaw. The man completed a graceless pirouette and went face down on Parnell's settee, his legs jerking in a spasm as all the receptors in his brain rebelled against the concussion. Rink leaned over the downed man, his fist cocked. I was about to step in and halt the final blow, but Rink had already figured the man was out cold and relaxed. He turned to me and his face was still rigid with battle determination.

Rink used to say I had a look when I went into battle. He called it 'my face': well, I could see it reflected in that of my best friend and I didn't like what I saw.

I grabbed at him, took his elbow. 'These fuckers almost spoiled everything.'

'What do you mean?'

'The killer. He was here.'

Rink jerked at my words. I held on to him. 'I shot the bastard, Rink.'

'You did what?' Rink began hauling me towards the exit.

I held on.

'He's gone, Rink. He went over the balcony.'

'Son of a bitch!' I couldn't tell if he was angry with me, or that he'd been distracted by the two thugs here and missed the action. 'Where is he? Show me.'

'In a minute. Hold up, will you?' I jabbed a hand back at the two bruisers. 'We have to sort *this* first.'

'They're done.' I'd never seen Rink acting petulantly before. It wasn't an image that suited him.

'We have to find out who sent them.'

'Isn't that obvious? It was Chaney. The frog-gigging asshole...'

'The killer isn't going anywhere, Rink. Just give me a few seconds with this guy here and we'll know for sure.'

Rink was shivering with pent up adrenalin. But he relented. 'You'd best be quick. The racket we've made, half the block will be on the phone to the police. We don't want to be here when they arrive.'

I ignored the man on the settee. He was still out cold, but the one I downed was wide-awake. Not that he was fully cognizant, because the agony of his dislocated femur was making him feverish. His face was a pale oval in the dimness, and beads of perspiration poured off him in floods. When he saw me stoop over him, his mouth opened in terror.

If I considered my actions I would have stopped then and there, but I needed answers and I needed them quick.

Placing one hand on his chest to hold him down, I used the other to dig into his dislocated hip. I could feel where the end of his femur had jumped out of the socket. Even through his jeans I could sense the pulsating heat of his injury. He was already in intense pain, my probing fingers made it grow tenfold. He yowled but I clamped my palm down on his mouth.

'If you think that hurts, just think what I'll do to you if you don't give me what I want.'

His eyes bugged.

'Who sent you after us?'

He moaned, working his mouth beneath my palm. He wasn't trying to bite me. I took some of the pressure from his mouth.

'If I tell you he won't be happy, man!'

'*I'm not happy.* Take your pick who you'd rather piss off.'

'It was Sean Chaney. He offered us good money to sort you out.'

'And you two were the best he could afford, eh? Why am I not afraid?' I relaxed a little more. There was no fight left in this man. I let go of his hip and rested on my heels. 'Why'd he send you here to hurt some old guys? Why not just call us out in person?'

The man looked past me to where Rink stood like a silent shadow in the doorway. 'It was him, man. The way he treated Chaney that day on the train. Don't you remember?' He directed his next words at Rink. 'You *humiliated* him and he's got a rep to protect. He wanted to humiliate *you* by beating those under your protection. We saw you that day at the funeral, but it wasn't the time or place. Instead we hung around and then followed the old guys back to this apartment. We knew it would only be a matter of time before you showed up here. We missed you the first time, it's why we came back.'

'You didn't miss us last time. You gave up the chase, hoping for an easier go at the old guys first. You cowardly piece of shit,' I said.

Without warning, I hooked my arm around his ankle and bent knee. I twisted savagely. The bruiser howled, but then his face slipped into a calmer state as he realised I hadn't ripped his leg off entirely. The pop of his joint realigning was horrible, but must have brought him some relief. I dragged him up. Shoved him towards his friend. 'I'd love to put a bullet in both of you. Wake up your buddy, and then get the hell away from here before I change my mind. And here's something else: tell Chaney he'd best leave town.'

When I turned to regard Rink my buddy was gone. I glanced back at the shambling thug who was hopping on his good leg as he struggled to waken his colleague. For what they'd planned to do to Parnell and Faulks, they'd have deserved a bullet in the skull, except their corpses would only complicate matters. I thought it best to leave him to it: I wanted them out of here before the police descended on Hayes Tower. There was the more pressing urgency of making sure that neither Rink nor I were tied to the dead man lying at the back of the building and I didn't trust the thugs not to blab as soon as they were pressed. I thought about offering to help carry the sleeping brute out of the apartment, but saw that he was coming around. I gathered up their dropped weapons and shoved them in a sideboard drawer, covering them with some of Parnell's belongings. By the time I was done, the two men were stumbling from the apartment. 'Best you get a move on,' I said, showing them my SIG. It proved good motivation, as did the approaching police sirens.

I closed Parnell's door as best I could, then backtracked to close the door I'd left open in the neighbouring apartment. When next I looked the men were piling into the elevator, wary of Rink who stood looking over the balustrade. He was unconcerned by their presence so close by, and didn't give them as much as a look.

I jogged towards him.

He turned and saw me coming.

'You said you shot the killer.' He nodded at a sprinkle of blood on the railing. 'But did you kill him?'

I had no firm answer, and judging by his face I could tell I wouldn't like what I found when I leaned over the railing.

The point was, I found nothing.

If Markus Colby had fallen to the earth six floors below us, then he'd landed on his feet like a cat, because there was no sign of him.

29

'Let's get outta here.'

'Give me another second, Rink. I just want to check down here.'

Sirens were filling the air, echoing back and forth from the high-rise block and the smaller apartment complexes across the way. We were risking being caught red-faced—if not red-handed—though it was necessary to check that Markus wasn't lying out of sight against the lowest point of the building. There was a pebble drainage gulley adjacent to the wall, with a slight overhang formed by the first balcony that butted out over it. When we checked I expected to find that when the killer slammed to the ground, the impact had bounced him against the base of the tower and his body would be found there.

It wasn't.

There was no sign of where the body hit the dirt either. There was no indentation, no sign of blood. I scanned the building overhead. The lights on each landing threw the outer walls into shadow so there was no indication of blood that I could tell. Unfortunately, now that the sounds of conflict had ended, the residents of Hayes Tower had come out on the landings, hailing each other as they tried to determine what had just occurred. A couple of the more courageous tenants were already scouting out the uppermost corner of the building, calling out to anyone in the rooms that might be injured. Thankfully no one looked down at where we lurked at the foot of the tower, but it was only a matter of time. Rink was correct: we had to get out of there, and quick. My only concern was that Markus was still there somewhere, injured but possibly a danger to the unlucky resident who came across him. We should have completed a check of each landing on our way down, cornered and finished the bastard once and for all. The opportunity was missed. Now we had to get away.

'Let's go,' I said.

Rink led the way, loping across the fallow ground. He moved with a determined ease that I couldn't match. The battering I'd taken during the car crash manifested in aches and pains throughout my body. I ignored them all and jogged after Rink. He reached the tall mesh fence, pausing while I caught up to him. Maybe he could tell I wasn't working at one hundred percent because he cupped his hands to help boost me over. I stepped into his palms and experienced a heady sensation as he heaved me up. I grabbed at the top of the fence, swung over and began scrambling down the other side. Rink swarmed over the obstruction like it was barely there. We ran, using the fence as a guide, avoiding obstacles on the fallow ground that would trip us in the dark. Andrew's car was parked beyond the adjoining book depository stockyard, half a minute away at most. A quick glance back over my shoulder assured me that any responding police cruisers were at the front of the building, and as yet there were no flashlights seeking us out.

'Our detective buddies are going to suspect it was us,' I said between breaths.

Rink didn't respond. I was stating the obvious.

'Without a body, there's no sign of a crime. Maybe it's a good job the killer escaped, considering the circumstances.'

'I'm glad.'

I shook my head as I ran, fighting to conceal a smile. The only reason Rink was happy the killer had escaped was that he could have his own shot at him.

I reassessed my earlier concern. The cops didn't know about our connection to Parnell yet. 'I don't think we need worry about Jones and Tyler,' I puffed. 'There's nothing in the apartments that they can use against us. We can always deny being there, and if they find prints or DNA we can claim it was from previous visits. Don't know what we can do about the blood from where I shot Markus, though.'

'His blood won't mean a damn thing if he's not already on record. By the time they can make a match, the bastard will be dead. That's if they ever find his body to match it to.' Rink had reached a connecting fence. This one wasn't as tall as the one we'd climbed earlier, and he went over it without stopping. I had to grab at the wire, shove it down and then straddle it before dragging myself over. I hadn't felt as sore for months: not since taking a pounding from a lunatic called Samuel Logan who didn't share my sensitivity to pain.

'I hope those idiots got clear before the cops arrived.' I was referring to Sean Chaney's heavies. If there were a scale for measuring criminal excellence, those guys wouldn't even hit the lowest level. If they were caught fleeing the scene then they'd immediately do one of two things: concoct a totally ridiculous story surrounding their innocence or blame everything on us. I trusted it would be the latter. Best-case scenario was that they got well away, but time would tell. I had to stop worrying about them and concentrate on the main issue. Despite shooting Markus Colby or Peterson—or whichever name he was using—and the man tumbling from the tower block, then somehow he had survived. It told me something I hadn't considered before: that he was more resilient than I gave him credit for. On most counts his victims had been elderly and not exactly a match for an armed man, some of them—in particular Takumi—were infirm and it didn't take a pro to murder them. I'd been thinking of him in terms of a reckless amateur, who'd managed to avoid capture before now due to his anonymity, Yukiko's reluctance to speak about what occurred all those years ago helping him, and a healthy dose of luck. Now I had to see him as a dangerous and capable adversary.

Making it to the car, Rink drove. He used a service alley to edge out onto the next street up from where all the activity was. Immediately he looked for another, and he turned into it to take us further across Potrero Hill and out of the cordon of response vehicles. I was thankful that Jones and Tyler were unaware of Parnell's status as a future victim in their homicide investigation; otherwise the cops would have descended on Hayes Tower en masse. The report would have been of shots fired, of a commotion in an apartment, but when they found no evidence of either the police activity would be scaled down. There was still that damned sprinkle of blood that might cause alarm, but with no assailants, victims or complainants in evidence, I expected that the matter would be filed and that was all. There was always the possibility that Markus was still in the vicinity and that the cops would locate him, but I didn't give that much credence. He was a dangerous and capable adversary, as I'd just concluded, and it wasn't likely that he had hung around after such a lucky escape.

Hayes Tower would be out of bounds to him for the rest of the night, and in all likelihood there would be a police presence there the following day as officers conducted door-to-door enquiries. My regret was that it was also a no-go area for us and that we'd lost the advantage for trapping the killer. I trusted that Harvey Lucas would come through for us though, and that if our suspicions were correct, in that the killer was Charles Peterson's firstborn son, then he would find him. Next time we would take Markus in a frontal attack that wouldn't be messed-up by outside interference.

'What do you propose we do about Sean Chaney?' I asked.

Rink had directed the car back towards downtown now that we were well away from Hayes Tower. He had tucked in behind a Fed-Ex delivery vehicle on an evening run. Behind us was a taxicab with two female passengers. There wasn't a cop car in sight. 'Nothing yet. I think we let his dimwit heavies report back and see if he takes up your advice to leave town. If not, we'll show him the error of his ways...once Markus Colby is squared away.'

'I can't help feeling we brought this on ourselves. We went after Chaney first. It's no wonder he sent his boys after us in revenge.'

'Cause and effect,' Rink said. 'Chaney shouldn't have muscled Jed Newmark in the first place. It's his fault. He started this, *we'll* finish it.'

I didn't reply. There was an answer for everything if you looked deep enough, and then twisted it to suit purpose. It made me consider who was to blame for the larger picture we were involved in now. We saw ourselves as the good guys, but I guessed that Markus also fancied himself as the great avenger, doling out justice to a group of murderers. Was he acting any differently than Rink, in that each was a son who wanted revenge for their slain father? What Andrew and the others did to Charles Peterson was horrendous, and if the shoe was on the other foot we could have been hunting them down. But the saving grace in all this was that Peterson had kicked everything off when he'd preyed on those innocent girls. Following Rink's line of logic there was only one person to blame and that was Charles Peterson. His son was his emissary in the here and now, still intent on causing pain to his victims and their families, and—as a result—definitely the bad guy.

There are always circles within circles, some overlapping and converging, that serve to bring lives into conflict. That, I understood, was what had happened here in San Francisco. But it was also the way of the world. There was nothing I could do about it other than try to end the Rington versus Peterson loop before it continued through further generations. I knew that Rink had no children, but what if Markus Colby had a son? If that were so, we could find this war raging into eternity. I rejected that idea as not even worthy of a joke.

30

Markus's pain had gone through the entire spectrum of intensity, ranging from agonizing to numb shock and all the way back again. Now it was somewhere in the middle, with an occasional flare towards the uppermost level, particularly if he attempted to move too sharply. Sweat beaded his brow and his flesh felt clammy to the touch, but otherwise he was clearheaded enough that he didn't expect impending death. That didn't stop him cursing his injury, or from thanking his luck.

When he was shot, the impact had spun him, and he'd gone over the edge of the balcony. Without doubt it had saved him from the second fatal shot that was on the cards. Even as he fell, some primal instinct for survival had made him release his pistol and grab for support. His right hand had clawed at the wall, then fixed around a metal protrusion, possibly a bracket at the base of the balcony rail. Whatever it was, he'd clung to it though the weight of his falling body had almost wrenched his arm out of its socket, then hung precariously for a few seconds while his feet scrambled for purchase. His fall had taken him into the open space of the second level down. It had been agonizing building up the momentum to swing onto the next landing, but preferable to the pain he'd suffer if he fell the remaining five floors to the hard dirt below. Enduring the torture in his muscles he'd managed the swing and had collapsed on the cold tiles, breathing heavily. Above him the sound of a struggle was dull to his ears, and he would have liked to lie there for some time in order to recover. The pain shooting through his side galvanized him though and he struggled up to his knees, clamping his left palm over the wound to halt the blood flow. Every muscle fibre in his right arm throbbed, but he used it to hook over the balustrade and help him to stand. Then he'd staggered towards the stairs and went down them as fast as his feet would carry him. Each step sent a new stab of pain through his frame, but there was nothing for it. He had to get away because the racket upstairs was sure to bring a police response. He couldn't leave by the front door. His gun was out the back where it had fallen from his fingers.

He discovered the gun and slipped it inside his pocket, the shape cumbersome and awkward and pulling down on the fabric. If the cops saw him, the weight in his pocket would be as much a giveaway as the blood streaming from between his fingers. At a loping run, he traced his way to the main street via the access passage he'd noticed pedestrians using earlier, and then hurried for his car at the far side of the tower. He drove away just as the first wail of sirens cut the air.

He had shed his jacket on arriving home at the crooked house. In his bathroom, he lifted his shirt to inspect the wound. The stranger's bullet had struck him in the ribs on his left side. Only the fact that he'd been moving as the bullet hit, his body torqueing to one side, had saved his life. There was a deep groove in the flesh, a bloody set of lips in which the teeth were the exposed bones of his ribcage. The pinkish bones were scoured, one of which he was pretty certain was cracked. Luckily the bullet had struck and rebounded off the curve of the bones, otherwise his injury would be more telling. Really he should seek medical assistance, but he'd no way of covering up for the fact that he'd been shot: any surgeon worth his salt would immediately recognise a gunshot wound, and was duty bound to report it to the police. So soon after the reports of gunfire at Hayes Tower he'd be hauled in for questioning, and it would only be a matter of time before a determined investigator began probing him for answers concerning the other shootings in town. He could point the finger of accusation back at the surviving conspirators, but it wouldn't help. Vigilante justice was never tolerated, however well meaning. He'd go to prison. Unlike his earlier contingency where—should they be arrested—he could have them murdered in their cells, he'd have no way to get at the others then. Not while he was on the same side of the bars as they were. In all probability they would be sent to a different prison than him: if he was caught he'd end up in a

Super Max, while they would do easier time at another less-secure facility.

He couldn't go to hospital, because he couldn't go to prison. That brought his work to mind and the fact that he was due to report for duty at six the following morning. No way he could go in like this! There was no alternative this time; he'd have to call in sick. At least on this occasion he wouldn't have to lay things on thick. He'd tell his superiors he'd been in an accident, fallen down the stairs and broken a rib. Once he was strapped up, should they require proof, he would appear to have a genuine case for absence. Perhaps he should start looking at his injury as a boon, instead of the hindrance he first feared. Off work and incapacitated, who'd ever think he was involved in the spate of killings that was about to happen?

He snorted at his egocentricity. Right then he had barely the energy to think straight, let alone continue his agenda. His ribs hurt, but *everything else* hurt too. No, he shouldn't think like that. His other injuries were superficial and he wouldn't allow them to stop him. They were only sprains and scrapes, nothing to worry about. Once he cleaned and dressed his ribs he'd dose himself with antibiotics and painkillers. Then he'd get on with his plan. The night was young, and one thing he was certain of was the bastard who shot him wouldn't expect him coming so soon.

He thought about the stranger. He was a dangerous enemy. He'd proven that quite succinctly. He had survived a house fire; a car crash; and, most recently, avoided his bullet. When he'd turned up at Takumi's house Markus had assumed that the man was a hired protector brought in by the murder ring, and now he was sure about that. There was no other reason for him to be waiting at Parnell's apartment. As to the man's background, Markus had no firm idea, but he took it as fact that the man had experience with firearms, and was probably handy in a fistfight. Markus relished meeting the man toe to toe in battle, and had no doubt who would be the one walking away— despite his injury. But there was no harm in raising his odds of winning. Next time they met he would have to ensure that he held the ace hand. From a drawer he fetched a length of ceramic fashioned to a wicked point, electricians' tape wound around the flaring end to act as a handle. He'd taken the shiv from a prisoner who'd tried to sink it below his ribs one time, and now thought he'd employ it in similar fashion. He stooped down and concealed the makeshift blade in his boot. Just wait until he had the stranger at his mercy; he couldn't wait to see the look of surprise on his face when Markus jammed the blade into his ribcage.

Next he thought about the two muscle-heads, and what their reason for assaulting Parnell's home meant. Had the thugs gone to Hayes Tower to hurt the old man—as he'd first reasoned—or to settle a private score with the stranger? If it was the latter, it added an entirely new dimension to the proceedings. Was it something he could use to his advantage? Markus knew people who knew *other* people, and was sure that a few well-placed telephone calls would identify who the tough guys were and whom they worked for. From there he would learn the identity of the stranger and with that knowledge he would be in a position to take the initiative.

Before anything else, it was imperative that he cleansed his wound. The cut in his flesh wasn't his main concern but the damage to the ribs beneath: an infection in the bone could prove life threatening. He pulled off his shirt, wincing as the bloody fabric tugged at the torn skin. Blood had streamed down his side, pooling at his waistband and staining his trousers. He took them off, as well as his underwear and went to the shower stall. The shower was an antique that barely dribbled warm water, but he stood under it, washing the blood from his body and watching it swirl down the drain. Watching the water go from red, to pink, then to translucent, it felt like his agony was washing away with the tainted water. He felt a little stronger.

When he'd set off on his mission he had understood that injury might be a possibility, and had compensated for that by purchasing a First Aid kit. Apart from the crepe bandages and a tube of antiseptic ointment, it was wholly inadequate for the injury he bore now. So, naked and dripping water, he headed downstairs to the kitchen and rooted among the bottles and containers beneath the sink. He found what he was looking for and screwed off the cap, even as he headed for his living quarters. He lay on the settee, propped on his right elbow, and using his left hand he poised the bottle over the wound.

He really wasn't looking forward to the next few seconds.

He took in a few quick breaths, steeling himself. His martial arts training told him that pain was but a figment of the mind and that a man who controlled his mind controlled pain.

A label on the bottle indicated the hydrogen peroxide was only four percent proof: when it hit his wound he would swear it was pure rocket grade fuel. His scream was short-lived, but only because he collapsed into unconsciousness.

He slept fitfully on the settee, the memories coming fast and furious to build a nightmare montage of his past. At first he saw events through the eyes of his younger self, and there was no distinction where he segued from one scene to another.

He was a small boy, hiding under his bedclothes as a man he didn't recognise entered his room, rocking on his heels as he swigged from the neck of a liquor bottle. The guy stank of sweat and piss, and the vest he wore over drooping boxer shorts was grimy. His stubble was grey, his forehead mottled by a birthmark. When he pulled back the blankets and leered down on Markus, his slug-like tongue lolled from between a gap in his upper teeth. 'Howdy, boy?' The man slurred, as he dumped the empty bottle on the floor, transferring his hand to fumble at the front of his shorts. He teased out his penis. 'Come on out from under there and say hi to your new daddy.'

Markus was about twelve years old. He was down by a culvert drain, floating twigs on the gush of muddy storm water. He was head down, intent on the voyage of his make believe pirate ship, and didn't at first hear the other boys gathering on the dirt embankment above him. A stone struck his shoulder and Markus yelped. He turned quickly, his hands making fists. Then he staggered back as another stone struck him in the forehead, the blood immediately flowing into his eyes. Bastard, bastard, bastard, *the other boys from his class were chanting. They rained more stones and broken branches down on him, and Markus fled from them. He ran until he fell gasping and crying in the dirt of his front yard. His mom was sitting in her chair on the sagging porch and when he looked up at her,* seeking sympathy, all he received was the same bitter twist of her mouth and stone hard glare as he ever did. 'Get the hell up outta the dirt,' she snapped at him. 'Look at the state of you. You been running from them other boys again? What'd I tell you, boy? You don't run from no one but me.'

In his dream there was no transition from where his mom got up out of her chair, brought her switch, and where she had him inside the house, whipping the skin from off his back.

'You don't run away. Your goddamn father ran away from me, left me carrying you in my belly. I guess he just wasn't the man I'm gonna make of you, boy. In future you will fight, you'll fear no one. No one but me that is!'

Markus was older. Eighteen. He stood looking down on the shriveled woman lying on the floor in the kitchen, barely recognizing her as the woman who'd ruled his childhood with equal measures of disregard and an iron fist. She was pathetic, curled up like that in a pool of her own vomit, reeking of hard liquor and cannabis smoke. He stared at the sunken face, the dull eyes, and he gave her as much sympathy as he'd ever earned from her. He walked away, not sure if she was dead or alive, and didn't care. He went looking for his father instead.

He had learned his father's name—Charles Peterson—and he had the one photograph his mother possessed of the man, one where he was standing with a group of soldiers outside the entrance of a concentration camp. But they were his only leads, and he did not have the savvy or avenues to discover the man's whereabouts. In his dream, he stared at the photograph, but the man standing in uniform and staring back at him was his own image.

A man begged for his life. Markus was an adult now, bigger and stronger than the punk who squirmed on the floor. The lank haired man, who leaked blood from both nostrils, wore striped prison clothes. In life he had not done so, but this was a dream that tinged memory, and here the discrepancy meant nothing. When Markus had forced the names of the lynch party from Mitchell Forbeck it had been on the outside, but now he lay in a darkened cell as Markus hit him again and again. With each punch or kick he learned a new name, and the list was long.

Markus was standing on a grassy knoll, looking down on a ramshackle house surrounded by trees. In a blink he was at the door and he watched his hand rise up to knock on wood in need of a lick of paint. Unlike it had in the real world, this door swung open to his touch and he stepped inside uninvited. A man was standing at the opposite side of the room, both hands held out towards Markus, begging for his life. Again—as in the photograph— this man wore Markus' face, but in the deep part of his mind that told him the oddity was not real, Markus knew this man to be Nicolas Peterson. His half-brother.

'Get out of my way,' Markus snapped.

'You bastard! My mom had nothing to do with his death.'

Even in a dream state Nicolas' words stung him anew, the 'bastard' word more than anything.

'I said, "Get out of my way".'

'Leave her be.'

'She deserves what she's going to get. She's as bad as the men that strung our father up. Her silence allowed them to get away with murder.'

'Don't you get it? He was a monster. He deserved everything that came to him.'

'No. That's a lie. You're a liar just like your whore of a mother.'

Markus was in the bedroom now, and Michaela Douchard was already dying from the bullets Markus had fired into her. His half-brother, Nicolas was slumped at the end of the bed.

Markus looked at the gun in his hand.

He didn't regret killing them. They were liars and players in the conspiracy to blacken his father's name. He only regretted killing them so quickly. He should have made them suffer the way his dad had. Drilling them full of bullets quick like that was too good for them.

Markus turned around.

The stranger was standing in the open doorway.

No. This was not what happened, Markus' brain screamed.

He lifted his gun, but the stranger was faster.

A bullet punched Markus in the side.

He fell, spinning once again over the balcony of Hayes Tower.

The ground rushed up to meet him and this time he did not snag a hold of the balustrade.
Flames erupted around him, fed by the rushing wind to a blazing conflagration.
Markus fell screaming.

He jerked awake. He sat up quickly, blinking in confusion all around his living room, unable in that brief moment between nightmare and wakefulness to recognise his home. The memory of the gunshot still rang in his brain, a resounding echo. The imaginary flames left their prickling memory on his exposed skin. He grabbed at his side; fully expecting to find the wound fresh and pumping blood, but the hydrogen peroxide had done the trick and sealed the torn veins. His breathing was ragged, an effort that made his ribs ache. He looked around, searching for the stranger. He wasn't there. He'd only been a figment of his feverish mind. But they would meet again. Next time Markus dreamt, he hoped it would be about the stranger's violent death.

31

Bridget Lanaghan's living room put me in mind of a museum to the Flower Power movement, and I would have found it strange but for learning earlier that her daughter, Judith, made a living selling tie-dyed shirts and scarfs, bangles and bead necklaces to the tourists at the historic Ferry Building market place on The Embarcadero. It was apparently market day tomorrow, because Judith had commandeered the sitting room to lie out and catalogue and order her wares. Her elderly mother was one of the ladies I'd met at Andrew's funeral, and the friend that Yukiko had mostly turned to for support. They both sat side-by-side on a comfortable settee made slightly constrictive by the bundles of brightly coloured clothing draped over its arms. Looking at Yukiko I was also reminded of the literal translation of her name: Snow Child. She was very pale; almost as colourless as the white funeral garb she still clung to. With the backdrop of neon blue, shocking pink and fluorescent green, she was almost translucent in contrast. I could see that Rink was worried for her.

A year or so ago Yukiko had suffered a heart attack, but her strength of will and character had seen her through the dark times. Now, with her beloved husband gone, I wondered if she would survive a further episode, or if she would merely give in to the inevitable. I'd heard similar stories before, where a grieving spouse gave up their hold on the earth, wishing only to join their lost one in the afterlife. I'm not sure, but Yukiko never struck me as the quitting type, and while she had responsibility I didn't think she'd allow herself to succumb to her broken heart. I watched as Rink crouched before her and took her slender fingers in his huge hands, but I had to turn away to allow them the moment of tenderness. I had an urge to jump on an airplane, to go home to the UK and tell my own mother, Anita, how much I loved her. Things had been a little fractious between my mom and me—all my fault, I admit—after my dad died and she remarried. Once my brother John was born, to my young mind I was shunned, and it took me a long time to understand the truth. My mom's aversion wasn't because she couldn't accept me as part of her new family, but quite the opposite. When she looked at me she saw my father, and she couldn't bear the loss she suffered. Sometimes I thought that Bob Telfer, my stepfather, shared similar misgivings whenever I was around, but his were based upon the knowledge that he'd forever be second best in his wife's affections.

The maudlin thoughts were only fleeting. I wasn't about to run away, not while the people here needed me most. I went and stood at Rink's shoulder, so that I too could convey strength to the old lady. Rink had just come in from the kitchen where he'd informed Yukiko of our suspicions, out of earshot of Bridget and her family. In a show of pure friendship Bridget had allowed them privacy, but was there to hold Yukiko's hand when she came back. It felt a little unfair that Bridget was not allowed into our ring of trust, but probably best that she knew nothing of what was going on, other than that Yukiko was in possible danger. To spare her and her family, we'd already decided to move Yukiko, and Rink was currently talking into our line of thinking. The gravity of the situation was setting in with Yukiko, and was what was most likely making her feel sick.

She couldn't go home, and she would not be happy hiding out with Parnell and Faulks at Lake Chabot, not while the old men's presence would force memories of what happened in the basement at Rohwer each time she looked at them. Rink had suggested taking her to a different hotel, but to do that would mean him staying with her, and halving our opportunity to take down Markus Colby. Briefly I'd wondered if, perhaps, it wouldn't be such a bad idea to take our suspicions to Detectives Jones and Tyler, and allow them to bring the murderer to justice, but we knew what that would mean to the three survivors and rejected the idea.

The solution was staring us in the face. We had the assistance of McTeer and Velasquez to fall back on. Yukiko didn't have to stay in the same lodge as the old guys, but one close by. Spreading our forces between two locations would strain our friends' system of round the clock protection, but hopefully this would end soon. All we needed now was for Harvey to get back to us, point us at Markus Colby and we could get this over with.

I hadn't really been eavesdropping their conversation, so didn't hear exactly what swayed Yukiko, but finally she allowed Rink to help her to stand. Younger by ten years, and sprightlier, Bridget pushed out of the settee without assistance and the two friends hugged each other. While they were saying their goodbyes, Rink nodded me outside. I followed him out onto a stoop overlooking a sloping flower garden. The house was on the upper edge of a residential district dominated by three-story houses laid to sequential rows. Rink had parked his father's car at the kerb, the way the other residents did here. From our vantage I could see the headlights of vehicles crossing the double-decker Bay Bridge towards the heights of Yerba Buena Island and on towards Oakland. Some distance to our left spotlights picked out Coit Tower standing proud over Telegraph Hill. Way out on the bay was Alcatraz Island, the cliffs and abandoned penitentiary looking like a half-sunken battleship under the wan glow of floodlights. We took in the sights in a moment of companionable silence, the flower scented breeze warm on our faces. Then Rink took out his cell and rang a number from memory. All the way across country it would be late now, edging midnight, but it seemed that Harvey was still on the case. He answered immediately. After checking that no one was in earshot, Rink hit the speaker button so that we could share his phone.

'You know, guys,' Harvey said after we'd made our greetings, 'sometimes it's best to go way back to basics. Despite our triggerman taking a jaunt out to Arkansas, and another to South Dakota, it makes more sense that he lives in San Francisco—or near enough that he has a base from which he works that allows him easy access to the city. As you know, I told you Markus Colby dropped off the radar following high school, and we assumed to do that he'd have to have built himself a new identity. The most likely was to take his father's surname and I've checked for Markus Peterson—with no luck.

I've been searching records all over the Internet and getting nowhere, when I should've been concentrating on one thing: his goddamn social security number.'

'Ain't that the first thing you shoulda thought of, Harve? Man, you're slipping.' Rink winked at me.

'I know, it's freaking private eye one-oh-one, but I got caught up in all the fancy searches at my fingertips. But, hey, I've still come through. I went back to the records and discovered something interesting. Colby's social security number hasn't been recorded anywhere since his disappearance, but...wait for it...his father's has. As you know, Charles was never reported missing, and with no record of his death, his social security number was still active in the system. It looks like our bad boy has been living off his daddy's identity for the last twenty-odd years.'

'Sounds like he's been planning something for years, brother,' Rink said.

'Looks like it,' Harvey said. 'I just didn't get why he waited so long until going to Michaela Douchard for answers. I guessed there had to be a catalyst, something that got his blood boiling. Hunter, you still there?'

'Yeah, I'm listening.'

'You remember that guy you asked Rink to get me to look at, the extra name on the cops' list.'

'Mitchell Forbeck.'

'That's him. I checked him out, and you're correct in thinking he was another victim. He was killed only a few days before Tennant, and—judging by how long they've laid out there—Michaela Douchard and Nick Peterson. Ballistics show that the gun used on Forbeck is the same as that used in the subsequent shootings...uh, sorry, Rink, but it was also used on your dad.'

Rink didn't respond one way or the other, but I could tell his mind was working furiously.

Taking the silence as his hint to carry on, Harvey said, 'You're probably wondering what the hell Mitchell Forbeck has to do with the other victims? Well, I found the link. Forbeck and Tennant were cellmates. They both shared prison time together.'

'You think that Tennant told Forbeck what he'd done all those years earlier?' I asked.

'You know what inmates are like; they share all their dirty little secrets with their buddies. If you listen to them speak there are only two types of guys in prison: innocent men and hard cases. The first type cry about the miscarriage of justice that put them away, while the second big themselves up so that nobody thinks of them as an easy target.'

I was jumping ahead, stealing Harvey's glory, but I couldn't wait. 'So Tennant made himself the big guy by bragging about his exploits to Forbeck? Are you telling us that Markus was in the system at the same time and heard what had happened?'

'Not *in* the system, guys,' Harvey crowed. 'He was working *for* the system.'

'A fucking prison guard!' I felt like kicking myself. The jacket and baseball cap Markus was wearing when he shot at my car had lodged in my memory, and I saw it now. Not unlike a police uniform, but with enough to differentiate one from the other. At the time I'd mused that it might have been a security guard's uniform but had decided that it was too easy to get hold of one to be important. For all I'd known then, Markus could have snatched the uniform from a pile of laundry or a washing line as he'd fled the scene of the house blaze.

'He's not a corrections officer in the sense that he works from any single location. He's a subcontractor, tasked with prisoner transportation.' There were some indistinct noises, as if Harvey was searching through some papers. 'I printed off some work schedules: our boy *Charles Peterson* was on transport duty when Mitchell Forbeck was taken to a parole hearing shortly before his release. Is it such a leap that the two could have got talking, and Forbeck mentioned his buddy Tennant's claim to fame to him?'

Rink interjected, 'So, as soon as Forbeck was released, Peterson sought him out for more detail, and that led him to Tennant?'

Admittedly I had to agree it was a plausible scenario. 'Where he tortured the details of everyone involved out of him.' I chipped in. 'Not only does Tennant give up the names of the lynch party, but also why they went after his father in the first place. My bet is that he visited Michaela Douchard to learn if the accusations were true. Maybe that's why he killed her and Nicolas...when he discovered his father wasn't the pillar of virtue he believed. Before that he was only out for vengeance, but when Michaela told him the truth about his "dear daddy" it threw him over the edge. It would explain why he escalated the violence so soon afterwards: he's trying to clean shop, guys, to get rid of anyone who knows what his father was *really* like.'

'That means he's definitely gonna try for my mom again,' Rink said. 'And more important that we get her away now.'

I shook my head. 'Your mom's safest here, Rink. If we take the bastard now.'

Harvey butted in, telling us the base from which Markus worked. 'Looking at these work rosters I have in front of me, he's due in on the early shift. You could set up close by and take him as he goes to work.'

'He won't be in work tomorrow,' I said. 'I shot the piece of shit. Not badly enough to finish him, but he'll be in no fit state for a day's work. In fact, you ask me, he's crawled back to someplace he feels safe.'

'That'll be his daddy's house then.'

'You have an address?' Rink asked quickly.

'Yeah. I got it from his personnel file. Double checked it to make sure it wasn't a bogus address Markus was using alongside his bogus identity.' Harvey was basking in the glow now, and I could picture his grin as he gave us the location. 'You going there now, guys?'

We shared a look.

'There's no time like the present,' Rink said.

'Am I wasting my time telling you guys to be careful?' Harvey asked.

'You know us better than that, Harve,' I said.

'Amen, to that,' he laughed.

32

Markus Colby came away from his meeting feeling empowered. Not from learning the identity of the stranger—he still hadn't learned a name—but at his discovery that he'd been correct all along and his nemesis had been drafted in by the murder ring. He was a friend of Jared Rington, the son of the ringleaders, Andrew and Yukiko. Sean Chaney had an intense hatred of both men. Apparently, a tit for tat quarrel had erupted between them after they'd mistakenly identified Sean Chaney as the one responsible for Markus' crimes. Mildly insulted that they thought a lumbering idiot like Chaney capable of what he'd accomplished, he also was thankful that they'd been distracted. It had allowed him free rein for the past few days while they had squabbled with Chaney and his men.

Markus would have liked the meeting to be face to face with Chaney himself, instead of with the thuggish brute that agreed to meet with him. But he was an advocate of the axiom that beggars can't be choosers. In his trade he'd met many people on both sides of the law, and it had only taken him a couple of pinpointed calls before discovering the identity of the two men he'd seen staking out Hayes Tower. One of them was still out of commission, having had his hip dislocated, but the second had recovered from the fight, albeit his face showed signs of who'd lost. A contact playing the middleman had brought Markus and the thug together, and, after Markus plied him with hard liquor, the thug had spouted all that had happened in the past few days. Chaney, he learned, had been attacked while travelling on the BART system, set-upon by Jared Rington before his friend intervened by shooting Chaney. His ego damaged, Chaney had responded by sending his guys to Parnell's apartment earlier this evening. They'd been beaten soundly, but that had only inspired more rage from Chaney, who now demanded a final resolution to the problem.

Markus wasn't so forthcoming with the information in return, but he'd told the man that it might be mutually beneficial if they worked together to bring Rington and his buddy down, and had sent him back to Chaney with that message. Not for a second did he intend cooperating with Chaney's knuckle-scrapers, but the extra manpower would be a great distraction to their protectors while he concentrated on finishing off the final trio of conspirators. He was not foolish enough to give his name, only a cell phone number he could be contacted on: he was certain Chaney didn't have the resources required to identify him from it. Even if he did, what would Chaney do with such information? Chaney was planning on killing Rington and his friend, and wouldn't jeopardise his liberty for the sake of bringing Markus to justice. Another maxim he believed in: 'honor amongst thieves' was bullshit. But, if it meant saving their ass, most criminals learned to keep their mouths shut. Anyway, once this was over with, he'd make sure that Chaney didn't whisper his name in the wrong ear; he'd pop a cap in the fucker as easily as all the rest.

Having set his plan in motion he drove towards home. Now he was a couple of blocks from the crooked house and made a stop at a drugstore to stock up on some essential medical supplies. The hydrogen peroxide had done the trick, cleansing and anaesthetizing his wound, and—once he'd come round from his faint—he'd rubbed in the antiseptic salve and dressed and bandaged his ribs. He'd tested himself, going through a set of pre-arranged karate moves and found that he was able to function at almost his usual level. Still he required a new stock of dressings, plus some stronger painkillers wouldn't go amiss. He went round the store, collecting the items on his mental list. He added some adhesive sterile strips and then diverted to the cooler-cabinet and grabbed some caffeine-laced drinks and a pre-packed sandwich. It was going to be a long night, and important that he stay alert and strong. As an afterthought he also selected a large bottle of glucose-rich Gatorade.

After paying, he lugged his purchases to his car and placed them on the passenger seat. Getting in and out of the vehicle was mildly painful as the action compressed his ribs. Gingerly, he backed on to the seat, ducking low for clearance, and then drew his feet in. Even pulling the door shut hurt his side. He swore under his breath, telling himself that pain was simply a frame of mind and to ignore it. He controlled his breathing, and sure enough the pain dissipated. As soon as he was settled, he reached for his bag of goodies and delved in it. No harm in aiding his frame of mind: he tore open a packet of painkillers and deposited six of them in his palm. He chugged them down with a draft of the Gatorade. While he was feeling better, he decided it was a good time to phone work and book a few sick days.

He took the phone from his pocket, but paused as he raised it. His screen saver carried the same image he'd showed to Andrew Rington minutes before killing him. He had found the photograph in his mother's purse the day he'd walked away from her, leaving her to perish in her own vomit. Other than the clothes he stood in, and the few dollars he'd stolen from her bag, they were all he'd taken away with him when he left. In the shot his father proudly posed in his military uniform. The original had included four guards standing outside the entrance to Rohwer Relocation Facility circa 1940. But when he'd scanned the photo into his computer he had cropped the image so that only his dad was evident. His father looked remarkably like Markus, tall and broad, with a dash of Nordic heritage in his pale eyes, high forehead and stern jaw. He often gazed at the picture, staring into the eyes of his father, determining whether Charles was staring back at him, and if he was proud of the son he'd never known. 'It's almost done, Dad. Only three more of the bastards to go and all the lies will be over with.'

He sat back briefly, breaking the connection that threatened to hold him, and prepared to key the digits that would take him to his work control room. The phone began vibrating in his palm. He checked the screen. Displayed upon it was UNKNOWN NUMBER. There was only one call he was expecting, but he acted noncommittal. 'Who is this?'

'You gave a friend of mine this number an hour ago: apparently you have a business proposition to make.'

'Is that you, Chaney?'

'Please, try not to use my name.'

'You're worried someone could be listening in?'

'In this day and age you'd be a fool not to. I'm pretty sure my phone's secure, it's yours I don't know about.'

Fair comment, Markus thought. Unlike him, Sean Chaney was well known to the police and there was always a possibility that they were listening in to his communications. Markus had stayed under the radar to date and wanted things to remain that way.

'Don't worry about mine,' Markus said.

'So?'

'Like I told your friend, we share a common problem. By working together we can eradicate it quite successfully.'

'How can you be sure we have a *common problem*?'

'Look, quit the bullshit, okay. You know we have because your fucking lackey just told you all about it. Otherwise, why'd you return my call?'

'The thing is,' Chaney replied. 'I don't understand your interest in this: you didn't make that clear to my friend.'

'Let's just say we have the same competition. Does *that* suffice?'

'There's no need for sarcasm, buddy. I only want to know why you're involved.'

Markus exhaled. 'Here it is then: the two guys you want out of your hair are equally troublesome to me. You know who I'm referring to, right?'

'I do.'

'Good. I propose we work in partnership to eliminate the opposition.'

'Eliminate is a strong term.' Chaney was silent for a few seconds and Markus tried to determine what was giving the man pause. Before he could decide one way or the other, Chaney came back on the phone. 'But it does describe my intention. How do you suggest we get this done?'

'I take it you know where our rivals are holed up?'

'I have addresses, yes, but no current whereabouts for them.'

'It doesn't matter about that. I know a way to draw them out.' Continuing in couched phrases, he explained what he required Chaney to do, and when.

'It seems a bit...extreme.'

'But something you're willing to do?'

Again a pause followed, with Markus waiting patiently for the man to make a decision. When none was forthcoming he added some motivation. 'You want these two men gone. Have your boys do as I asked, and I'll see to eliminating our rivals. It's a win-win deal for us both.'

'We'll see. I don't even know who you are; how can you expect me to trust you when I know nothing about you or your background? For all I know you're an undercover cop trying to sucker me into a conspiracy charge.'

'Do I sound like a fucking cop?'

'I need something more from you than that, buddy.'

'Haven't you been following the news?'

'You're talking about all those old bastards? You're the one that capped Andrew Rington?'

'Among others.'

'You already did me a huge favour there. But, it was also because of that I ended up with a bullet in my leg, and why two of my guys had their asses kicked tonight.'

'You can't hold any of that against me. Rington's son and his friend are the ones you should blame. It was them who came after the wrong guy. This is your opportunity to get them back...good and proper, man.'

Chaney grunted, and Markus could almost feel the smile in the man's next words. 'If you're the man you claim to be, you've *definitely* proven your worth.'

'I am.' Markus smiled. 'And after tonight you'll be even more impressed when I hand you their heads in a basket.'

'That I look forward to, buddy.'

'We have a deal then?'

'Deal.'

33

While we made our final plans in the kitchen of Bridget Lanaghan's home, I used the time to run through the ingrained habit of cleaning and checking my gun. I could disassemble and rebuild my SIG blindfolded, and going through the routine this time I did so in a methodical fashion, without once having to take my mind off the coming events.

'I'm not worried about what we have to do, but how we're going to avoid being arrested afterwards,' I told Rink.

My friend was in a dark place, one that ensured he had no fear of incarceration, and all he cared about was neutralizing the threat to his mom, and avenging his dad. He only shrugged as he too worked on his weapons. The Glock he'd employed earlier was his weapon of choice, as well as a Ka-bar combat knife he had honed to razor-sharpness. I had brought my gun with me from Florida—carrying it in a hotbox under 'official papers' that would satisfy the scrutiny of Homeland Security, supplied to me by my old CIA handler, Walter Conrad, when he'd employed my services a few moths ago. I should have handed back the papers at conclusion of the job, but Walter didn't ask, so I didn't offer. I had no idea how Rink got his hands on his weapons, but he was resourceful and acquiring firepower must have been his first task after he'd fled his mom's bedside at the hospital that time. Watching him, though, he did not show any enthusiasm for either gun or knife, and I guessed that he preferred to end Markus's life with his bare hands. If it weren't for the fact that Markus had shown a penchant for firearms and edged weapons during the previous murders, I'd have been happy to go along empty-handed too. There was less chance of forensic evidence pointing back to a murder weapon if either of us ended up snapping his spine with a kick.

Rink checked his mom was okay.

While he was inside, I waited in his father's car, allowing them their privacy.

When Rink slid in beside me his eyes looked dry and hard.

'Ready?' I asked.

'I've been thinking about what you said, about avoiding the cops. We can take the bastard at his house, but we can't do him there.' He nodded. 'The trunk's a tight-fit but it will have to do while we take him out in the hills.'

We shared a look. This wouldn't be the first time we had abducted a killer and taken him to a place of execution. This time was different though. I didn't like the unfamiliar feeling creeping through my gut. On those occasions we'd been acting on sanctioned orders, to take out a known terrorist or war criminal. Much of what we had learned about Markus Colby— or whichever name he went by now—was based on supposition and hastily strung together theories.

'I'll do it myself,' Rink said.

'Like hell, I'm coming with you.'

'Just remember that we are the good guys, brother.'

'Yeah,' I said, wondering how many of the original ring shared my misgivings when lynching Charles Peterson all those years ago.

On the way to Markus's house we stopped off at a hardware store, the sign above the door stating: NO JOB TOO SMALL— WHATEVER THE HOUR. I wondered if their promise included abduction and execution. Avoiding the CCTV cameras as best I could, I grabbed a hessian sack, a crow bar and rolls of electricians' tape. Waiting to pay, my basket looked like it contained a serial killer's hand-kit, and I'm sure my face was burning as I handed cash to the teller and scuttled out the store.

Rink drove to within a couple of blocks of the address on Clarendon Heights supplied to us by our friend. Harvey learned that Markus's house had been built by his grandfather, before leaving it to his son in his will, and Markus had taken possession of it under his dad's credentials. It struck me how easy it was to bamboozle officialdom where business was conducted at the end of a telephone: no one would pick up the disparity in age where the impostor didn't present himself in person. What did surprise me was that Markus worked for a security company, subcontracting to the Federal Bureau of Prisons, and that their checks hadn't been more thorough.

My purchases were in a plain plastic sack. I lugged them along, while Rink led the way, then I waited at a corner of the street while Rink went ahead to survey the house and terrain. It was late by now and there were no civilians out on the street, but we had to be careful. He returned within minutes.

'Everything's quiet. The house looks dark, but for one light in an attic room. I watched but there was no one moving about inside. I think the asshole has left on the light to deter intruders.'

His final comment was meant in humour, but neither of us laughed at the irony.

'What about a vehicle?'

'Nothing, but there's a drive that goes up one side to the back of the house. It hasn't seen a tyre track in years.' He handed me the keys to his dad's car, taking the sack from me. 'Put it around the back, out of sight. By the look of things, Markus doesn't bother pulling his vehicle in, but just leaves it parked on the road.'

I left to fetch the car, and when I drove back, Rink opened the wooden gate to allow me to pull into the driveway. Looking up at the house, I noticed it tilted slightly to one side and wondered if it was going to topple on me if I disturbed the ground by driving on it. I took it easy—not because of the fear of collapsing buildings—so that I didn't churn up the turf that had grown over the original drive. I found that there was room at the back to turn the car, and left it nose out for a quick getaway. Beyond the parking space, the garden sloped steeply, down to a stand of overgrown trees and shrubs in need of a visit from a tree surgeon, before the ground dropped abruptly into a gulley. A road ran through the gulley, but at this time there was no traffic on it. While I was engaged with the car, Rink closed the gate and then came to join me.

'What if he doesn't come back here tonight?' I whispered.

Rink shrugged. 'Parnell and Faulks are out of the way, and he has no way of knowing where my mom is. He'll come back here at some point tonight. It's just as you said: he'll want to be somewhere he feels safe while he licks his wounds.

I indicated the uppermost room. Just because Rink had spotted no movement, Markus could be lying on a bed up there. 'Maybe he's already here.'

'Let's go find out, shall we?'

I drew my SIG. Passing the sack to me Rink drew out the crowbar. He used the jemmy, inserting it between the back door and frame and exerting pressure, to spring the latch. We entered, finding ourselves in a kitchen cum utility space. The room was in darkness, but there was enough ambient light to tell that Markus spent little time on cleaning chores. The room would best be described as a hovel, full of clutter and mismatched furniture, reeking of spoiled garbage. We moved through the space carefully, avoiding making any noise, or maybe to avoid contracting a disease. Passing the refrigerator, my shoulder brushed against a handwritten list with a pen hanging from a string attached to it. I glanced at the note but couldn't read it in the gloom. Probably his shopping list, I assumed, and moved on. The door into the hall was partially ajar, something jammed in the narrow space. Checking, I found that a pile of dirty clothing had been left there, and it stank of sweat, mildew and decomposition. No way was I going to delve among it, but I thought that if I inspected it closely, the rotting stench would be from blood spilled during one of the previous murders. Until now, I'd been giving the asshole too much credibility. I'd deemed him resourceful and clever, an enemy not to be underestimated. Now I understood he was a complete whack job who hadn't even bothered to discard the items likely to prove his guilt during any investigation. That didn't mean he was any less dangerous, but part of me that had thought of him as misguided, a man merely seeking retribution for his wronged dad, was pushed to the back of my mind. To me, he now represented a sicko who deserved what he was about to get.

We moved into the hall, stepping carefully over the clothing and watching for anything that could be knocked over and alert Markus to our presence. We found that the old house was similarly constructed to Rink's parents' place, with a sitting room, den and dining room all clustered around a single vestibule that served each room. The front door was midway along the vestibule, shut tight. More or less opposite it was a set of stairs that was sandwiched between the supporting walls of the sitting room and den. The stairs doglegged at the next landing, but we couldn't make anything out of the upper floors from this position. Before going up, Rink went one way while I went the other, checking each of the ground floor rooms: who knew if Markus could have been in any of them? It wasn't a chance we could take before continuing up. I discovered Markus had converted the den to a makeshift gymnasium, complete with weights and punch bags. More telling was an upright post, around which thick rope had been wound tight. The rope was compacted, frayed and flecked with brown stains I recognised as dried blood. The item was a *makiwara*—a punching post used by traditional karate practitioners to toughen their hands for combat. It surprised me that someone with a hatred of the Japanese people should embrace their martial practices. Judging by the time he'd spent at the makiwara, Markus was not one to be taken lightly. In the back corner of the den cum gym I found another door. A rusted padlock held it shut, and I ignored it, deciding it was access down to a cellar. By the look of things, Markus visited the cellar as often as he did the kitchen.

We regrouped at the bottom of the stairs. I mentioned Markus's apparent interest in karate-do. Rink's lips turned up at the corners, but he didn't comment. He just went for the stairs.

I covered him, before I followed up the stairs rapidly, placing my feet to the edges of the steps to avoid making too much noise. The carpet was frayed and probably hadn't been re-laid since the days of Markus's grandfather. At the first landing we found a series of four bedrooms, all of them deserted. A bathroom turned up something more interesting. There were spatters of dried blood on the hardwood floor, more streaking down the edges of the porcelain sink. I checked the detritus lying in and around a wastebasket and saw wadded rags, dark with blood. There were also strips of adhesive, and part of a frayed bandage. It looked like Markus had indeed been injured by my bullet and had applied rudimentary dressings to his wound here. We shared a knowing glance. We had the right man. Immediately Rink turned for the final leg of the stairs. He went up them with his Glock extended, sweeping the area at the top. I mounted the stairs, still lugging the plastic sack, but cocked an ear to the lower floor. If Rink was correct and Markus wasn't home, nothing said he wouldn't arrive at any second.

Rink didn't hang around. He grabbed the handle of the only door before us and shoved it open, stepping immediately into the cramped space of an attic room. A quick scan showed us that his summation was correct: Markus wasn't home. But there was more proof that we had found the right man.

There was a cot pushed up against one wall, an ancient wardrobe as crooked as the house, a small table and an old TV set with a turquoise-coloured surround that was probably all the rage in the 1970s. There were boots and shoes cluttering a corner, as well as stacks of laundry, that, this time, were clean and laundered—including what looked like a spare correctional officer's uniform. But these items weren't what held our gaze. On the wall above the unkempt cot a frieze had been formed from many photographs around a central poster. In some dives I'd been in, the poster had often been of a female tennis player scratching her butt, but here was something totally different. An old photograph had been enlarged, blown up to a proportion where it was pixelated and grainy. But when viewed from the doorway it was apparent that the image showed a large man in military uniform, standing proudly beneath the gates to Rohwer Relocation Facility. The soldier was slightly side-on to the camera, as though he stood at the end of a group of people but they had been cut out of the picture. His bespectacled face was tilted towards the photographer, and a smirk pasted his face. The glasses reflected the overhead sun, making his gaze unfathomable, but judging by the smile alone I recognised something cold and snakelike about him. For the first time, we looked upon the face of the man who had started everything. We looked into the face of Charles Peterson and I hated him.

It was bad enough standing before the sickening smile of the beast, wondering what was going on inside his head. Had he already began preying on the girls when this picture was taken, or was his crimes still ahead of him? He was a sick-minded son of a bitch, and he curdled my guts. But his image was nothing compared to the smaller pictures tacked around him. They were on glossy paper, the likes of which are churned out of a computer printer. Each picture was marginally blurred, as if the camera wasn't the highest of quality, and I guessed that the images had been snapped on a cell phone. I looked from each picture to the next, never concentrating on one for long, because I was looking into dead faces. Not only had Markus murdered the members of the execution party, but he'd also snapped evidence to bring back to his dad. He had formed a shrine of sorts, dedicated to the worship of a child-molesting monster. Now my feelings for Charles and Markus couldn't be described in words: 'hatred' wasn't near strong enough.

I placed a comforting hand on Rink's shoulder.

He was trembling beneath my fingers, his entire body quaking, like pressure building in a hot water tank, ready to explode. He was staring at a cluster of pictures on the wall, each of them taken from a different angle as Markus had stood over Andrew Rington. In the background of more than one of them, Yukiko lay with blood pooling around her head. Rink began cursing under his breath. It was unlike him, but I could understand the change in his character.

34

Markus pulled up outside his house at Clarendon Heights.

He left the vehicle in its customary position adjacent to the kerb. Getting out he felt better than he had earlier: perhaps the glucose and caffeine rush from the energy drinks had helped, but he preferred to think it was more to do with his Zen state of mind—ironic that one who hated the Japanese people so much should embrace their teachings. Much of the pain was relegated to a deep place in his psyche, now that the thrill of anticipation was on him. If Chaney's men came through, he would have his third shot at the stranger within the next hour or two. His primary agenda was to punish all the members of the murder ring, but until his nemesis was out of the picture then that would prove difficult. He couldn't wait to have the bastard in his sights and to kill him. Maybe he'd make him suffer and shoot him in the ribs first, before placing a more telling bullet between his eyes. Or better yet, he'd beat him with his hands and feet, and then he'd use his concealed ceramic blade to cut him to ribbons...then shoot him.

He could feel the shiv against his ankle as he moved, slightly uncomfortable but also a welcome sensation. He felt for where he'd pushed the gun into his jacket pocket, smoothing his hand over the cool metal and on to the crosshatched grip of the butt. For ease of carriage he'd unscrewed the suppressor and it was now in his opposite pocket. He glanced up and down the road, searching the nearby houses for any sign that his neighbours were up and about, but at this late hour he found most houses were in darkness. He glanced at his crooked home, not for the first time thinking that it looked like the Bates House from *Psycho* the way it perched up on a knoll. The place was in darkness as he'd left it, but for the one light up in his room at the top. Had the light just flickered?

He stood, peering up, but the momentary disruption to the

light leaching from beyond the blinds was not repeated. Nothing, he decided: an insect flying close to the bulb could cast a large enough shadow to cause the effect. Still, he walked up the path to his front door with his hand resting on his gun.

From a pocket he pulled out the key and inserted it in the lock. For some reason he found that he was taking things very quietly, teasing the lock to open. Maybe there was more to the flickering light than he originally thought. He eased the door open and entered the vestibule, his keys replaced so that he could close the door with one hand while holding his gun with the other. He stood in the darkness, listening. He stood like that for one long pent up breath. He could hear the ticking of water through pipes, the settling of the old wooden beams, but that was all. Feeling foolish, he relaxed, placing the gun back in his pocket and reaching for the light switch. He flicked the switch over. Darkness prevailed.

'Crap!' He had only replaced the light bulb a month earlier: *this old house took up more of his goddamn time than it was worth.*

He thought about going directly up the stairs to hit the light switch at the next landing, but decided against it and headed for the kitchen where he was sure there were spare bulbs in a drawer. He only made it a couple paces before his boot crunched on shards of glass. Now that was *wrong!* He wasn't the most house proud of people, and it was probably many weeks—if not months—since he'd run a vacuum cleaner along the hall carpet but he'd be damned if he'd allowed broken glass to litter the floor. He crouched, feeling around and felt a prick of his fingertip. Ignoring the brief flare of pain, he snatched up the offending shard and held it close to his face. He could already feel the curve of the thin glass, but he pulled out his cell and pressed a button, scrutinizing his discovery under the pale blue light from the screen. He looked up and back at where the ceiling rose hung empty. The freaking bulb couldn't have been screwed in tightly enough, and had worked its way free over time. He scowled at his theory, figuring the chances. It didn't surprise him, not when the rest of the place had been deteriorating round his ears for years.

He continued on to the kitchen and reached for the light

switch. Once more he was rewarded with enduring darkness.

'What the hell is going on?' he demanded into the pitch shadows.

What were the odds of two goddamn bulbs blowing in short succession? Fucking *nil*. Paranoia shrieked through him.

He turned back for the hall, adamant now that he'd be better off heading directly for his room, where he'd stashed the extra ammunition he'd come to fetch, then get the hell out of there. Something caught in his peripheral vision and he swung back. He stared across the breadth of the kitchen; the familiar shapes of the table and cluttered worktops were not what had caught his eye. He looked beyond them to where the back door was, wondering at the slither of city light down its edge. He took a step that way, angling his body for a better view and was sure that the door stood open an inch or two.

He rested his hand on his gun once more, teasing it partway from his pocket. The door had been opened, probably for the first time in years and he was sure as hell that he hadn't done it. He took another step that way, before turning abruptly and peering back towards the hall. He remembered again the flicker of shadow from his room and understood that it wasn't something as mundane as an insect moving about up there. He felt a cold blade wedge through his gut at the realization that whoever was up there had seen the results of his work. He didn't fear discovery, because in time he'd like the truth to be uncovered, he only feared it coming too soon. His wasn't the best neighbourhood, he knew, and it had its inherent problems like any other. Burglars were known to prey on the old houses here, seeing them as insecure and an easy target. Markus wondered if a thief had noted the house's apparent abandonment and had entered seeking anything worth stealing. He couldn't discard the idea, because even burglars could be swayed to drop the police a tip concerning a greater crime than theirs. He had to stop whoever was up there, no doubt about it. He brought the gun fully out, and began stalking along the hall.

At the stairs he paused.

Burglars didn't normally break light bulbs on their way through a house. He looked up into the solid wedge of darkness above him, feeling a flare of excitement.

What if it wasn't a burglar who'd found access to his home? What if it was someone else entirely?

He half expected to see the stranger appear from the gloom, as he had in his recent nightmare, the flashes of gunfire lighting up his features as he came at Markus. He almost welcomed the scene, because this time he was ready for him.

Knuckles pounded on the front door.

He was caught in a moment of flux: what should he do? Answer the door or check for the intruder? What if both were connected and the person banging at the door was a distraction to allow the one inside the house to steal up on him in the dark? He understood now why the bulbs had been broken—it was a deliberate act in order to confuse him.

He took a tighter grip on his gun, and placing his back to the wall next to the door, he kept an eye up the flight of stairs. Then he snatched his gaze away for the briefest of seconds to peer through the dingy glass in the door. A shape moved beyond the murky glass: a shadow only, cast by the headlights of a vehicle parked on the street.

The banging came again. 'Charles Peterson?'

'Who is it?' Markus yelled.

'Police. Open up.'

How the hell had the police made the connection to him? Whoever it was upstairs must have called them, he realised. They had seen the photographs, been horrified by their discovery and had immediately telephoned the police.

There was more banging on the door. 'Open up, Peterson.'

There was no possible way that he could allow himself to be arrested. Not yet. Markus had single recourse, and it forced his hand.

He lifted his gun and fired, directly through the wood. He was wise enough not to shoot through the door, as the cop out there would not stand directly in the line of fire. He angled his shots so that they passed through the worm-eaten walls to either side of the door. He heard a yelp of pain, and the thud of someone going down hard on the porch. There was a corresponding shout from another person more distant. He knew the likelihood of other cops surrounding the house was very high, but he also doubted that they would have come in force based only on a tip off. They would wish to investigate first, and then arrest Markus after establishing just cause. Markus quickly pulled the door open a few inches, peering down at the cop rolling on the porch in agony. He saw a man in a navy blue suit, with dark hair that had flopped over his pale face. Markus ignored him, seeking instead the source of the second voice. He spotted a large fair-haired man rushing towards the house, his gun held out in the two-handed grip as he sought to cover his fallen comrade, and to find a viable target at the same time. When the big cop caught sight of Markus it was too late. Markus fired directly at the cop and hit him high in the chest, knocking him down. The cop let out a yowl that was more anger than it was pain, and Markus realised he was probably wearing a bulletproof vest. He fired again, seeking to hit the man in a more telling place. The cop came up to his knees, and then scrambled for cover. He was yelling at Markus to drop his weapon, but didn't yet return fire.

Markus stepped out of the door.

He quickly scanned around, seeking the hiding places of other cops, but saw that other than the one car drawn up at the rear of his own vehicle, no other cruisers were on the scene yet.

He smiled, the momentary concern of before replaced by savage satisfaction at having defeated the cops sent to interrogate him. They would definitely call in reinforcements, but not if he snatched that opportunity away from them. He looked again for the big cop and saw that he'd managed to place a shrub between them. The bush offered no protection from Markus's gun, but did make targeting more difficult. Markus fired two rapid shots into the greenery, and saw the big cop throw himself flat. He wasn't sure if he'd killed him or not, but immediately turned his attention to the nearer detective.

There was a gun lying out of reach of the man. In any case, he didn't look capable of lifting it. Markus could now see that his shots through the wall had been deadly—or would prove to be so —judging from the copious amount of blood pouring from the man's neck. The cop had both hands on the wound, and his mouth was opening and closing in silent shock. His dark eyes were pools of despair as he stared up at his slayer.

Markus pointed the gun directly at the cop's face.

He pulled the trigger.

The gun cracked noisily.

Aimed directly at the cop's skull, the 9 mm round would kill him, but Markus's aim was knocked askew at the last second.

He did not see where the bullet struck, but it was not in human flesh from the resounding *crack!* Markus let out a shout of anger, as much at missing his shot as at the man that grappled with his gun hand. He felt his wrist twisted violently, somebody trying to tear the gun from his grip with such sudden violence that it tore skin from his fingers.

Rage struck Markus in a flash flood. He should never have taken his attention off whoever was lurking in his house. Now he'd allowed himself to be captured. Goddamnit, no! He would not give up. He struck out, throwing all his weight against his attacker. He rammed his elbow backwards, but though he struck, the body was too prepared to be hurt badly. Instead he pivoted, hard and fast, and head-butted the face of the man struggling with him. It wasn't the stranger—it was Jared Rington. The man was momentarily dazed, and Markus plucked his hand free. He swung to gut shoot him.

Another gun blazed, someone coming down the stairs fast. Markus skipped back and on to the porch, almost tripping over the fallen cop, missing his opportunity to finish Rington. Thankfully the man's large body blocked the doorway and thwarted his friend's aim. But now Rington was going for his gun. He could still kill him and quite possibly the stranger as well. But then the fair-haired cop joined the shooting party. His shots were ill aimed, and punched into the walls of the house. Rington ducked back inside, swearing loudly, and Markus understood the notion of discretion being the better part of valour. Caught in the sights of three guns he didn't stand a chance. He turned quickly and leapt from the porch, charging across the unkempt garden for the low wall. The cop had no clear target through the foliage and Markus capitalised on his blind shooting, knowing that it would also pin down the other two men.

'Goddamnit, Jones!' someone yelled. 'Hold your fire. He's getting away!'

The cop either didn't hear or didn't care. He fired again at the house, just as Markus went over the wall and landed on the hood of his car. He was inside it in seconds, the car squealing away from the kerb, leaving behind twin ribbons of rubber on the asphalt. As he forced the car round the first bend, Markus was grinning savagely. He was adrenalized, the blood raging though him. Now *that* was just the kind of warm up he required for the night ahead.

35

The last thing either of us expected was for Detectives Jones and Tyler arriving at the front door. Their appearance warned of untold problems to come, but there was nothing to do but follow through with our course of action and kill Markus. By grabbing Markus when he did, Rink assuredly saved Tyler's life, but I wasn't sure that would win us any brownie points in the eyes of the law. Tyler was too shocked to understand he'd survived such a near miss—let alone recognise us as his saviours—but Gar Jones was still alive and fully aware. Perhaps aware was a poor choice of words, because he was indiscriminately firing his weapon at the front of the house, causing us to retreat while Markus made his escape. It was a response born of shock and panic, and I wasn't sure if he even realised he was allowing the murderer to get away.

The roar of his car peeling away from the sidewalk meant that we'd missed an opportunity to finish Markus. But not entirely. If we could follow him now, we could still catch the bastard. The only problem being saving a life was always more important than taking one in my estimation.

'Hold your fire, Jones. For God's sake, your partner's dying here!'

The bullets stopped punching through the open doorway.

Jones was considering my words, and I had to keep him thinking.

'You know we're not your enemy. The bastard who just shot Tyler is. He's getting away goddamnit, and Tyler's bleeding to death.'

'Show yourselves,' Jones shouted back.

Rink was dabbing at a raw patch on his cheek where Markus head-butted him. By the look of him he was wishing he'd twisted Markus's head back to front instead of going for his gun hand. 'What do you think?' I asked him.

'Think I should've killed the fucker when I had the chance,' he said. But then his gaze fell on the shuddering form of Detective Tyler on the porch, and his expression changed. He'd made the correct decision, after all. The man was severely wounded, but without Rink's intervention he would have been dead by now. Tyler still stood a chance. 'Jones. We're coming out,' he shouted. 'Get over here and lend a hand with your buddy.'

We put our guns away, and moved outside, our hands empty so that Jones was under no illusion of our intent. Jones approached us; he had a palm slapped to a wound on his outer left thigh, but in his other hand he held his service pistol aimed at us. He was a man torn by indecision. I hoped he'd be a friend to Tyler before he was a cop. His features showed a range of emotions as he checked us out, anger, rage, but something else too. It was the look of gratitude that I was glad of, but not something we could rely on. The detective would have called this in and other uniformed officers would be descending on the house, and they would arrest us in a heartbeat. It made our need to get away more urgent.

'Here, quickly,' I commanded. 'You must put pressure on the wound, or he'll be gone in minutes.'

Jones had only one decision to make. Arrest us or not. If he did so then he'd miss the opportunity to save his friend. Thankfully he didn't consider making one of us administer assistance to his fallen comrade. That was his duty, he understood. He placed down his gun on the porch while he pushed both palms down over Tyler's hands. Blood still pulsed between all twenty interlaced fingers. 'Hold in there, buddy,' he said. 'Help is on its way, okay. You'll get through this.'

'You called an ambulance, right?' Rink asked.

'Coming,' Jones whispered, without taking his gaze off Tyler's pale features. 'It's coming.'

'Good,' Rink said. He nudged me. 'We're leaving.'

'You can't. You have to wait here.' Jones' face was stricken, as if he did not want to be alone with him when Tyler slipped away.

'We have to stop the bastard who did this. You know how it is, Jones,' I said. 'If your buddies arrive while we're here, they'll waste time arresting and processing us. There are still people in danger from that murderous son of a bitch. Do you want him to hurt others the way he has your partner?'

The big cop stared down on his friend. Tyler tried to say something, but all that issued from between his lips were scarlet bubbles. But his intention was emphatic enough. Jones turned and looked at us in turn. 'You'd best go out the back way, or else you'll be stopped.'

We shared a moment, and for the first time our attitudes were one of mutual respect. He mirrored my nod of acknowledgement. Then we turned away and fled round the side of the rickety house to where we'd left Rink's father's car. Rink had grabbed the sack and its contents we'd brought, and he slung them in the back. He got in the passenger seat, while I started the engine. Our original intention to grab and execute Markus somewhere far from prying eyes was now redundant. Now it didn't matter how many witnesses there were, our hand had been forced to take more direct and immediate action. First we had to get away from there.

I threw the car into drive and set off, but only made it as far as the side of the house before noticing the baleful wail of approaching sirens, and over the rooftops of the houses opposite the stuttering gumball lights rebounded from the trees on the next ridge over. I hoped that one of the sirens and set of lights was from the ambulance on its way to save Tyler.

Jones' warning to leave by the back made sense. If we went out by the same route I'd driven in, we'd be seen and chased down. There was nothing for it, then. I reversed quickly, popped a turn on the hard stand at the back, and then angled towards the overgrown shrubbery. I caught a look of resignation from Rink reflected in the rear-view mirror, and I could only shrug. I battered through the foliage, hearing branches gouging the metal work, leaves and flower heads blizzarding over the windscreen as the car tore through. A sapling bent beneath the fender, snapped, and I hoped it caused no major damage to the undercarriage. The next obstacle was a weathered wooden fence, but it was smashed to kindling, and I pushed the car unhindered now down a rugged slope of couch grass and plants I neither cared to identify or worry about. The drop off to the road was the trickiest manoeuvre to perform, and it was as much luck as skill that sent the car off the hillside at an angle, so that the two offside wheels found traction on the asphalt before I pulled at the steering and weaved off the embankment onto hard ground. As it was the resulting contact made the car slew and bounce like crazy, but I grimly held on to the wheel and forced it under control.

'Good job we're dumping the car after this,' Rink said.

He was right. The chances were that I'd caused unthinkable damage to the chassis and the car would never be roadworthy again. As long as it took us to where we were going, that was all that mattered now. There was a whine from the engine that hadn't been there before, as well as a rhythmical thud each time the front left wheel completed a revolution, but otherwise the car kept going. I pushed it as fast as I dared, taking us down a steeply sloping avenue towards lower ground, intent only on evading the police swarming towards Markus's house. Towards the bottom of the decline, I slowed, and drew up at a crossing. Waiting there we looked like any other car on the road—so long as no one made a closer inspection—and we didn't receive as much as a glance from the cops in the marked cruiser that shot by with its sirens screeching.

'So far so good,' I said, clichéd but true. Once the cop car was out of sight around the next bend I pulled out, heading in the opposite direction, intent on gaining a route to Bridget Lanaghan's house before the police cordoned us in. It was apparent to us both that Markus would have reconsidered his plans now that his identity had been discovered. With Parnell and Faulks safely out of his grasp that left only one other he could target. He'd be going for Yukiko.

The temptation was to drive fast, but that could attract too much attention, so as much as it pained me I kept to the speed limit, heading across town to the Lanaghan house. Thankfully traffic was sparse by now, so there were no major holdups, and even the traffic lights fell in our favour. We made it to Bridget's leafy neighbourhood in a little less than ten minutes. It felt like ten minutes too long. Rink was gritting his teeth, his features set rock solid the entire time. We didn't concern ourselves with debating what if's, because it would have been a waste of energy. There was little likelihood that Markus could have arrived before us, because his priority would also have been avoiding the police cordon, before coming here. There were no guarantees that he even knew about the connection between Yukiko and Bridget Lanaghan's home, but it wasn't a chance either of us would take. Yukiko would have to be moved elsewhere. Probably it would be best that Bridget and the other members of her family were taken somewhere safer until this was resolved. As I pulled up outside the well-kept garden, Rink was out the car and rushing up the path for the front door before I'd engaged the parking brake. As fast as he was, the door opened before he got all the way there, and standing in the opening was Bridget's daughter, Judith. Even from the length of the garden I recognised the woman's concern in the way that she plucked at her tie-dyed skirt. I couldn't hear what she said, but their discourse lasted all of about five seconds before Rink was charging back towards the car.

'My mom's house. Now!' he shouted even as he was lunging inside the car.

Without argument I hit the gas.

'What's happened?'

'Why does my mom have to be so goddamn stubborn all the time?' he demanded by way of reply. It didn't explain, but I could read the subtext behind his words.

'She has gone home?' I asked.

'Where else? *The hard-headed old goat...*' Rink punched the dash. 'Mom talked Mrs Lanaghan into driving her home. Judith phoned, to check that they made it there safely as she expected her mom home ages ago. She got no answer, Joe. Dear God, what if Markus went straight there and has hurt her already?'

Earlier my resolve to stay within the speed limit had been tested. Now it simply snapped as I floored the pedal, aiming to get to the Rington family home in record time. There was always the idea that Markus didn't know where Bridget lived, but the same couldn't be said for Yukiko's home. The bastard had been there before.

I tore along streets. I recalled Rink's joke when he'd bemoaned the opportunity to do a *Bullitt* when evading Chaney's men that time, but we got it now. Andrew's car wasn't a super-charged Mustang like Steve McQueen drove in the iconic movie scene, but it did the job all the same, ramping off each intersection as we hit the downward slopes. Something had been knocked loose as I'd negotiated the hillside behind Markus's house, and now it rattled and clanged and the engine was making a high-pitched shriek. I didn't slow one bit. We cut across town and screeched on two wheels around the penultimate corner before reaching Yukiko's street.

'Oh, no!'

Rink's dismay was well founded. Over the roofs of the residential neighbourhood the sky was painted a baleful orange. A huge plume of smoke billowed into the heavens. It didn't take a genius to guess the source of the fire or its instigator. Markus had previously shown his penchant for flames as a method of murder when he set Yoshida Takumi's house ablaze.

'We might make it in time,' I tried to reassure my friend, but they were empty words. I arrived at Takumi's place just after Markus had set the place on fire, but looking at the immensity of the flames gouting over the rooftops this blaze had been going some time. Anyone caught within such a conflagration would be charred to cinders by now.

I spun the car onto Yukiko's street, almost hitting a group of neighbours watching the fire. They leapt out of the way, and I pulled hard on the steering taking the car away from them. Clear of them I hit the brakes and the car skidded to a halt. The crowd was made up of people that had spilled from their beds at sounds of alarm, as they stood in pyjamas and dressing gowns, watching with open-mouthed awe as the roof of Yukiko's house collapsed down into the charred guts of the building. The roar of crashing timbers was echoed by their gasps. Flame ribboned into the sky, a million sparks dancing on the breeze. Over it all was Rink's tortured shout. 'MOM!'

He battled his way out of the car, and I was a second behind him as he plunged towards the burning house. I raced after him, and with his long-legged gait he was gaining distance, and there was no sign of him slowing. He was about to dash directly into the flames in search of his mother. There was no other recourse: I threw myself after him, wrapping my arms around his thighs and took him down. We hit the roadway, my elbows and knees slamming the concrete paving, but the pain was nothing to what Rink must have been enduring in his heart. He struggled and kicked to free himself from my grip, still intent on charging into the conflagration, but I crawled up him, holding him down. I knew that if he meant to, he could clamber up and carry me into the flames with him, but he wasn't about to do that. His actions had been driven by a moment of intense anguish. Our tumble, followed by my exhortations for him to calm down finally impinged on his mind. It was safe to release him, and we both scrambled up, conscious of the concerned neighbours moving all around us. Distantly came the warble of sirens as fire trucks responded to 911 calls.

Rink spun, facing the crowds. 'Was she in there?' he demanded. 'My mom, Yukiko Rington, you all know her right? Was she inside the fucking house?'

At first he didn't receive a reply. The people were too stunned by the fury in his shout.

'Was my mother inside the house?' he roared again.

'She was with that lady there. The one sitting in the car.' An old man pointed out. He was holding a leashed poodle and was the only person in the crowd fully dressed. 'They arrived after the fire had started. Your mom asked me to call nine-one-one, so I ran back inside...'

Rink wasn't listening to the man, he was already charging towards Bridget Lanaghan's car. She had obviously approached the house from the opposite end of the street judging from where she'd parked a hundred yards further along. The hood faced us, as did the windshield, but the smoke billowing across the road made it difficult to see anyone inside. I nodded thanks at the old dog walker, before sprinting after Rink.

I covered my face with my jacket as I charged through the smokescreen, feeling the intense heat of the fire carried along with it. Sparks clung to my clothing, and as I cleared the choking cloud I batted them out. Rink seemed mindless of those that glowed brightly on his shoulders. Catching up to him as he bent to peer inside the car, I slapped the points threatening to ignite his clothing. He didn't even notice.

He craned back and let out a shout of denial, his hands slamming down on the roof of the car. I pushed by him and discovered the source of his torment. Bridget Lanaghan sat in the driving position, both her hands folded in her lap. Her head had lolled forward and she looked as if she was sleeping. But for one thing: the blood trickling from a wound behind her left ear.

Leaning in, I pressed the tips of two fingers to her carotid artery just below the left jaw. I couldn't find a heartbeat. But the slow trickle of blood told me that there might yet be hope. Gently I eased her head back, taking the pressure from her throat and I checked again. It was faint, but I found a steady pulse.

'She's still alive,' I said. 'We have to help her, Rink.'

'We have to find my mom,' he corrected.

36

Despite having just shot his way through a police cordon, Markus made the San Mateo Bridge with little drama, and sped over it towards the lights of Hayward, having negotiated the tollgates without raising suspicion. Then it was a short run up the Nimitz Freeway to San Lorenzo where he cut across country to the MacArthur Freeway and on towards Chabot Regional Park. Despite the route, he didn't have a clue as to how close he'd come to Parnell and Faulks's hiding place, he was heading further into the national park where Sean Chaney had called an emergency meeting. His new business partner had come through for him, but in a more satisfying manner than he could ever have expected. He was keen to meet the man. As he gained a route through the wooded hills, he phoned Chaney back and was directed on to Redwood Road, and then, a couple of miles along, down a track towards the shores of a second expanse of water called Upper San Leandro Reservoir. Markus guessed that the area could be well populated by campers and had noticed signage on the way in directing visitors to various staging grounds and campsites, but where he was heading looked less travelled. The area served him well for what he had in mind.

The trail led between dense groves of eucalyptus trees, the grass and chaparral alongside the trail bleached of their natural colour by his headlights. Then he was in a gulley, its steep banks strewn with boulders, and he was forced to switch back and forth as he followed the zigzag route down towards the water. He wondered how the hell Chaney knew about this place, but the answer was obvious enough. This probably wasn't the first time that the gangster had made someone disappear without trace. How many shallow graves held rivals of Sean Chaney out in those woods? How many enemies had been sunk to the bottom of the lake?

The road ended at a wide turning area formed of hard-packed dirt. It was currently home to three vehicles; a black SUV, a panel van, and a tan coloured Lincoln sedan, all of them deserted. The turning area was at the end of a peninsula that jutted out above the still waters of the reservoir. The car's headlights petered out in the empty void over the lake, but closer by they highlighted an occasional night-flying bug that zapped by like a mini-meteorite. Way off on the far side of the lake was pinpricks of light from widely spaced dwellings or campsites. They were sufficiently far away that Yukiko Rington would not be heard should she decide to scream for help.

After parking the car and shutting off the lights, he headed for a secondary trail. It wound deep into the woodland at the edge of the lake. He was beginning to wonder where he was heading, if he'd missed a turn in the trail, when he made out a darker silhouette against the nightscape. The trees grew in clumps there among the ravines of the shoreline, causing indistinct shapes in the dark, but there was something looming ahead that was more geometrical, and as he approached it began to take shape as a large log structure with a peaked roof. Markus paused, studying the building, and couldn't decide what it might have once been used for. His best guess was that it had been employed as a focal house, a meeting place for some group or other. Perhaps its patrons had partied there, and the sounds of music and laughter once rang from beyond its walls. Whatever its previous purpose it was immaterial now, because the sounds destined to come from it soon would be in direct contrast to those happier times.

He passed a sign nailed to a post and driven into the earth. Tough grass and briar had grown up around the noticeboard, and the wood looked stained and warped, and in the darkness he could barely make out the yellow lettering on it. By the look of things the warning sign had been there for years, which gave some indication of how derelict the structure must be when it had warned of danger all those years earlier.

There was a rusty padlock and chain hanging from a latch on one side of the door. It had been unlocked, the opposite hasp standing open. Markus paused, wondering—not for the first time—if he was walking into a trap. He knew little about Sean Chaney's trustworthiness, but when all came to all what did it

222

matter? If the son of a bitch planned to double-cross him in any way then he'd just have to deal with the consequences. He felt more than a match for Chaney and the kind of half-witted punks he had at his disposal. He still had the gun he'd used on the cops back at his house, though he'd failed to fetch the extra ammunition he'd gone back for. His gun still held four rounds: he'd checked. His ace card was down his boot, his ceramic knife. Let Chaney try to pull a stunt and he'd cut out his lying tongue.

He shoved the protesting door inwards, lifting the warped wood to clear the accumulation of dirt and decomposing leaves that had invaded the gap beneath. He leaned to look inside. The interior was as decrepit as the outer shell, the old floorboards mostly rotted away, and showing hard earth beneath. Stacks of ancient furniture had been piled down one side of the room, cleared by God knew whom, but he doubted it was by Chaney and his gang. They were all at the far end of the large meeting hall, a storm lamp casting yellow light upwards from where it sat on a table painting their immense shadows on inner peak of the roof. He guessed the large, bald man sitting behind the table was their leader. He'd taken the privileged position for more reason than he simply could. Propped next to his chair was a walking stick; it appeared that Chaney's leg was troubling him yet. Maybe it was for show, indicating how hurt and humiliated he'd been by their mutual enemies.

As Markus entered the hall he felt the change of pressure in his eardrums. This room had been locked tight for some time, he guessed. He worked his jaw, popping his ears as he strode towards Chaney. Chaney studied him as he approached, his gaze steady, unmoved by Markus's appearance. The others were more wary, and more than one of them flexed their hands, perhaps expecting a sudden shoot out to erupt.

Coming to a halt, Markus crossed his arms on his chest. He looked down at Chaney, ignored the others.

'You don't look anything like I was expecting,' Chaney said.

'What were you expecting?'

'Don't know. Murderers don't usually look like you.'

Markus didn't understand where Chaney was leading the conversation. Murderers came in all shapes and sizes, all creeds and colours. Markus had met many of them in his time. 'You expected me to look insane perhaps? Maybe have a swastika or pentagram seared into my forehead? Sorry I don't meet your expectations, but—if it helps—I don't consider myself a murderer. I'm an avenger.'

'Whatever,' Chaney said. Leaning on his stick he rose up to meet Markus eye to eye. He was an inch or so too short. 'It's not important what you call yourself. All that matters is that you're here. And that we can get on with killing the bastards who shot me.'

Markus peered past him to the dark space beyond. A wall had been erected, dissecting the hall at about the three quarter mark. In it was an open door.

'Is the Jap bitch through there?'

Without turning Chaney nodded.

'I know it wasn't in the original plan to snatch her, but she turned up just as we were burning down her house. It was too good an opportunity to miss.'

'You did right.' Markus included the other men in his glance. They relaxed marginally. 'If anything's going to draw our enemies out it's her.'

'Good.' Chaney tapped his stick against his wounded thigh. 'I look forward to meeting those two bastards again. If all continues to plan they should be on their way here soon.'

'You've left instructions of our terms, as I asked? You did mention that I want Parnell and Faulks as well?'

'They'll bring them. It's like you said, Jared Rington isn't going to put anyone before his mother's safety.'

'Have you learned the name of Rington's friend yet?'

'Nope,' Chaney said. 'But there's someone down in the cellar who will tell us.'

Markus smiled, but it looked more like a grimace. Cellars were not his favourite places. But to reacquaint himself with the lying sow behind his father's murder he'd make an exception. The terms he'd asked Chaney to relay were simple. He said that if Parnell and Faulks were brought to him, then he'd give back Yukiko. He hadn't promised that she'd be alive.

37

Yukiko had the impression of an echoing space around her, though the sack pulled tightly over her head made it difficult for any of her senses to operate sufficiently enough to make a considered decision. The rough hessian chafing the tip of her nose and forehead smelled strongly, but under that she could detect a loamy aroma of rotting wood, must and vegetation. The ground beneath her was solid enough, but felt as though she sat beneath some great overhang of earth poised to tumble down and crush her beneath its colossal weight. She wondered if this must be how it would feel to lie in an open casket, waiting for the grave to be backfilled on top of her, burying her in its cold embrace. Is this how her dear husband had felt as she stood over his grave, dropping a handful of soil onto his coffin lid? She hoped that his soul was not trapped within his casket, but had been set free to fly to the promise of heaven. Had he though, had he been embraced by his God, or sent for judgement for what he did to Charles Peterson all those years ago? Was she to be judged next? The sensation made her shudder. Though she next forced the disgust from her, and tried to sit a little straighter. It wasn't an easy task with her hands bound between her shoulders, a loop thrown over her head and secured under her chin. Doing so made the rope nip at her wrists and throat, but she didn't care.

Something very important had struck her.

These men intended to kill her, but she was not afraid.

If they only desired her dead, they would have killed her back at the house when first they'd surprised her and knocked Bridget unconscious. They had an agenda to complete first, and while they played out their game there was an opportunity at escape. While there was a way out—however slim her chance at freedom might be—there was still hope. Jared would not rest until he had come to save her. Joe would not rest. He too was a

225

good son. Hope emboldened her. It reaffirmed her determination to see this through to the end. She would be strong, the way her ancestors were strong. But if she were wrong—if she were to die—she would be brave and face her slayer. That also was the way of her ancestors.

She guessed who was behind her kidnapping. Never had she got a look at her captors because the sack had blinded her too quickly, but she was under no illusions of who they were. The big one who'd sat next to her all the way here, poking her with the point of a walking stick to check she was still conscious, was Sean Chaney. Her understanding brought a trickle of unease she could not give complete description to: she should fear the man, for if anyone should wish her harm it should be him. It was because she pointed the finger of blame at him that her son, Jared, had hurt him. Jared had not told her the specific, but she thought that before this Sean Chaney had not walked by aid of a stick. Yet she did not fear Chaney. He was a bully and a coward, one who had not stood up to Andrew—a man twice his age. But she did fear whom it was that Chaney intended handing her to. No. It wasn't fear of the man himself, but what he might do to her. Would he punish her the way he had the others? Tennant and *poor* Takumi? As firm her resolve was to face death with her chin held high, the thought of immolation sent a qualm of abhorrence through her tiny frame. She could not discount the irony here; Charles Peterson had died in a cellar, and now it seemed that history would repeat itself. She did not expect pity: the son would do anything to complete his mission to avenge his father's death. But then, there was irony in that statement as well. Her son also had a father to avenge.

It would be easier for Rink to concentrate on his mission if she was not a shield before his enemy.

She must be stronger. She had to get free so she did not burden her son.

She pushed up from the stool on which she'd been sitting. She twisted at the ropes around her wrists. Oh, how she longed for the vitality of youth once more. Her old woman's arms did not have the strength to loosen her bonds, her arthritic fingers unable to untie the knots. Yet, she had to try.

'Sit down.'

The voice snapped from above her.

She knew that voice. It was the same one that taunted her husband as she'd sneaked up on the killer, intending knocking him out with the vase she'd silently lifted from the hallway cabinet.

His boots rang on the short flight of stairs down which she'd been carried earlier.

'I said *sit down*, bitch.'

Before Yukiko could respond to the order, hands grabbed her shoulders and forced her down. She resisted momentarily, but she was nothing in his hands. She fell back, but was stopped short by the seat of the stool smacking against her backside. The hands holding her steadied her with brusque efficiency. Then the hands moved away. Yukiko sat, her arms aching as she twisted them to a position where it would relieve some of the pressure on her throat. She lifted her head as best she could.

'Am I not allowed to see the face of my murderer?' she asked.

'All in good time.'

Yukiko thought that there was no good time. It was a poor expression. Though she would not tell him so: it would only give him satisfaction.

'First,' her tormentor went on, 'you're going to listen to me.'

'It's difficult hearing anything from beneath this hood. You may as well take it off; you're going to kill me anyway, so what's the difference if I see your face?'

'You've already seen my face, that's not the reason the sack's staying put. It stays because I fucking say when it comes off. *Not you.*'

Yukiko would prefer the hood to be removed sooner rather than later. The more time she had to study her surroundings, and to formulate a way out of his predicament the better. Still, there was little she could do while the brute was here in the cellar.

'What are you planning on doing to me?' The question surprised Yukiko, because she had not formulated it in her mind before asking.

'I'm going to kill you. What else?'

227

Yukiko would not allow herself to slump: she would not show she was fearful.

'You have nothing to say to that?' asked her captor. 'That's probably best, because there's nothing you can say that'll change my mind. When I set off on this, your death was always marked.'

'I'm not afraid to die.'

'Maybe not, but that doesn't mean a thing to me. I'm going to kill you even if you beg and plead. Your lies murdered my father and that's unforgivable.'

'Your father died because he was a rapist and child molester.'

Without warning a blow to her head knocked Yukiko off the seat and she went down hard on her side. The slap was more of a shock than that it held power, but pain screamed through her frail body from the collision with the floor. Before she could recover, hands grabbed her and hauled her back on the stool. She sat gasping for a long moment. Fingers grasped the collars of her blouse and yanked them tight. She was pulled forward, and even through the sackcloth she could feel the heat of anger radiating from Peterson's son.

'Those are the last lies you'll ever say about my father,' he growled.

'Charles Peterson was a sick monster who beat and raped little girls. You do understand that don't you? You know what kind of monster you've sanctified?'

Her captor let out a wordless growl.

Suddenly Yukiko felt weightless, and it took a moment to realise that she'd been lifted bodily from the seat. By the time understanding struck she was already on her back and unable to avoid the kick aimed at her body. The boot slammed her in the gut, forcing the wind from her lungs.

'Hey, for Christ's sake! Take it easy, will ya? We need her alive.'

A second set of feet descended the stairs, accompanied by the pecking of a walking stick on each alternative step.

'We don't need her. All we need is that they believe she's still alive,' her tormentor snapped.

'They might ask for proof,' Sean Chaney pointed out.

'Then I'll send them her lying tongue gift-wrapped in a fucking box!'

'Don't ruin this now, buddy. We're close to winning this battle. But if you lose it with the old girl...' Chaney leaned close to her. 'Kicking her like that, she'll be dead in no time.'

'She's tougher than she looks. I already pistol whipped the old bitch once and she survived.'

'Trust me. She won't last long like this.'

While Yukiko was still gagging, her abdominal muscles clenching in response to the kick, she was snatched up by her feet and dragged across the floor.

'So give me a hand here, goddamnit,' her abuser said.

Both men must have held her then, because she had the impression of more than one set of hands lifting her back to her feet. She was thrust against an upright pole this time. One of her captors jammed a forearm across her chest, holding her secure.

'I can't...breathe...' Yukiko wheezed.

The pressure went from her chest, but it wasn't a token gesture of pity. It was so the man could press both hands against her shoulders. Something slithered down over Yukiko's head, coiling at the nape of her neck. While she was still trying to make sense of the new sensation an arm was shoved behind her back. The rope between her shoulder blades parted with a deft cut of a knife. Her hands dropped but didn't part, and she realised that, though the rope that cinched her hands to her throat had been severed, she was not free. Still her position was not as untenable as before; at least now she had some freedom of movement in her upper body. It made breathing much easier, but still each exhalation came as a soft pant.

'Don't move.' The order came from Chaney. His voice was gentle. Was there a hint of remorse in the man? Something that she could play on, use to her advantage?

The sack was yanked off. In reaction Yukiko screwed her eyelids tight, expecting to be blinded by a sudden invasion of light, but when she opened them again she found she was still in darkness. She blinked around, unable to make anything in the gloom that hung over them all. It took a few more seconds before her eyes began to adapt to her surroundings, and now she could make out faint lamplight creeping down the stairs from the room above. She was standing against an upright beam that supported sagging rafters. Overhead the ceiling was missing many of its original planks and bars of yellow light cut inside the cellar at oblique angles. They fell across Sean Chaney's features as he faced her, making the big man look like he was wearing camouflage paint. One beam reflected in Chaney's right eye, and it made it soulless, pitiless, and Yukiko realised that there was no hint of mercy she could depend on from the brute. Her resolve wasn't aided when Chaney nodded upwards and Yukiko followed his direction and saw the rope suspending off the rafter above: the same rope that had been dropped over her head a few moments ago. Even as she realised what her captors intended, the murderer yanked the other end of the rope, pulling it taut and ravelling in the length noosed round her throat. Yukiko went up on her tiptoes. She gasped. But then she could breathe once more. She settled on her heels.

'Don't worry. I won't hang you yet,' said Peterson's son. 'There's something else to do first.'

The man was to her left, swathed in deep shadow. She could not make out his features, but she caught a glint of something metallic. He was holding aloft something that Yukiko believed was the knife he'd cut her rope with earlier. Or more likely it was a gun. His father had been shot during his hanging, the bullet fired by her husband. She thought that the son intended replaying Andrew's original part in the hanging. But she was wrong. She felt liquid spray onto her chest, droplets of it splashing under her jaw. Only when he passed the item through one of those bars of light did she fully understand what he intended. He was holding a can of barbecue lighter fuel and was squeezing its entire contents onto Yukiko's clothing. He was playing the part of Bruce Tennant.

Despite her previous resolve to meet death bravely, Yukiko flinched.

'What's wrong?' He gave the can another squeeze, sending a ribbon of fuel over Yukiko's legs. 'You don't want this circle to end the way it began? You chose to burn my father, so why's it so wrong if I do the same to you?'

Yukiko flinched again. Not at his words but at the memory

of the flames and smoke gouting from the cellar at abandoned Rohwer. In nightmares she had often pictured the torture, the intense agony that Charles Peterson must have endured. In reality she had not paid witness to his demise, because she had stayed in the car with Rose. But in her dreams she watched the flaming, kicking torch-like figure jerking at the end of a chain, as if she'd been in the cellar with the others. In the nightmares the face eaten away by flame had always been hers. She had always believed those images had been conjured by guilt, as he sought to come to terms with her part in Peterson's slaying. Now she believed otherwise: they had not been a vision born of empathy for the man's suffering but a portent of her own death.

'Don't...do...this...' There was a hint of pleading in her voice, and it grated in her own ears.

The murderer took out a cigarette lighter. He rasped a thumb over the wheel and it sparked brightly in the dark. He rasped the wheel again and a guttering flame stood an inch tall. He held the can of fuel in his other hand, aimed at Yukiko's face so that when next he squeezed it the ribbon of ignited fuel would engulf her like napalm.

'Don't.' Yukiko imagined her face in flames, the flesh melting horribly, peeling from her skull in charred ribbons. It wasn't something she would allow. 'Don't do this. If you're going to kill me, then kill me, but *not like this.*'

Her captors shared a look. They both nodded simultaneously. Yukiko screwed her face tight, as if that would save her the agony. She stood there, stoically, with only the slightest shiver of her body betraying her terror. 'So be it. If you're going to do it, then do it!'

'Oh, sorry, Yukiko. I'm confused. Are you saying this isn't how you'd like things to end?' Her would-be killer grinned, his teeth now flashing in the glow of the flame. He cast down the fuel can and allowed the flame to gutter out. 'You don't? Good, because neither do I.'

Yukiko shuddered out a breath.

She relaxed her features slowly, setting her gaze on her tormentor as he moved into a beam of lamplight.

'By the time I'm finished with you,' he said, taking out his knife, 'you'll wish you had taken the easy way out.'

Yukiko saw his face clearly for the first time, and more than the blade in his hand—or the continued threat of immolation—it was his features that sent a flutter of dread through her heart.

38

Over the past few years I'd been inside the Rington's house on dozens of occasions. I couldn't equate the smouldering heap of timbers with the neat home that Yukiko and Andrew always kept. Fire crews were on the scene. They had fought to contain the fire, but all their valiant attempts were for nothing. The house was burned to the foundations, and all that remained were charred heaps unrecognisable as the furniture that once decorated the rooms, and the stubs of the walls that once contained them. Even the stone chimneystack had fallen, brought down when the roof collapsed. It was as if someone had taken a painting of the neighbourhood and dropped a splash of ink on the canvas, obliterating the once beautiful space where the house stood. I had to shake the image—as unreal as it seemed—this was not oil on canvas but a real place. Those people who once lived there were also real. People I'd grown to love as much as I did my own flesh and blood. As I observed fire fighters sift among the wreckage, seeking out hotspots to dampen down, I felt as if one of those hidden embers had lodged in my heart. I would not allow it to be smothered, because I wanted it to flare into being and fuel me in the hours to come. Since this started I'd concerned myself with avoiding the notice of the police, but that caution had hindered me. Now it was a case of the law be damned. This was a personal attack on my loved ones and no one would stand in my way to avenge it.

I looked at my friend, and my rage must have been nothing in comparison to his.

Rink stood as solid as a granite boulder next to me. He hadn't moved in some time as he too surveyed the wreckage of his family home. I wondered what memories he had of the place, but at the same time knew that was not how his mind was working. He was not thinking of the material worth of the place, but of the spiritual. More than the fact his mother had been snatched from her home, this was where his father had died, and the burning of the place was the ultimate insult to his memory.

Bridget Lanaghan had not recovered from the knock on her head before the paramedics arrived. Thankfully she was only unconscious, and the medics were able to stabilise her and reassured us that the prognosis for a full recovery was good. My greatest regret was that she had not been able to tell us anything before the ambulance left, but I'd live with it. Better that she was looked after, and brought back to health than I encourage her to speak while so poorly. Others could answer my questions.

There were still a number of neighbours moving in the distance, beyond the cordon set up by the fire trucks and their unravelled hoses. I looked for the dog walker. I hoped he could tell us more about what he had witnessed. He had seen Yukiko and Bridget Lanaghan together, but he said that the fire was already underway by then and that Yukiko had asked him to call the emergency services. But had he been walking his dog before that? Had he seen any others near the house, a vehicle of some kind? I wanted confirmation that Markus Colby was responsible for this...or was it someone else? I could not see the man with the dog. Perhaps another neighbour had seen something. I was about to move away from Rink's side, to go ask, and did not expect the verification that came next.

Beyond where we'd abandoned Andrew's car, there was another. It was familiar to me.

The lights from the fire trucks danced across the car's windshield, but I could make out the form of a man inside.

That spark in my heart flared.

I touched Rink on his elbow.

'The sand-coloured car is back,' I said.

That was all the motivation either of us needed. We headed for the car, despite the presence of so many witnesses around us. As we approached, the driver started the vehicle and completed a reverse U-turn in the roadway. He did not speed off, but waited until we were back in Andrew's car and also made the turn. Then he led us away. There was no urgency to get away, no attempt to lose us, he wanted us to follow.

Finally, a few blocks away, he pulled into the forecourt of a vehicle repair shop that was closed for the night.

He got out the car, leaning on the open door as he checked around. There was no one about, only the occasional car passing on the street. He'd have been better off doing this where there were plenty of others.

Rink and I approached him. It was the bruiser that Rink had knocked out in Parnell's apartment at Hayes Tower. He knew he wasn't a physical match for either of us. He flicked back the tail of his jacket to show the gun on his hip as he stepped into the open. We didn't bother showing ours.

'What are Chaney's terms?' Rink demanded.

There was no need for preamble. It was apparent what had happened back at the house. Our warning that Chaney leave town had fallen on deaf ears and the bastard had gone through with yet another repercussive attack. Why he'd chosen to snatch Yukiko was out of character though. It didn't surprise me when the man spoke next.

'Your mother for Parnell and Faulks.'

'What the hell does Chaney want them for?' Rink demanded.

'He doesn't. His new friend does.'

It didn't take any thinking about. It was obvious who Chaney's new buddy was.

'So it's true then? Shit does stick to shit.'

I smiled at Rink's summation.

'When and where?' Rink went on.

The big guy had been holding something in his opposite hand, concealed behind the open car door. For a millisecond I thought he was going to haul out another gun and force us into his car, but that wasn't it. He threw a folded map on the floor at Rink's feet. Rink didn't bend to retrieve it.

'Two hours.' The man nodded down at the folded map. 'X marks the spot, as they say. Be there with Parnell and Faulks and you get your mother back. No cops. No weapons. The first sign of either and your mom dies. Understood?'

'Understood?' Rink asked me.

'Crystal clear,' I said, half turning as if to retreat to our car. Then I turned back. 'Actually, there is one other thing...'

The man lifted his chin, a reflexive jerk at my question.

My hand came up and my SIG cracked.

'...why are you still standing up when you're dead?' I finished.

The question was lost on the thug. My words had arrived after the bullet that drilled his left eye and then fragmented against the orbital bone, sending slithers of white-hot lead into all corners of his cranium.

The man tipped backwards, landing in a billow of grit on the garage forecourt. Apart from a little blood around his eye socket there was no hint of the untold damage within his skull: that was the beauty of a soft-nosed slug. No blowing off of heads.

'Whatever happened to the idea of *not* shooting the messenger?' Rink asked.

'It was kill him now or kill him later. Either way he was going to end up dead. This way we gain an advantage...and a nice new car.'

'You're a step or two ahead of me,' Rink said as he bent to retrieve the map. 'What have you got in mind?'

'Let's get this asshole in the trunk first.'

I popped the trunk of the big sedan, and there was room even for the bruiser to fit inside. We couldn't leave him here. Neither could we leave behind Andrew's car. While Rink drove it a couple of blocks away, I checked that there was no one around who might have witnessed what had just occurred. Thankfully there weren't. I'd already taken note that the only CCTV camera in sight was positioned to cover the entrance of the auto shop, and was directed away from us. My car was an import with a stick shift, but the big sedan was an automatic. But I'd driven enough of them—Andrew's car included—that the different driving experience gave me no problems. I eased the car out of the lot, and drove to where I'd agreed to meet Rink. He was waiting by the kerb, Andrew's car hidden from sight behind a row of shops like a mini-strip mall. He'd left the keys in the ignition, I guessed. This time tomorrow the car would be gone, stripped of its parts, the remainder burned on some vacant lot. He got in our new acquisition; slinging the weapons he'd brought on the back seat. Immediately I set off, my subconscious radar sending me towards the bay.

'I've figured out your plan, brother,' Rink said, as he unfolded the map. 'They aren't expecting us to arrive for two hours. They'll think that we'll have to go fetch Parnell and Faulks and will be preparing a welcoming party for us. They won't be expecting us coming right now.'

'That was my plan,' I agreed. 'So long as the idiot they sent wasn't supposed to call them when he delivered the message, we've a good chance of surprising them.'

'Did you check if he had a cell on him?'

'None.'

Rink searched in the glove compartment but there wasn't a phone there. 'Maybe he was going to use a call box.'

'I doubt it,' I said. 'They probably expect that you'll do exactly as you were told. They know how much your mom means to you, and think you'll hand over the old guys without question...'

I left that hanging on purpose, gauging his response.

'Well that isn't going to happen,' he said. I didn't think so, but thought it best to check. The reality of the situation was—if we did make the exchange—all that would result was the deaths of all three of the original lynch party. Markus Colby would kill Yukiko and both the old men first chance he got. He'd have already tried to have us killed by then, his reason for recruiting Chaney and his gang. The rules of honor meant nothing to Markus, and what goes around comes around. Fair enough. The gloves were about to come off: actually they already had when I placed a slug in the guy back there. If he wanted dirty fighting then that was what he was going to get.

'Someone will be watching,' I said. 'But they won't be alarmed when they see this car arrive. Our buddy in the trunk probably had instructions to go back to lend extra firepower at the exchange.'

'They won't see me coming,' Rink said, and it wasn't an empty boast. 'As we approach, let me out. They're only expecting to see one guy in this car. They won't be watching their backs for another.'

'Where am I going?' I asked.

Rink arched an eyebrow at the map he'd unfolded in his lap.

'Somewhere I know well,' he said, stabbing a finger at where someone had literally marked the map with a red 'X'. I was surprised to note it was near Chabot Lake where we'd left the old men with Velasquez and McTeer. Rink went on. 'When I used to visit my parents, my dad and me used to go hiking out there all the time. Right there—' he touched the map once more, a half-inch from the 'X', '—there used to be an old lodge house. I just bet that's where they have my mom.'

'Makes sense,' I said, pushing the sedan towards the Bay Bridge. 'Let's go get her back.'

39

Snow Child had never actually seen snow.

Or if she had it was when she'd been too young to remember it now. She had seen it in picture books and in a movie at the cinema once, but never the real thing. Snow was brilliant white, but when she'd watched that movie it had looked grey on the screen. Everything looked grey in that movie, in one shade or another. The snow then had looked like the ashes at the edge of the fire she now poked at with a twig. The ashes and cinders fascinated her, the way they looked almost solid to the touch, but actually crumbled to powder as fine as talcum when she probed them with her stick. She wondered if snow disappeared when touched. Maybe that was why she was called Snow Child. She prided herself on her ability to disappear so she could not be touched. She was better at hiding than Rose or any of the other girls, and that was the only thing that kept her safe from the guard with the bayonet. Usually.

This time she was so focused on the ashes in the fire pit that she was unaware of his scrutiny. Or the way the cold winter sun glinted on the lenses of his spectacles as he studied her from the corner of one of the dormitory sheds. There was always noise here in the Rohwer camp, always the sound of the tread of marching feet, so his were lost among the others as the guard approached her from behind. The first she knew of his presence was when the cold gleam of his bayonet flicked the twig from her hand and it dropped among the cold cinders.

Yukiko was terrified of the blade.

She let out a wordless cry, even as she twisted around to stare up at the giant towering over her. She fell on her back, the ashes puffing round her: snow falling up *towards the sky.*

He was in silhouette over her, but the lenses of his spectacles flared with an errant beam of light, giving him the look of a Tengu—a mountain demon—as he bent to inspect her.

She thought that he must know.

Had he been aware that she had hidden under the piles of laundry in the washhouse? Had he known that she'd witness his attack on Rose, and had he taken secret pleasure in the knowledge? Had he come now to make sure that she never told another soul about what he'd done?

He placed the tip of his bayonet against her cheek.

'What are you doing?' he growled.

'I'm...playing...'

'In the dirt, just like a little yellow rat?'

'It's not dirt it's—' she was about to say snow, '—ash.'

'It's filth.' He stared down at her. 'You're filthy. Look at your clothing, your face. You have dirt all over you. Get up.'

She couldn't rise for the steel glinting in her vision.

He leaned down and grabbed the front of her jacket.

'Up I said. Now get over there. To the washroom and get yourself cleaned up.'

He did not release her. He held on to the front of her coat. Staring at her from behind the colourless lenses. He cocked his head left to right. She felt filthy, but not due to the ash, but the salacious way in which his lips puckered.

'You're a small one, ain't you. How old are you?'

Yukiko couldn't find the words. Her throat was pinching shut.

'It doesn't matter.' He propelled her towards the washhouse, her feet barely touching ground as he half carried her there. Yukiko desperately tried to scream. If she screamed someone would come and stop the monster. If she screamed loud enough her dad would hear all the way from Tule Lake and he would come back to save her. But panic had struck her dumb. The big man pushed her inside the washroom, pausing only to check over his shoulder, ensuring that no one had seen him carrying her there. Then he followed her in.

Yukiko could feel fat tears streaming down her cheeks. They dripped from her elfin chin, pattering on the collar of her rough cotton jacket as she shivered uncontrollably. They did not move the guard to pity, if anything they excited him all the more.

'Get them off. Those filthy clothes. Off. Now.'

He prodded her with the tip of his bayonet, hooking it under the centre button of the three on her coat.

'Take it off, or I'll cut it off. I might not be too careful and may also cut off your hide.' He prodded again with the bayonet.

Her fingers trembling, Yukiko plucked open the buttons and shrugged out of the coat. It fell in a heap behind her. All she wore beneath was a shapeless off-white shift that covered her to the knees. Her legs had the benefit of knee length socks and sturdy black clogs, but her bare arms were like twiglets protruding from the cuffs of her shift. The tip of the guard's tongue flicked over his dry lips. He made a noise as if he was clearing a bug from his throat.

'Take all of it off.'

'P...Please...'

'Off.' His voice had dropped an octave. She would never know if the hoarseness was through anger or longing.

The door creaked open and a lady stepped inside the washhouse.

Yukiko did not know the lady's name. She only knew her as the older sister of her friend, Harumi.

The guard spun, immediately lifting his gun and aiming the fixed bayonet at the lady.

'Get out,' he snapped.

The lady feigned misunderstanding. She bowed, bowed, bowed, entering the room, talking gently in Japanese. She went past both Yukiko and the guard, heading for the shower cubicles. She gave the guard a shy tilt of her head as she went by, bowed her lips in a smile. Harumi was twelve years old, while her sister was that much older at fifteen. To a child as young as Yukiko, a fifteen year old was a grown woman, a lady, in comparison. But to the monster she would still be a child.

The guard lowered his rifle, and he turned to look down at Yukiko.

'Filthy yellow rat,' he said to her. 'Get outta here...and keep out of that damn fire pit the in future. Next time I'll make you scrub yourself raw.'

Yukiko grabbed for her coat and fled for the door.

She hauled it open, her only wish to be as far away as possible.

Yet she stopped and sought the eyes of the lady.

'Domo arigato,' Yukiko whispered. Thank you very much.

The lady looked back at her, her features a well of desperation now. Yet she straightened herself as the guard approached her, shoving her further inside the cubicle. There was no door. The guard turned around, pulling off his spectacles and shoving them into his jerkin pocket. He caught Yukiko watching.

'Out,' he mouthed silently.

Then he smiled at her, a silent promise that one day he would have his time with her.

Yukiko fled.

She did not see the lady again. Not alive, anyway. Two days later the lady was found hanging in a closet, shamed into taking her own life after what she had tolerated on Yukiko's behalf. She should not have been shamed: her actions had saved the little girl.

Years later, Harumi would marry Bruce Tennant. In the decades that since passed Yukiko had forgotten much about Harumi, but never had she forgotten her sister, the lady who gave her own innocence to the beast in order that the Snow Child remained chaste.

She also remembered the look that Charles Peterson cast after her as she'd fled the washhouse.

It was the same one his bastard son wore now.

He also promised that he'd have his time with her, after he'd checked out the shouting and gunfire above.

40

For some time I'd held the impression that Markus Colby was someone who had followed misguided reasoning when setting out on his murder rampage, and that deep down, he saw himself as the good guy avenging a supreme wrong. Was Markus any different from Rink in that respect? Both men were out to avenge their murdered fathers. Well, the answer was right there before me now. Rink's actions were driven to save life as much as they were to take Markus's, whereas there was nothing to vindicate the killer. Markus had beaten, hanged, shot, stabbed, injected and burned his victims, and had taken satisfaction in their deaths. But now he'd overstepped the mark by a long shot. By taking a vulnerable old woman, he'd committed the inexcusable. He'd stooped to the level his father had when he'd also targeted the vulnerable and innocent. I knew that Rink desired nothing more than to see Markus dead at his feet, but he'd never stoop that low. And he sure as hell wouldn't take any delight in the man's death. He would only be relieved.

Though, if he failed to save his mother, nothing would console him.

I thought briefly of Yukiko and her staunch belief in *giri*, and concluded that it was Rink's burden of obligation to end this seventy-year loop of violence. The way I saw things, by extension that obligation was also mine. I was prepared to do anything to safely free Yukiko and end the threat to her. By throwing their lot in with Markus Colby, Sean Chaney and his men had just signed their death warrants.

I let Rink out of the sedan a good quarter mile from where we'd been instructed to deliver Parnell and Faulks. He'd taken his gun and knife with him as he slipped away into the trees. He was gone from sight in seconds, and I knew that next time eyes were laid on him they would be a split second from death. I had my SIG, but I'd also grabbed the gun from the dead thug in the trunk when I'd searched him for a cell phone. The extra firepower would come in handy. While Rink went for his mom, I was to play disruption on the enemy lines. In hindsight, maybe I shouldn't have shot the messenger so quickly. Better that I'd disabled him first, demanded to know their numbers and strengths, and gained us an idea of what we were up against. But that's me: 'Impulsive' is my middle name. Fuck the numbers, I decided, if I didn't have enough bullets there were plenty other ways of killing men.

It had taken time to get to Upper San Leandro Reservoir, but by my reckoning we weren't expected for a little more than an hour yet. Though the messenger and his sand-coloured car would be. I drove the car down a winding track towards a turning circle on a promontory overlooking the lake, driving with the lack of caution one returning to his friends would show. The headlights were on full beam for a reason. As I arrived I saw a cluster of vehicles, one of which I immediately recognised as the one that Markus Colby had so recently fled Clarendon Heights in. A van, and two other cars, could hold a number of men, but I didn't think that was the case. Lit by my main beam was one sentry, standing smoking as he waited for his buddy to get back. As he saw me coming, he stepped out, flicking his cigarette butt on the hard grit in a shower of sparks. He took another ungainly step and I saw it was the man whose leg I'd dislocated back at Hayes Tower. I must have done a reasonable job at realigning the joint, because apart from some pain in his grimace of welcome he didn't look too unwell. Shame. He was holding a hand cupped to his forehead, attempting to disperse some of the glare from my lights. Because of the stark beams he couldn't make out my figure beyond them, but he recognised the car. He waved with his other hand. The mug wasn't even armed—or if he was, his weapon was tucked away.

Parking the car, I made sure the lights stayed on full. Throwing open the door, I climbed out, but I remained bent over so he didn't notice the disparity in height between me and his pal, and moved round for the trunk. I waved for him to follow. I popped the lid and it gave me some cover as he moved past the lights and alongside the car. My lights would have ruined his night vision, and the few seconds it took for it to adjust would have to do. I didn't want to shoot this man. Not that he didn't deserve a bullet, just that it was too soon to announce my arrival to the others further out in the woods.

He came around the car, wondering what I wanted to show him. I was leaning inside, covering the form of his dead friend. By the hiss of his breath I hadn't fully concealed the corpse. He began to step away, to fumble with his coat as he went for a gun in a shoulder rig. Snapping a sidekick into his damaged leg, I followed it by ramming the point of my elbow into his throat. His busted knee buckled, and he began to fall, but his shout of alarm was wedged behind the collapsing cartilage of his voice box. He forgot about the gun as he tried to reshape his throat with his fingers. I almost felt sorry for the punk. Almost. But there was no place for pity now. Grabbing his chin in one hand, the crown of his skull in the other, I twisted it like a large stopcock.

The trunk of the sedan was spacious, but not large enough to contain both corpses. I left the second thug lying where he fell, and the trunk lid open. If any of their pals should spot them, then all the better. It would help throw confusion and fear into their hearts, make my job all the simpler. I didn't wait around but began a slow run down a path that led towards the abandoned hall that Rink mentioned earlier. Partly I wished that more of the gang had been waiting at the turning place, because that would have meant fewer surrounding Yukiko when we arrived. Not that superior numbers concerned me, but the fact that any one of them might choose to employ Yukiko as a human shield.

Out there in the woods, approaching from another direction, Rink would be figuring a way to reach and safely free his mother. By now, he should have been in place. It was down to me to make his task achievable. While he employed stealth, I had to cause discord and panic, draw the bastards to me instead of barricading themselves within the lodge. I began snatching at the branches of trees as I jogged, making noise that any listeners might hear, but which would also confuse them. A determined enemy wouldn't make such a noisy approach, would he? Their attention would be piqued, but their response would not at first be deadly while they came to check things. Or that was the plan.

Plans and me don't always work out.

A gun blasted from about thirty yards ahead of me on the path.

The accuracy of some handguns is notoriously poor, but that wasn't what saved me. The darkness, the lack of surety of the gunman, the racket I was making, all helped throw off his aim. In fact I'm not full sure he fired directly at me, but perhaps into the air to warn the others. Whatever the case I kept running, unimpeded by injury, using the flash of gunfire to lead me to the gunman. Someone crashed through the bushes, getting off the trail, looking for cover. Now that bullets had been fired there was no requirement to hold my fire. I lifted the appropriated Glock I'd taken from the messenger and fired at the rattle of fronds. I tracked the movement, aiming a foot or so in front of the source of the rattle of breaking twigs. A grunt, followed by a body hitting the earth rewarded me. Covering the fallen man, I moved to check on him. When I arrived, I found a thick-necked punk lying on his back, his eyes glazing as he stared up at the night sky. I didn't know the man's face, and for the briefest of moments thought about the irony of how this man had died, having not seen the face of his killer either. Scum like Sean Chaney gathered men like this around him, like fleas to a mutt. The man had a life, hopes and desires of his own, yet he'd died needlessly to appease his boss man's selfish ends. This punk wasn't an enemy; he was simply a faceless drone to be dropped before I reached the big kahuna himself. There would be more just like him.

From somewhere to my right a voice queried loudly. The words were indecipherable, more of a shout of alarm than anything. I ignored it and went on, winding my way along a path between tall conifers and maple trees, the grass springy underfoot. Via Markus Colby, Sean Chaney's instructions had been implicit—bring Parnell and Faulks, no cops, no weapons. Well one out of three wasn't bad. Yet the abruptness of gunfire might force Markus or Chaney to go through with their threat that Yukiko would die if we welched on the deal. I didn't think that would be the case. While confusion reigned, they'd keep her alive. I hoped. But then, that eventuality couldn't be relied upon, certainly for any great length of time. I had to hit them hard and fast.

With the Glock in one hand, my SIG in the other, I advanced, moving now with more caution as I approached a clearing, a warning sign marking the entrance. *Danger* it said in faint weatherworn lettering. Never a truer word was said. Someone hidden in the lea of a sagging building opened up with a submachine gun. I'd heard enough of them in my time to recognise the weapon as an Uzi SMG. The gun had a cyclical rate of fire of around six hundred rounds per minute. The guy was panic-shooting and bled the thirty-two rounds in his magazine within four seconds. Still, it was a long four seconds while I threw myself to the ground and listened to the shredding of foliage above me. As the rattle of gunfire stopped, and the gunman cursed, fumbling to eject and reload a fresh magazine, I came up and put two bullets in his body, one from each of my guns. Another one of the faceless drones went down, never to rise. I experienced no sense of irony this time. I was in that zone where all that mattered was to kill or be killed, and any man pointing a weapon at me was to be cut down. Fourteen years black ops had conditioned me to the frame of mind, and it could only serve me now.

There was shouting from within the decrepit building now. I caught a flash of light, but someone had the good sense to douse the lamp, to make them difficult to target. Some gung-ho fool came running out, firing blindly as he raced to gain a flanking position on me. Crouching in the tree line, I targeted him, put a cluster of rounds through his upper thighs and he pitched face first on the deck. He wasn't dead—not yet—and he started howling blue murder. My intention for not killing him outright. If I'd nicked a femoral artery he wouldn't be screaming for long, so I had to make the most of the disconcertion the others had to be experiencing. With no idea where Yukiko was being held, I couldn't blindly fire into the building for fear of hitting her. Better that I draw the others out, offering Rink room to move.

I fired once, presenting muzzle flash, but immediately

scooted away, placing a tree trunk between the lodge and me. At the far corner, a man leaned out and fired at where I'd crouched seconds earlier. He loosed half a dozen rounds. I waited until the last to let out a startled yelp, before shaking the bushes next to me, as though falling back. I made a loud moan, as I moved silently out of the way.

'I got the bastard,' the gunman crowed.

'Careful,' another cautioned. I hadn't been aware of this man, hiding out behind a pile of logs to my left.

'I heard him fall,' the first said. 'I got the fucker.'

'Take it easy. He might still be alive. Chaney said he had a buddy with him; watch out, man.'

'We have to get Boyd out of the way. We have to stop his goddamn screaming before he brings the other to us.'

'Leave him, there's nothing you can do if the bastard out there is still alive.'

The gunman had a sense of loyalty usually found lacking in these types. He came out from hiding, first checking on his fallen comrade, before seeking out where I'd fallen.

'Cover me, I'm going to check.'

In less than a second, the gunman came at a crouching run, his gun held out in both hands as he honed in on the spot where he thought I'd gone down. I ignored him momentarily, watching as the second one lifted his head above the stack of logs to follow his progress. On my left he made for a poor target, but I'd trained myself to shoot with both hands. My right hand's better, but the left's not too shoddy. I squeezed the trigger of the Glock and it bucked in my hand. A cloud of blood and hair puffed from the top of the man's head and he sunk below the line of logs. The running man skidded to halt, barking out a curse, as he understood they'd been suckered. He swung his gun, shooting at my muzzle flash, but that was okay. My arm had been outstretched, well away from my body, and it was through empty space that his bullets flew. Calmly I lined him up with my SIG and shot him in the face. Throughout, the leg-shot man, Boyd, hadn't stopped screaming. But he'd realised he was not yet dead. He clawed his way around, lifting his gun, and he fired at me.

I was running at him.

One of his bullets punched my shoulder. I've been hit there before and know just how agonising and debilitating such a wound can be. Without thought I understood that his round had not found flesh, but only the cloth of my jacket. I barely missed a step as I fired with both guns, a double tap to his central mass as I charged by him and pressed myself tightly to the lodge wall. I smelled mildew and rot, a heady aroma tinged by the more acrid cordite wafting in the breeze. From within there was harsh whispering. Two voices belonging to Chaney and Markus. There followed a thud of feet on stairs. I slipped my SIG in my belt, checked the Glock and found the mag still half full.

Judging by the number of vehicles on the turnout I'd expected more defenders than those I'd gone up against, but didn't doubt that Rink had accounted for some of the others. I could only hope he'd reached a good position, now that I'd compromised mine.

'You out there,' a voice bellowed. 'Drop your gun or—by God—I swear the old bitch will die.'

I recalled Sean Chaney's bullfrog croak from the BART carriage.

'Isn't going to happen, Chaney,' I called back. 'Your best bet's to hand her over—unharmed—and you'll be given a chance. If I come in there I'll be shooting. You understand that?'

'Come in, I'll kill you.'

'I'm not interested in you. It's that other bastard I want. You there, Markus?'

'He's with the old woman,' Chaney shouted. 'He'll do her in a second. Do you hear me? Come inside and the Jap bitch dies.'

'If that happens, I swear to you, Chaney. You'll beg for death before I'm finished with you.'

'Like I said: come in. I'm not about to be suckered like that time on the train.'

'You've had all the warnings you're getting. This time I won't be going for a leg shot.'

'You shouldn't have last time,' Chaney crowed.

He fired and bullets punched the wall. The timbers halted most, but some cut through the rotted wood or found chinks between the caulking. Good job I'd already flattened myself to the dirt floor. As chunks of wood jumped in the air above me, I rolled clockwise and placed myself belly down in the gap in the doorway. Chaney was a huge amorphous silhouette, darker than the darkness around him. From my prone position I fired.

I'd lied to him.

I did go for a leg shot.

Blood puffed from the matching hole I put through his previously injured thigh. It was a supreme insult, just to show the bastard what I thought of him. He roared at the ignominy, swinging his gun on me, but I'd already continued my roll and out of his sight. I came to my feet, pressing against the logs once more.

Chaney dragged himself further inside, cursing like mad.

There was another noise, a scuff above me. From a tree bole a figure detached and clambered up onto the roof.

I grinned.

'Chaney,' I called. 'Are you ready to hand Yukiko over yet?'

'Fuck you! The old woman's going to die.'

'Then there's nothing more I can do to spare your life,' I said.

From further back there came a crashing of shingles as Rink broke a way inside. Immediately I sprang for the door. Offering cover I dashed in, just as Rink dropped through a hole in the roof and landed behind Chaney. In Rink's hand, he'd switched his gun for his Ka-bar. It glinted dully, casting a burnished flame in my buddy's normally dark eyes. Chaney was caught wrong-footed, stumbling on his game leg, as he swung at the new threat, offering me his broad back.

Chaney fired. But his gun was empty, his bullets spent on the wall. He looked down at the useless weapon on hearing the dead man's click.

I could have easily shot Chaney dead, but this was primarily Rink's gig.

He had first dibs on Chaney for taking his mom.

He rammed the blade through Chaney's open mouth with such force the tip of the blade jutted an inch from his bald pate.

Chaney fell backwards, landing flat on his back, dead.

Rink yanked the Ka-bar free with a sound not unlike Velcro

torn apart. With a deft shake of the wrist he shedded the blood from the blade, a move reminiscent of the Samurai *chiburi*—or blood shake—manoeuvre as he cleans his katana sword before returning it to its scabbard. He kept his knife firmly in hand.

Then he turned to face Markus Colby who'd crept up from a cellar behind him.

Markus also gripped a knife, but it was held to Yukiko's throat.

41

'Put down your weapons,' Markus said.

He was a big man, easily as tall and muscular as Rink. In comparison Yukiko was diminutive. She made the hole in a human-shaped doughnut, while he was the outer ring, and I was pretty certain that I could've shot Markus a dozen times without as much as nicking her. But I couldn't take the chance. Unless my first shot killed him, the killer would ram his blade into her throat and that would be it.

Rink didn't look at the man; his attention was on his mother, checking that she had not been harmed. Her hands were bound behind her back, and a noose over her head. Out of sight behind her, Markus gripped the trailing rope. He had the strength to yank her off her feet and hang her in front of us.

'I won't tell you again.' Markus pricked the skin of Yukiko's throat, and a bead of blood slipped below her blouse collar. In the gloom it looked like a beetle had scuttled for cover under her clothing.

'We'll do it your way, Markus,' Rink said.

He dropped his Ka-bar on the hard-packed dirt, kicked it away. Then he pulled out his gun and also tossed it away across the room. It clattered where it fell among some stacked furniture.

'What's the plan, Markus?' I asked. 'We throw down our weapons and you shoot us, and then you kill Yukiko any way?'

'Possibly,' Markus said. 'Maybe I'll just walk out of here with her, use her for cover until I can get to a vehicle, and then release her. But that won't happen unless you put down your *fucking* gun.'

There was little chance of him releasing Yukiko. In all likelihood he had a gun stuffed in his belt, concealed from us by Yukiko's body. He'd wait until we were unarmed, then jab her in the throat, throw her into our arms to stall us while he brought out his gun and shot us in the head. It was an untenable position we were in. No way he could expect me to give up my weapon.

Rink gave me a nod and I threw down the Glock.

Markus's eyes narrowed marginally.

I just bet that he was expecting me to resist further, so he had an excuse to use the blade on Yukiko a little more.

'Let my mother go,' Rink said.

'You're not in a position to make demands,' Markus told him.

'We've done as you said and put down our weapons. Let my mother go,' Rink repeated.

'You didn't do fully as I asked. You were meant to bring me the other two murderers. Where are Parnell and Faulks?'

'Safe from you,' I said.

Markus stared at me. His face was rigid. He shifted marginally, and I guess he was thinking of last time we met and how much it had hurt.

'Who the fuck are you anyway? What has any of this got to do with you?'

'I'm Joe Hunter. I'm Rink's brother.'

I didn't expound. I didn't need to tell him that Rink and I were as close as if we shared the same blood. Let the fucker wonder. All he needed to know was that I was prepared to fight tooth and nail to save my friend and his mother.

'You think you're a bad ass,' he sneered.

'I know what I am. I also know what you are. Coward.'

'Fuck you,' he said, not rising to the bait.

'Let my mother go. I'll bring you the old men in exchange for her.' Rink had straightened, showing Markus his palms.

'That isn't an option now. I can take Yukiko, and I can find the other two in my own good time. I don't need anything from you except to *shut the fuck up.*'

Inwardly I smiled. Not that it was a happy situation by any stretch of the imagination, but Rink's words had got the rise I'd been hoping for from Markus. I wanted him angry, and his mind confused by conflicting messages. He didn't know that Rink was bluffing—he would no sooner hand over the two old guys than exchange Yukiko's life for his.

'Let her go, Markus. It's over now,' I said. 'The police know your identity and they will catch you. You can help yourself by sparing Yukiko now.'

'I killed a cop,' Markus pointed out. 'Nothing will help me. I'll go to prison for life for killing him, so I might as well take the others. It's not as if they can extend my sentence beyond life, is it?'

'You didn't kill a cop. He survived. There's still a way to end this peaceably.'

'I don't want peace. I want the ones who murdered my father dead.'

'Hurt my mom, and I guarantee you'll never see life beyond *these* walls.' Rink's tone had changed. He was no longer attempting to reason, but trying to goad Markus into making a move on him, not on his mother.

But Markus wasn't playing.

'How do you suppose that's going to happen? Seeing as I'm calling the shots now?'

'The second you use that knife on my mom, I swear to God I'll be on you. I'll rip your fuckin' head off your shoulders.'

Markus laughed. He glanced at Yukiko. 'Must be great knowing you have such a loving son? Pity my dad didn't get the same opportunity.'

'Your dad was a piece of shit,' Rink snapped.

'Your dad was the piece of shit,' Markus came back. 'Gave me great pleasure when I killed the bastard. As it will when I skin your mother alive for what you just said.'

Yukiko and I had been holding eye contact. She appeared incredibly calm for being seconds from death. For the first time she said something. 'Kill me, but let my son go.'

Markus glanced down at her. 'You're the one who dies. I'm not interested in *him*.' He did then what many would do by reflex: he used the blade of the knife to indicate Rink. The knife was away from Yukiko's carotid artery for no more than a second, but it was the break I'd been waiting for. I snatched my SIG from my waistband, concealed from view all this time from Markus. I fired.

I was shooting to hit his hand, but my aim was poor and rushed.

The round hit the steel blade of the knife and shattered it into glittering shards. Some of the exploding splinters hit Yukiko, digging into her shoulder, but some also hit Markus in the face. He roared in surprise, leaping back from the old woman. He was still holding the rope.

Then everything happened quickly.

There was a blur of bodies.

Markus hauled back on the rope, but Rink was also moving and grasped the knot before the noose could cinch around Yukiko's throat. Pulled with force the rope could tear her skull from her frail body.

Off balance, Yukiko was already falling.

Rink scooped her up in his other arm, wrestling to wrench the rope from Markus's hands.

I couldn't get a clear shot at Markus for the tussling bodies.

Then Rink broke free, hauling his mother from the murderer's control and turning away.

Yukiko gasped for breath, her chest heaving.

Rink's face was ashen as he looked down at his mother as she struggled for life. After everything, was her existing heart condition going to be the deciding factor?

'Get her out of here, Rink,' I shouted. 'Leave this bastard to me.'

Markus had fled towards the rear of the room, an indistinct figure in the dimness. Through the hole in the roof where Rink had made his unexpected entrance starlight was our only mode of illumination. I shot at him as he leapt behind the piles of furniture. Markus returned fire.

I backpedalled, moving to keep my body between Markus's aim and my friend as Rink carried his mom through the portal into the open air.

Furniture crashed down as the murderer fought to find a way out of the building. But he was stuck back there. I fired, now that Rink and Yukiko were out of the way, and began moving for him once more.

Markus fired twice.

I shot back, heard him curse. But he wasn't hit, because there was no pain in his voice, only frustration.

He fired again, and I heard the unmistakable clack of the slide staying open.

He swore again. There was no sound of him slapping in a fresh magazine, or racking the slide to arm the gun.

'Are you out of bullets, Markus? Now that's a real shame.'

'Fucker, I'll still kill you.'

'Come on then,' I shouted back. 'I've been looking forward to this.'

He didn't understand at first.

I waited.

'Well, punk, aren't you going to come out and face me?'

'You're armed.'

'I don't need a gun for the likes of you.' I threw my SIG to one side. What Markus didn't know was that I too was out of bullets, but let the bastard think I was giving him an honorable go at fighting his way free. In truth I'd have preferred to put a couple rounds through his skull, but I was happy to go man to man. Plus, it would've become evident that I was out of ammo the second I tried to flush him from the furniture piles, so why waste energy and place myself in the compromising position of having to clamber over chairs and tables to get at him? 'Come out, Markus. Show me what you've got.'

42

Markus came forward, but he paused as he checked me out. I had the door to my back and presented only a solid silhouette to him. Perhaps he thought I was still carrying another concealed weapon.

'Quit stalling,' I told him. 'You were happy to beat old people to death, not too keen when you're up against someone your own age?'

'I don't fear you.'

'You should.'

'I want to know something...'

I thought he was going to ask why it was so important for me to stand between him and the Ringtons. He wouldn't understand. But that wasn't it. He surprised me with his next question.

'What happens if I win?'

'Then you're free to walk out of here,' I said. Not that I was planning on allowing that to happen.

He studied me and I returned the favour. His body language betrayed him, even in the dim starlight. I could tell that he was bunching himself, readying himself to make his attack, thinking maybe he had a good chance of escape after all. He was a big guy, fit, powerful and relatively healthy—but for where I'd shot him in the ribs, but that had proven a minor injury. He was obviously tough, being employed in the transportation of dangerous felons you had to be reasonably handy in a fight, and the presence of the makiwara back at his house told me he practiced his unarmed skills regularly. The thing was, it was one thing throwing your weight around when manhandling shackled prisoners and old men incapable of putting up much resistance, quite another when facing someone determined to hit you back. I fancied my odds at being the one to walk out.

Then again, what the hell did I know about betting?

Markus lunged at me, planted one foot firmly on which to pivot and threw a high roundhouse kick at my head. I was surprised by the unorthodox attack. Reflex took over and I ducked, but Markus's shin scuffed the side of my skull and rocked me for a second. I dodged too late, got a shake of Markus's head in return. He laughed as I swiped at the raw patch above my ear.

'Bastard,' I called him.

Markus danced back. Light on his feet, his hands held in a boxer's guard.

'Wish you saved one of those bullets now?' Markus sneered.

'You got lucky, punk. Care to try again?'

Markus nodded. Then he launched the same kick a second time. At the last second he adjusted the trajectory of his shin so that the kick swept low under my guard and slammed my ribs. It was some kick: like a baseball bat delivered to a side of beef. I winced, trying to conceal the agony.

'That puts us on an even keel now,' he said. 'You damaged my ribs, I damaged yours.'

I snorted at his bravado. 'Is that all you've got?'

'Plenty more where that came from,' Markus crowed.

'Let's do it then.'

We both threw a blinding combination of blows, using fists, legs, and elbows and we were well matched. Knuckles slammed flesh, knees rammed guts and shins whacked each other's thigh muscles. Within seconds I was bleeding from my mouth, and Markus had a huge bruise growing on his right cheek. Then Markus got in a low sweeping kick, similar to one Rink favoured during his knockdown karate days and I went down on my back. The fight wasn't over. Not by a long shot. I threw a kick from the floor, forcing Markus to hop back out of the way. He stood ten feet away, waved me back to my feet.

I lunged up like a Gridiron footballer attacking the line of scrimmage. My opponent could have easily avoided the attack, but it appeared he was eager to get to grips with me. We crunched together like sumo wrestlers, each pushing and jostling, grabbing at each other's clothing. But it was a momentary clash, until I reared back and then drove my forehead directly into Markus's face. There was a crunch of cartilage and, as we broke apart, Markus's nose had taken on a new position. Blood flooded over his top lip, looking like oil in the darkness. He swiped at his face with the back of his wrist, then spat blood and mucus on the floor. My blow wasn't one allowed in a karate tournament, but straight from my soldier's repertoire. The shape of the battle was about to change.

Earlier I'd called Markus a coward: he proved me wrong in the next instant, because he didn't lie down but came back at me. If anything the broken nose seemed to spur him to greater action. He threw a couple of looping overhand punches at my head—both missed—but then he drove in with a straight cross that slammed me forcefully. The only thing was that I'd dipped my face at the last second and Markus's knuckles impacted on my forehead. The forehead is one of the hardest points of the human anatomy—much stronger than the weak metacarpals of a hand. Markus jumped back shaking his hand, and more droplets of inky blood spattered through the bars of starlight streaking the old meetinghouse. He was swearing, and I saw him glance at his fist and followed the movement. The skin was torn at his knuckles, bone glistening through the ruined flesh. I checked and found a smear of blood on my forehead, but I was confident that this time it was all Markus's. My skull still felt like a ten-pound hammer had struck it.

If his hand was broken then Markus was now severely hindered, but he saw his fight for what it was: a matter of life or death. He let out a loud bark of anger and threw a kick at my groin. A subtle twist of my body ensured that Markus's kick missed its intended target, but his foot whacked my inner thigh almost as painfully. His elbow struck with lightning speed, ramming into my ribs. Good job the blow struck my good side or the fight might have ended then. Markus watched as I stumbled away from him, almost losing my footing before I was able to catch myself. He allowed me the time to right myself. He shook his head in disdain of his enemy: he was actually playing with me.

'To think that I worried you'd be a deadly opponent,' he said.

No not playing, I realised, the bastard only wished to prolong my agony.

'I'm not done yet,' I snarled.

It was difficult to breathe, but I sucked it up. Went back at him, throwing a jab kick at his knee that he avoided, but a backhand strike to his face that got him full on.

Now it was his turn to back away, while he shook the cobwebs from his head.

'Worried again?' I asked.

Markus swung away from me, and I wondered if he was as keen to continue as before. He began glancing around, seeking something to use as a weapon, and I saw his gaze alight on a pile of old furniture stacked in one corner of the room.

'Do your worst, bastard,' I said.

'I'm going to,' he said, reaching for the pile.

Furniture began to topple as Markus rooted around for something he could wield. He finally spun back holding an old chair with his good hand. It was an ancient thing, and looked like a folding deckchair but made from slats of wood. He swung it at me, but his stance and aim proved ungainly and he missed. I hopped in and threw a kick, demolishing the seat of the chair and leaving Markus holding part of the backrest. Markus let out a grunt of satisfaction: he was now wielding something he could control; a weapon he thought might raise the game in his favour again. He lunged in, stabbing at my throat with the broken spar. Weaving aside I threw a left-right combination into Markus's face. It snapped the man's head back but he clubbed at my body and I had to retreat to avoid broken bones. Markus came after me, confident he had me on the run, his club whistling with each swipe. I dodged once more, but struck out with a knife hand blow that impacted with Markus's wrist. The length of wood spun away and was lost in the shadows at the other side of the large room.

Markus wasn't deterred. He went immediately into attack mode, landing a kick to my chest and followed through with a powerful punch to my chin. It caught me squarely, and only because I was moving backwards, riding the force of the blow, saved me serious injury. Galvanised by his success, Markus threw his opposite hand, spearing with his open fingers for my eyes. I twisted under the attack, catching Markus's extended arm over my shoulder and butting in with my hips, jacking

Markus on his locked elbow and spun him over my shoulder and on to the hard-packed floor. Dust billowed at the impact and Markus let out a hiss like steam escaping a ruptured boiler. Momentarily stunned, he was at my mercy.

But I stepped back.

It was best that I had. Where he'd fallen, he was in reaching distance of the Ka-bar ditched by Rink earlier and had snatched it from the floor and swiped at my gut.

He raised an eyebrow my way, licked the blood off his lips and gave me the tiniest of smiles as he rose up from the floor.

I was breathing hard, blood leaking from my nostrils invading my mouth. Each time I exhaled, droplets misted the tiger-striped atmosphere. I glanced once at the junk pile, then back at Markus, but I was loath to move. He stood up straighter, shaking his head.

'What's up? You think I'm going to stab you from behind?'

'I wouldn't put it past you. I still think you're a coward.'

'I'm going to look you in the eyes when you die.'

'Ditto,' I claimed.

Markus moved in a blur, his right hand whipping out in a backhand slash that took a flap of skin from my right deltoid as I reared away.

Markus stalked me, laughing as blood flooded my shirtfront. I would have spat on him if I didn't loathe the habit. He adjusted the knife for the *coup de grâce*. He had a smug sheen to his face: you'd think he was King Arthur and had just drawn Excalibur from the stone judging by the look of satisfaction he exuded. By the way he held the knife, and the way in which he kept it close to his body, he had as much knowledge of knife fighting as he did unarmed combat. I hoped that I hadn't made a huge error in allowing him a go at me.

I was also an accomplished knife fighter, but I was without a weapon. Quickly, I ripped off my jacket and shirt and wound them around my left forearm. The blood helped the cloth adhere to my skin. My night vision had now adjusted to the murky interior and my opponent was a silhouette against the monochrome background of decaying walls and trashed furniture. I readied for his attack.

Markus made an expeditionary probe with the knife. He

barely came within a foot of my body before withdrawing. I rolled my head, loosening the kinks in my neck, but that was my only reaction. I had read the lack of commitment in Markus's attack. 'Come on, arsehole,' I grunted, 'let's get down to the real business.'

'I aim to.' There was no commitment to his words, and I knew he was trying for the sneak attack. When it came, I was still a half-second too slow to react.

His arm whipped forward, the Ka-bar zipping from his extended hand like a flash of blue flame. Only the fact that I was already sailing on adrenalin saved me. Reflexively I dropped low and the blade sailed through the exact place where my head had been a moment earlier. But the handle struck my head and left a fresh wound in my scalp. 'Son of a bitch...'

It surprised me that he'd thrown the knife, giving up a major advantage. But Markus crouched down and his hand slipped into his boot. When he came up, it proved he wasn't as stupid as I'd thought, because he was clasping a homemade shiv and there was a gleam of familiarity in his eyes. He'd chosen to throw away the Ka-bar so he could employ his personal killing weapon on me. He must have noted the recognition in me, because he came fast, ripping up at my gut with the tip of the blade. As I dodged to one side, Markus moved with me, angling the blade as though it was an extension of his thumb and he was hiking a lift. Unchecked the knife would pass over my left shoulder and into my neck below the ear.

I was prepared for the secondary attack. I pivoted towards the knife; my cloth-covered forearm impacting with Markus's wrist, even as I swung a looping elbow strike into his chest. The force of the blow staggered Markus, but not enough to flatten him completely. Markus disengaged, then jabbed at my chest, but immediately reversed the trajectory and went for an overhand thrust at my face. What followed was a blur of action that stuttered through the beams of starlight, reminiscent of dancers moving through strobe lights. Markus jabbed and slashed; I moved defensively, my bandaged forearm and cupped palms redirecting his attacks. Nevertheless I was an unarmed man against a skilled practitioner with a super sharp blade, and fresh spots of blood grew on my chest and hands.

I was breathing loudly as he slashed and stabbed. My posture had contracted slightly, and I was growing heavy-footed. Conversely Markus was moving with more grace. His face was set in a death's head grin. I was damned if he didn't appear to be enjoying the fight. The cloth around my arm was now a shredded rag. I desperately jumped away from Markus, shaking my arm. Blood spattered the floor from a wicked gash on the back of my right wrist.

Finally Markus had got through with a telling strike. There was a flash of his teeth at the knowledge that he had his quarry on the back foot. He came at me again, more determined than before. He obviously wasn't enjoying the fight as much as I'd assumed and was now ready to finish things having drawn sufficient blood.

Get my arse into gear, I stepped up the pace of my defensive tactics, and each was now delivered with a corresponding counterattack. As I blocked his stab, I struck with my other hand. As I redirected a sweep of Markus's blade, I kicked at the man's supporting leg. As Markus speared at my gut, I rammed my stiffened fingers into his throat. I had to take him apart bit by bit—or more correctly destroy Markus's ability to attack. I ignored the slash of his blade through dermis, concentrating only on avoiding anything that could maim or kill me immediately. Cuts to my chest and arms now leaked blood, as did one on my left cheek. I disregarded them, concentrated on injuring him in turn. My blows were aimed at the muscles of his upper arms, his deltoids, to his inner and outer thighs. Markus began to seize up as his limbs shut down. If he couldn't move, he couldn't wield his blade.

Up until then I'd been too busy warding off his stabs and had avoided striking his face or groin, but now they became targets for my punches and kicks. I knocked a couple of teeth out, kneed him in the balls. The shiv hung limp in Markus's hand as he bent forward, gasping.

An uppercut knocked him back on his heels.

'How does it feel now?' I demanded through gritted teeth. 'Like those little girls felt at your father's hands? And as Andrew and the others did when you brutalised them?'

Markus opened his mouth to reply, but there was nothing I

wished to hear from him. Before he could form words, I drove into him with a kick that lifted the murderer from his feet and threw him backwards into the stack of furniture. Chairs toppled over him, half concealing him from view. I charged in, throwing aside the clutter to get a clear target, and crouched to deliver a right cross to Markus's face. There was crunch of teeth as Markus's jaws were rammed together. I wasn't finished. I threw a left, and heard the crack of a bone that signified a broken jaw.

Surprisingly Markus wasn't finished either. He swiped his blade at my chest, scoring a fresh line across one collarbone and almost adding another to my cheek. It won him a second's respite and he came to one knee, jabbing at my groin. I butted the knife away with a jab of a knee. Pivoting, I rammed a back kick into Markus's face and the murderer crashed back among the heap of furniture. His broken jaw now hung loose, blood and saliva in drooling ribbons on his chin. His eyes were rolling, going in and out of focus. The shiv clattered among the legs of broken chairs and ended on the earthen floor, out of either of our reach.

I stepped back, lining up a kick to the man's prone body. A hand was placed on my shoulder. I could feel the heat radiating off Rink in waves. 'It isn't over until he's dead,' I told my friend, aching still to crush Markus beneath my heels.

'He's finished, Hunter,' Rink said: an echo of something he had told me the day we became firm friends. On that occasion I'd been poised to deliver a finishing blow to a more honorable opponent than the one lying before me now.

'You're going to allow him to live...after everything he's done?'

'The circle of murder has to end.' Rink stooped down to pull the unconscious man into the clear. Then he hefted the noose he'd taken from around his mother's throat. 'But we do this the way we originally planned, okay?'

I looked down at the despicable piece of human crap at our feet. What Rink had in mind was too good for the bastard, but what could I say? First and foremost, Markus had always been Rink's burden of obligation to deal with.

43

Detective Jones had cautioned his younger partner to go easy and to await the arrival of appropriate back up before trying to affect an arrest on their murder suspect. Finally they'd pieced together the connection between the wives and sisters of the murdered men, and this had led them to records of others ensconced at Rohwer Relocation Facility. Cross checking had brought them to a marginal note in the file of one Charles Peterson, who had apparently been re-posted following complaints from his fellow guardsmen that he was brutalising some of the camp interns. Following Peterson's trail, they found other mentions of assault on females during his civilian life until a point in 1970 where the man had disappeared from the records. It was only in the recent years he'd shown up again, supposedly forty years younger, and working at the same correctional facility where both Bruce Tennant and Mitchell Forbeck were incarcerated until a few short weeks before their deaths. Though they had no proof that Peterson was their man, they'd shown enough circumstantial evidence to raise an arrest and search warrant.

A back up arrest team of uniformed officers were already en route to the scene, but Tyler had proven too enthusiastic for his own good, and instead of listening to good sense had wanted to snatch a headline or to impress their bosses with a quick arrest. Whatever his reason was, it had forced a rash decision and look where it had got them. Both of them injured and their suspect at large and causing further terror. Tyler could still expect headlines but not the kind he'd longed for, and the attention coming their way would be less than impressive—except for its volume of recrimination.

Not that it would mean a lot to Tyler in his current state. Jones had the horrible feeling that his partner would not survive the night, let alone live to regret it in the coming days.

Tyler had been loaded onto a gurney and whisked off to emergency surgery. The medics who had arrived on the scene had worked furiously to stem the bleeding, and had stabilised him, but that was all they could do outside of an operating theatre. Jones recalled the last time he'd watched another ambulance tear away with sirens flashing, and things had not ended well then. Yoshida Takumi hadn't made it to the hospital, and he doubted that Tyler would either.

Jones looked down at the blood that drenched his clothing, and he studied his hands. They looked as if he was wearing crimson gloves. He had done all he could to assist his friend, compressing the wound in his throat to stop him bleeding out, but it was almost hopeless. At first the blood had jetted out, then slowed to a milder pulse, but not because the bleeding was under control, but that there remained little to be squeezed out of Tyler's failing body. He checked his own wound, and was thankful for the ballistic vest he'd worn under his shirt. When the suspect shot him, the bullet had flattened against the vest, knocking him down with the force, but it had not punctured his flesh. He had a major haematoma due to grow on his chest, judging by the pain, but for now he could live with that. The suspect had shot him again as he'd crouched behind the shrubbery, this time nicking his left leg, and the burning sensation of his wound was little more than a distraction. A medic had patched him up, but he'd refused further treatment and had stayed to secure the crime scene and the incriminating evidence discovered within the house.

It was almost two hours since the shootout and the house and surrounding neighbourhood of Clarendon Heights had taken on the look of a carnival. Lights flashed everywhere, vehicles came and went in processions, and people had come from their beds to watch the excitement. Uniformed officers held back the ghoulish crowd of onlookers, who stood beyond the crime scene tape in their PJ's and dressing gowns. Journalists and TV crews were also in attendance, and more than once Jones had brushed away a microphone that had been thrust under his chin.

What would he say to their demands for a quote anyway? That the SFPDs hunt for their multiple-murder suspect was a complete screw up? It was as far as he was concerned. It had taken two vigilantes to do more than the SFPD had achieved, and despite everything he even owed them for both his and Tyler's lives. There was no doubt about it: the killer would have murdered Tyler outright if they hadn't grabbed him as he was about to execute the injured detective. Jones wasn't even sure that he would have survived the next shots fired at him as he'd taken ineffective cover behind the bushes, if it hadn't been for Hunter and Rington's judicious actions.

Jones was a cop through and through. But he was also a man who laid much faith in the goodness of others' hearts, and he was grateful that good men had come to his aid. It was his reason for keeping the two men's names quiet when other officers arrived at the scene. Maybe his decision would come back to haunt him at a later date, but right then and there, he'd kept their secret. He had said that Charles Peterson had shot them then made off. The officers tasked with hunting down the fugitive were at a loss to where he'd gone, but were currently checking CCTV footage from all the major routes out of the city. In his colleagues there was an overriding sense of urgency to catch Peterson, but Jones wasn't fearful that he would continue his killing spree. In fact, he had the sense that the elderly residents of his city were safe from the beast now. Aiding that assumption was the cell phone message he'd received minutes ago.

He had been surprised to hear the phone ringing from his pocket, and had plucked it out, trying not to smear Tyler's blood over the screen as he fumbled it up to his ear.

'You might be surprised to hear from me,' Joe Hunter said. 'But you gave me your phone number that time I met with you at the station.'

'I'm surprised, all right,' Jones said, as he'd glanced about, checking he wasn't in earshot of any of his colleagues. 'But not because you remembered my number.'

'You're surprised I'd call you at all.'

'Have to admit it, Joe. I thought that you and your buddy would disappear and that would be it.'

'There's some unfinished business we need your assistance with.'

'Yeah, I had that impression the second you called. Where is he, Joe? Where's Charles Peterson?'

'Markus Colby,' Hunter corrected him. 'That's the killer's real name, but he has been using his dead father's name. Don't ask me why, or what his motives for the murders were because I won't tell you. Only understand that he was misguided and chose to attack people for his own demented reason.'

'It was to do with something that happened at Rohwer, wasn't it?'

'Like I said, I'm not telling. The thing is, if the truth ever comes out then good people will be harmed.'

'And that's why you've chosen to silence him.'

Hunter didn't reply.

'Where is he?' Jones didn't expect to ever find out. The cop part of him was disappointed, but the man who owed Hunter his life wasn't so sorry.

'Can we trust you to be discreet?'

'I've covered your asses this long,' Jones said.

Hunter had laughed. Then he'd given Jones a location to meet him, and express instructions to come alone.

'Can I trust you?' Jones countered. 'For all I know you're leading me to a trap. After all, if my buddy, Tyler, doesn't make it through the night, I'm the only man who knows what really happened here.'

'Despite our differences in approach,' Hunter said, 'we're on the same side.'

Hunter had then disconnected the call and Jones had stared at the phone for a few seconds before placing it back in his pocket. That was when he'd noticed the copious amount of his partner's blood on his clothes and hands.

He turned away from the house and the hive of activity within and walked away, brushing off a question from a uniformed sergeant. 'I've got to go get cleaned up,' Jones said. 'I'll be back soon.'

In his car he pulled off his jacket and slung it on the back seat. Under the dashboard light his homicide detective's badge winked back at him from where it was fixed to his belt. He pulled it off too and placed it on the back seat and covered it with his soiled clothing, but his service firearm stayed put on his hip. Then he'd driven away from the scene, heading out towards the reservoir beyond Chabot Lake. His in-car set was tuned to the hubbub of radio chatter between the crime scene and SFPD headquarters. As he was crossing the Bay Bridge he heard a coded announcement that sent a wedge of ice into his heart. He could barely breathe for seconds afterwards, and tears misted his vision, causing the taillights of the vehicles in front to blur. He dashed the tears from his eyes, mindless that he smeared blood across his cheeks.

The journey was completed in a daze, but he finally found he had to concentrate as he moved off the hillside road onto a steeply descending track that wound its way down to a promontory overlooking the still waters of the reservoir. As he drove onto a turning circle his headlights picked out a group of vehicles, and a man leaning against the trunk of a tan-coloured sedan. Joe Hunter was bare-chested, and myriad cuts decorated his arms and body. He'd made an effort to clean off the blood but he still looked like a savage.

Despite the mistrust he'd intimated earlier, he was happy that Hunter had not set him up and that his friend Jared Rington wasn't poised to shoot him from the darkness. He parked alongside the nearest car, recognising it as the one in which the killer had fled Clarendon Heights, and got out. He swayed in place as the blood rushed to his head, but then he went forward. Hunter met him, studying his face.

'You okay, detective?'

'Just Gar, okay? Or Jones. I'm not here in my official capacity.'

'Suits me fine,' Hunter said.

Jones pressed a palm to his face, scrubbing at his cheeks and forehead, stimulating the blood that had drained from his features during the drive over. Hunter watched him, a frown creasing his brow. Jones looked down at his hands and saw that they were still stained with his partner's blood.

'Your friend didn't make it?'

Jones shook his head. 'I tried to save him, but it was...' His features crumpled and for a second or two it was a struggle to hold his emotions in check. Hunter stared at the floor, but he finally looked up and met Jones's gaze.

'I'm sorry to hear that. Tyler was a good man. So are you, Jones. I'm sorry I was such an obstructive arsehole to you. It's like I said though: good, decent folk would have suffered if I told you what I knew.'

'That doesn't matter now. Not when you've done the right thing in the end. I'm not interested in what happened in the past, or what sent Colby on his killing spree, I'm only pleased he's been stopped.' He approached Hunter. 'Show me where the bastard is.'

Hunter moved away without another word, leading the detective between a steep gulley over which loomed the crowns of maple trees. The earlier clear skies had filled with clouds bearing in from the distant mountains, driven by strong winds. Stars winked in and out of the gaps in the clouds, while the moon was a faint halo low on the horizon. Night would soon give way to dawn, but darkness prevailed for now. It suited Jones, both his mood and his intention.

They approached a large log structure, and by its decrepit state Jones could tell that it was seldom visited. He thought that it would be unlikely for anyone to discover what Hunter and Rington had done if they hadn't purposefully led him here. That was discounting the various corpses scattered around the building.

Jones looked at Hunter for an answer, but received nothing in return.

He looked up at the sagging roof, the walls that were overgrown with briar and moss, and then at the open door through which he was about to step. For a second he faltered, before his mind flashed back to how Markus Colby had stood over his mortally injured partner poised to execute him like an injured dog. He recalled the grin of pleasure on Markus's face as he began to squeeze the trigger, and that made up his mind. He walked over the threshold in full knowledge that there would be no turning back.

Jared Rington was standing with his back to him, and he barely turned to acknowledge his presence. In the gloom Jones could just make out another figure beyond Rington, a small Japanese woman he recognised as the man's mother. She was sitting on a chair, looking pale and weak from whatever she'd endured.

Lying on his back, his mouth wide in an eternal shout was Sean Chaney.

'What the hell?' Jones whispered.

'They were working with Markus,' Hunter explained. 'Chaney and his gang. They kidnapped Yukiko in order to flush Rink and me out. Don't know if you heard any reports about an arson blaze this evening? That was Chaney's crew; they attacked Yukiko's house, set it on fire then snatched her on Markus's behalf.'

'I was too busy trying to keep Tyler alive,' Jones admitted. 'But, yeah, I did hear something over the airwaves.'

'We had to kill them,' Hunter went on. 'Self-defence you understand? And to release Mrs Rington who they were planning on murdering.'

'Where's the other one? Markus Colby?'

Rington pointed, and Jones saw the murderer standing further back in the hall. Markus had to be a giant of a man to stand so tall. It was only when Rington fully moved aside that he seen the rope around the man's neck. He moved forward, a sound of dismay in his throat. He got to within feet of Markus when the man's eyes snapped open.

'He's still alive.' Rather than a question, his words came out in a relieved statement as he saw that Markus was perched on an old wooden chair. It looked rickety enough that any injudicious movement by Markus would send him to a neck-snapping death.

'We're not murderers,' Rington said. 'The others died in the heat of battle, but we couldn't kill him in cold blood. He's all yours to do with as you wish.'

Then Rington led his mother away, joining his friend by the exit door. Hunter had collected a sack of some kind, and Jones realised that both men had cleared the room of any evidence that they'd ever been there while awaiting his arrival. He once wondered how they had got away with the other killings they were suspected of, but it was clear to him now: they were careful. And they had never killed anyone who didn't deserve killing, so their involvement was never fully investigated or was covered up entirely. He wondered now what the outcome would have been if he hadn't gone to Markus's house at the moment he did. If the man standing before him hadn't subsequently murdered Tyler, would he have been happy to cover for them in the same way? Would they be as happy to cover for him?

He was sure they would.

He stared up at Markus.

Then he wandered back to where Chaney lay. A gun was in the man's dead hand. It was the same model as the gun on Jones's belt, but a quick check showed him that it was empty. He fed one bullet from his gun and into Chaney's.

He returned to Markus, saw how difficult it was for the man to remain upright on the stool. He unloosened the rope holding him upright and Markus collapsed to the floor. Jones stood over him in the much the same way Markus had stood over Tyler.

There was pleading in the man's eyes, but he was unable to form words through what was undoubtedly a broken jaw. Drool pooled on his chin. He was pitiful, but there was no pity in Jones's heart. Markus Colby was responsible for eight murders that he had learned of, all of his victims brutalised for the man's demented pleasure, but it was the face of his friend, Tyler, that came to mind as he studied the broken man at his feet. Jones thought of how Tyler had peered up at him, a look of complete faith that his friend would save him painting his face, even as the blood bubbled out from under Jones's hands. Jones had been unable to save him. He saw that as the ultimate failure.

But he could avenge him.

He shot Markus in the head.

44

I was never sure how events would play out when bringing Detective Jones to the abandoned meetinghouse, or if duty would win out and we would be brought up on charges. Only as we walked away, and I heard the single crack of a gun, did I suspect that we were safe from prosecution. It was sickening, considering the events that had led to that moment, but I have to admit to being relieved. I was happiest for my friend, because all the way through I'd been worried that he would give in to his base emotions and execute Markus himself. I knew Rink would be tormented by such a decision and he'd carry the guilt with him for the rest of his life. I didn't want him to suffer the way his parents had, and looking at the way in which his problem had been resolved I concluded that it was the best for all of us. Perhaps Jones would regret the impulse killing of Markus, but maybe he had a different sense of justice than we had.

We hadn't waited for Jones to join us, but had driven away, seeking somewhere far from the reservoir to dump the sand-coloured car. I'd already hauled the two men from it and laid them with the others outside the lodge, as well as the man I'd killed on the path. For all intents and purposes it would look like a shootout had taken down everyone around and in the lodge. It was better that Jones covered his own tracks and wasn't seen with us. He would be resourceful enough to find his way back to the city having destroyed any trace that he'd been at the old lodge, we concluded. We found a minor lake a couple of miles distant, and after stripping all identifiers from the car, Rink sent it into the deep water and we watched it sink without trace just as the sun broke over the eastern peaks. I had lugged the plastic sack along with me, and inside it was the rope that had bound Yukiko's wrists, and the hessian sack that had blindfolded her. In the bag we also placed our guns and Rink's

Ka-bar, and my bloodstained rag of a shirt. I loaded it with rocks, and then hurled it far out into the depths of the lake. Afterwards we walked back to the motel at Chabot Lake, Rink carrying his mom in his arms the entire way.

Velasquez was sleeping when we arrived, but our buddy, McTeer, was fully alert and he met us at the door with his pistol drawn.

'There's no need for that anymore,' Rink told him. 'Markus is finished.'

Rink took Yukiko inside and sat her down on a comfortable couch.

'How are you doing, Mom?'

'I'm fine, Jared,' she said. 'Please stop fussing.'

I hadn't realised that Parnell and Faulks were up and about until I heard their collective whoop of joy as McTeer relayed them the news. The two old men came towards us from the depths of the lodge, their faces painted with a thousand questions. When they saw my semi-naked state, the small cuts all over me, they came to a halt, their mouths open in shock. I held a palm up to them. 'Remember what I told you back at the cemetery that time? Best you don't ask anything, then you can't slip up and say something you might later regret.'

'Just tell me it's true. I'll be happy with that.' Faulks still appeared jittery but this time it was with excitement.

'It's over with. You can go home now. How's about you gather your things together while me and Rink get cleaned up.'

Velasquez appeared from a back room. His dark hair was sleep mussed, standing up like a cockerel's crest at one side. His gaze seemed clear enough though, and he held his pistol in a firm grip. When he saw who was causing the fuss he relaxed. 'Does this mean I get to go home too?'

'First flight out,' Rink promised, including McTeer in his glance. 'I need you both back at the office and back to work. I don't have money to burn you know.'

Within hours both our vows played out. Rink and I took turns to shower—me tending to my minor wounds—then to dress in spare clothing, before organising taxicabs to take the old men home and our colleagues to the airport. We couldn't leave San Francisco just yet. Not before Rink made sure his mom was okay. It would be difficult for her, now that Andrew wasn't with her, but she had proven a resilient old bird and I trusted she'd be fine after a few days' rest. She still had her friends close by, and I guessed that Parnell and Faulks would always prove sympathetic ears if she needed to talk with anyone about what had happened. Yukiko smelled of lighter fluid that Markus had sprayed her with, but she did not want to shower here. She wanted to go home. She cried when she recalled her home was no longer there.

I accompanied the old guys back to Hayes Tower. The police had been and gone from Parnell's apartment, and it seemed like his landlord had seen to the replacement of the locks after Sean Chaney's men had burst their way inside. Parnell checked around the apartment, and seemed pleased that it had not been totally wrecked. Who'd have guessed that two big men had been beaten up in his living room? The only sign of conflict was in the way the settee had been pushed against one wall, from when Rink had knocked his opponent unconscious and the big guy had flopped down on it. He offered me a seat, but I declined.

'I can't thank you enough, Joe,' he said, extending his hand.

'You might want to think about that next time you join a lynching party,' I said, tempering my delivery with a grandiose wink that brought a faltering smile to Parnell's face.

'We know now that what we did was wrong,' Faulks said.

'No. Charles Peterson deserved everything he got,' I said. 'So did his son. Best that you forget all about the both of them now. The police might question you yet. Don't admit to anything, okay.'

I shook hands with both old men, before leaving and hailing another cab to take me back to Chabot Lake. Enough time had passed for Rink and Yukiko to talk. That's why I'd chosen to go with Parnell and Faulks: I didn't want either Rink or Yukiko to hold back on their emotions while there was an observer nearby. That was their way. Hopefully by the time I got back, they'd have come up with some kind of plan for the future. Knowing Rink, he'd want his mom to come back to Florida with him. Knowing Yukiko, she'd refuse. I guessed that Andrew had left her well cared for in his will, and the insurance would pay out on her home. She'd be set up again in no time.

When I arrived back at the motel, Yukiko was sleeping in one of the rooms vacated earlier by the men.

Rink was watching TV with the sound turned down low.

'Something you gotta see, brother,' he said. There was a tone to his voice I had not expected.

'What is it?'

He didn't reply, just indicated the TV screen.

It was tuned to a local channel.

It showed a news crew at a crime scene, reporting live as firemen bustled about behind them.

I didn't immediately recognise the abandoned meetinghouse in its current state. Not now it was barely a heap of smouldering embers. The fire crew were still dampening it down, but already investigators were poking around in the steaming wreckage.

More than did the chattering reporter's words, the tickertape banner playing across the bottom of the screen told me everything.

Murder suspect Markus Colby AKA Charles Peterson had fled from police after fatally shooting one detective and wounding another, where he'd then come into conflict with local underworld figures at their remote hideaway on the shores of Upper San Leandro Reservoir. The police had no idea as yet why a furious gun battle had broken out during which Colby had slain a number of men, before being killed in a shootout with Sean Chaney. At some point a lamp had been broken and ignited some spilled accelerant and had burned down the lodge house. They were questions the chief investigator hoped to answer following further investigation.

The reporter then approached a large, fair-haired homicide detective overseeing the proceedings and asked his opinion. The man looked tired and drawn, a little ruffled by a long night of extraordinary occurrences, but he still mustered a few words: 'No one knows what was in Markus Colby's mind that would drive him to do this. But I will say that it matches his modus operandi. During previous attacks he has employed firearms, bladed weapons and fire against his victims. He was a brutal killer, but on this occasion he met someone equally as dangerous. I'm sorry that I missed the opportunity to arrest him for his crimes, but I will add this: I'm satisfied that his terrifying murder spree is over with now, and the elderly residents of our good country can rest a little easier in their beds.'

It was a slightly scandalous comment to come out of a police officer's mouth, and it shocked the reporter to momentary silence. By the time the interviewer formed a second question, Detective Garforth Jones had already moved away.

I looked at Rink, wondering if I wore the same stunned expression he did. I exhaled slowly. I had come to terms with the fact that Jones had taken revenge on Markus over the slaying of his partner, but I hadn't expected this. But who was I to complain? Jones had found a way that exonerated us all. If ever there was a burden of obligation it was now on Rink and I never to mention Detective Jones's involvement in this to anyone.

'You think anyone will buy his story?' I asked.

Rink shrugged. 'Maybe if Markus hadn't murdered Detective Tyler things would be different. Now, I'm not so sure. Perhaps someone will suspect something, but who's going to dig too deeply? Cops have a way of closing ranks to protect their own. Jones got his partner's murderer: one way or another, that's all that will matter to them.'

'You sure about that, buddy?'

He looked wistfully at the bedroom door beyond which lay his elderly mother. She had survived everything that had happened to her, but being forced to reveal her secret would likely finish her off.

'I hope so, for my mom's sake,' he said.

THANKS AND ACKNOWLEDGEMENTS

As usual there are people who I must thank for their unflinching encouragement and support while writing this book, and as usual the list is a long one. So, without further ado, I say a huge thank-you to: Denise Hilton, Luigi Bonomi, Alison Bonomi, Thomas Stofer, Sue Fletcher, Eleni Fostiropoulos, Swati Gamble, Alice Wood, Pete Nicholson, Richard Gnosill, Gary Jones, Paul Tyler, Col Bury, Lee Hughes, Jim Hilton, David and Karen Hilton, Jacky and Val Hilton, Sheila Quigley, Adrian and Ann Magson, Raymond Hilton, Sue Harding, David Barber, Ian Grahame, Trevor Turner, Martin Fell, and all my author-type friends throughout the world. Also, a huge thank-you goes out to my readers: without your support, all the efforts of the above would be for nothing.

I would also like to say a posthumous thank-you to Sensei Ronnie Whittle, the person who taught me the concept of *giri* and all that it stands for. I carry a burden of obligation to you all.

ABOUT THE AUTHOR

Matt Hilton quit his career as a police officer with Cumbria Constabulary to pursue his love of writing tight, cinematic American-style thrillers. He is the author of the high-octane Joe Hunter thriller series, including his most recent novel *The Lawless Kind*—Joe Hunter 9—published in January 2014 by Hodder and Stoughton. His first book, *Dead Men's Dust*, was shortlisted for the International Thriller Writers' Debut Book of 2009 Award, and was a *Sunday Times* bestseller, also being named as a 'thriller of the year 2009' by *The Daily Telegraph*. *Dead Men's Dust* was also a top ten Kindle bestseller in 2013. The Joe Hunter series is widely published by Hodder and Stoughton in UK territories, and by Down & Out Books and William Morrow and Company in the USA, and have been translated into German, Italian, Romanian and Bulgarian.

As well as the Joe Hunter series, Matt has been published in a number of anthologies and collections, and has published novels in the horror genre, namely *Dominion, Darkest Hour, Preternatural, The Shadows Call* and a young adult novel called *Mark Darrow and the Stealer of Souls*. Matt also collected and edited both *ACTION: Pulse Pounding Tales Volumes 1 and 2*.

Matt is a high-ranking martial artist and has been a detective and private security specialist, all of which lend an authenticity to the action scenes in his books. He is also very interested in the paranormal and has accompanied Ghost-North-east and Near Dark Paranormal Investigations on a number of their investigations.

Matt is currently working on the next Joe Hunter novel, as well as a stand-alone supernatural novel.

www.matthiltonbooks.com

OTHER TITLES FROM DOWN AND OUT BOOKS

See www.DownAndOutBooks.com for complete list

By Anonymous-9
Bite Hard

By J.L. Abramo
Catching Water in a Net
Clutching at Straws
Counting to Infinity
Gravesend
Chasing Charlie Chan
Circling the Runway

By Trey R. Barker
2,000 Miles to Open Road
Road Gig: A Novella
Exit Blood
Death is Not Forever

By Richard Barre
The Innocents
Bearing Secrets
Christmas Stories
The Ghosts of Morning
Blackheart Highway
Burning Moon
Echo Bay
Lost

By Eric Beetner and
JB Kohl
Over Their Heads (*)

By Eric Beetner and
Frank Scalise
The Backlist (*)

By Rob Brunet
Stinking Rich

By Dana Cameron (editor)
Murder at the Beach: Bouchercon Anthology 2014

By Stacey Cochran
Eddie & Sunny

By Mark Coggins
No Hard Feelings (*)

By Tom Crowley
Vipers Tail
Murder in the Slaughterhouse

By Frank De Blase
Pine Box for a Pin-Up
Busted Valentines and Other Dark Delights
A Cougar's Kiss (*)

By Les Edgerton
The Genuine, Imitation, Plastic Kidnapping

By A.C. Frieden
Tranquility Denied
The Serpent's Game
The Pyongyang Option (*)

By Jack Getze
Big Numbers
Big Money
Big Mojo
Big Shoes (*)

By Keith Gilman
Bad Habits

(*)—Coming Soon

OTHER TITLES FROM DOWN AND OUT BOOKS

See www.DownAndOutBooks.com for complete list

By Richard Godwin
Wrong Crowd (*)

By William Hastings (editor)
Stray Dogs: Writing from the Other America

By Matt Hilton
No Going Back
Rules of Honor (*)
The Lawless Kind (*)

By Terry Holland
An Ice Cold Paradise
Chicago Shiver

By Darrel James,
Linda O. Johnston &
Tammy Kaehler (editors)
Last Exit to Murder

By David Housewright &
Renée Valois
The Devil and the Diva

By David Housewright
Finders Keepers
Full House

By Jon & Ruth Jordan (editors)
Murder and Mayhem in Muskego
Cooking with Crimespree

By Andrew McAleer & Paul D. Marks
(editors)
Coast to Coast (*)

By Bill Moody
Czechmate
The Man in Red Square
Solo Hand
The Death of a Tenor Man
The Sound of the Trumpet
Bird Lives!

By Gary Phillips
The Perpetrators
Scoundrels (Editor)
Treacherous

By Robert J. Randisi
Upon My Soul
Souls of the Dead
Envy the Dead (*)

By Ryan Sayles
The Subtle Art of Brutality (*)
Warpath (*)

By Anthony Neil Smith
Worm

By Liam Sweeny
Welcome Back, Jack (*)

By Lono Waiwaiole
Wiley's Lament
Wiley's Shuffle
Wiley's Refrain
Dark Paradise

By Vincent Zandri
Moonlight Weeps

(*)—Coming Soon